THE BATT

The Inferno
of Erif

THE BATTLES OF LIOLIA

The Inferno of Erif

WRITTEN & ILLUSTRATED
BY
WILL MATHISON

To Mace,

Hope you enjoy the adventure.

Will Mathison

THIS BOOK IS DEDICATED
TO MY GOOD FRIENDS
WHO HAVE EXPERIENCED TREMENDOUS LOSS
AND
TO EVERYONE WHO HAS LOST SOMEONE THEY
LOVE TO CANCER.

IN THEIR MEMORY AND SO THAT OTHERS CAN
CONTINUE TO FIGHT
IN THEIR HONOR,
ALL OF THE PROCEEDS FROM THE SALE OF THIS
BOOK WILL BE DONATED
TO
RELAY FOR LIFE.

CONTENTS

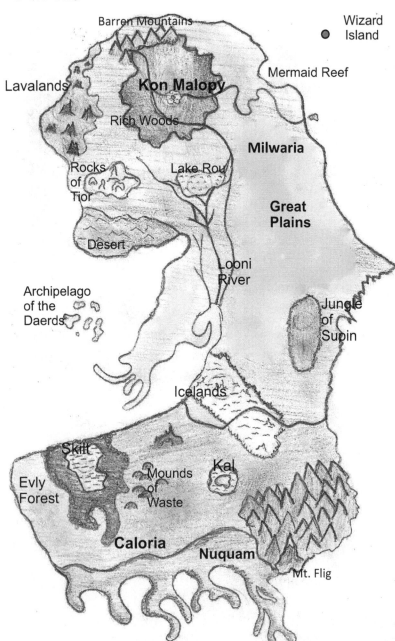

Liolia

Barren Mountains

Wizard Island

Mermaid Reef

Lavalands

Kon Malopy

Rich Woods

Milwaria

Rocks of Tior

Lake Rou

Great Plains

Desert

Looni River

Archipelago of the Daerds

Jungle of Supin

Icelands

Skill

Mounds of Waste

Kal

Evly Forest

Caloria

Nuquam

Mt. Flig

It had been half a year since Speilton had seen his village crumble to a pile of soldering embers. Since that traumatic day, autumn's orange leaves had fallen, leaving the trees bare and lifeless as winter came. Then, the snow and ice that had once encased the trees melted away, along with many men who had perished in the war that winter. But now it was spring, and just as the delicate flowers began to bud, Milwaria was strengthening, growing, and preparing for the harsh days ahead.

Speilton stood at the top of Sky Tower and peered over the Rich Woods. The green, luscious trees were full of blooming flowers and vibrantly colored birds. The young king came here often. He enjoyed the isolation and cherished his time away from the rest of the world not that he didn't enjoy his new family. He loved his brother and his sister. His heart had burst with joy with the realization that he had a family once more. Even though his true, royal name was Visveres, he wished to be called Speilton, the name he had always used. So to his friends and his family, he was known as Speilton Lux, one of the two Kings of Milwaria. Still, many others called him Visvires, thinking it best to refer to him by his royal name.

What Speilton really hoped to escape, after climbing the many steps to the top of Sky Tower, was the war. Every day, people were dying across the land. Every day, horrible creatures such as Dnuoh, the large black Hound of Flames, were slaying innocent people. The main enemy and the greatest threat to Milwaria though were the Wodahs, the ruby-eyed, smoke demons that made up the Calorian race.

In the sun the Wodahs appeared to be human, but once they were enveloped by the dark they took their true form as creatures as black as a moonless, midnight sky. They attacked in thousands, torturing and destroying anything in sight. The worst of them was Sinister. The Milwarians were afraid to call Sinister by his true name - *Retsinis* - which was said to curse the speaker. Sinister was the invincible leader of the Calorians and would stop at nothing to destroy the Milwarians' peaceful way of life. The Calorians were the threat that kept every Milwarian up at night wondering if they'd see the next day.

It had been a while since any one had seen Sinister. Some believed he was recruiting new allies, while others claimed he was recuperating in Nuquam after his fall from Sky Tower. Nuquam was the only other country on the continent of Liolia and was uninhabited since it was a place of thick fogs and mysterious monsters. Regardless of Sinister's current location, everyone knew the Dark King would be back and devastation would soon follow.

For now, Speilton stood atop the Castle of Kon Malopy, gazing across the beautiful land of Milwaria. The view showed him what he was fighting for and what he would lose if he ceased to believe in victory. This view and his friends and family were the core reasons why he continued fighting.

As Speilton gazed over the green tree canopy and the purple haze of the Barren Mountains in the distance, he replayed his adventure across Milwaria in his mind. Almost every day he thought about those two weeks, and his life before that time. Speilton tried to piece his childhood together. He searched his memory to recall anything he could about his parents or being taken away to Kal. His oldest vivid memory was when he was barely five years old. He laid on his back gazing into the night sky with his best friend,

Faveo. He remembered seeing a flash of golden light dash across the sky. "Look!" Speilton cried a second before the flash disappeared.

""What? I don't see anything," Faveo said.

"It was a shooting star, just above the Gemini constellation!" Speilton announced.

"Really? I was looking there, but I didn't see a shooting star!" Faveo declared.

Speilton felt as though the shooting star, which only he could see, was a sign. The shooting star made him feel like he and Faveo were not alone that night under the stars.

Speilton recalled when his old village was destroyed, crumbled to ashes, and Faveo was lost in the raging fires that the Calorians had created. That day still haunted him. The flames crept deep into his dreams and turned them into nightmares.

Once his village was gone, Speilton left Kal and hiked through Caloria with his blue dragon, Prowl. Prowl grew or shrank depending on how much she had eaten. Along the way he met Ram, an escaped Knight of Milwaria, and his loyal tiger, Burn. Together they journeyed into Milwaria, fending off Calorians. They had been lucky for a while and succeeded in several battles before Burn was killed. The death was heart-breaking, though the three were forced to continue. After many fights and narrowly escaping danger countless times, they reached Kon Malopy, the capitol of Milwaria. At Kon Malopy they helped the Milwarians defeat the Calorian army. Only after the war did they discover that Speilton was the lost King of Milwaria who had been taken away as an infant to be protected from the Calorians.

Speilton once again had a family. His brother, Millites, had been fighting the Calorians for years even though Millites was only fifteen, two years older than Speilton. Their sister, Teews, was Queen. Teews was fourteen, and Millites would not allow her to fight for Milwaria. Millites was very protective of his younger sister and feared that if she were to be killed in battle, there would be no Lux family heir. The loyal Second-in-Command, Usus, would be a fine leader, and Ram, the General, could protect them, but the loss of their leaders would be fatal for Milwaria. The Calorians would see it as an opportune moment to attack with all their forces.

But for now, in these short moments atop Sky Tower, all was peaceful and quiet. For a moment Speilton felt like he was back in Lorg, his old village on the tiny island of Kal. The only sound was the chirping of the birds and the wind whistling through the trees. Speilton closed his eyes and let the cool spring air blow through his dark-brown hair. Though he would never admit it, Speilton enjoyed life more when he was back in Kal. In Kal there were no Calorians and no war. Though life was not easy, it was much less frightening and dark than this new world.

At least he had Millites and Teews along side him. And he knew that he could always trust Ram, Usus, and Prowl. In the uncertainty of his new life, they were the only people keeping him sane. He was very grateful to have them.

Then, a loud horn blared which signaled battle and dozens cheered in response. The clatter of the men grabbing swords and shields cut through the soft morning air. A flock of birds took to the sky, squawking in a frenzy. The horn blast and the ferocious cheer of the Milwarian warriors echoed across the forest and traveled to the Barren Mountains.

What has happened to this world? Speilton wondered. *Our lives change in a single second. Everyones' joy changes to fear at a moments notice, and the boys who one played merrily on the streets are forced into armor. What has happened to this world that causes even the rats to abandon crumbs in search of safety? This world seems to be intertwined in a nightmare, one that cannot be awakened. Yet in this nightmare, people really suffer and evil triumphs. This nightmare is reality,*

Speilton heard feet patter up the stairs. He turned to see Prowl emerge from the doorway. She had recently been fed and wore a thick silver helmet that covered her neck, forehead, and snout. She clutched a saddle in her grinning mouth and set it down before Speilton. Prowl was ready, eager for a fight and to prove herself a warrior once again. The young king picked up the saddle and tied it around Prowl's waist before climbing onto her back.

"Alright, Girl. Let's go!" Speilton said, as the blue dragon leapt up onto the open window sill. Like a gargoyle, Prowl perched for a second, letting the cool breeze whistle across her turquoise scales. Then she unfurled her massive wings and leapt into the spring breeze. As they flew over Kon Malopy, Speilton looked into the open courtyard to see warriors dressed in full armor marching out of the castle. Speilton followed them from high in the air as they hiked down the steep slope of Kon Malopy to meet a swarm of women and children in the village. Wives looked for their husbands, mothers looked for their sons, and young children ran to find their fathers. Many wept and begged for the warriors to stay, but in the end, the warriors marched on … out to war.

What has happened to this world?

The Calorians were defeated at Kon Malopy, but the war continued….

The soft wind whistled through the trees. The sun had long since set, and the birds had finished their last songs. Owls hooted in their trees, the only sound in the night except for five Milwarians.

They sat around a bonfire in the woods, the rest of the camp silent and asleep. But these five could not rest. Battle and war were staring them in the face. A battle that would be remembered throughout history was closing in. That is, if there would be any history for the Milwarians after this.

One thought was on all of their minds. Survival. They were surrounded by the merciless Calorians and unsure of their next move. They could not surrender and give themselves up to the Calorians since both King Speilton and King Millites were with them. And if they were captured, there would be no one else to take the throne but their sister.

Speilton and Millites were only thirteen and fifteen. The throne had been handed down to them after their parents disappeared in a battle. Now they were having to lead an entire nation during its darkest hour.

Because of this, they couldn't sleep. Huddled around the fire with Speilton and Millites was Usus. Usus was the Second-in-Command and twenty years old with amazing skill. Andereer, who was in charge of battle strategy, and Toroe, who was in charge of artillery, were also there discussing battle plans.

"There is no possible way for us to escape this camp without being spotted. We must fight," Andereer announced.

"Would you risk losing so many men? The dark of night is their realm. To fight now would mean to lose many?" Usus asked.

"If we're all going to die soon with the fall of Milwaria, why does it matter?" Toroe grumbled.

"Wow, really optimistic. That really lightened my mood," Speilton said sarcastically.

"What he says is true," Millites sighed, "but we must have a strategy. We can't just waste our lives."

"Then what do you say we should do?" Andereer questioned.

"I agree that we must fight. But we must come up with a reasonable strategy," Millites said.

"What would be the safest way to act under these circumstances?" Speilton asked.

"We could attack straight on with all of our troops at a certain point in the Calorian's ring of warriors."

"No, no. That plan would leave our backs vulnerable. The Calorians could easily sneak up from behind," Andereer said.

"What about splitting up into four groups and surrounding them from four points?" Millites asked.

"Again, too risky. They would notice our movement, and we would be spotted which would mean certain death."

"Then what do you propose we do?" Speilton questioned.

"Fire from a distance. More lives would be spared," Andereer said.

"I'm not so sure," Toroe sighed. "Our artillery isn't strong enough. We have two catapults and about two dozen archers, but that's not enough to stop them. We need to wait. Soon enough we'll have a new weapon, twice the size and strength of any normal catapult. It's being constructed right this second."

"Great, but how is that supposed to help us now?" Usus asked.

"Well, what if we wait here patiently until we have a viable plan. We'll remain vigilant so that they can't sneak up on us," Speilton suggested.

"It seems like that is the only thing we *can* do," Usus agreed.

"All in favor?" Millites announced. Everyone but Toroe raised their hand.

All eyes rested on Toroe, and even in the small light of the fire they could tell something was wrong. His body was rigid, his mouth agape, and his eyes were rolled back in his head. Before any one could react, he toppled over into the fire, a black arrow planted in his back.

Millites rushed over, "It's the Calorians." He pulled Toroe out of he fire then pulled out the arrow and smelled the tip. "Poison" he muttered.

Twinge, twinge, twinge! Three more arrows silently landed all around them.

"We're under attack!" Usus announced as they all drew their swords.

"I'm sorry Toroe," Speilton whispered resting his hand on the Artillery Chief's back.

"Well, it looks like we're not going to be making the decision about how to fight," Andereer added, as a horrifying cheer exploded from the woods all around them. The Calorians were coming.

"I'll wake the others," Millites announced taking off towards his tent. The king whistled and a golden dragon emerged from the twisted branches of a tree. He leapt, and the dragon dove perfectly underneath him so that Millites sat on his back. "Go to the bell tower!" Millites commanded.

The dragon bolted through the air. Yes, this is the dragon that was hatched after the battle at Kon Malopy. This playful, young dragon was the son of Comet, Millites' previous dragon who was killed by Worc, the King of the Daerds.

This young dragon, Hunger, was smaller than his mother had been and was about the size of a lion. Hunger had a hard shell that covered the top of its face like a helmet and branched into three horns higher up on its head. The helmet formed a sort of beak, and inside the large mouth were two rows of razor blade teeth.

Hunger had two hind legs and used his clawed wings to crawl around. His neck was covered in spiny thorns, and his tail ended in a club of knife long spikes. But the most amazing thing was his ability to change colors; red for anger, blue for mourning, green for injured, purple while strategizing, yellow for pride, and a golden brown all other times.

As they dashed through the sky, the dragon was deep purple, anxious to get to the ancient bell tower that had been used here in the Rich Woods for years.

Behind them, a tent burst into flames and a few Milwarians were awaken by the noise. Over all the commotion of scurrying for weapons, the Calorians cheer for blood thirst rang out.

When they finally reached the bell tower, Millites and Hunger realized that they weren't the first. A dozen Calorians were scouring the walls, armed with arrows pointed towards the sky. There were two levels on the tower, one twenty feet from the ground, and the other only ten feet above that. Hunger darted forward and landed with his claws extended on a Calorian, grabbed another in it's jaws, then scorched three more with his flaming red breath. Millites leapt from Hunger's back and pulled himself up onto the top level. As a Calorian rushed forward, Millites knocked him over the steep, rocky ledge with his sword. The old tower shook as Hunger smashed a Calorian into the wall with his spiked, club-like tail below.

Millites leapt over the deep hole in the center of the tower and grabbed onto the rope that hung down. As he descended into the hole holding the rope, the bell rang loud and clear. The sound was so deafening that some of the Calorians stumbled over the edge. Millites dropped the remaining five feet to the ground level, and rushed out of the tall tower. As he flung the door open, five Calorians charged through. Millites stepped back, and began fighting all five at once. He flipped one onto the ground, kicked another, disarmed one, and cut down the other two.

As he rushed outside again, he met a friendlier sight this time. Hunger was waiting for him. Millites climbed onto the golden dragon's back, and they took off into the sky.

Back at camp, the battle had begun. Milwarians had rushed from their tents and filed in behind Speilton and Usus. As the Calorians rushed out of their hiding places in the dense woods, they were suddenly ignited by blue flames. Prowl, Speilton's faithful dragon and loyal friend, landed next to him. The king unsheathed his sword, and took his invisible shield which shines as bright as the sun in daylight, and rushed forward, the Milwarians right behind him.

The two sides clashed, but even before they'd started, the Calorians had the upper hand. The front line of Calorians held long, spear-tipped staffs that were lit on fire on the other end. As the Milwarians rushed forward, the Calorians spun their staffs and struck the tired warriors with their flames.

With Speilton in front, they were able to shatter the first row of defenses and charge through the Calorian warriors with ease. Speilton was an exceptional swordsman, a trait shared by every Lux. Millites, Teews, and especially Jupiter, their father, were also finessed and highly skilled. Jupiter was said to have been invincible in any sword battle. Though, even he had been defeated. In a battle, he simply disappeared. No one ever claimed responsibility, and since he was a very powerful king, his slayer would've been awarded great riches in Caloria. Still, no one claimed responsibility.

Even after many years, his body was never found. Some people said he had retreated, while others claimed to have seen him rise into the air as a spirit, and cross over into the next life.

But whatever the cause, he was gone, and Speilton promised himself every day that he would not die. He would not leave Millites alone to fight the war like his father had left him.

Suddenly, a burst of screams - just like before - rose from behind them. Usus spun around to see another line of Calorians closing in all around them. It wasn't looking pretty.

Hunger's wings pumped as he dashed through the air. He drifted over the tall trees, glancing through the underbrush at the Calorians underneath. Everything was dark and quiet, yet teaming with Calorians.

In the distance, they could see the flickering red light of the Calorian's torches. These lights guided them to the battle scene.

Hunger started to shake. "It's okay. I know it must be hard for you to fly this late," Millites whispered to the dragon.

But that wasn't the reason Hunger was shaking. He sensed something, and Millites realized it all too late. "CRAAAAW!"

A black crow with teeth as large as daggers, spikes the size and shape of a Great White's dorsal fin, and three times the size of the poor dragon, crashed out of the night. Millites saw the fear in Hunger's eyes as the creature used one taloned foot to grab the dragon by the neck, and the other to grab his waist. Millites was thrown from Hunger's back, and as he descended, he had horrible deja vu. Hunger's mother had died that same way, by the claw of Worc, the King Daerd. As Millites fell, Hunger and Worc left his sight.

Millites experienced excruciating pain as he tumbled into the tree canopy. His arm cracked off a few smaller branches from the top of the tree, but the farther he fell, the thicker the branches got. He lost complete track of time. It was ten seconds of banging and cracking, smaller twigs scratching, and wondering which way was up. It felt like an hour.

When he finally reached the ground, he could only lie there. His entire body ached. It had been a miracle he hadn't broken his neck. Millites breathed in deeply, trying to fight through the pain. His body was shaking as he propped himself up against a tree. As he laid there, his mind replayed Hunger being torn away from him. He remembered seeing the anguish in Hunger's eyes as he was dragged away by the very same creature that destroyed his mother.

Finally after a few minutes, the pain had eased slightly, and Millites' eyes slowly came back into focus. Shoving the image out of his mind, he opened his eyes.

Nothing. Absolute darkness wrapped around his body. In the distance he could hear the Calorians take up another battle cry, but here, the trees blocked out all the small light that the stars and moon created.

His heart raced. What if they fought and lost? They needed someone to lead them. And once the battle was over, the Calorians would come back this way. He'd be helpless, and easily captured, and…

The next thing caused his heart to stop all together. Two blood red, glowing eyes appeared an inch away from his nose. Before he could react, a hand grabbed him by the front of his shirt and lifted him up against the side of the tree. He dangled a foot off the ground, his back pinned to the thick bark.

"Hello, Retsinis," he spat.

Flickering lights appeared around them creating a wide circle. They were Calorians, and they all wanted to watch the death of their greatest enemy. Their torch lights lit up the scene.

"HA! You dare speak my name? I thought it was illegal in your country."

"I'll say what I wish to say," Millites growled."

"What is this? Do you wish to show allegiance to my name? You're not thinking about joining me are you?" he laughed maniacally.

"I'm not afraid to say your name. Neither am I afraid of you," Millites grumbled with much more bravery than he had.

"Fine, so you don't fear my name. But do you fear death?" The Lord of Darkness reached for something on his belt. Millites didn't even need to look to know what it was.

The King Calorian held a curved black dagger to Millites' throat. "I'll make this as slow and painful as I can. My Calorians haven't had a good show in years."

THWUNK! An arrow struck the tree, only inches away from Millites face. *Oh great! More Calorians.* Millites thought.

But it wasn't a Calorian. It was Speilton, fumbling a bow and arrow. No wonder the shot hadn't been so good. It was meant to hit Sinister, but that didn't exactly happen since archery *wasn't* Speilton's expertise.

Luckily, it distracted Sinister just enough for Millites to land a crushing kick right in the Lord of Darkness's chest. Sinister stumbled backwards, but once he got to his feet, he was ready. In one hand was his black sword and in the other was his element wand of darkness.

"Speilton dies first," Sinister muttered as Speilton began to slowly back up, sword drawn.

"No!" Millites ran forward but Sinister was faster. A black substance exploded from his wand and crashed into Millites, throwing him into a tree. A black band of scratchy rope wrapped around his body.

The King of Darkness used his element of darkness to bind MIllites to the tree. The element wand had been given to Sinister months ago by Venefica, a witch and enemy of the Wizards.

Millites tugged against the harsh rope as Sinister announced, "Now, it's time for your playmate."

This time the darkness came out slowly and drifted to the ground. In seconds, it had grown and condensed to form the shape of a puma.

"Rarrww!" it growled, stalking toward Millites who was scrambling to get free.

"And now, it's just you and me," threatened Sinister as he walked up to Speilton.

"You don't scare me," Speilton's voice quavered ever so slightly, but Sinister noticed.

"Not very sure with words are you, young king? Let's see how you are with a sword."

Sinister leapt like a cat on a mouse. Speilton rolled out of the way as the sword struck the ground. He turned and engaged in a ferocious fight. The air was filled with the sounds of clashing swords, and Sinister's *helpful* remarks. "You're pathetic, weak. So are the Milwarians. You know its almost over...the war. Can't you feel it? This is the final chapter. And once it's over, whose side will you be on? Are you willing to die?"

The puma stalked closer to Millites. Froth dripped from its mouth, and its eyes were wild, red, and missing a pupil in one eye.

Millites was sawing away at the rope with his small knife that he kept in his pocket for emergencies. This qualified as a good reason to use it.

The puma sat back on its haunches. The hair on its back stood straight up, and even more froth (if that was possible) dripped from its blood-stained fangs.

Pop! The last rope broke and with a hiss, the puma leapt. Millites rolled forward, and the puma lunged over him as Millites lifted his blade and drug it across the creature's chest. It howled, flipped and bashed against the tree, dissolving into black dust.

Speilton's sword flipped into the air and clattered to the ground ten feet away. But it was ten feet too far.

"Your skills need improving," Sinister remarked. "Though sadly, it seems like your time is up."

Sinister raised his sword, ready to strike Speilton. The Calorians began to cheer, but their attention was so distracted by the prospect of the end of King Speilton, they didn't see a plan at work.

"NO!" Millites threw himself against Sinister, and they both tumbled to the ground. (Hey, I said it was a plan, not a good plan.)

Millites scrambled to his feet first, drew his sword and brought it down on Sinister's chest. He felt it sink halfway through the armor, but suddenly stop. That blow should've gone straight to his heart.

"Ah, so you've noticed my new armor ... Monticore hide. It's thick, yet lightweight. Very efficient," Sinister boasted as Millites strained to pull his sword out of the armor.

Sinister struck Millites across the face, and the king crumpled to the ground. The Lord of Darkness pulled the sword from his armor with ease.

"The King's sword!" he announced, tossing the sword into the jeering crowd of Calorians. "And now, I put King Millites to-"

A red ball of flames exploded in between Sinister and Millites. A blue shape darted out of the sky and began circling the Calorians, spitting blue flames into the crowd. The circle of Calorians began running around in a frenzy with flames dancing across their backs. But Sinister dismissed the chaos and walked straight through the flames, ready to end Millites. The good king could only stare up at Sinister as he walked toward him.

Suddenly a pitch black creature landed between them. At first it appeared to be a Daerd, a huge, black, spiked crow with fangs. The bright green eyes and deep red blood dripping down the neck showed it to be Hunger, now black in complete fear.

Now, dragons are many things: energetic, dismissive, prideful, boastful, lazy, stubborn, and slightly deadly. Fearful is not one of them. The young Hunger to landed in a swarm of flaming Calorians and stood up to the King of Evil.

"Back away beast. This isn't your fight," Sinister commanded. Hunger lowered his head, stared Sinister straight in the eye, showed his sharp teeth and growled.

"Then die."

"CRAAAAW!" called a figure from above that blocked out half the stars.

11

This time, Millites was ready. He leapt on to Hunger's back, and they darted into the sky as Worc crashed where they had been only seconds before. The giant crow looked up, spotted them, and continued the chase.

As they began to fly, Millites rested his hand on Hunger's gash. The scales had been torn away, and Worc's talon had cut into Hunger's unprotected flesh below.

Millites caught sight of Speilton climbing aboard Prowl and taking to the sky. Then, suddenly he remembered something.

"Hunger, one more stop," Millites said as they dove down over the flaming Calorians. Finally, Millites found the one for whom he'd been searching.

"I believe this is mine," Millites said plucking his lightning bolt bladed sword out of a Calorian's hand.

They flew up next to Speilton. "What's the next move?" Millites asked.

"Why are you asking me? Don't you usually decide what to do?" Speilton smirked.

"Well, I don't have any ideas."

"Then, since you mentioned it, I do have a plan. Sort of."

"Go on."

"But it's going to be dangerous," Speilton added.

"Good, that's just the way I like it."

FISH, SOUP & STEAK
~ 2 ~

"Hyah! Here, you big crow!" Worc snapped his large jaws, his wings pumping after Prowl. The dragon and the giant crow dodged through trees, swerving through, under, and over the canopy. Somehow, it always ended up this way - with Worc right on Prowl's tail. Except this time, they needed the chase. The only problem was that they had to wait for Millites. Right now they were trying to waste time and distract Worc, without losing speed.

Down below on the ground, Millites was rousing the warriors. "Men! Fall back!" A trumpet sounded as Millites struggled to get the men to follow him on Hunger. "Get on your horses or just run. Everyone follow me."

The Milwarian warriors scrambled, with the Calorians closely following. The two armies had been intertwined only seconds before. Now, the Calorians followed them, cutting down the men from behind. At this rate, Millites knew they weren't going to make it.

Millites glanced over his shoulder to Usus who was flying along side him on the back of his golden griffin, Flamane. "Can you hold them off?" he asked.

Usus nodded his head and told the king, "You continue on. We'll fall in behind you." The Second in Command flew back over the Milwarians and landed just in between the armies of good and evil that were fighting while running after Millites. But without any commands or any one leading them, many Milwarian warriors were falling easily. "Men, ready," Usus commanded, "We must protect. Get ready to fight, for your country."

And that small group of a dozen warriors prepared themselves for their last stand.

Speilton was nearing his target. Worc was still steaming on behind him. "Hurry," Speilton muttered to the army of Milwarians that were being led by Millites.

Speilton dodged a grove of trees, and his target came into view. Up ahead was the bell tower. It was an ancient tower that had been rousing troops out of beds for decades. The stone walls were now old and weathered and were overgrown with vines (some of which had been burned away, thanks to Hunger). For generations, this tower had stood as a mark of endurance, in a camp that was as old as the Rich Woods itself. Too bad it was about to be destroyed in a few seconds.

Down below Prowl, the Milwarians were charging after the tower. Millites drifted over them, egging on the warriors. He looked up and gave Speilton the thumbs up. Speilton did the same, then took off towards the tower, Prowl flying at top speed. They were going to make it.

Ceeruuunk! Two massive boulders flew up from behind Prowl, hurtling from the catapults, and crushing into the tower with a massive *THUNK*.

The tower shuddered, and many of the bricks clattered to the ground. The boulders rolled into the center of the tower and dropped to the ground. Phase one, complete.

Now all they had to do was get Worc to… Massive jaws clamped onto Prowl's tail. Worc swung his head wildly, thrashing Prowl around in the sky. Speilton struggled to hold on. They were so close to succeeding, yet they'd been stopped here.

Prowl struggled to take control, while being tossed this way and that. Finally, she was able to turn her body, just enough to billow a jet of flames into Worc's face. By now, Prowl knew it wouldn't kill the King Daerd (since his feathers were fireproof), but it stunned him just long enough for Prowl to launch herself back into the air.

Worc was ready. He pressed in so close behind them that Speilton's body stung from the heat given off by the flaming Daerd.

They reached the crumbling tower, and Prowl hardly had a second to react. She caught hold of the piled bricks and kicked up just a few feet higher. Those few feet probably saved their lives, as Worc crashed through the tower. The bell rang one more time before collapsing onto the Calorian army.

The bit of wall that Prowl was clinging to dropped away and crashed down like the bell. The blue dragon groped for a second, searching for solid ground. Prowl and Speilton fell a few feet before the dragon unfurled her wings and drifted to the ground.

Worc's limp body collapsed to the ground amidst the rubble and crushed Calorians. The blue flames that had covered his body spread, catching the tower's overgrown vines on fire.

The plan had worked. But Speilton and Prowl couldn't celebrate yet. They still had to get all the Calorians through.

Prowl cleared a path through the flames to allow the Milwarians to flee, although she left a few flaming boulders on either side to keep the Calorians from rushing in to attack.

As the Milwarians disappeared into the forest, the Calorians didn't try to pursue them. The battle was already over, and even though the Milwarians had won, they knew they would still be there to fight another day.

The sun rose into the sky for the first time since the battle had begun, but the Milwarians were long gone. Usus's group of twelve men (now with only six) caught up with the main army, their duties fulfilled. It hadn't been a victory, but they'd survived. In this war, that meant as much as a win.

After a few hours of walking they made a new camp to heal the injured. There they ate lunch and regrouped. They took attendance to see who was no longer with them, and had a ceremony for Toroe and all of the others who had been killed. The sun was setting when the survivors of the war marched up to Lake Justice, a huge body of water surrounding Kon Malopy, the capitol of Milwaria.

After crossing a thin path leading through the lake and to the castle where a great battle had taken place half a year ago, they came to the village and fields that lay at the base of a circle of cliffs. The soldiers were met by a cheering crowd, as they usually were after every battle. They looked for their families and ran to them in the crowds. The families looked for their fathers and husbands and children, though some were never able to see them again. But for those who were reunited again, it was a very special time.

Millites, Speilton, Usus, Andereer, the two dragons, and the griffin walked up the steep slope to the castle.

Kon Malopy is made up of four walls connected by towers to create a square. The insides are a labyrinth of twisted halls with rooms branching off in all directions. In the center of the castle is the Banquet Hall, and above is the tallest tower in all of Liolia, the continent in which Milwaria and Caloria are settled.

As Millites, Speilton, Prowl, and Hunger entered, Teews, their younger sister and Queen of Milwaria, leapt forward and wrapped the two kings in a warm embrace. The two dragons scampered into their den, hoping to find dinner ready for them.

"Millites! Speilton! Are you all right? How was the battle? Did you win? It's been so boring here with-" but Teews never got to finish her eternal flood of questions.

"How's Ram? We needed his strength and courage today," Millites blurted out.

"Oh, I'm very worried about Ram. According to my research of his symptoms, I believe he has the Rush from breathing in too much Calorian smoke. An elf is up there right now trying to help him. Usus walked in just before you and went up to check."

Millites and Speilton drew in a sharp breath before running towards the stairs that lead to Ram's room.

"NO!" shrieked Teews grabbing the boys' arms. "The infection from the Rush is highly contagious. Nicholas, the elf who's been caring for him, has been instructed not to allow you in the room."

"But how was Usus able to go up there?" Speilton asked.

"You know that Usus is good with potions and elixirs."

"So you're implying that we aren't good at making those things?" Millites asked with a smirk on his face.

"Honestly, you guys are pathetic at potions. I would never trust you to help," Teews laughed.

"Wow, thanks," Speilton said sarcastically, "So, what are we supposed to do?" Speilton questioned.

"Well, you must be starving!" Teews suggested.

So, the Kings washed up, walked down to the Banquet Hall and sat at the table that was made into the shape of a sword. The second they sat down, Chef Bone Appateet appeared out of the kitchen and drifted over to the table. "Ah, hello

King Millites, King Speilton. I assume the battle went well?"

"Hardly," Millites scoffed.

"Ah, well, you know what they say. Better luck, um… later… or something like that," joked the rotund chef as he laughed, his curled mustache bouncing as he did it.

"I believe it's 'better luck next time'," Speilton offered.

"Oh yes, of course. So, what would suit your tastes this evening?" Appateet asked, happy to change the subject.

"I would love to have a little rose petal soup. You know how I like it spiced with your special ginger seasoning," Teews smiled.

"And you?" he turned to Speilton.

"Grilled salmon sounds really good right now," Speilton said.

"King Millites?" Bone asked.

"Steak, rare with a lot of your good au jus, please!" Millites licked his lips.

"Right away. I'll be back in a moment," the chef said bouncing away.

"So, Millites, did you see a weak point in Sinister's armor?" Speilton asked.

Millites and Speilton had been trying to find a weakness, a chink in Sinister's armor for months. "Unfortunately, no. I'm not any closer than when we started."

"So he has new armor now, right?" Speilton asked.

"Yeah. It's too thick. If we can't determine how to destroy him soon, all of our men will be dead."

"How many casualties did we have today?" Speilton asked, not sure he wanted to know the number.

"One hundred and seventy two."

Speilton's jaw dropped.

"Here, I'll let you two talk. If I'm not allowed to fight in the war, I don't want to hear all the details about what I'm missing. Unless, of course, you'd like *my* opinion," Teews moaned. "I'll ask Bone Appateet to deliver my soup to my room," she sighed walking up the stairs.

Millites knew that despite her protest, he had to protect his sister since her responsibility at the castle was more important. He continued as if he were unfazed by her frustration. "Sinister's new armor is made of Monticore hide. My sword got stuck halfway through it."

"What about his back?" Speilton asked.

"Covered in chainmail, laced with thick strips of leather. No chance of breaching him there either."

"So, what's your plan?" Speilton wondered.

Millites wasn't able to answer because at that moment, Bone Appateet flew from the kitchen and plopped down Millites' steak, Speilton's fish, a bowl of bread, and a fruit salad.

"Dinner is served!" Appateet announced as he raced up the stairs to Teews' room.

"So, the plan?" Speilton asked again.

"If we can't beat Sinister, we must defeat the Calorians at their roots," Millites sighed.

"What?" Speilton asked dropping his fork in surprise. "How are we going to get there and do… that! It's impossible, insane."

"It's the only way!"

"That's even more difficult than killing Sinister! I'd rather kill him myself. I can fight the Lord of Darkness to the end. We can't risk failing that mission."

"No! No one is going to fight Sinister! Especially not you!" Millites commanded.

"Are you saying I'm not allowed to fight him, or I'm not able to?"

Millites didn't respond.

"So only you are able to fight him. Not me, not anyone else, you won't even let Teews help."

"We can't all die! Milwaria needs a leader and a warrior and a Queen. I took on the role of both warrior and leader when I was barely five. Though from the very beginning, I've been mostly a warrior. When people asked for good news, I had none to give. When people asked for advice, I had nothing to offer. Now that you're here, you must be the leader. You must be the one who lives and stays alive. You are an inspiration to the Milwarians. I must be the warrior. That's all I know and have ever known. I must be the one to risk my life. It's a decision I made in the beginning. Because, Speilton, in the end, Milwaria doesn't need a warrior to lead them. Milwaria needs a leader to guide and inspire them," Millites concluded.

Speilton just sat there. Now it was his turn to not have anything to say. Luckily, he was spared by Usus who flooded down the stairs, followed by a young boy at his heels with long blond hair. Something about the boy's face seemed distorted and a little strange to Speilton, but the thought left his mind as Usus gasped, "Ram has been horribly taken by the Rush. Only Rilly can save him now!"

The next morning, after a light breakfast, the royalty ventured into the Rich Woods. The sun had just completely peaked above the horizon, and nature was bristling around to get everyone up and ready for the day. They first walked out of the huge front doors, newly repaired after the last battle it had encountered, and walked onto the cobblestone path that led down an easy incline connecting the village with Kon Malopy. The castle was set upon a ring of high cliffs which gave it an advantage in battle.

Once reaching the village, men and animals alike halted and dropped to their knees in respect to the kings and queen, and a few other royal knights and servants who rode along behind on brilliant white horses. Millites stroked the soft, thick mane of his noble pet lion, Rorret, as they marched forward. They were followed by Speilton on Prowl, and Teews on her Clydesdale. After parading through the village and cutting through the traffic, they took off across the tiny strip that connected the island to the land. Crossing the stretch brought back bad memories for Millites. Many good men died here on this stretch. Many Calorians died here too. The place reeked of death, of tragedy, and of victory.

They were all happy to reach the Rich Woods. Once entering, everyone is taken under its spell. At first it seems like a dark area. Then you'd see light peeking out of little gaps in the leaves, throwing dancing shapes onto the forest floor. The next thing you'd notice are the trees with their round bases and twisted, gnarled branches and long, glassy bushels of different shades of green leaves. Then, there are the other plants. The vibrant flowers and tall weeds that swish and sway in the cool breeze and the tall shrubs and shorter trees with fruits and leaves unique to that one tree add to the color and splendor.

There are also the sounds of the tiny birds chirping in a frenzy in the trees. Thin deer fawns trot through the forest as their mother shows them which fruits are tasty and teaches them not to eat certain berries. That's how the Rich Woods was every Spring. It didn't matter that Liolia was in the depth of a war. It was always that amazing. No less.

When the group finally arrived at Rilly's, the sun was perched straight above. Rilly was the oracle the Milwarians depended upon to provide cures for life-threatening situations and knowledge of the mysteries of Liolia. Even before reaching Rilly's shack, they saw the Forest People (elves, dryads, fauns, and satyrs) leaping in a happy dance in a circle. The Forest People had always gathered near Rilly. No one knew why, but the first of the Forest People who reached the Rich Woods did so, and so did their children, and their children, and on until this very day.

In a small clearing in the middle of the forest was a small shack, a fire pit, and a tiny well. This was Rilly's house. As the party approached the shack, the wind around them blew and spun. Petals on the ground, blades of grass, loose leaves, even a few dried fruits were whisked up into the sky and began to spin around in a vortex of wind. Slowly the vortex took the shape of a humanoid figure. As the wind slowed, the leaves and petals and fruits all assembled themselves together into the shape of man.

No one was afraid. No one backed down. The man was no enemy. "Hello Rilly!" Millites smiled.

"I have been expecting you. Please, come in!" the wind man gestured.

As Millites, Speilton, and Teews entered the shack, leaving the servants to watch the animals, they noticed a large, hovering object in the air above an empty cauldron. The rest of the room was dark.

Once he looked closely at the sphere, Speilton saw an image of Ram lying, moaning, in his bed, Usus and the elf at his side.

"Rilly, what is that?" Speilton asked amused.

"It's a sphere, a shadow of time from my book," Rilly answered casually.

"So, is that..." Speilton gestured to the image on the sphere, "what is happening right now?"

"Yes. I assume it is for that reason that you came?" Rilly asked as he stirred the empty cauldron with a stick, causing the sphere to disappear.

"Usus said you are the only one who can help him," Millites explained.

"He's right. The Rush is horrible to go through. Horrible, horrible, disease. Even more horrible to get rid of." Rilly began to shuffle through his potions and elixirs. "Nearly always fatal. Breathed in too much Calorian smoke, I presume."

"Yes, it was only a few days ago. He was surrounded by Calorians and fought them off, but was overcome by the smoke as they evaporated," Speilton explained.

"Ah!" Rilly drew a clear vile of purple liquid off one of his shelves. "Well, this should cure him. Give him one tablespoon after every meal for two days. Let him rest."

"Thank you!" Teews said as they all turned around to leave.

"Everything happens for a reason," Rilly mumbled.

"Excuse me?" Millites asked.

"Ram became sick for a reason. He caused you to come to my hut. There is another important consideration for your coming here."

"What's the other reason?" Speilton asked confused.

"So that you could learn how to succeed in the war," Rilly quickly responded.

"Are you saying that you know how to defeat the Calorians?" Millites asked.

"Really? Why didn't you come to Kon Malopy to tell us?" Speilton wondered.

"My body is linked to this area. My soul is unable to leave this land. I can only communicate with you when you are here."

"So, do you know how to destroy them?" Speilton asked. " Do you have a plan to defeat the Calorians?"

"Yes. My book tells of the history of Liolia. It tells the past, the present, and the future. It tells of all the steps that must be taken to reach a victory, but some pieces are harder to pull out of the book than others. Some pieces I can't pull up at all, for the magic containing the piece is too strong for me.

Those parts tell the outcome of the future. The farther ahead into the future I, the more difficult it is to determine. But the past can easily be unlocked from here," Rilly shrugged.

The wind man floated over to a thick book with a rotting leather cover. Rilly opened it and flipped through the pages. "Ah, here we are!" Rilly sighed, pressing his finger down on a page. He shut his peach eyes and focused silently. Slowly a thin stick rose out of the page like a branch, until it reached a foot long. Rilly snatched it up and tossed it into the cauldron. He walked to the side of the room and pulled out a bottle of green froth, with a star symbol etched into its side. Rilly poured the thick potion and began to stir the bubbling cauldron. At first he stirred slowly, then quickly. Suddenly, the liquid began to morph and change. It seeped away from the edges of the cauldron and began to form a sphere. The large circular disk rose up into the air, the green froth dripped from the sides but evaporated the second it touched the cauldron.

"Isn't that the same thing that showed Ram?" Teews asked, taken back by the colorful object.

"Yes, this is the same *substance*, but not the same sphere. This sphere is the first of two spheres that explain a story. But the one you saw before told a different story. It showed the steps that would cause you to come here. This one tells the steps of how to win the war, or at least lead you to a final battle between the Milwarians and Calorians," Rilly explained as the sphere slowly began to show a picture.

"So, this scene, what we're doing right now, is this in the book?" Speilton asked.

"No. This part is not. You see, this part is an outcome. I am only able to pull out the steps to a final journey. This sphere right here will show what you must do before your adventure. The outcomes are too powerful for me to pull out. The only way to see them is to actually experience them in person, or draw them out after they have already happened. Now, watch carefully. All of this is important," Rilly said.

The sphere began to glow brighter and brighter until the luminescence lit the whole room with sparkling light. Suddenly, sparks like tiny comets sprung from the sphere and glided across the room. Once finding a certain place, it detonated, creating a circle of fizzing light that hung in the air. The number of sparks increased rapidly, exploding every second. Then, piece by piece, the tiny explosions began to form a dome of sparkling light that surrounded the four of them.

The sphere that floated over the cauldron grew, filling up every space of the room. When the sphere washed over the four bystanders, they felt an odd sensation of complete numbness and weightlessness. Their minds lost all thought but what they were doing at the moment.

Suddenly, an image appeared in the haze of fizzing light. It showed three boys, one girl, and four animals marching across the plains. They appeared appeared to be Millites, Speilton, Usus, Teews, Hunger, Prowl, Flamane, and Brisk, Teews's Clydesdale, though the entire image was foggy, and they couldn't be sure. Suddenly the people in the image came to a castle, half washed over by the rising tide. The image blurred for a second before coming back into focus to show them all on a ship gliding out to sea.

The image changed as Rilly dropped in another stick from his book. This image was a different color, a red shade. It showed four men this time, Ram included, so the new image must've been a few days later. The pets weren't there with them, and neither was Teews and Brisk. Instead, there were six other creatures, meaning that in all, there were ten adventurers.

Speilton named the different creatures in his head. The animal with the body of a horse, but the torso and head of a human extending out from where the horses head should've been, was a centaur. The young girl who had crazy, frayed hair, and a dress that resembled a trunk, was a dryad. The small bearded man was a dwarf and the tall boyish, pointy-eared creature was an elf. The two goat-legged, horned humanoids were a faun and a satyr. Speilton knew that the Satyr was the one with longer, curled horns, and was buffer, shorter, and hairier than the other. Fauns were normally taller, more musical, very timid, and had tiny little stumps of horns.

The creatures and the humans seemed to be on a journey as the scene around them changed from dry desert, to open plains, to rushing rivers, to thick jungle, to icy tundra, to rocky gorges, to grim forests. Suddenly, a castle rose before the nine of them. *Nine* Speilton noticed, *There should be ten.* Speilton counted again but still got nine. Then two thoughts collided in his head. The first was, *that castle is Skilt!* The second was, *not all of us who go on the adventure will survive!* Speilton tried to determine who the missing person was and was still wondering if what he saw was really Skilt when the scene changed. The nine quickly turned into the woods and faced a cave, hidden in a thick growth of black trees.

The picture quickly disappeared, and the dome of light with it. All of it imploded into the cauldron in a loud CRACK!

"What…was…that?" Teews asked in a panic.

"It's worse than I thought. Much harder, much more dangerous," Rilly muttered.

"Wait! You mean that you've never seen that before?" Millites asked bewildered.

"Of course not! Each of those spheres can only be seen once."

"Then how did you know which page to look on? And how'd you know what we would see in that sphere?" Millites questioned.

"As for your first question, all of the spheres are in order of sequence. And for your second question, I didn't know what we'd see. I just knew that it would show how this war would end," Rilly said picking up the book to show the rest of them. "Each page has a tiny sentence written in the Ancient Language. It's like a title or a caption, but that's all. I had no idea what we'd see exactly."

"We're not going to make it. Someone's going to die," Speilton mumbled.

"What?" the three asked simultaneously.

In the sphere, at first it showed ten people, but once they reached the castle," (Speilton couldn't admit to himself it was Skilt) "there were only nine," Speilton choked out. "We can't go. It's too dangerous!"

"Speilton, my young king, there's no other choice. The fate of Milwaria was decided at the beginning of time. It is all laid out in this book. You can not change history, or things may go horribly wrong. This is the only way," Rilly pleaded.

Speilton said no more, so Millites asked, "Rilly, what did it mean? I got the beginning of the first image. We must go to Mermaid Cove, but where was that boat sailing?"

"It stumped me, too, at first, but then I noticed that it must have been sailing towards the Wizard's Island, far off the coast of Mermaid Cove. It's a small island but almost impossible to reach. On that island, the Wizard Council joins together to discuss matters every full moon. And, it just so happens that the next full moon is …" Rilly pulled out a scroll from his desk with what looked to be the shimmering image of the moon at that very time (full except for a thin sliver) "in three days!"

"So that means that we must talk to the Wizards," Millites suggested.

"Yes, they will probably make everything clear," Rilly said.

"But what about those creatures? We should probably start looking for them soon!" Teews suggested.

"That, I will take care of. Four of the creatures were the Forest People," Rilly offered. "Now, you must be on your way if you are to reach the island in three days."

And so the three walked out of the hut, climbed onto their animals, and took off into the forest, Ram's medicine deep in Millites' pocket. Though this trip had become much more than helping Ram.

His eyes began to blur. His stomach swam. Speilton slowly began losing consciousness as he slipped off Prowl's rigid back. No one else around him seemed to be affected. But the dizzier he got, the farther away he seemed to slip from them. The tall trees of the Rich Woods rose to a towering height, and Millites, Teews, and the rest seemed to be slowly moving away. His eyes spun, his head ached, his stomach flipped, and suddenly, he noticed he was all alone.

Speilton felt he was being watched. Peeking eyes were staring at him in the low shrubs. He could sense their gazing watch. He could hear their deep raspy breathing, and he could feel the perspiration slowly rolling down gnarled, etched skin. He could even sense their depraved souls begging for death.

Speilton began to run, wand drawn before him, but the more he ran, the farther away from his destination he seemed to be. "Show yourself," he called.

Suddenly, he heard a deep groaning growl behind him. He turned just in time to see a wolf-like creature with huge, bulging blood shot eyes and claws that arced into foot-long sabers, and blood-matted fur. The creature lunged off its perch high up in the tree. In midair it dissolved into a wisp of black smoke, which twirled and coiled back into the forest. Two more wisps of smoke drifted next to the first. Then the wisps began to morph and take the shape of a bird, then, a cloaked man. Speilton couldn't figure out which it was. A ripped cloak was laid over a bird-like figure. It had two wings jutting out from under the cloak, and tail feathers fell down below it. The chest hidden by the cloak could still be seen. It seemed to have rotted over the bones, showing a ribcage with either flesh webbed so tightly that the bones were very easily seen, or their was no flesh at all.

The three creatures drifted toward Speilton who was struggling with all his might to get away. Though no matter how hard he tried, his feet were glued to the spot.

"Why do you struggle?" one of the creatures asked. Since Speilton couldn't see the creatures' faces, and the voices seemed to echo with a harsh and raspy tone off of the trees around him, he had no idea who was talking.

"We are the Versipellis. Though you don't know us, we know everything about you. We have been watching you since the day you were born."

"Why have you come here? What do you want with me?" Speilton asked.

"You were created to do great things. And if you join us, we could help you reach your ultimate potential. We have come to negotiate."

"Negotiate what?" Speilton asked.

"Your life. We've come to offer you a chance to live. With your loyalties to the Milwarians, failure is inevitable. But with the Calorians, you could become a hero."

"I'd never become one of them," Speilton spat.

"Are you so sure?" the Versipellis asked in a raspy, earthy tone. "Milwaria is dying," the Versipellis announced. "In two years, it'll be nothing more than a barren wasteland. You must believe us."

"I don't believe you," Speilton seethed. "I would never become a Calorian."

"You would be great leader of the Calorians - respected and revered. You are already possess the most powerful characteristic of a Calorian."

"How?" Speilton questioned.

"Your wand of fire. It's the Calorians' best weapon."

It was true, and Speilton knew it.

"You were raised there for most of your life. While the Milwarians wouldn't protect you, Caloria did. For years, you lived in Caloria. It is your true home."

"But the Milwarians are my family, my friends. I couldn't leave them," Speilton insisted.

"Are they really that good to you? Millites doesn't think you're good enough to fight Sinister. But with the Calorians, you would be fighting right alongside the Lord of Darkness."

"I'm not a traitor. And besides, even if I did join, which is, by the way, never going to happen, I would be the only human in the army."

"But you're not the only human. There are many others, all of whom have been sent on … special assignments. Such as, Anthony Jackson, the human who organized the raid of Lake Rou." Speilton remembered that horrible battle. "And Incertus. His assignment is very precise, though, very dangerous. His time is coming soon. Though, if he fails, it will be easy for us to roast him in the fires."

The other two Versipellis laughed coldly. "Not that you would ever be treated like this," The Calorian continued, "You could become the most famous human ever to join Caloria. You would receive the ultimate significance. Besides, who cares what the Milwarians think of you? This is your chance for a new life with opportunity."

"No, I'm a Milwarian, and that's how I'm going to stay!" Speilton declared.

"You're going to regret that, King Lux." The voice seemed to come from all three of them this time.

The Versipellis dissolved into wisps of smoke again, but this time coiled all together. They formed a huge funnel cloud which drifted toward Speilton, engulfing him into its swirling tornado of smoke. "You'll regret that!"

"Speilton! Speilton, wake up! We're back at the castle," Millites shook Speilton awake. "What were you dreaming about? You were moaning. Are you alright?"

"Nothing, it was nothing," Speilton insisted.

Speilton just couldn't bring himself to tell Millites about his dream. Although they were brothers, they were just beginning to form a trusting relationship. Millites and Teews had experienced great loss, also, and were given incredible responsibility for their country. How could he possibly tell them that the enemy was trying to recruit him without losing their confidence in him. He couldn't find the courage to tell Millites that something horrible was happening. What would Millites think of him if he knew that he was being offered a new life in Caloria? Would Millites believe that he was truly dedicated to Milwaria as they were losing the battle? Or would he look skeptically on him afterwards?

No, he couldn't tell him, not yet. For now, the Versipellis had to be a secret.

THE FLOODED CASTLE
~ 4 ~

After giving the medicine to Nicholas to administer to Ram, and loading up the animals with food and water, they all started back into the forest. This time they walked east once reaching the Rich Woods. During the long journey in the thick forest, Speilton had to ask, "Millites, what are the Versipellis?"

"The Versipellis? Where did you hear about them?" Millites asked.

"I just … read it in a book, up in Flame Tower," Speilton fibbed.

"Well, the Versipellis are three dream spirits of death and darkness. They travel from world to world, just like the Wizards from the Wizard Council. But instead of helping countries in need, they inflict horrible appearances and plot the downfall of the good nations. On each world they pick a single person and use them to tip the balance of good and evil, plunging the lands into death.

"They can sense when someone is weak. They are cunning and try to persuade their victims to come to the dark side. It's always a bad omen. It usually means that death lingers closely around the victim. In the end they always lead to the destruction of goodness and light."

"And, what, exactly, do they look like?" Speilton asked, his voice a bit shaky.

"Well, they are shape shifters. Their true form is a cloaked bird - pretty weird. But they also like to take the shape of a sort of serpentine human with freakish reflexes and arms like giant blades," Millites added flippantly.

"So, are they easily destroyed?" Speilton asked, hoping that if they could be destroyed, the whole thing would just blow over without him ever having to get this curse of death.

"No, they're actually very hard to kill, possibly harder to kill than Sinister himself," Millites said.

Speilton was shocked, not knowing what to say.

"You…you haven't seen them have you?" Millites asked, obviously noticing that Speilton was completely pale.

"No!" Speilton shot out quickly.

"Good! That's the last thing we need!" Millites exclaimed.

Speilton suddenly wanted to tell about his odd dream, let them know that they were all in serious danger, but he held it all in. The urge boiled inside of him like the urge to chug down an iced cup of water after gorging yourself with chili peppers.

He knew he couldn't tell them. If he was cursed, then the fact that death lingered around him would spark uncertainty. Would they alienate him or would it only make them want to protect him more, leaving them vulnerable to fall prey to the cold clutch of death. He must destroy the Versipellis himself and end them once and for all.

Luckily, his thoughts were interrupted as they entered into a farming town. It had grown late in the afternoon, so many of the workers were just finishing up. As the group trekked through the village, men and women looked up from their plows and fields to see who these strangers. Even the dogs froze in the middle of digging their holes, the cats woke from their afternoon snooze, the pigs stopped rolling in the mud, and animals of all kinds stared at the strangers. The first to get to them were the children. The youngest ones reached their arms up as high as they could to touch the velvet strips laid upon the animal's back.

The older kids stroked the manes of Rorret, Flamane, and Brisk, and the leathery blue scales of Prowl. As they looked up, they saw Hunger twirling and circling, billowing fire in loud arcs, obviously trying to show off.

The men and women rushed out of their houses and buildings to bow before the Kings and Queen. A jester leapt into the air as his friend began playing a lively song on his accordion, and a small boy did tricks with a scrawny monkey. As the jester juggled three hard, leather balls, the boy's monkey was suddenly distracted halfway in a back-flip, so that the hairy creature landed on his head. Teews giggled as the monkey hurtled through the air and snatched one of the jester's balls, and toppled to the ground, gnawing furiously on the hunk of leather. The jester scowled at the boy who ran to pick up the little, growling ball of fur, but then, noticing the pleasure and laughter of the Kings and Queen, told the boy to put the monkey down, and pretended as if it was all part of the play. The jester began to throw the balls back up into the air, letting the monkey snatch them. Everyone laughed at this. When the song that the jolly, round man was playing ended, the boy picked up the scrawny monkey and pried the soggy balls out of its mouth.

After many of the farmers offered the Kings, Queen, and their animals crops and meat, they were given rooms in the village inn. There they slept through the night. The next morning they were given more of the villagers' crops and milk before setting out for Mermaid Cove once more.

They walked all day, taking a break every hour. Their hike was slow and uneventful. The sun had just begun to shrink below the horizon behind them as they stood aloft a steep hill, casting a long shadow over the valley below them. When they looked down below, they saw a castle half buried in the rising tides of the Ocean. Perched on the top of the castle was a large ring of pure sapphire with a translucent canvas stretched out in the middle with figures and odd shapes. Speilton couldn't really make out what it was, but it interested him a great deal.

When they reached the bottom of the hill, a guard dressed in complete pearl and sapphire armor marched forward and asked them, "Friend or foe? Oh, my Kings! My Queen! Sir Usus! To what do I owe this honor?" the guard bowed politely.

"We have come under secret circumstances and need to speak with Neptune as quickly as possible," Millites informed the guard.

"Of course! Right this way, your majesties!" The guard directed them to the shoreline, pulled out a coral encrusted sword, and brandished it high above his head. Suddenly, the foam on the edge of a rising wave formed into two jets of water which rose into the air forming an archway. At first, Speilton could see the ocean and castle through the arch, but in a few seconds time, the flickering shape of a tunnel formed between.

"Right this way, follow me!" The guard entered the archway and Speilton, Millites, Teews and Usus, and the creatures followed.

The inside of the tunnel was a swirl of rushing water that rose over their heads. The path was crowded, since mermen and mermaids were entering the tunnel from the watery sides. Speilton noticed the odd way that the creatures moved, surprisingly fast in a sluggish sort of way, since the dorsal fin was laid flat and dragged as they scooted forward in short little lurches. As the Kings and Queen trudged forward on the damp, sandy ground, bits of water dripped off of the mermaids, and water that dripped from the walls and ceilings dampened their clothes. The warm, soothing waters from Mermaid Cove offered calm feelings. After walking about a quarter mile they descended a flight of steps and noticed that the next room was flooded.

"What's happened?" Teews asked.

"Oh, it's nothing! It's just to refresh the mermaids. The water doesn't affect humans. Here watch!" the guard told them as he stepped down into the water which suddenly spread, creating a cavity in the pool of water. Reluctantly, Teews followed, stepping gingerly as the water pushed away.

As they began to walk on, Speilton asked the guard, "So, if everyone else is a mer… person, then why are you human?"

"Well, mermaids can't stay out of water for very long. That's why this place is flooded," the guard said very matter-of-factly. After turning a corner, they came to a huge coral doorway which was opened wide and came to a large courtyard filled with merpeople, or mers, as they were known in Liolia. They walked across the courtyard, took a right into a room with tall diamond and coral-encrusted columns and turned left into a room where the walls were the sea itself. On the other side were colorful, dazzling fish. At the end of the passage were two golden doors. Outside were two guards, both mers.

"Tell King Neptune that the Kings and Queen are here." As the guard escorting Speilton, Millites, Teews, and Usus said this, one of the guards rushed into the room.

Though Neptune was called *King* Neptune, he was really more of a Duke, in control of a territory, almost like a governor.

The guard returned less than fifteen seconds later and swiftly spoke, in a sort of melodic voice, "Please, your Majesties, enter."

As they entered the large room, King Neptune, sitting in his tall blue velvet throne, welcomed them. "Please, sit down." He gestured to a round table in the center of the room as he walked down to sit with them. "Tell me, why have you come?"

"I'm sorry, but that is secret. But I will tell you that it could lead to ending the war," Millites said wistfully.

"But why is it you came here? What do you want with me?" Neptune asked.

"It's not you we want. It's a boat. We need a boat," Speilton said.

"Well, I'm sorry. I have no more boats to lend. They are all being used in the war. The only other ship is the Night Seemer."

The Night Seemer was a fabled boat, the swiftest, best armed, largest ship in all of Milwaria. And, it had the newest artillery weapon every invented, the cannon. They had placed many of there ingenious weapons aboard the ship, making it one of the best boats around.

"We must use it. It is crucial that we have a ship by tomorrow," Usus argued.

"I will not give it over. It is the only protection we have here in case we are attacked. The mers have many enemies, all of whom would attack if we were vulnerable. There have been rumors that the Anglers are gathering." The Anglers are a group of horrifying, water dwelling creatures with muscled, slimy, scaly skin. "And Cetus has come back! He could attack any second now. We stopped him once, but we do not have the ability to stop him again. I'm not taking that chance. Why can't you ask Selppir, he hasn't helped out in the war at all! Half of the boats he has just sit there -"

"You will just give us that one ship, won't you?" Teews asked in her soft, sweet manner.

Neptune's eyes suddenly went out of focus and an ear-to-ear smile spread across his face. "Of course," was all he could say before he slumped back into his chair and passed out.

"How did you? What just?" Speilton stammered.

"Oh, it was nothing," Teews hummed stuffing her wand of love into her pocket.

"Nice job!" Millites admitted as they left the room and walked back to the guards.

"Are you going to be staying with us for long?" the guard asked.

"Just one night," Usus said.

The guard walked over to a mermaid and whispered something into her ear. "Right this way your Majesties," the mermaid said as she bowed.

They followed her up a wide staircase. The mermaid bounded up the stairs two at a time. After climbing up two flights, they took a right through an archway. "Here we go," the mermaid said. "This suite is for Queen Teews." She gestured towards a door. "This one's for Millites. Over here is Speilton's, and finally this is for Usus'."

As they entered their rooms they all said goodnight. They had a long day ahead of them, so they retired early. The mermaid came into each room to make sure everything was to their satisfaction.

Speilton had been lying there in his bed pondering so many questions. Some of them were too horrifying to ask anyone else, but he finally decided to ask just one. When the mermaid entered his room he asked, "What is that big ring on the top of the tower?"

The mermaid was surprised by the sudden question, but responded by saying, "Well, the webbing inside of the ring tells of our history. The ring lines up perfectly to the rising sun on the summer and winter solstices. On those days, the images inside the ring are thrown across the hill. It's truly amazing. Everyone in the castle watches."

"What type of images does it show?" Speilton asked.

"It shows things like … our first victory over the Anglers, and our taming of the huge sea monster of destruction, Cetus, and the saving of the dolphins from the sharks," the mermaid added meekly.

"Thank you," Speilton said as he laid down on his bed and instantly fell asleep.

Dark figures loomed in the shadows. Speilton reached for his wand, but it wasn't there. His feet were rooted to the spot by an invisible force. As he stood there gaping, even more dark figures crept through the damp, moldy corridor. As he stood there, he began to hear a horrifying sound. It started softly but then grew louder. It was the sound of wailing, of screaming. He heard anguished cries, and sharp objects scratching against the stone walls. After a minute, all of these sounds began to jumble together and started to get louder and louder. Whoever or whatever was making that sound was getting closer. Soon the sound was so loud, it was almost unbearable. Just before Speilton expected his eardrums to burst, he felt a cold, gnarled, worn, clawed hand grip his shoulder, and the sound stopped. A shiver ran down his back as his body turned around to face the figure. It was the Versipellis but, this time, in a different form. It resembled a tall, lean, hunchbacked corpse who had been buried covered from head to toe in a black sheet. The sheet began to mold and rot onto the corpse, practically becoming part of the body. The Versipellis smelled of rotting flesh. Speilton tried to close his eyes and look away, but every time they closed, some mysterious force seemed to pry them open. Speilton then noticed what was opening his eyelids. It was the Versipellis's eye, the one thing that had to be destroyed to destroy the Versipellis itself. The Versipellis stared straight through Speilton. The eye was wide open, twitching, and blood-shot. It seemed full of fear, as if being held against its will by an evil master. Speilton almost felt pity for it, but once he looked into the eye, his head swam. The eye had hypnotic powers, and for a second, Speilton had fallen under its spell.

"You have been chosen…" The Versipellis growled in its ancient, hushed voice. "Your destiny awaits…"

The Versipellis took its clawed hand off Speilton who stumbled to the ground. As he began to crawl away, the Versipellis's gnarled hand shifted into a long machete. In one powerful leap, it sprung onto Speilton.

Speilton shot upright on his bed. Cold sweat was rolling down his body. He was panting so hard. "Grrrrrrr…." Speilton almost leapt out of his skin, but then noticed the sound had come from Prowl who was curled around the side of his bed.

The brilliant blue dragon was snorting out rings of greenish smoke that danced across the ceiling before disappearing. It was stuffy in the room, and hot. Speilton was drenched in sweat. He knew he couldn't fall back to sleep. He had to think but not in here. So he stood up, dressed himself, lit a candle, and stepped into the hallway. The corridors were empty, and Speilton's shoes hardly made a sound on the magical flooded floor. He climbed up flights of stairs that continuously spun in a circle. There seemed to be no end to the staircase. Speilton was about to turn around when the stairs ended in a large circular room. The walls were made of grey bricks, covered with clumps of colorful coral. In the center of the room was a ladder that led to a hole in the ceiling. He felt cool air rolling down into the room through the hole and the distinct smell of salt water lingered in the air. He walked across the room to the ladder. As he climbed the rungs, he looked up and saw glittering stars lighting up the sky. It was still night. As he reached the top of the ladder and walked out onto the roof, he realized he was on the top of the castle.

On his left he saw the steep hill on which he had stood not very long ago. On his right was a vast ocean. And above him was the large ring. Speilton knew that this was as good a place as any to think. Speilton sat down facing the ocean and the stars that reflected off of its watery surface. A cold wind whipped across Speilton's face, but it seemed to calm him. His mind emptied itself as he stared across the water.

Speilton began to make out images on the sea. The longer he sat, the more vivid they appeared. For a second, Speilton thought it was an army, or group of creatures hovering below the waves. He almost jumped up to alert the castle of an attack, but then realized it was the reflections of the images on the canvas with the moon creating the light. He saw the image of mers attacking sharks. He saw a King being presented with a crown. He saw a tremendous beast with huge arms and tentacles attacking a fleet of ships. On one ship was a man with a finger pointed straight at the creature. He saw the Night Seemer surrounded by ships, all sunk after a battle. As Speilton sat watching each of these images, his mind wandered, and he toppled over to sleep.

"Speilton! Speilton! Wake up, it's time to go!" Teews, Millites, Usus, and Rorret were standing over him. Prowl was hovering a few feet above him, staring down. "Are you okay?"

Speilton sat up, "Yeah, I'm fine."

"What are you doing up here?" Millites asked.

"I couldn't sleep. I needed some fresh air," Speilton moaned rubbing his eyes.

Prowl drifted down onto Speilton's lap. The blue dragon was a very special type, and changed size depending on how hungry she was. On a full belly, she could grow to nearly ten feet long. But with out having eaten in a while she was now the size of a Labrador Retriever. "Are you hungry girl? You look like you could eat a feast!"

"We have food on the ship. But we need to get going. We've been looking for you all morning, and it's put us behind schedule," Usus said.

They all fled down the twisting steps, circling around and around and around. Finally, they came back to the main steps which were once again crowded with mers. They raced through the crowd with Rorret at the front to clear a path. But to Speilton's surprise, once they entered the courtyard, instead of going back the way they had entered the day before, they turned left past a fountain with water that contained magical healing powers and ascended another flight of stairs.

They turned left again and walked down a long corridor. At the end was a harbor filled with mers rushing about. They were carrying yards and yards of rope onto the ship and preparing the sails. The Night Seemer had masts over one hundred feet tall, and huge sails with the painted emblem of a lion and a unicorn standing back to back in the middle of a sun, the emblem of Milwaria,

symbolizing that bravery and justice are the key to light. The sides of the ship had three levels of cannons with five cannons on each level, thirty cannons in all. Also, on the sides was the zig-zagging image of a serpent surrounded by black paint.

As the Milwarian leaders were standing there looking at the ship, two mermen walked up. The taller of the two bowed so low to the ground that his nose nearly brushed the wooden planks of the pier.

"Hello, Your Majesties. My name is Rolias, the Captain of the Night Seemer."

"Captain, yeah right!" the shorter, plumper one said.

Rolias gave the shorter one a little kick, if you could call it a kick.

"What do you mean? He is a Captain isn't he?" Usus asked.

"Well… every other captain is off fighting in the war. So he's the best we've got."

"You'll have to do. We need to get to the Wizard Island as fast as possible," said Millites.

They all boarded the ship, and as the last mers going on the voyage climbed aboard, other mermaids and mermen waved good bye. After a few minutes their sail caught the wind and they were blown out into the ocean. Prowl, Hunger, and Flamane flew to the top of the masts and ate their breakfast of huge chunks of meat in the crow's nest where the crew had left it for them. Rorret and Brisk went down below where they ate carrots and meat out of small tubs. Speilton, Millites, Usus, and Teews went down two levels and ate off a long table mounted firmly to the ground and had bread, cheeses, apples, and milk. After breakfast, they all walked on to the main deck.

"Ahoy!" the shorter man cheered as he steered the ship. "Rolias has a question."

Rolias pounced down the steps and walked over to Millites. "So ... where exactly are we sailing?"

"The Island of the Wizard Council should be somewhere around here," Millites suggested pointing to a place on Rolias' map.

As the sun crept higher and higher, Speilton's stomach grew sicker and sicker. The constant lurching and swaying of the ship flipped and tossed his stomach. Speilton spent most of his time with his head hanging over the side. But it actually worked out, because he was the first one to see the fog that was crawling towards them.

"What is that?" he asked.

"What's what?" Millites said.

"That fog over there. What's it covering?"

"We're almost there," Millites whispered, then shouted. "Rolias! Head over to the fog over there!"

"What fog - oh, you mean that fog. Yeah, I saw that a long time ago. Puffer, turn right!" Rolias said to the round man at the wheel.

The ship turned, and they all headed towards the fog. As soon as they reached the edge, wind seemed to stop. The sails fell limp and the boat stopped. Usus and Millites called up to the rig monkeys who help with the sails and ropes and told them to go down below and row. Slowly but steadily the ship trudged on. Once inside the fog, they were met with tall rock spires that appeared out of nowhere. They were able to avoid the rocks but scraped the bow, nearly crashing on a half-sunken ship. The Night Seemer shook violently but stayed intact. The ship slowly crept through the dense fog.

"Okay, that was too close," Millites stated as he began to climb up a rope ladder to the top of a mast. "I'm going to scout ahead."

"No! We can't divide up. What if you get lost in the fog? What if you're attacked? Who knows what's out there!" Teews tried to persuade Millites.

Millites reluctantly came back down. And again they took off into the fog.

After several more close calls, Speilton saw an object looming high up in the sky - the top of a tower. Below it, behind one more rock spire, was a wall of razor sharp spiked rocks jutting out of the side of a tower wall.

"Stop! Stop the ship!" Speilton screamed as he charged down the stairs. "Stop rowing! Stop!" The rig monkeys stopped suddenly but not without asking a billion questions. Speilton didn't answer any of them, but instead raced back up the stairs to the top. "What's wrong? What are you doing?" Millites asked.

All Speilton had to do was point ahead of them at the wall. "Oh no!" Millites muttered. "Did you tell the rig monkeys to stop rowing?"

"Of course! That's what I just did."

"Then why are we still moving?"

Speilton ran to the side of the ship and noticed that it was true, they were being pulled toward the razor rocks by strong current.

"Drop the anchor!" Speilton called.

Rolias ran over to the anchor and it plunged into the water with a loud *plunk*. As the anchor sank and sank, the ship gained more speed and grew closer and closer to the rocks.

"Come on, come on!" Speilton urged.

With a heart-stopping jerk, the rope became taut but didn't catch hold of anything. It wasn't long enough.

There was no time to think. The men hurried away from the front of the ship, hoping to survive the crash. Suddenly, the boat jerked to a stop. There was a loud creaking sound, as the ship moved ahead a few more inches, before stopping altogether. The men rushed to the side of the boat and peered down into the water.

"We're rising!" One man announced.

"The ship is on a rock pillar," Another said.

"It's lifting up the ship!" All of the men began talking over one another, pointing down into the water and explaining their theories. But none of them were right, as they all figured out the reason a few seconds later.

Usus stood outside the Captain's quarters, holding his wand out before him. Speilton noticed him first and ran to show Millites and Teews. Slowly, the men began to realize what was happening.

The Second in Command was the one who had saved them. Usus had used his wand element of stone to raise the floor of the Ocean up in a pillar. The Night Seemer was stuck on the pillar, just like many ships were stuck on reefs. But this time, running aground was like a miracle. It had stopped them from hitting the spikes.

Usus finally stopped his concentration, letting the ship rest on top of the pillar, with only a foot of its hull in the water.

A cheer rose from the boat in one loud outburst. After everyone thanked Usus, they decided what they should do next. Since there was no way to walk onto Wizard Island, they decided they had to fly onto it.

"We'll watch the boat," Rolias told them, "You can go ahead and fly." Millites jumped on Hunger, Usus leapt onto Flamane, and both Speilton and Teews climbed onto Prowl who was at the time, the largest of the flying animals. Together they all took to the sky, looking for an entrance to the palace.

Every inch of the island was consumed by the palace. Gleaming white walls of polished stone began just behind the ring of sharp spires and arched up forming a half dome. The roof of the palace was round on the edges and peaked into four little cone shaped points.

After circling the area, Teews called out, "I found it. There's a light down there on the side of the steep wall."

She pointed to a tiny gleam in the fog. "There's only one way to find out!" Speilton suggested, as Prowl dove down towards the the the shimmering light. They landed on a mass of jutting rock about fifty feet by fifty feet. Built into the castle wall only a few feet away, was a huge ivory door trimmed with silver.

"Millites! Usus! We've found it! We've found the door!" Speilton called.

Speilton could hear the beating of strong wings. At exactly the second Hunger and Flamane landed, the doors began to slowly open. On the other side of the door an aged figure was standing there looking straight at them.

"Hello. I've been expecting you to come for many days. Please, follow me."

The old man was dressed in purple robes, wore a black velvet, pointed hat, and had a beard that brushed the man's knees. Together, they walked across the room which was crowded with dozens of odd objects in glass-pedestaled cases, such as shrunken heads, amulets, coins, books, and many other unusual things. Where the wall and ceiling met was a long line of tapestries with pictures on them. Speilton realized that it depicted the history of Liolia.

On the first drapery closest to the left of the door showed the creation of their world. The next showed the formation of the two countries, Milwaria and Caloria. The Wodahs (the race that makes up the Calorians) and other evil creatures were marching away from the humans and many other creatures like the ones seen in Rilly's sphere. The next showed the building of the countries of Milwaria and Caloria. After that, the tapestries depicted the Golden age of Milwaria, and the horrible years the Calorians endured in their wastelands and bogs. The next depicted the first attack of the Calorians which started the Endless

War. The rest showed battles over the next few hundred years. One of the most recent paintings showed Speilton on his adventure to reach Kon Malopy. To the right of that -Speilton couldn't believe it - it showed them, walking through the halls of the Island of the Wizard Council.

It showed what was happening at that very second. Though after that, the tapestries were blank. Speilton's heart stopped as he looked at them. There were only four left. The end of Liolia was growing near, one way or another. He tried to think about something else. As they walked on, Speilton couldn't help but ask the wizard, "Are you-" he was cut off.

"Am I Cigam? Yes, and you are Speilton." He said this without even turning around to see who had spoken. "I assume Rilly sent you?"

"Yes, he said that before we can go on our quest we must speak to you," Millites said.

"There is much you don't know, that you need to know, such as how to enter Skilt and destroy the Inferno of Erif."

So it was true! Speilton thought. *They had to go to Skilt.*

"But wait, what does this, Inferno of... whatever have to do with this?" Usus asked flustered.

"The Inferno of Erif has everything to do with this. The Inferno of Erif is the entire reason for your quest," Cigam said.

"But what is the Inferno of Erif?" Teews asked.

"It is the eternal fire that creates the Calorians."

"But I thought that you can create the fires anywhere. Are you saying that there is only one spot they are created?" Speilton asked.

"No, you're right. The fires can be created anywhere. It just takes a certain spell over a fire to turn it into a fire that creates Calorians. But the Inferno of Erif is the largest chain of Calorian-creating fires in the world. The fires are so intense that they can create five Calorians each minute, which is three hundred Calorians an hour, though most of them do not survive the first few hours." Cigam explained.

"So… where is the Inferno of Erif?" Speilton asked, terrified of the answer he knew he would hear.

"It's located in the heart of Skilt." Cigam said mysteriously. They were all quiet, letting the thought sink in.

"But… how are we going to get into the Calorian's castle?" Millites asked.

"That's where you need my assistance. The Wizard Council has created a magical entrance so that there is a path, a second path into every place. There is always more than one way to get into or out of a situation. The Wizard Council has even made sure that there is a way to enter secretly into Skilt, but the only way to find these hidden entrances is to look through this." Cigam stuck out his empty hand and called, "Kigethma!"

Suddenly a twinkle of light shot through the sky and rested on Cigam's outstretched hand.

"Yes?" said the squeaky voice of a tiny, three inch tall pixie sitting on Cigam's hand.

"Go fetch the Eye Stone," Cigam commanded.

The pixie took to the sky and whizzed out of sight. Five seconds later she returned with a ring around her waist. "Here you go, sir!" The Pixie announced, tossing the ring to Cigam.

"Thank you," Cigam turned back to Millites, Speilton, Teews, Usus, and the creatures. "Just look through this ring, the Eye Stone. It'll show you the entrance which will be somewhere in the Evly Forest. But beware, the passage will test you. The magical passageway will challenge in four different ways; skill, agility, strength, and determination. If one of you fails while trying to complete your task, he will be terminated and the remaining three will be sent back to the beginning of the entranceway." He handed the Eye Stone to Speilton who shoved it deep into his pocket. "Oh, and Millites, make sure to remember the tales of the great heroes. Their victories are more than fiction."

"What do you mean?" Millites asked.

"I am sorry, but that is all I can tell you."

"So when we get into the castle, how will we be able to find the Inferno of Erif?" Usus asked.

Cigam responded by flippantly saying, "I have absolutely no idea. That's for you to determine."

"Okay...how do we destroy the Inferno of Erif?" Millites asked, swishing the thought of having to search through the castle without any help around in his head.

"Kigethma!" "Cigam called.

Again, the twinkling light of the pixie dashed through the air and landed on Cigam's outstretched hand. "Yes?"

"Please fetch the vials of Aqua," Cigam commanded.

Again the pixie took to the sky, returning with a long string with four vials filled with blue liquid threaded to it. "Here are the vials!" the squeaky voice said as she dropped the string onto Cigam's hand.

"Thank you. Now, your Majesties, all you have to do is break this over the Inferno of Erif, and the entire fire will be extinguished. But once you destroy the fire, retreat as quickly as possible. After being destroyed, the souls of the unborn Calorians will rise from the smoke and cause the walls to cave in on the destroyer of the fire."

"And what happens if we fail or all of the vials break before we're able to use them to destroy the Inferno of Erif?" Speilton asked.

"Then the quest is a complete failure. The only other way to destroy the Inferno is by destroying the king. It is ancient Calorian tradition to use their king's life to determine how long the fires last. But just because the king and the Inferno are destroyed, does not mean that the Calorians can't find a new king and recreate the fires."

There was a long pause before Usus asked, "Is that all?"

"No, there's one more thing. When you go on the quest, prepare the warriors of Kon Malopy for battle. Have them follow behind you at a good distance. If things turn to the worse, you may need them. Make certain they aren't too close because they might give away your position. Have them travel under cover."

"Wait, if our warriors are fighting down in Caloria, then who will protect Kon Malopy?"

"The centaurs. Tell the centaurs to protect the castle. It is crucial that it is the warriors of Kon Malopy who fight at Skilt, because the humans are the bravest of all of the races. The dwarves will have an important job elsewhere. And one last thing before you leave. Millites, I have something for you."

Cigam walked across the room to the cluster of odd objects on pedestals. He stopped at an object in the middle of the room where inside a glass case was a foot long rod with strange markings on it, like an ancient form of writing. Standing next to the pedestal, Cigam rested his hand on the top of the case. Cigam closed his eyes in concentration. "Enclosire crawkiss widess!" Cigam muttered.

Slowly the glass case around the object began to twist and turn into a long spiral that started at the top and coiled down to the bottom. Suddenly, the spiral began to turn from transparent, to an opaque green color. They then realized that it was taking the form of a snake that lurched forward at Cigam.

"Flaremick!"

The snake instantly burst into flames and fell to the ground in a pile of ash. "My apologies. We need very tight security on some of these objects. Especially this one." Cigam grabbed the strange rod from the pedestal and walked over to Millites, Speilton, Teews, Usus, and the creatures. "Now Millites, this is Ferrum Potestas, the Sword of Power. It is a sword as ancient as myself. Hundreds of years ago it was forged by the Wizards to be granted to the race of men to use in troubling times. It's powers were meant to be used only for good, though the sword craved a balance. You see, Ferrum Potestas bends to the will of its master. If its master is pure of heart, it turns everything it encounters, virtuous. But if its master wishes to use the power of the Sword for evil, then its victims become vile, also. All that is needed is the slightest cut to cause this affect. Then, the power of the sword seeps into the victim's body, heals his wounds, and overcomes his mind and heart. The first victim of Ferrum Potestas becomes the strongest, for it uses more of the Sword's power to change its victims than any other afterwards. The first person to become cut is practically indestructible since the power of the Sword transforms him and gives him abilities unlike any creature before."

"Though, its powers do not stop there. The Sword of Power has the ability to control the weather and summon blazing strikes of lightning. Ferrum Potestas also has the ability to summon a huge beast from the Cave of the Magmors. This beast will be massive and deadly, with a impenetrable hide and unpredictable powers. The creature will forever be loyal to the wielder of the sword and follow him into any battle."

"Amazing," Millites exclaimed, "Though, how do we use the sword if it only appears to be a rod?"

"Before you can get Ferrum Potestas to take its true form and become its master, you must touch the blood of an animal strewn with the marks of darkness, fire, and light. The animal should be powerful and horrifying yet kind and loving. For the Sword to be empowered, the creature must have sacrificed itself. Until then, Ferrum Potestas will remain in this rod form," Cigam walked over to Millites and handed him the Sword of Power.

Suddenly, out in the distance they all heard a boom. Then it came again, a little closer and louder. Then, with a loud BAM! The west wall exploded into a cloud of dust. Cigam held out his hand, and suddenly, a three foot long staff formed in his clinched first. As Millites, Speilton, Teews, and Usus drew their wands, there was complete silence. Then, all evil broke loose. A stream of evil black birds flooded into the room. Blasts of light, fire, stone, love, and some strange substance that resembled melted wax flew towards the Daerds.

The first round stumbled out of the sky, knocking into other evil birds. But some of the surviving birds shot around the room, knocking over the pedestals. Millites leapt onto the blood-red Hunger and took to the sky of Daerds. Usus climbed onto Flamane, and the two shot into the sky to help Millites. Teews began fighting back the Daerds with a spear she had found in the ruins of the pedestals. Speilton was about to leap onto Prowl, when he saw Cigam, standing in the same spot. He was looking for something, waiting for something. It was a lady, a beautiful lady dressed in black with straight black hair and skin so pale that you'd think she'd never been in the sun her entire life, walked out of the flood of Daerds.

"Venefica! I knew you'd come," Cigam muttered lifting his staff to attack the lady.

But before he could attack, the lady merely swished her hand through the air, as if smacking a fly, and Cigam's body was thrown into a wall.

"Hello, old man," Venefica smirked. Cigam stumbled to his feet and thrust his staff forward towards the lady. Two orange coils shot out of the staff, intertwining in the air as they flew at the witch. But Venefica merely held out her hand, creating a swarm of black flies that contained the substance and plowed into Cigam, knocking him to the ground.

"Why? Why are you doing this?" Cigam groveled.

"You really don't know?" the witch mused. "I'd heard news that you were growing old, but I wouldn't ever have guessed that you were becoming this dim-witted," the witch scoffed.

"You and your fellow wizards mocked me when I was young. My father was powerful, more powerful than any other wizard. I was born with his powers, but you all underestimated me. You said that a woman, a witch, could never obtain the same amount of power as a male wizard. It was then that I swore that one day my powers would exceed yours. I endured the laughs and mocking despite my anger. After training as a wizard for many years, I realized that I couldn't learn anymore magic from you as a wizard. You are so limited. So, I went to a warlock."

Venefica smiled sinisterly. Cigam gaped in horrified astonishment as warlocks are the mortal enemies of wizards because of their use of dark magic. Speilton stood there, not knowing what to do.

"After learning all I could about dark magic from him, I dedicated my life to ruining yours. By helping your enemies, I destroyed those you were trying to help, thereby weakening you."

Cigam quickly grabbed his staff and pointed it at Venefica. "Not so fast!" Venefica jeered, lifting her hand. Suddenly a huge boulder that had broken off of the destroyed wall lifted into the air and soared at Cigam. At the last second Cigam created a gust of wind to push back the boulder. But Cigam was much older, and weaker than the young and sly Venefica. The boulder crept closer and closer to Cigam. Speilton saw Cigam's hand shaking from the extreme power he was using. Speilton realized that Cigam was about to give up.

Speilton immediately thought of a raging, out of control fire when suddenly a large jet of fire streamed from his wand and overwhelmed Venefica's back. The boulder fell to the ground as the witch roared with anger, and Cigam fell to the ground unconscious.

Venefica turned around to Speilton and roared, "How dare you attack me, you little louse? You're going to pay for that."

The witch stretched her arms high above her head and arched her hand and fingers as if holding an invisible ball with both hands. Suddenly a dot of darkness appeared in between her hands and began to grow larger. As it grew, it resembled a black hole. Finally, once the black hole was large enough to touch Venefica's hands, the witch slowly pulled her hands apart.

Speilton tried to create a ball of fire to send at the witch, but nothing came out of the wand. As Venefica lowered her hands, the black hole stretched apart into two circles. As her arms lowered to her waist, Venefica closed her eyes tightly. As she opened them, the dark black, beautiful eyes had turned completely white. Her black lips gaped open. Suddenly, the two black holes began to dissolve into long wisps of smoke that dropped to the ground. Then, Speilton realized that the smoke was slithering towards him. Slithering. The smoke wasn't smoke, but long black snakes.

Speilton shoved his wand in his left pocket, drew his sword, and took his shield off his back and strapped it to his arm. His shield was very special - invisible in the dark and gleaming as bright as the sun in the light. And in the darkened room the shield was invisible.

Suddenly, one of the serpents lurched forward at Speilton's leg and sank into Speilton's pants. If not for getting its teeth stuck on something in his pocket, it would have sunk into his skin. As the snake pulled back, it ripped the Eye Stone out of Speilton's pocket. The Eye Stone quickly dropped down the snake's throat. Before Speilton could react, the snake shot at Speilton's back. At the last second Speilton blocked the lurching snake.

While he was distracted, the snake first to attack curled around Speilton's leg and pulled it out from under him causing him to end up flat on his back. As Speilton began to lift himself off the ground, one of the snakes lurched at his face. Speilton quickly swatted the snake in the neck with his blade. The black serpent instantly vanished into a cloud of smoke. As Speilton climbed to his feet, the other snake struck at his sword hand. Speilton tried to leap back, but the snake's jaw sunk down onto the handle. It then pulled back, tossing the sword out of Speilton's hand. The serpent then shot forward again and again, as Speilton side stepped and blocked the snake back with his shield. It seemed to never end, until, by luck, Millites flew overhead shooting blasts of light out of his wand. The light passed over the shield, causing it to become as bright as the sun. As the serpent lunged again, it instantly exploded into smoke.

As it exploded, the Eye Stone which had been somewhere inside the snake, flew across the room and landed in the wreckage of magical items. As Speilton began to run across the room to retrieve it, Venefica smirked "Nice try! But it'll take a lot more than that to destroy my power."

Suddenly, all the light in the room vanished, leaving the room completely black. There were a few loud crashes, then, everything became quiet. Speilton began groping around on the cold marble floor. As he stumbled over a large book, that seemed to be vibrating, he cut himself on the sharp pieces of glass on the ground. After crawling over a broken stone, he came to where he'd seen the Eye Stone land. As he stretched his hand out to feel around for the Eye Stone, his hand rested on a round disk. Sadly, it was only a coin. He reached around and grabbed yet another coin. Then another, and another. The whole area was covered in them. But there was no ring. He then started grabbing a hand full of the coins, hoping to grab one that was more than another coin. Finally, in his fifth handful, he felt a ring. As he began to drop the other coins, he felt another ring slip around his finger.

That wasn't a good sign. If there were two rings, there were probably more. Speilton groped around the floor to see if he could find any other rings. After a few seconds, Speilton found one more ring before he heard a sound behind him.

Suddenly, a hand grabbed his shoulder. Speilton spun around to see Millites with his wand of light in the other hand motioning for Speilton to follow him. Speilton slowly stood up pocketing the last ring. As they crept through the darkness, led only by the faint glow of Millites' wand, Speilton realized that the others were already following Millites.

BANG!!! The mound of coins Speilton had been sitting on five seconds earlier exploded and was now reduced to ashes.

"We've been spotted! Run!" Millites screamed as he leapt onto Hunger's back.

Usus leapt onto Flamane's back, and both Speilton and Teews took off on Prowl. The four of them charged to the edge of the jutting rock, and leapt off the side head first. As they dove down, they heard the rapid beating of dozens of Daerds' wings. Millites took off around the right side looking for the ship in the fog, quickly followed by Usus. But since Speilton and Teews were the last to get out, they were separated from the others by the stream of Daerds. They were forced to fly in the opposite direction, closely pursued by a dozen of the evil birds. Speilton knew he had to get the Daerds of his tail. "Prowl! Fly into the maze of rock spires.

The great blue dragon took a hard left into the foggy areas clustered with dangerous stones.

Millites and Usus had become surrounded by a flock of Daerds. There was no way out. As they hovered in midair, looking for an escape route, Venefica appeared out of the wall of Daerds, standing on a purple, green, and black chariot pulled by two serpents of smoke. "Ah, so you thought you could escape, and you were so close, too. But you fell short. Now, Millites, hand me the Ferrum Potestas. Please?" Suddenly Millites seemed to have fallen under a spell. His pupils shrank rapidly and his hand slowly moved to the Sword of Power in his pocket. As if in slow motion, he held the sword of Power out to Venefica.

"Millites? Millites what are you doing?" Usus yelled .

But Millites was gone, he'd fallen under the witch's enchantment. Millites tried to fly toward Venefica on Hunger, but the dragon struggled against him. Usus knew he had to act fast.

Quickly, he created a stream of rocks to fly at Venefica. As the witch blocked back the rocks, the spell she had on Millites broke.

"If that's how you want to play, then fine! I'll just have to destroy you," Venefica muttered summoning another black hole of darkness.

But instead of separating it, she shoved it forward so that it whizzed towards Millites. He ducked down just in time to dodge the ball of darkness as it flew over his back and exploded into a group of Daerds. This was their chance. Swiftly, Millites and Usus darted out of the ring of Daerds and dove down towards the Night Seemer. They were pursued by Venefica and the flock of Daerds as explosions rang through the air around them.

In the distance, Millites saw the light of the ship. 'Over there!" he called steering Hunger towards the Night Seemer.

BANG! They were getting closer. BANG! Almost there! BANG!!! An explosion erupted right behind Millites, throwing them to the ground. The great, now green and wounded dragon crashed to the deck of the boat, and Millites crashed into the rope ladder before collapsing to the ground.

Luckily, Usus and Flamane had a softer landing, and right as he landed, Usus let the pillar of rock go back down to its rightful place, causing the ship to fall and splash down into the water. Then he pointed his wand up into the sky and created a shield of stone from his wand that covered the top of the ship. As Millites stood up, Rolias and Puffer ran to his side and asked, "What happened?"

"Do you need help?"

"What can we do?"

"Tell the rig monkeys to arm the cannons," Millites muttered. "The Daerds aren't going down without a fight."

Speilton shot from left to right dodging rock spires that seemed to appear out of nowhere. Behind him he could hear the horrible sounds of the Daerd's bones cracking and splintering as they crashed into the rock spires. After a minute or two, there were only three pursuing Daerds left. Speilton decided he had to return to the ship just in case they were in crucial need of help. "Teews! Can you get rid of those last Daerds?"

"You're asking me to fight? This is a first," Teews scoffed.

She turned around and shot a beam of love into the face of the closest one, causing the Daerd to flap so slowly and lazily that it plunged into the water. As Prowl turned a hard right, one of the Daerds crashed into a rock spire. But there was still one Daerd left pursuing them. Teews tried to shoot the last one, but it was a very fidgety Daerd and wouldn't stay in the same place for very long at all. Finally, she shot a beam of love at a rock spire which shattered on top of the Daerd, sending it into the murky water. Up ahead Speilton saw that the Night Seemer was enveloped by the rest of the huge flock of crows. They covered every inch of the ship clawing and biting at the wood.

Millites had just begun to create his shield of light over the boat, when a hole was punctured in Usus's shield of stone. Suddenly fire spilled from the hole as Speilton, Teews, and Prowl toppled out of the sky onto the deck. The hole automatically sealed itself behind them.

"How many Daerds are out there?" Millites asked as his light shield spread completely over the top of the ship.

"Enough to cover every square inch of the ship and your shields," Speilton said.

Suddenly, Usus collapsed to the ground and his shield of stone shattered, leaving only Millites' shield to protect them.

"What happened?" Speilton asked.

"He used too much power. His body couldn't take anymore," Millites said.

"What about you?" Teews asked.

"I don't know how much longer I can take it. You have to do something and fast," Millites struggled.

Speilton thought for a second, then figured out a plan. "Teews, follow me," Speilton said rushing down the first flight of stairs where Rolias, Puffer and the rig monkeys were cowering. "Everyone! Arm the cannons! Every single one." Speilton shouted.

"But there aren't enough of us to fire half of the cannons at one time!" a rig monkey called.

"Prepare all of the cannons. After you fire one round, fire the cannons next to it. We have to send the Daerds away," Speilton screamed as the men ran to each cannon, preparing them to fire. Speilton climbed back up the steps to see how Millites was. Sweat was rolling down his stained face as he struggled to hold up the shield. He couldn't hold on much longer. Speilton rushed down the steps to Teews. "How are they?" he asked.

"They're almost done. They've just started the second round of cannons," Teews informed Speilton.

"Okay, you go down to the hull and call up once everyone is done," Speilton commanded.

Teews raced down two flights of stairs and Speilton descended one. "All done?" he asked the rig monkeys.

"Almost, just one more," a rig monkey chimed in.

Down below, Speilton heard an, "All done!"

Finally the rig monkey grunted, "Ready."

Speilton raced upstairs to the deck.

"Okay. One... Two... Three... Fire!" Speilton shouted.

Suddenly an ear-splitting BOOM!!! echoed through the air, blasting away large groups of Daerds. After hearing several splashes, Speilton shouted again, "Fire!"

They heard several more splashes as the Daerds sank into the murky water. Then all the Daerds took to the sky, flying away from the deafening sounds. Speilton climbed up the stairs to check on Millites as the rig monkeys roared with applause. Speilton saw Millites begin to fall to the ground. Speilton caught him just before Millites banged his head. As Speilton helped him down, he reached down to grab the Sword of Power to put it in a safe place. As Speilton turned around and began walking towards the hatch that led to the stairs, the door suddenly slammed close.

"Leaving so soon?" came a cold, but soft voice from behind him.

Speilton whipped around to see Venefica standing over Millites' limp body, a dagger in her hand. "Give me the sword, or Millites dies!" Venefica muttered.

Speilton realized that he was trapped. If he didn't give her the Sword, she'd kill Millites. If he gave her the sword, the witch would use it to destroy the wizards or give it to Sinister to use against them.

As he quickly thought the situation over, he began to hear knocking on the door behind him.

"Speilton? Speilton are you okay? Open the door!" he heard Teews's voice calling.

"Give it to me or Millites dies!" Venefica growled.

Speilton slowly inched forward and stretched out his hand to give her the Sword. The witch reached out and snatched the sword out of Speilton's hand and leapt onto her serpent drawn chariot that sat on the bow of the ship. She gave a cackle, then took off into the sky.

As Speilton watched the dark shape of the chariot fly away into the fog, a large white blob darted out of nowhere engulfing the witch. The blob dropped down out of the sky and landed on the boat. Speilton pulled out his wand of fire and pointed it at the blob of light.

"Don't shoot!" the blob said as it formed into the shape of Cigam. "Hold onto this!" Cigam said handing Speilton the Sword of Power.

The wizard snapped his fingers and the door to the stairs opened wide. "Get out of here as quickly as possible. Start the quest in four days. Destroy the Inferno of Erif." But Cigam didn't get to finish because a ball of dark magic exploded in the spot where he'd just been standing. Venefica appeared behind them coming toward the ship.

A second later, Speilton saw the blob of light that was Cigam flash through the sky and collide with the chariot that Venefica had once again summoned. Behind him, Teews, Rolias, and Puffer climbed up the stairs and asked, "What was that all about?"

"I'll tell you later. But right now, we need to get out of here, fast!" Speilton commanded as everyone ran to their stations.

Millites and Usus didn't wake up until they reached Mermaid Cove. The dark surface of the water dazzled with the reflection of the stars until they reached the dock where the sun first broke the horizon. They were met by a roaring crowd of mers who all wanted to hear of the miraculous journey. They shared the stories from their own perspective, each one having a different twist. Obviously, Millites and Usus couldn't recite the entire story but told what they'd encountered as well as they could. They all agreed that it was Speilton who told it best. As they eagerly listened, they became immersed in the battle. They felt Speilton's tension as the snake coiled around him, and when he found more than one ring in the pile of coins. Luckily, Speilton grabbed the right one but decided to keep the other two.

Though each story was different, there was one thing they all had in common. Every single one of the stories was incomplete. Yes, they did tell about the battle on the ship and in the fortress, but they all made sure to leave out the part about Ferrum Potestas, the vile of Aqua, the Eye Stone, and their directions into Skilt. That was all best left unspoken.

They each had a tale that changed every time they told it. After hearing so many different explanations, the mers gave up and decided the only thing worth remembering was the battle.

The next day, Millites, Speilton, Usus and Teews rode out of the tall castle on their animals and trekked up the hill. They hiked all day before resting down in an old village. The younger children ran up to Hunger, each of them wanting to pet the leathery scales. Hunger turned away, pretending not to care, but his thin smile and sparkling eyes gave him away. They thanked the villagers for their hospitality before setting off once again.

The first star was shining when they reached Rilly's hut. Outside, around a dazzling fire, were five people. As Speilton, Millites, Usus, Teews, Prowl, Rorret, Hunger, Flamane, and Brisk approached, one of the five who proved to be Rilly stood up and announced, "Here are the four adventurers."

Another of the figures, a tall, blond long-haired boy rushed forward and bowed before the Kings and Queen. "Your Majesties, I am Nicholas."

"Rise, Nicholas," Millites said as the boy stood straight.

Speilton glanced at the boy's face and noticed something amazing. The boy looked to be about his age, maybe a few years older. "Nicholas, how old are you?" Speilton asked.

"Forty-seven, sir."

"What?"

Rilly stepped forward. "Nicholas is an elf. His life span is about twice as long as a human's."

"You're an elf? I thought they were supposed to be short," Speilton said before realizing he'd been rude. The elf had been caring for Ram. Speilton should have been thankful, instead of annoying.

Nicholas rolled his eyes. "Curse those gnomes. I see why you would think that. But the true story is that the gnomes, those pesky burrowers, disgraced our race with silly legends of short elves. In all honesty, we are actually larger than humans and much taller than those foot-tall trolls."

Speilton, now noticed Nicholas's pointed ears and felt awkward about stirring up this heated conversation. But luckily Millites saved him, "Are you willing to join the journey?" he asked.

"I have been waiting all my life to be given this opportunity," the elf said.

"So why should we take you? What can you do to help us on our journey?"

"In truth, I've come prepared. For years I have been planning for the time when I could get back at Sinister for what he did to my parents. He killed them after they had been disarmed. There is nothing more foul than attacking a defenseless person. And so, I want to teach him a lesson. I want to prove to him that he is wretched and evil. That in the end, he will be defeated," Nicholas said, his voice rising with frustration.

"He's brave," Usus announced. "But he must learn to turn his anger into something positive. Sorrow and fear can change people and cause them to become bitter and imbalanced."

"Wait, but Nicholas can also do more than fight," Rilly interjected. "He's also an inventor."

"Inventor? What is it you've made?"

"Well, many things. I love to tinker. I've created this collapsible knife that also contains a little saw, hammer, and pliers," Nicholas explained, drawing the useful mechanism out of his pocket. "I've created dart-tipped arrows that can fly very straight and smooth. The only quirk is that it takes a really stiff bow to shoot it, which makes it nearly impossible. Luckily, I'm a skilled archer. Also, I'm still working on a few other things that aren't completely finished yet."

"You'd make a wise addition to the team," Speilton said.

"Thank you," Nicholas said as he bowed before the kings and queen. Though he looked stern and solemn as he turned around, he was overjoyed inside.

"Who's next?" Millites asked.

A girl with a large mound of twisted, twirled pink hair stepped away from the fire as Nicholas returned to the log positioned around the fire. "Hello, I'm Ginkerry," the girl said.

"I like your hair!" Teews said walking up to the girl.

"Thank you!" she said. "It's naturally like this for us Dryads."

The girl's hair was full of flowers, pine cones, and what might've been a bird nest. She wore a long dress that dropped straight down to the ground. Speilton instantly saw the resemblance in the dress and a tree trunk since Dryads are spirits of trees.

"So do you want to join our quest, too?"

Suddenly, Rilly appeared behind them and whispered in Millites' ear, "Actually, she was the only one brave enough to go. At mention of the adventure all of the other Dryads returned to their trees."

"Oh," Millites said, "Ginkerry, why don't you tell us a little about yourself."

"Well, only a few days after my mother, a cherry tree Dryad, and my father, a Ginko Treep planted me, the Calorians raided the Rich Woods. Both of their trees were destroyed by the Calorians' flames. But luckily I survived, being only a seedling. Some of the other Dryads took pity on me and took me under their wings, though they don't really have wings. It makes more sense to say that they took me under their branches," Ginkerry giggled.

Teews laughed with her to make the little Dryad feel comfortable. "Okay, who wants to present themselves to the kings and queen next?" Rilly asked.

As Ginkerry walked back to her seat, a small, but gruff hairy man stepped out from behind the fire. He bowed lazily then stood back up, gnawing on a tuff of grass. "Who are you?" Usus asked.

"My name's Brutas. You can call me Brute. As you can see, I'm a satyr," he mumbled, trying to act bored.

"And why is it *you* want to help and join our journey?" Millites quizzed the grumpy satyr.

"I don't want to go with you, but it seems that I have to." He muttered staring at Rilly.

Rilly spoke, "When I found out that we needed a satyr, I expected some trouble. You see, every year the satyrs join together in one huge celebration in honor of their god, Pan. The beginning of the journey to the festival was a week ago, and I was scared that all of the satyrs had already left. But then I found one particularly grumpy and lost satyr, named Brutas, wandering around. It turned out that he had overslept and every one had left without him. So, being the only one left, he has to join the journey."

"Thank you for summing that all up leaf man," Brute grumbled sarcastically.

"You're very welcome," Rilly threw back.

"Okay, so do you like weapons?" Speilton asked.

"No."

"Battle strategies?"

"No."

"Survival skills?"

"No."

"Stealth moves?"

"No."

"Gathering food?"

"If the food is anything but grass; no."

"Running?"

"No."

"Anything that'll help us on our quest?'

"No, no, and no."

Teews perked up, "Is there anything you do like?"

"Yes, actually. Me, myself, and . . ." he stopped and stared upwards, "my horns."

Wow! Speilton said in his head, *This guy is no help.*

"Okay, next," Usus called.

No one walked forward as Brute returned to his seat.

"Is there any one else?" Millites asked.

"Metus, come on out," Rilly called.

"N-n-no," came a voice from the edge of the forest.

"Come on. There is nothing to be afraid of," Rilly urged.

A small head appeared from the forest's edge. The face was round with large eyes and a wild wig of curly hair. "What's he doing hiding back there?" Teews asked Rilly.

"He's scared of fire. And water. And the dark. And the light. And practically everything else."

Speilton couldn't blame him for being scared of fires. They were his worst fear, too. It was pretty ironic that he was given the element of fire.

Slowly but surely, Metus stepped out of the shadows of the forest and into the light. He wore no shirt, and his legs were those of a goat. Around his neck hung a flute attached to a necklace. He looked no older than about ten years.

"See, Metus, you're okay," Rilly urged.

"Why exactly did you choose him?" Millites whispered to Rilly.

"It's a long story. In short, once I told all of the fauns about the adventure, he was the only one that didn't scatter away."

"So, he actually did something brave?"

"No. He was the only one who passed out. Once he was awake, there was no time for him to escape."

"So, Metus, how do you... calm your self down?" Speilton asked.

"I p-play m-my f-f-flute," the satyr whimpered, lifting the instrument hanging around his neck to his lips.

He closed his eyes, breathed into the flute, and the most beautiful noise rang out. It relaxed everybody's muscles like a massage on all sides. The song filled their senses bringing them images each of their own favorite memories.

To Speilton, he felt the swirling, cool wind on a soft, warm day as he stared up at the starry night sky. He smelled the roasting mutton on the fire and heard the daytime birds giving their last chirps of the night, as the owl began its song.

In Millites' memory he felt himself nestled in his mother's lap as they sat on a large, velvet overstuffed chair before a warm fire in his old room. Millites' eyes began to flutter closed as he saw the large, grey bricks of the castle around him. His mother was whispering to him great stories about bold heroes who conquered armies or defeated dragons. And then, after each story, she'd whisper, "One day, you'll be riding alongside them."

Teews felt herself flying across flower-laden fields on the back of her mighty horse. The flowers' petals danced into the sky after Teews rushed through them in a wave of vibrant colors. Teews felt the warm air running through her light brown hair, and she heard the deep panting of her sturdy Clydesdale. She ran her hand down his soft mane and knew she was free to roam wherever she wanted.

Usus felt his arms straining as he pulled himself up onto the top of the mountain. His arms and legs shook from the effort it had taken to climb to the top, but the view itself was worth it. Before him lay lush valleys with glorious orchards, and other purple mountains much like the one he had just climbed. An eagle flew over his head, wanting to take in the same view.

But the dreams ended. Speilton's village was now destroyed, and Millites' mother was gone just like his father. Teews couldn't ride her horse alone anymore for fear of being attacked, and the mountainous peak Usus had climbed was now destroyed. It all was gone, as reality seeped back in, and the music stopped.

Everyone stood there dazed.

The other creatures' faces were full of sorrow after the realization that their wondrous, lost dreams were now just that - lost dreams.

The only one not shaken by the music was Metus. It was as if he'd heard the whimsical music so many times, he'd come to control his lost emotions.

Rilly broke the silence. "This music is not charmed or hexed in anyway. It is only an old faun lullaby that spurs the sweetest memories in the bystanders' mind. It is used to inspire and bring hope to the satyrs. It connects them with nature, joining them together."

"What caused you so much fear?" Usus asked Metus.

"I-i-it was in the fall. When the C-calorians attacked. I s-saw things."

Rilly explained, "Metus was a warrior. Though most fauns are horrified by battle, he wasn't. Metus was only nine, too young to fight. The satyrs tried to tell him to hide, but his ambition was too strong. He tried to fight but was taken captive. They tortured him, killed his brothers. But they kept him. Once the Calorians were defeated, he was left alone. Though saved, he was scarred for life."

As Rilly spoke, Metus stood there, firmly. His mind was somewhere else.

"There is a warrior in him. Deep down, there is ambition."

There was silence. The four creatures and the four rulers gazed at each other. "These are the four questers," Rilly said. "Rise Forest People."

The eight returned to Kon Malopy that night. The moon was large and bright in the sky since it was after midnight. They strolled through the village, meeting only the castle guards along the way. Up the path to the cliff-ringed castle, through the courtyard and into the empty banquet hall with a slowly dying fire they traveled. The four questers departed from the group and were guided to their rooms by a guard. The royals' animals crawled down a flight of stairs to their chambers as Millites, Speilton, Teews, and Usus went up a different flight of stairs on the far left which led up Spiral Tower.

At the top of the stairs was a long corridor with rooms on every side. They walked along it until they came to a door. On either side was a guard who protected the royal chambers. The two were covered from head to toe in thick red and purple armor. Neither said a thing but merely stood there. Speilton guessed that having to stand watch there all day could really take the life out of you, but the knights at least gave Speilton a feeling of safety.

Speilton pushed through the tall wooden, doors with golden banners and entered a small circular room. They were in the center of Spiral Tower. Each of the four walked through one of the five separate doors around the room. After saying good night, they entered their rooms. Millites, Speilton, Teews and Usus lay down on their beds. A servant darted in to lead the creatures down a floor to their beds.

The four rulers undressed, set their weapons and wands down on the tables next to them and got in bed. Millites, who had taken the things from Cigam with him, put them with the rest of his things. They each fell asleep easily.

Millites was suddenly awakened from a pleasant dream by a small creak in the corner of his room. At first he thought he'd imagined it, but then he heard it again, a little closer this time. A thousand thoughts shot through his head. *Maybe it was Speilton or Usus or Teews. Or maybe it was something else. If it is something then should I attack? It seems that the only reason that I'm still alive right now is because the attacker thinks I'm asleep. I should probably just wait a little longer.*

Then he heard the person, whoever it was, reach onto the table right next to him and pick up something. That was it. The other person in the room was stealing right under Millites' nose. In a flash, Millites reached for his sword, ready to point the blade at the thief.

But his hand fell short as a hard club bashed him in the head. As he slumped to the floor, the thief chuckled, "Not so powerful now, are you?"

A GUEST IN THE NIGHT
~ 8 ~

"Speilton! Speilton!" Someone was calling his name.

Speilton opened his eyes from a deep sleep to see Ram standing over him. At first he thought he was still on the journey to Kon Malopy that had taken place half a year ago. Then, noticing the fear in Ram's face, he was brought back to reality. "What's wrong?" he tried sitting up.

Ram talked in a rush, "It's Millites. No one can find him. He's not in his bed and his weapons and the things you got from the Island of the Wizard Council are missing."

Speilton was met with a mixture of feelings with the realization that his brother was missing and Ram was alive and healthy.

"Ram! You're okay! The potion worked?"

"Yes, I'm fine. But you've got to listen to me. Do you know where Millites is?"

"No. He didn't tell me anything."

Speilton leapt out of bed and charged into Millites' room. Teews and Usus were standing around the bed. "Are you sure that the entire castle has been checked?"

Teews nodded solemnly. Usus looked down at the bed and noticed something new. "Speilton, come look at this." He motioned towards the bedsheets.

Speilton saw it too and knew that something horrible had happened. On the sheets was a single drop of blood. Speilton reached forward and touched the tiny dot. It was wet, which meant it was fresh.

"Millites has been kidnapped," Speilton announced solemnly.

"But how? The guards would have seen the thief and stopped him. Unless..." Usus and Speilton locked eyes as they both came to the same horrible realization. They rushed out of the room and darted into the long hallway where the two guards still stood, leaning against the wall. "What happened last night?" Usus asked them.

Neither moved.

"Did you see anyone last night?" Teews asked.

"Answer us!" Speilton stepped forward, grabbed a guard by the soldier's shoulder and shook him vigorously.

That's when their worst fears were proved to be true. The guard slumped to the ground, landing on his stomach, and exposed a long gash in his back. Blood was still slowly rolling out. Speilton removed the man's helmet to reveal a face as pale as snow and eyes which rolled back into the top of his head.

"The guards couldn't save Millites," he murmured.

"Ram, go get some warriors and find these two guards' families. Tell them... what has happened," Usus commanded as Ram took off down the hallway.

Speilton gazed at the dead guards and remembered the words the Versipellis had spoken at their first encounter. They'd said something about a person, a human who had joined the Calorians. They said he had a crucial job. This must've been it. No Calorian would be able to sneak into the great castle of Kon Malopy on his own. No, it must've been a human. A traitor.

Speilton was about to tell Usus his theory, but suddenly noticed he couldn't since it would require him to tell about the Versipellis' curse.

Then Speilton remembered that the Versipellis said if the traitor failed, it would be easy for them to roast him in the fires close by. This could be a clue.

The Versipellis made it seem that if the thief who had taken Millites failed, they would cast the thief into a fire in the blink of an eye. That meant that whoever the traitor was, he had to be going towards or to a place full of flames. Speilton did a mental check of all the places in Milwaria he knew that were filled with fire. The answer came to him almost immediately since he'd been there countless times. The Lavalands, which were one and a half days trek to the West. He'd figured out the most likely location, but now the problem was figuring out how to tell Usus without giving away his secret.

He knew that the Versipellis were strongly involved. The only reason they entered the war was to cause one side to fail. They could've chosen to help the Milwarians, but of course, they picked the stronger, blood-thirsty, power-hungry army to join. And now they were using him, Speilton (Visvires) Lux. He was the key to this whole thing. If he held strong and fought against the Versipellis, he could save the Milwarians. But if he was weakened and went scurrying for help every time the Versipellis showed their ugly faces, he would fail, and Milwaria would topple with him.

So far, he was failing. Speilton knew he needed help, guidance. But then, he would also have to tell everyone that it was his fault. It was because of him the Versipellis entered this war. It was because of him the Versipellis were watching them, plotting the downfall of Milwaria. It was because of him Millites was gone. If he told Usus, everyone would loose faith, both in him, and in a positive outcome of Milwaria.

As Millites said, once the Versipellis locked sight on a target, there was no doubt they would die, and their country along with them.

That brought Speilton back to his problem. How was he going to get a search party to travel to the Lavalands without giving away the Versipellis' Curse?

While he thought, Ram stepped back into the corridor and approached Speilton and Usus. His face was pale and tight, but his eyes were red, obviously from crying.

"Their families have been alerted. They are arranging the funeral," Ram informed them. "Now, the real question is, what is the next step. Where is the kidnapper?"

Speilton knew the answer, but he couldn't tell. He had to figure a plan out, fast.

Usus spoke up. "The kidnapper was most likely a Calorian, and probably acted alone if he was able to sneak in. The first thing he did was probably look for help. I propose he went south, closer to Caloria."

Ram interrupted, "But what if that was exactly what he wants us to think. I think he went the opposite way."

"He couldn't have gone North. A Calorian would never be able to sneak by the guards. Ever since the siege on Kon Malopy last year, the Looni River has been safely guarded," Usus reasoned.

Ram thought about it for a second, "Then maybe he went East. It would be the place he'd least expect us to search for him. Besides, there is so much undeveloped land between here and there."

"What do you think?" Usus asked.

It took Speilton a second to realize what Usus was asking him. The expression on the Second-in-Command's face showed that whatever Speilton's answer was would be the path they'd follow.

Millites had said that the Milwarians needed a leader. That would have to be him, Speilton Lux.

This proved what Millites had told him. Usus was willing to fly headfirst into any situation just at Speilton's word. In a way, this made Speilton feel even worse. He was cheating all of them, keeping secrets. All the while, they were willing to do whatever he said.

He couldn't tell them. He knew he owed it to them, and telling them the truth could help them all. Though, it could just as well cause their demise. Speilton would just have to wait. If the worst came, he would confess. But would it already be too late?

He had to think fast. He couldn't just bring up the possibility of the Lavalands being the destination too suddenly. Speilton panicked, "Well, um … maybe we could … split up. Yeah! We should split up into four groups. One could go East, another could go South. Just in case, one could go North, and maybe the fourth could go to the Lavalands."

"Great! Lets go downstairs and gather some men. We'll head out immediately," Usus announced as he started down the stairs, swiftly followed by Ram. It was as simple as that. No questions, no misunderstandings. Speilton's word was law. This was a lot to juggle.

He followed Usus down the stairs. Four groups were jumbled together. The warriors were called in immediately. Most were missing armor or weapons that had been forgotten in their haste. But here they were, ready to serve their country.

Three of the groups consisted of the Knights of Milwaria. The other was made up of Speilton, Usus, Ram, and since Millites couldn't tell her not to, Teews.

Though, there was another close call. "How about the four of us go south, the most likely way the Calorian went," Usus proclaimed.

"No!" Speilton shot out.

"What? Why not?" Ram asked.

"Well…"

Here it was again. Speilton had to think fast.

"Maybe we should…er…check on Onaclov. We need to see that they are safe and nothing unusual has happened to him or the dwarves in the Lavalands." Speilton suddenly remembered something Cigam had said. At the time it had seemed insignificant. But now, it might save them all.

"Remember what Cigam said. He told us something about an important task the dwarves must fulfill. If we head in that direction, we might be able to figure out what that is. Besides, we need a dwarf for our quest-"

"That I don't get to go on, since the 'prophecy' didn't show me." Teews sulked.

Speilton excused Teews comment, "It's worth a try. Who knows? We just might find him along the way," Speilton added.

Usus glanced at Ram. "It makes sense. The faster we get along on this journey to save Milwaria the better chance we'll have at succeeding. If we wait too long, we may miss our chance." Usus explained.

"But what are our chances of finding Millites?" Ram asked.

Almost definite! Speilton thought to himself.

"Well," Ram said, "There have been many mysterious things happening around that area. It would be a key place to investigate."

"Great! It looks like we're going west!" Teews declared, "That is, only if I get to go along."

They embarked mid morning with the other three groups. At the end of the narrow path leading through the lake, the four split up, going their separate ways. The party heading north took Rorret along with them for extra protection. The group going east took Flamane, and the southern group took Hunger. Speilton's party had Prowl. All the other travelers rode Milwaria's fastest, strongest horses.

As Speilton crawled through the dense forest on Prowl's back, he asked "Ram, how are you feeling this morning?"

"Oh, yes. With all that has happened, I feel that I am completely healed. Nicholas was a wonderful caretaker."

It was nice to have Ram back.

The sun was sitting atop the Barren Mountains as they walked out of the forest and began their ascent. The slopes were covered with thick pine trees that made homes for squirrels and birds. Large rocks jutted out of the sides in random places, though there weren't enough to create a steep slope. Hiking the mountain was easy, though strenuous. They reached the summit as the sun began to sink. All was silent and peaceful, until there was suddenly a distant outcry. "What is that?" Teews asked as the screeching grew louder.

They all looked up the mountain to see … only a flock of birds, squawking and flapping away in a frenzy. "Oh, it's only some birds," Usus said.

But Speilton knew better. He'd seen birds flying in large groups like that, but they always had a formation. Those birds were crazy, swarming, and out of control. Speilton knew something had spooked them.

And at that moment, the horses reacted. All three horses whinnied and shook, prancing and dashing, their eyes wide with fright. Prowl fell to the ground darting nervous glances in all directions. "What's wrong?" Speilton asked.

Prowl peered up at him with a horrified expression. Speilton looked up in the direction in which the birds had flown, and found what was causing *all* of the fear. High up on the mountain, outlined by the sky, was a dark figure riding a horse-like creature with a long, snakish neck, claws instead of hooves, and bared fangs. It was a Hakesorsees, the Calorian's version of a horse. But the rider wasn't a Calorian. He was a traitor.

"Usus, I think we've found the kidnapper."

THE CURSE FESTERS
~ 9 ~

"Let's go!" Usus commanded as they bolted up the summit.

The figure heard his voice and disappeared over the ridge of the mountain.

The royals' horses took a few steps forward, obeying their masters. But, they had minds of their own, and they made sure they used them. The three horses pulled away, trying to run back down the mountain. Ram was able to overpower his horse, and Prowl stayed firm, but the other two horses thrust their riders off their backs and ran.

"Are you okay?" Speilton asked as Usus and Teews picked themselves off of the ground.

"We're fine," Teews said.

"Go on. We'll catch up," Usus urged.

Ram glanced over to Speilton. "Ready?"

But Speilton never answered because suddenly, another squawk was heard.

They all turned around to see a dark figure cross through the sky. At first they thought it was a cloud of retreating birds, but then they realized there were three birds flying towards them at an unrealistic speed. The closer they got, the larger they grew. Three black birds.

Neither Teews nor Usus nor Ram knew what they were. But Speilton did, because as they approached, he noticed a single, bloodshot, bulging eye quivering on each of the birds' chest.

One word echoed through his head - Versipellis. His secret was about to be broken.

"Run!" was all he could manage to say. Ram's horse dashed up the hill.

Speilton looked back only once to see the awestruck Usus and Teews staring at the creatures. "No," he screamed.

But it was too late. The three birds shot into the ground, thrashing dirt and wood onto Usus and Teews. Speilton road on and watched as the decaying, hideous bodies of the Versipellis slowly formed next to the unconscious Queen and Second in Command. Earth and the broken remains of trees and bushes lay on top of them like a deadly cocoon. Though Speilton horribly wished he could help them, he knew that with the three Versipellis standing over them, he would be no help.

Prowl kept running up the mountain as the Versipellis suddenly changed once again. But this time instead of birds, they were raging storms of fury that ripped up the ground and trees around them. In only a matter of seconds, their deed was done. They left Usus and Teews then turned their attention to the real target, Speilton.

Simultaneously, the Versipellis slowly turned their moldy, linen wrapped faces to Speilton. For a split second, Speilton made eye contact with one of the deathly eyes.

It was too much to bare. The eye seemed to pierce him like a sword, and he soon had to turn away, setting his attention on reaching the traitor and saving Millites.

Luckily, Ram who rode next to him, never turned around. His attention was on the traitor, and the traitor only

Speilton, Prowl, Ram and his horse all reached the top of the mountain, a ridge that fed off to forested slopes on both sides. Behind them, the Versipellis made their move. As the demons dashed up the hill in pursuit, Speilton turned around and thrust Prowl into her fastest speed. Ram saw them pulling ahead of him, and thought it best to catch up. They began down the other slope, when Ram suddenly froze. The traitor had come into view.

Speilton looked back to see a mixture of feelings on Ram's face. Fear, sorrow, and confusion. Speilton couldn't figure out why.

But in the next instance, that seemed to be the least of Speilton's worries because suddenly, the dark shadow of the Versipellis loomed over the hill and darted after him. In only seconds, one of the creatures had caught him. Prowl spun around and rose up onto her haunches, striking the Versipellis in what should've been its face. Instead, it went right through, as if the demon bird was made of smoke.

The second Versipellis struck, crashing into Prowl's side. The blue dragon went sprawling as Speilton was thrust into the air and down the mountain. Speilton tumbled and rolled, being poked by pine cones and beaten by the rocks. Every few feet, his knees or arms would collide with a tree, though it hardly slowed down his momentum. This side was much steeper than the side they'd climbed.

Finally, after many broken bones, countless bruises and dozens of scratches, he collided with a tree which caught him full force in the chest. As Speilton blacked out, he saw the fearless Prowl taking flight, the Versipellis hot on her trail.

Ram couldn't recover from the shock. Below him, he saw a man evil enough to attack and kidnap the king of a nation. All along, Ram had had his suspicions, but this proved them to be true. The traitor, the thief, the one causing so much pain and horror, was his very own brother. "Incertus" was all he could say.

How could Incertus do this? He remembered years ago, when his brother had made his decision to become a Calorian. He remembered their fight, and how he had been overpowered. But most of all, he remembered his brother leaving.

Ram had never expected to see his brother again since he assumed Incertus would be killed off. All those years, he'd been longing to see him again. But now that the time had come for them to be united, he wished it hadn't happened.

Ram was scared. He didn't know what to do. But he knew he had to do what was right. He had to stop Incertus.

His horse took off down the mountain, being careful not to slip and fall. At the same time, Incertus was riding just as fast away from them. "Incertus!" he called.

His brother looked back, and just as shocked as Ram had been, Incertus froze. In his mind, Incertus recalled the fight they had, his leaving, the despair.

It gave Ram just enough time to catch up, and for Incertus to regain his composure. "Ram, what a pleasant surprise."

"It doesn't have to be this way. Come back with me," Ram urged.

He could see fire raging in Incertus' eyes, and now that they were closer, he noticed how he'd changed. Incertus was skinnier, much skinnier. He'd seemed to be starved half to death. His hair was long and dirty, and an untidy, though short beard crawled out of his chin. All over his body were gruesome scars that Ram knew hadn't been there before.

"It's too late. I have all of Caloria beside me. The war will end soon with Caloria the victor, and I will prosper alongside them," he growled.

"Incertus, I'm sorry. Please come back."

"Sorry, sorry for what? What is there to be sorry for? I will be the one to live once this is all over."

"I'm sorry, that you had to go through this. I'm sorry that you weren't treated like everyone else. I know that's the reason you left. To escape.

You didn't like your life. You didn't want to live and die afraid. You didn't want to go through the struggles that everyone else had to. So you sought another life. And I'm sorry that I couldn't stop you."

The fire in Incertus's eyes grew wilder, fiercer. "How dare you? I never needed to be stopped! Because now, I will live, while all of you suffer from the Calorians."

Incertus lunged forward on his Hakesorsees and drove his rusted sword towards Ram's heart. Ram parried the blow and jumped off his horse. Incertus struck again, though it, too, was reflected. Ram didn't want to fight. He blocked the shots, but couldn't bring himself to attack.

"I will destroy you! For Caloria! For Sinister!" the traitor screamed.

"What have you become?" Ram mourned, backing away from a wild swing.

For a second, Ram thought about leaping onto his horse and escaping Incertus' attacks, but he saw something that changed his mind. Incertus's Hakehorsee slithered toward Ram's horse opening its fanged jaws for a bloody bite. The horse saw the demon in time to leap up and kick the Hakesorsees in the mouth. The sleek, black creature reacted quickly. It hissed, and shot its wild head toward the horse's neck. A strangled whinny was the last thing that was heard from the steed.

Ram turned back around to see Incertus charging at him. He had only a second to duck below the sword. In a flash, he thrust his sword against Incertus' blade so that the two weapons were locked together, one pushing against the other.

"Incertus! I know you're in there somewhere," Ram said, looking his brother straight in the eye. "I know the real you is in there. The one that used to laugh, and have fun, and be carefree.

The one that I used to love to play with as a child. The one that didn't care what others thought about him. The real you, that I always looked up to and admired. The real you that I want to have back."

The rage of fire in Incertus' eyes disappeared. The sword slipped from his hand and clattered to the ground. "Ram," he whispered, "I'm, I'm...sorry. They were going to kill me if I didn't obey. It was a mistake. I...I'm sorry"

The fire had been replaced by tears.

The two stood there, awkwardly staring at each other. Incertus spoke up. "Where are Mother and Father?"

"They died a few months after you left." Ram's eyes filled with tears, though it wasn't just because of his parents. He had learned to accept their deaths but was overcome with emotion knowing that he had his brother again.

The two embraced. When they pulled away, Incertus held out his hand. Resting in his palm was a ring with a large blue stone in the middle. Written on the stone in gold was an 'I' standing for Imperium, their last name.

"It belongs to you," he said.

"You ... you still have the ring?"

"How could I lose it? For a while, it was the only thing keeping me sane."

The Imperium Ring had been handed down to the oldest child for generations in the Imperium family. It had most recently been given to Incertus, but now, it was going to be given once again.

"I can't take it," Ram said. "It has to go to the oldest. That's you."

"I know. But at this rate, I think I've disgraced myself from being an Imperium. Now ... I'm a Calorian."

His eyes were once again filled with tears as he tossed Ram the ring.

"But Incertus, you could still prove yourself. You said the Calorians were right beside you. That means you have information."

Incertus' eyes sparked to life. "I do know some things that could assist you. The Calorians have two armies that are about to embark. One is going to the Lavalands by boat. They have a fleet of over a hundred ships, each carrying about twenty men."

"The other army is coming by land and is twice the size."

"What is their destination?" Ram asked.

"Kon Malopy."

Speilton woke up to see a menacingly dark sky filled with massive clouds. He lifted his head off the ground and sat up, though suddenly wished he hadn't. His ribs must've been broken, along with countless other bones. It all came back to him. The rolling, the collision, the Versipellis. He sank back down to the ground. All was calm as he lay there.

Suddenly, Prowl appeared out of one of the dense clouds, one of her wings bent. She painfully circled to the ground. Speilton soon figured out why. The three Versipellis darted out of the cloud and began heading down the mountain. Speilton peeked around the thick trunk of the pine tree to see where they were going. Down below, was Ram, standing there next to the traitor.

"No!" Speilton whispered.

He knew Ram couldn't take all four on by himself. He had to help, but what could he use? His sword, no good. His shield, no way.

His hand closed around his wand. His arms felt as though every bone was broken. He pointed the wand at the diving Versipellis, imagining a raging fire. Suddenly, flames spurted from his wand as the Versipellis flew past. The flames, which usually shot in a single short burst, wouldn't stop coming as the fire kept screaming toward the trees.

Speilton pulled the wand away hoping it would end the stream of fire, but the flames kept shooting, now reaching into the trees around him. Images of his lost village flashed before his eyes as he had a horrible deja vu moment. He had seen flames spread across trees in a fury before. And the two instances, now, and then, mixed together. It was happening again. Except this time, he had caused the fire. The flames spread across the surrounding vegetation that stood around him. In only a matter of seconds, it would spread into a massive forest fire.

As the flames finally stopped spurting from his wand, Speilton looked up towards Ram. What he saw sent a chill up his back. One of the Versipellis was stopped by the spreading fire. But then, the table turned. The Versipellis looked right at Speilton with its blood-shot eye, and it spoke. Though it was over a hundred yards away, Speilton could still hear the frosty, raspy voice, as if it were whispering in his ear. "Did you really think it would be that easy?" it said.

With that, the horrible eye rolled back into the Versipellis' forehead, onto the top of the rotting cloak and down its back. The fire went straight through the demon, igniting the trees. If the Versipellis could smile, it did now. "It's never that easy." It said again.

And now, the forest was on fire. The flames spread to the ground, igniting the pine-straw. Smoke filled the air. Speilton came to a sudden realization. If the flames reached Teews and Usus before him or Ram, the two of them could do nothing to stop it.

He looked down at Ram and knew he could either save him and risk losing Usus and his sister, or he could try to save Usus and Teews and risk loosing Ram. He couldn't think straight. The flames brought back memories of his burning village once again, making the choice that more frustrating. His mind kept wandering to his old life.

Speilton had lost his family before. It had ruined him. But then he was given a second chance. He couldn't stand losing his family again.

Despite his pain, Speilton began running up the mountain, hoping to reach his older sister and the Second in Command before the fire did.

"Incertus!" The Versipellis screamed. "Kill Ram Imperium and leave."

Flames had suddenly ignited behind the one eyed demons, but the tension in the air was too thick for anyone to notice.

Incertus looked over at Ram, then looked the Versipellis in the eye. "No. You no longer have power over me."

"How dare you!" The Versipellis seethed. "As long as you're a Calorian, I have supreme power over you."

"That's the problem. I'm not a Calorian. I'm a Milwarian."

The Versipellis responded. Its voice sounded both happy, sinister, but definitely not surprised. "Then you will die like one, your brother alongside you."

One of the Versipellis took to the air as the others rushed towards Ram and Incertus. Ram, expecting the Versipellis to stand and fight, drew his sword and pivoted, never taking his eyes off of the creature closest to him.

This was exactly what the Versipellis wanted, and their plan might've worked if Incertus hadn't been sharp enough to know the demon's ways.

Incertus spun back around towards the third Versipellis who had taken to the sky. He was just in time to see it crash into the side of a tall burning

Oak tree. The crippled tree began to topple over as the Versipellis let out a jaw-clenching shriek of jubilation. The burning tree fell towards them, as ash and burning bark peeled off into the smokey sky.

Incertus had a single second to think. And in that single second, he understood his destiny and fate. In that single second, he lunged towards Ram knocking him so hard that he toppled over and rolled a few feet. In the *next* second, the tree crashed to the ground, marking Incertus' final resting spot.

Ram sat up and saw the burning tree smoldering on the ground. He let out a cry of anguish, both over the death of his older brother, and over the pain in his legs. Though Incertus had sacrificed himself for his brother, he had not saved him completely. The tree had landed on Ram's legs, burning and crushing many bones.

The Versipellis stared down at the wreckage. "Tut tut tut. Such a pity to see him *dead*. It seems that our work here is done." And with that they took to the sky, leaving Ram alone, struggling in the center of a fiery wasteland.

Speilton took off down the mountain. He could hear the fire crackling in the trees behind him as he got closer and closer to Usus and Teews. But the fire was catching up. Running down the mountain, he stumbled and crashed, but he had to pick himself up if he wanted to reach them before the fire did.

Suddenly, he asked himself, *Even if I'm able to reach them, what am I going to do?* Just then he reached the wreckage that Usus and Teews were stuck in, and Speilton began to dig into the wood and stone, hoping he wasn't too late.

He wasn't. Usus had already started the work and after a few seconds he burst from the mess screaming, "You have no idea how many ants there are in all that wood."

Speilton laughed, he actually laughed, and Usus joined in with him despite the fact that they were in mortal danger. Teews began unburying herself.

"Oh great, my clothes are a mess! I guess if I'm going to be a warrior now, that's a small price to pay." They would have laughed at this, too, but Usus suddenly noticed the flames streaking down the mountain. "What happened?" he asked.

They were all brought back to reality. Even though it was a horrible idea, it was Speilton's only one at the moment. "Run. Maybe we can get away from the flames long enough for them to die down or something."

The three bolted down the hill, hoping to outrun a forest fire.

They didn't make it.

"Help! Any one. Speilton, Usus, Millites, somebody, please!" Ram called over the roar of the flames that were spread all around him. He was lying on a patch of dirt, though everywhere around him was fire or black smoke. Tears streamed down his face. Even when his life was so close to ending, the only thought in his head was his brother. He had finally gotten him back after all these years, only to have him snatched away once again.

The swirling flames grew larger and closer, filling the air with a dense cloud of smoke. Ram stayed as close to the ground as he could, hoping to find some clean air. All the while, he gazed out into the flames, praying that every swirl in the smoke was someone coming to save him.

As a burning tree limb crumbled and fell from high above him, a savior did come. A streak of blue flew through the flames and huddled around Ram. Prowl fixed her wings and tail around

the injured knight forming a tent around him. Ram looked over to his side to see Prowl's head safely tucked under one wing, and her eyes winced as the burning branch fell on her back. Her scales - like all dragons' - were fire proof. Still, they did not protect her completely.

In a second, Prowl whipped herself out of her tent-like position, slithered under Ram, tossing him onto her back, and dashed up into the air. They weren't safe yet. Ram had to hold his breath in fear of swallowing some of the smoke that billowed and swirled all around them. Prowl darted around looking for… something, but Ram couldn't tell what. His head began to ache as he tried to hold his breath. Nausea sunk in and he couldn't tell which way was up in this cloud of smoke. Finally, when all seemed lost, Prowl lunged one last time, and they both felt cold droplets on their faces. Ram exhaled and breathed in sharply and was surprised to swallow nice clean air. The cold droplets woke him up like a bucket of water being dumped on his face.

The slow beating of Prowl's wings as they flew forward created a cool breeze on his face. After a few more deep breaths, he noticed they were in a cloud. The water vapor that hung all around them made it hard to see, but it wasn't nearly as bad as the smoke. He looked around to see that the cloud went on a good distance, but from where he was he couldn't judge exactly how large it really was.

Ram shifted his position now that he felt better, and his hand rested on a cracked, singed scale on Prowl's back. As he looked he noticed many more missing scales across her body.

He was quickly reminded of all that had happened. Knowing that his brother had sacrificed himself, Ram knew that he couldn't let his death be in vain. He couldn't throw his life away, a life that Incertus had saved with his own. He reached down, and stroked Prowl on the top of her head. "Thanks," he whispered.

Prowl grunted in recognition.

They flew on through the cloud in silence. The cool air and frigid rain helped cool them down after their saga in the flames. But now, all was fine and silent...

When suddenly a bolt of lightning streaked through the sky, letting out a cracking BOOM!

Prowl dropped out of the sky. At first Ram thought she'd been hit, but as they departed the cloud, he realized that they had reached their destination. There were others in need of rescuing, and they were about to get it.

Flames were surrounding them on all sides, and it was because of him, Speilton Lux, whose worst fear was fire. Ironic, aye? It began pressing in on them.

"Speilton? What's our next move?" Usus asked.

"Uh, does getting stuck in the middle of a forest fire happen often when you're a 'warrior'?" Teews asked. "You know, for future reference."

"That's if we have a future," Usus responded morbidly.

"Actually, this happens often when you're a warrior. Well, if you're around me."

A tree branch collapsed between the three of them, blocking Teews from the other two. The queen shrieked as the flaming bark caught the pinestraw on fire. "Jump onto the dirt patches," Usus commanded Teews. "You'll be safer there."

"Al...alright," she whimpered.

There was a sudden thud as Prowl and Ram appeared. "Ram! You're alive!" Speilton cried.

Ram didn't dare get off and stand on his broken legs. Instead he called from Prowl's back over the roar of the flames. "What's our next move?" Ram asked.

Speilton couldn't think. His skin burned and his head was filled with smoke and confusion. "Uh...how many people can Prowl carry?" he wondered.

"My guess is two, maybe three at a time. How far has the fire spread down the mountain? Do you think she can fly some of us down there, and get back before the rest of us roast?" Usus asked.

"On the way down I saw that the fire has spread to the base of the mountain where the trees seem to stop. Still, it's over a mile away." He coughed, the smoke getting to him again like it had the others.

"Okay, can we please get a plan?" Teews asked, "Is it just me or is it *hot in here?*"

Another tree collapsed, much too close to them. "Yeah, it isn't just me," she murmured.

"That's it," Ram muttered. "It's over,"

"For some of us," Usus shot out, "Ram said Prowl could carry *two* of us. Speilton, Teews, you two are royalty. Milwaria needs you. Ram and I are just… there to help. It is you that will save our people. It's only fair that you should-"

"NO!" Speilton stopped Usus, "If one of us is going down, we're all going down together."

Ram objected, "Speilton, you know you can't argue. It was meant to be this way. You must leave. You too, Teews. Speilton, Milwaria needs a leader. And Teews, they need your kindness and grace. You two must leave."

"But-" Teews tried.

"No." Ram interrupted. "It's decided." Speilton glanced toward Prowl. She slowly nodded her head.

"I'll miss you," Speilton walked over and hugged Usus.

"Good luck," Usus said. "Milwaria depends on it. You better not mess this up."

They smiled. Even in the face of death, Usus was joking around.

Speilton was about to take a leap onto Prowl's back, when there was another crack.

Except this time it wasn't a tiny branch but a tree that was large enough so that when it collapsed on Prowl she crumbled to the ground, a burning heap of ash on her back.

"Prowl!" Speilton cried as the blue dragon's eyes fluttered closed. Ram, who had been thrown from her back, struggled over to her, pulling himself and groaning. "She's still breathing, but I don't know for how long."

"What are we going to do?" Teews whimpered.

The flames seemed closer than they had before, and they were denser and hotter showing more signs of death. And they all knew that soon, they would bring death.

Suddenly, there were three flashes in the sky. At first they appeared to be lightning, but they *all* knew that it must've been some other force since the flashes came from the ground and darted up into the clouds. They were amazing, yet frightening. No one knew what they were.

And that's when it began to rain.

It wasn't just a small drizzle, it was a storm that came suddenly and soon enveloped them in a swirl of rushing water. In a matter of seconds they were soaked wet to the bone. Ash and rain battled against each other in the sky, leaving behind smoke. But the rain brought soft air and a cold breeze.

They all felt like crying, and laughing, but didn't know which to do first. The rain had saved them. Bolts of lightning shot out of the sky in loud crashes, but no one was scared. The electricity just seemed to make the clouds of rain seem even more powerful. Speilton leapt up into the air in joy as the flames died down. Teews danced on the smokey ground. Usus joked and laughed. Ram even let out a few hurrahs in between groaning over his extremely painful legs. The battle between the fire, and the weather had ended, and the rain had won. Even this small victory was enough to save Milwaria for now.

Finally, the storm passed, leaving them in a smoldering, steaming, hazy, and wet pile of scalded trees. They could hardly see more than ten feet away, but it was enough to find each other. As they huddled next to the injured Prowl, no one spoke.

Speilton was horrified. He knew that if anyone had anything to say, they'd ask what had happened, who the three demons really were and how had the fire started? And then he'd have to tell them everything.

But the next question was the last thing Speilton had expected. In all that had happened, he had forgotten the true reason for this adventure.

Teews was the first to speak. "Where is Millites?"

TIME TO REGROUP
~ 10 ~

The smoking, destroyed land was bathed in complete darkness when they found the dead Hakesorsee. They'd been searching, hiking over the wet chunks of smoldering trees. The ground was charred white and black, and small fragments of wet, yet warm ash floated through the air.

The sun was long gone, and with no supplies they were forced to walk on in silence, the stars and moon being their only source of light.

Usus limped, Teews had what seemed to be a broken arm, many of Speilton's ribs were cracked, and Ram's legs were nowhere near strong enough to support his body so Prowl was forced to carry him on her aching back. The blue dragon's shoulder's and neck were burned, and many of her scales had cracked.

Still, their search for Millites led them on through the darkness.

After three hours, Speilton stumbled over. His hands landed on something warm and soft. Speilton felt the wet hair of the horse-like body and jumped back in surprise., "I think we've found him." he muttered

They could all remember first seeing Incertus riding away on his Hakesorsee. Hanging on its side were two large bags. They had no doubt that one of them contained Millites.

Speilton reached out, groping for a bag. His hand grabbed one, and he pulled it off of the Hakesoree's body. Speilton found a few long wooden poles with a leather tarp wrapped around them, some dry chunks of wood, a small first aid kit (which only contained a few bandages, and thread and needles,) and a flint and steel that had been stuffed down deep into the bag.

"Not in this bag." Speilton announced, his heart racing.

Speilton grabbed the other bag, hoping that this one had Millites. Slowly he opened the bag, trying to pull the bag off of whoever was inside. He finally came across what he was looking for. The King rolled out of the bag. "Millites." Speilton rested his hand on the king's head. He was still warm. As he moved his hand across Millites face, he felt something wet and sticky. Red blood was crusted over a deep gash in his cheek.

"He's injured, badly."

Usus went for the bag of supplies and pulled out the dry wood, and flint and steel. He rested the wood on the ground and created a spark. After a few seconds, they had a small fire.

Speilton pulled Millites next to the small flames, careful to keep his distance. The light showed several wounds all over Millites' body, including the deep gash on his cheek, a broken arm, and a huge bruise on the side of his head.

"Teews," Speilton began, but the queen already had the needle and thread, and went to work on stitching up a gash in Millites' arm. As she laced the needle in and out, tears slipped down her cheeks. Millites winced in his unconscious state, but at least he was alive.

Their stomachs growled as they tried to dry off next to the fire, and Teews wrapped up Millites other wounds with bandages. After awhile they began looking around, though most everything was ruined and wet. They were all glad that Teews was with them especially since she was so skilled and patient at nursing their wounds.

Teews suddenly stopped and gasped. "His pulse, I think it has slowed down. I think he's only getting worse."

"What should we do?" Usus asked Speilton.

"Well, we can't go back to Kon Malopy. It's too far away. We could continue onto the Lavalands, but the terrain would be very difficult to hike."

"Ram? What is wrong? You've been… quiet, "Teews said.

Everyone looked over to Ram who gazed up at him. "The kidnapper, he … he was my brother."

"What? How did that happen?" Usus asked.

"He was scared. He expected the Milwarians to lose and didn't want to get killed with everyone else. So he sided with the Calorians. I had no idea what happened to him. I'd expected him to have been slaughtered, but he was assigned this mission."

"Then he is a traitor," Usus snarled.

"No. He realized the errors of his ways. The Calorians, they changed him. But he came back. Then, these … creatures, attacked us. He sacrificed himself to save me, but my legs were still injured in the process."

"I'm so sorry," Teews said hugging Ram.

"I had no idea," Speilton whispered.

"He'll forever be remembered as a hero," Usus announced.

Something rustled in the wet wood. All of them spun around and looked to the top of the hill. Four figures disappeared over the ridge. "Something is here," Speilton muttered.

"Should we run now?" Teews asked.

"We can't leave Millites."

THWUNK! A spear landed right in the fire. The flames traveled up the rod.

"Can we run now?" Teews whimpered.

Speilton drew his sword in response. They were going to fight.

A figure appeared at the top of the mountain, followed by three others. They appeared to be riding on a tall creature that stood on its back legs, though the creatures had long forearms that brushed the ground.

The creature growled deep, and frighteningly. The rider yelled "Yah, yah!" in response, and they took off down the hill.

Its front legs dug into the dirt and threw the body forward as the back legs pounded at the ground, kicking a cloud of wood into the air.

Speilton raised his sword higher, and everyone else shrunk behind him since none of them had weapons.

The creature got closer, kicking up more dirt into the air. In a matter of seconds it was so close Speilton could hear the creature's loud breathing.

Speilton was ready to strike when … a spear hissed out of the air and caught his blade. The sword was thrown from his hand as the creature met them. "Whoa! Whoa!" the rider commanded as the creature pulled to a halt. The rider turned so he could see Speilton. "Visvires Lux, are you?" the rider asked as if every word pained him.

Speilton stepped forward. Even though he was scared to death, he acted bold. "Yes, I'm Visvires," Speilton said.

A smile spread across the rider's face. That couldn't be good.

"We have come to help."

Speilton woke up suddenly as if someone had shaken him awake. His first thought while in his limbo stage between awake and asleep was that he was back on his quest with Ram, trekking to Kon Malopy. But as always, reality seeped back in and he remembered all that had happened.

He remembered first seeing Ram's brother at the top of the hill, as if it had just happened. He could still feel the scars that covered his arms and legs where the rocks and bark had torn after his fall down the hill. He could still hear the crushing thud as he hit the tree full force in the chest and the icy voice of the Versipellis as it spoke those frightening words. Then he remembered seeing, hearing, smelling, tasting, and feeling the flames. The flames he had created. The flames that had caused so much devastation.

Speilton vaguely remembered his ride here. The Native tribe known as the Isoalates had brought him and the others here. He remembered that Ram had been positioned on the back of a friendly creature with four beady, insect eyes, a tubular mouth and long neck. The creature had the back legs of a sturdy horse and the front legs of a small rodent that hung down in front. Millites was carried away on a stretcher held up by two Isoalates. Usus, Teews, and Speilton rode on the back of a large slower creature with a long, though heavy set back and six thick legs that held up the weight. There was plenty of room for them to ride on the creature's back, though the fact that it was dragging a large wagon for Prowl to rest on was amazing. Even though it was able to pull and carry everything, the six legged monster kept grunting and growling out of its ugly face with a short snout, underbite, and tusks that jutted straight up.

Through the night they crept on. Even though no one knew where they were going, neither Speilton, nor Teews, nor Usus, nor Ram, nor Millites said a word. Slowly, very slowly, they all drifted off. Speilton was the last one awake.

Finally, as the sun peaked above the horizon, illuminating the burned, scarred world, Speilton's eyes again shut, as he left his life in the hands of the six legged beast.

Speilton awoke inside a dark room carved out of cracked grey stone. Shimmering light was cast across part of the wall coming down a rocky path that led to the main cavern. Since he'd been asleep last night he had no idea where he was.

Speilton sat up, but he soon regretted it. A sharp pain went through his chest, and he collapsed back onto the fur pelt that made up his bed. "Owwww!" he choked in pain.

A figure suddenly appeared in the doorway and walked to Speilton's side. He reached for his sword, but it was nowhere to be found. Speilton could only wait for the figure to make the first move.

Speilton felt a hand rest on his head, and he automatically pulled away. "No, no, my king. You must rest," the figure whispered.

"Who are you?" Speilton asked, his voice shaky.

"My name is not important. All you need to know is that I'm here to heal you. I'm an Isolate."

"Where are we? Do you know where my brother, Millites is? Is he alright?"

"So many questions. Yes, I have seen your brother. He's healing, slowly. As for where we are, this is the volcano of the Tawii tribe, the last known tribe of the Isolates."

"Wait, are you saying that there is more than one tribe of Isolate?" Speilton asked.

"No, what I'm saying is that there *were* more than one tribe. Many years ago we were all in one large group, known as the Isolates. But then..." the Tawii dropped his gaze and walked to the side wall and grabbed something off a shelf.

"But what?" Speilton asked sitting up in anticipation, but then collapsed back in his bed after the sharp pain in his chest.

The Isolate walked back over to Speilton. "Then the settlers came," he whispered as if it brought back horrible memories. "The Isoalates quarreled. Some wanted to leave, some wanted to stay. Some wanted to fight, some wanted to join them. The Isoalates split into a hundred different tribes. The ones that joined the settlers were enslaved and died off. Others fought and lost. And yet others fled, and were never heard of again. Over years and years, we are the last ones standing."

"What did the Tawii want? To hide?" Speilton asked.

"No, our goal was to survive."

Wow, Speilton thought, *I can hardly imagine a life where my highest goal was to survive. I can't imagine being the last of my kind.*

But then he realized that he could relate since he was the last survivor of Kal. Some how, this was encouraging. If he died, so would Kal. Every other villager in Lorg had been lost. They were all victims of flames.

Flames danced before his eyes. At first they were the flames that engulfed Lorg and Kal. But then they became the flames that caused them all to be in this situation. His flames. "It's all my fault," he could't help saying.

"No, don't say that my king. Just rest," the Tawii's soothing voice said. "But first, drink this," as he handed Speilton a small vial he had taken from the far wall of shelves.

Speilton was so exhausted and absent minded at the time, he took the elixir without question.

"Now, sleep," the Tawii said as he sat down on the ground and lit a fire. Flames rose up into the air as Speilton's eyes slowly closed. Since the fire was far away from his bed, and sleep was closing in fast, he didn't care. As he gazed into the soft flames, the last thing he did before falling back to sleep was to vow to never use his flame wand again.

INTO THE DWARF MINE
~ 11 ~

Three days passed, which were three days for the Kings, Queen, General, Second in Command, and Dragon of Milwaria to regroup in the volcanic fortress of the Tawii, but also time for every soul in Caloria to ready themselves for their final deadly attack. The clock was ticking, and the Milwarians were losing time.

After those three days, Millites cuts and bruises, Speilton's broken ribs, Teews and Usus's lesser injuries, and Prowl's injured wing were on the mend thanks to the Tawii's great effort. But those three days weren't enough to heal them completely. They still needed time, and Ram still couldn't walk.

His legs were scorched and broken, and needed time to heal. But time was one of the many things they did not have.

Ram kept regarding himself as a geezer, too feeble to fight. "No, you're strong and agile," they kept trying to tell him. Every one of them knew that they needed him. Not only because he had the element of wind, but he was the inspiration and had the experience. Ram was the wisest, and he'd been through the worst. They could never leave him.

So it was settled. That morning they gathered up their things. They packed every shield, sword, arrow, spear, plus the two rings, Eye Stone, and the Sword of Power.

Before they left, Speilton went back into the room where he'd stayed. The Tawii was there, laying new animal skins out. "Hey, er ... thanks. We would've died with out all of you."

"You're welcome," he said as he continued to adjust the sheets, "I'm just not sure why you must leave so quickly. You are not healed."

"Well, its complicated. The end of the war is close at hand. The outcome depends on succeeding or failing our quest. We need to begin quickly, because according to the prophecy, the Milwarian army is supposed to be gone while the Calorian army attacks Kon Malopy. It's strange, but for some reason, it has to be that way.

"Anyway, we haven't found an army willing to protect Kon Malopy. And if we don't leave here and find one soon, Milwaria will meet its end."

The Tawii whispered something under his breath. Speilton wasn't sure, but he thought it had something to do with "a calling". Then, the Tawii looked Speilton directly in the eyes. "I will not fail," the Tawii man promised before leaving the room.

They emerged over the last rocky, obsidian hill, and below them was a sight that amazed every one of them. Even though they'd seen it dozens of times, it still made them "ooh and aah."

They crossed a black wasteland of cracked rocks of all sizes, and volcanoes that rose high above the rest of the obsidian chunks. But now, below them was a vast valley with luscious groves and fields. Small huts dotted the landscape hidden in the fruitful vines. A lazy river wound its way through the center of the valley, coming from the Ocean that spread from left to right as far as the eye could see. A black sand beach lay between the the orchards and the Ocean, wrapping the two areas together. And on the beach was a flat dam that spread across the river. It was a water purifier, an invention that could only be made possible by a single race - the dwarves. In the center of it all, rising above everything, was a volcano.

A winding path wrapped around it leading to the top where a single tower rose from the volcano's mouth. The valley stretched about three miles, and the ocean was about a mile from the base of the far wall that they were standing atop.

To Speilton, it was magic. He'd been told it was simply the mix of the fertile, volcanic soil, and the Ocean water. But no matter the reason it was amazing. It was Igniaca.

They climbed down the last hill, and the deep black stone quickly turned to tall grass. Each tiny blade was the deepest green, and it wasn't just because it was spring. Speilton had visited Igniaca in the fall, and the grass had still been this deep green.

When they reached the orchards, the first people began flooding out of their huts to gather around royalty. Some of the people were humans, others were dwarves, but no matter the race, they gathered to celebrate the arrival of their leaders. The closer to the castle, the denser and larger the crowd grew. They all cheered and laughed.

"Thank you for all you do!"

"All hail the Kings!"

"Ram, good to see you again!"

"Keep faith!"

"YES! I touched King Speilton!"

When they finally reached the volcano that sat in the center of the valley of Igniaca, the crowd split, revealing a steel door one hundred feet high. The bolts creaked and groaned as the doors slowly opened. The crowd stepped back and gasped.

To them, it was just as amazing as it was to the kings, queen, Second in Command, and General, who had only seen it happen a few times. Past the door was top-secret, priceless gold, gems, inventions, and information. In other words, it wasn't open to the public. But obviously, royalty was worth opening the door for.

The doors didn't open all the way and reveal the secrets within. But they did open just enough for a young man and three dwarves to walk out. The man had golden-blond hair, a goatee, and a young face. He was about twenty years old and wearing a set of silver armor. At his side, dangling from a utility belt was an axe, a dazzling sword, and the element wand of lava. The man was Onaclov, King of the Lavalands. Though the native race in the Lavalands were the dwarves, he was human and liked it that way.

Onaclov got down on his knee and bowed. Then he leapt up and grabbed Millites in a bear hug, "Millites, it's so good to see you," he said as he began to walk over to Speilton. "Speilton, how've you been?"

"Great. Well, I guess if you don't include almost getting killed half a dozen times," Speilton said.

"Nah, let's not include that," as he walked over to Teews and leaned over in a steep bow. "My Queen," he said with mock reverence.

"Onaclov." she responded, blushing.

Onaclov shook Ram's hand, then stepped forward and did a half shake, half hug type of thing.

Then he saw Usus and his eyes narrowed. He stepped back, and the two engaged in a stare down. The tension was broken by Onaclov bursting out in laughter. "Usus, I haven't seen you in forever."

"It *has* been a while," Usus agreed.

"Onaclov and Usus had been allies since birth. They'd grown up together, faced challenges together, and escaped death, together. But that's a different story."

"So, I came down as soon as I heard you were here. What's wrong?"

"Well..." Speilton noticed the crowd listening in on their conversation. "It's probably best discussed inside."

The doors shut behind them. Now, you'd expect the inside of a volcano to be dark. Well, it's not dark if it's lit by lava. The circular room was as large as an arena, nearly one hundred yards by one hundred years, and four hundred feet tall. In the center of the room was a thick column that stretched to the ceiling, but this was no ordinary column. It held up this entire room and was made from volcanic rock. The small cracks in the stone revealed magma inside of it, and the tiny gaps of lava lit the room up. Still, it all looked safe. Metal pipes held the rock chunks together, and there was a large, thick tub that surrounded the column to catch any oozing magma.

But, possibly the *most* amazing part of the room was that it was teaming with dwarves. The small men raced across the room with pick-axes, jewels, and cords of rope in hand. They were even racing along the walls.

The inside walls of the volcano were ringed with paths. Small ladders led from one to another. There were at least twenty or thirty circular pathways that were built into the wall, suspended in mid air. Even at the very top level, dwarves were grabbing jewels and weapons, and building another path at the very top.

They went through the area where jewels and precious metals were sorted, the blacksmith room where Liolia's finest weapons were created and countless other rooms before climbing a steep stairwell and coming to a smaller room with four columns in each corner, and a large table in the center.

"So, what happened?" Onaclov asked.

Millites began telling the story. He told about the fight with Sinister, and their narrow escape. Onaclov couldn't help but smile at the part where they destroyed the bell tower. He told Onaclov about the visit to Rilly's hut, the prophecy, and that they needed six creatures, one of them being a dwarf.

Teews told the next part of their adventure; their journey to Mermaid Cove, how she 'persuaded' Neptune to let them borrow the Night Seemer, and finding the Island of the Wizard Council.

Usus explained to Onaclov that Cigam told them that it must be the humans that fight the final battle, and that there were two armies planning to attack Kon Malopy. He told Onaclov about the Eye Stone, the secret way into Skilt, Ferrum Potestas, the need to possess certain animals, and the overall power of the Inferno of Erif.

Teews told how Venefica and a storm of Daerds ruined the palace, how they escaped from the island, and how she shot down Daerds with her wand. Next she explained how they fired the cannons, and told about Cigam and Venefica's final battle.

Speilton's heart started to beat rapidly. He knew what was coming next. Should he tell them he was the one the Versipellis were after? Should he tell them it was all his fault? But then he saw the pain in Ram's eyes as he began the next part of the story. Speilton just couldn't bring himself to tell Ram his brother's death was because of him.

Ram explained his sickness and how Nicholas saved him. He told Oncalov how Millites had been kidnapped and how they realized that the kidnapper was his brother, Incertus. "But then..."

"But then, what?" Onaclov asked.

"We were attacked by some creature."

Teews chimed in, "Yeah, it buried us in a pile of dirt."

"They killed my brother," Ram mourned.

"Did any one see the creature?" Onaclov asked.

"Well, I was stuffed in a bag the whole time," Millites said.

"They were moving too fast. I couldn't tell," Usus said.

"Me, either," Teews added.

"I… I can't remember. I was too distracted by …" Ram stopped, and they all understood.

Everyone, but Onaclov. "Why were you distracted?"

Teews whispered in his ear, "His brother was lost in the battle."

"Oh, I'm so sorry I had no idea," he said, then looked down in sorrow.

There was silence, broken by Prowl tossing and turning in her sleep on the floor.

"So, no one saw the creature?" Onaclov asked.

"Oh wait," Usus realized, "Speilton - Speilton saw the creature. He tried to stop it with his wand but…it started to malfunction."

"Don't worry. It'll never happen again. I already promised myself that I'd never use it again."

"What?"

"I just can't control it. I'm not ready. I nearly killed all of us." All of Speilton's emotions that he'd been feeling the last few days poured out. "It just doesn't make sense. Why did I get the flame wand? It's like a bad joke. It was because of fire that my village burned down and lost everything."

"But if it hadn't, you'd have never found us," Teews offered.

"Yeah, well, life was a lot easier when the only thing I had to worry about was trying to shoot a deer."

"Speilton, I know this is hard for you. Having to take command as King after, your village..." Millites stopped himself before he said *too* much.

"Speilton, we *will* discuss this later, but right now, we need to know what the creatures were," Ram said.

Speilton could see the pain in his eyes. Ram *had* to know what had attacked them. He wanted to know who to blame. Who had taken his only brother.

"Well, they were..." Speilton couldn't do it. "They were cloaked, black, spirits or something like that."

"It wasn't the Versipellis, was it?" Onaclov asked, and everyone else sat forward in their chairs.

"No," Speilton responded quickly.

"Maybe they were some type of new creature. A new ally for the Calorians most likely," Usus suggested.

Everyone agreed, and after that, Speilton remained quiet for the rest of the meeting.

"Okay, now I have some information to share," Onaclov announced. "Two days ago we got news that Kon Malopy's artillery machine, recently named the Avenger, was completed after five years.

"Also, I have received word from Cigam that the Island of the Wizard Council has dropped into the ocean. Hundreds of worlds are losing battles. The darkness itself is destroying entire planets, and everywhere, their islands have been destroyed. Areas of Liolia have been destroyed, along with a few other countries on other planets. Let me see, there was Tangool, um . . . Latoe, Atlantis, and Kakle or something. My point is, I don't think that we'll be getting much help from the Wizard Council for a while."

"Great, what else could go wrong?" Millites wondered.

"So, our next step is getting you a dwarf," Onaclov announced. "I'll call up our finest. CRINGE!!!" Onaclov called.

A tall (compared to most dwarves), red-bearded dwarf marched up the stairs. He wore a thick helmet that covered his eyes with thin, tiny bars of a jail. Four horns protruded from the helmet, two in front and two in back. He wore normal dwarf clothes, heavy chained armor, a thick belt holding a hammer and pick axe, and thick, metal-soled boots. On his chest was a golden badge with a single pick axe depicted on it, which was the sign of a miner.

"Yes, my King?" the dwarf bowed.

His eyes widened as he saw King Millites and King Speilton.

"This is Cringe, my Second in Command and chief of the mining crew," Onaclov announced.

The dwarf took a clumsy bow.

"Cringe, go grab our finest dwarves. These good people need to take one on their journey."

"Yes, King Onaclov," Cringe began to hurry away.

"Oh, and that does mean Ore, too."

Cringe froze as if he'd been shot in the back. "Are you sure? That dwarf has never been good for anything." Cringe argued.

"Cringe, you must bring *everyone*." Onaclov commanded.

"Of course, my King." he said, though his voice had a slight edge to it."

"Now, we need to send a messenger to tell everyone in Kon Malopy you are safe, Millites."

"And to tell them to gather all of their troops, and ready every artillery vehicle, including the Avenger," said Onaclov.

"Are you sure?" Ram asked, "We must cross through the Calorian wastelands, and you know how hard it'll be to pull catapults through that."

"But what about the Avenger? We have been waiting years for it to be finished. We can't abandon it in our darkest hour."

"Fine, we will take only the Avenger, and leave the other catapults behind to fight at Kon Malopy. Then, we must leave in the morning to get a centaur from the desert," Millites announced.

"But how is the army going to catch up with us?" Usus asked.

"We could meet each other, in the Jungle of Supin?" Ram offered.

"No, the jungles are too crowded. It'll be impossible to find them in there. And it'll be to hard to drag the Avenger through." Speilton said.

"Well, the jungles are too small, and the Great Plains would be far too large to find them. I say we meet in the Icelands," Usus decided.

"Agreed," Ram said.

"But what of the Four Forest people? How will they find us?" Usus asked.

"The desert would be about three days away for them. That's where we need to go next if we want a centaur. But to be honest, I don't think I can stand it that long in the desert," Ram grumbled.

"What about one of the rivers? That'll be about a two-day journey for them, and we can get there in about the same time," Millites suggested.

"The old ruins. We can meet up at the old ruins on the edge of the Sintel River," Usus announced.

"Perfect, they'll know where that is," Ram said.

"So, now onto other matters. Battle strategy," Millites said. "There are going to be three battles. One at Skilt, which'll be fought by the humans. One at Kon Malopy, again. And there is also a fleet of ships coming to attack here at the Lavalands. Once they have taken you over, they will procede to destroy Kon Malopy.

"The Mers could fight at sea," Usus offered.

"But how are we going to alert them on such short notice?" Onaclov asked. "I may be able to help you with that."

"How can the Lavalands battle on the seas? Isn't that mainly Mermaid Coves' responsibility?" Ram asked.

"It's a project we've been working on for a while. You see, we're so close to the water and could easily be attacked from the ocean. That's why we created a fleet of sturdy ships. I think seven or eight in all. The ships are pretty simple. No fancy cannons or anything like in Mermaid Cove, but they're fast. They're in a large room somewhere under the volcano. We have them on rollers, so we can take them to the water in case of an unexpected attack. Though they've never gotten a chance to fight."

"Well, it looks like it's their lucky day. There's a battle coming soon." Millites said.

Soon, two messengers were on their way to Kon Malopy, and Speilton, Millites, Ram, Usus, and Teews were in a room with twenty dwarves. Onaclov wasn't with them, since he had to check on a rockslide that had happened on one of the sides of the volcano.

"So, here are the best of the best when it comes to dwarves," Cringe announced, as all the dwarves bowed to their Kings and Queen.

Every Dwarf wore a badge depicting their specialty. A pick axe for miner, a flame for black smith, a diamond for jeweler, coal for engineer, a feather pen for inventor, and so on.

"So, dwarves, as you probably already know, we are looking for a dwarf to accompany us on a quest," Millites informed them as the dwarves tried their best to look tough and brave.

"Now, I think you all should know this," Speilton said. "One of the questers will die. The future has been written, and there is a chance that person could be one of you. To join us is to put your life on the line."

A few of the dwarves shrank back, but most stayed firm and solemn. "Are you willing to join us?" Usus asked the crowd.

"Aye!" they all called back.

"So, what type of dwarf do you need? We've got blacksmiths, miners?"

"No, those won't help us. We need some one strong...someone brave. We need a warrior," Millites decided.

"Oh, no. We don't have any warriors," Cringe apologized.

"Yeah we do. Ore's a warrior," one of the dwarves shouted out.

Cringe's face turned red, and he looked down at his feet, an angry expression on his face. "Yeah, Ore, the *worst* of the best," he muttered under his breath.

"So, who is this Ore?" Ram asked.

A short, REALLY short dwarf stepped out from the back. His eyes were wide, and his beard was less scraggly, long, and burned than the others. On his head was a round helmet with two curved horn's like a viking. He wore leather armor, and a huge, two-sided weapon was strapped to his back. On his badge, was an axe and a hammer, the sign of a warrior.

"Yes?" the dwarf asked.

"So, Ore, are you the only warrior here?" Usus asked.

"Well, yes. I'm the only warrior in the volcano, at least. There are others outside the volcano that fight, but I'm a guard in here, actually, the only guard in here now that the others have…"

"Yes, yes, so sad," Cringe grumbled cutting off Ore's ramble. "Are you sure Ore is who you're looking for? He fails at even the simplest dwarf skills. We have many other great dwarves, inventors and jewelers. Or, you could take me. I have the most experience. I could assist you."

Speilton looked back over to Ore, and saw a frightened expression in his tiny face. In that one look, Speilton noticed dozens of things. He remembered after the meeting with Onaclov, how he had to command Cringe to gather Ore. He recalled how happy and amazed Ore had been while talking to the Kings. Also, in that glance, Speilton noticed a long rivalry. Ore had always been beaten by Cringe in everything. Cringe was the Second in Command and treated Ore like he was inferior. He had no respect for Ore's talent. Only seconds ago, Ore had almost gotten a shot. Victory was so close at hand, but it had been snatched away and stolen by Cringe once again. "We'll take Ore!" Speilton announced.

The dwarves' jaws dropped, Ore's included. "But, Speilton, what about Cringe?" Millites asked.

"Ore's a warrior, he deserves a chance, and on our quest, the assistance of a miner wouldn't help. We need a warrior. We need Ore."

Millites looked at Speilton and knew that there was more to this, though he decided not to ask yet. "We'll take Ore," Millites agreed.

The dwarves cheered, Ore beamed with pride, and Cringe glared at the dwarf with the intensity of the sun. Ore could only smile back.

A LAND WITHOUT WATER
~ 12 ~

"Are you sure you need to leave so soon?" Onaclov asked.

"It's best we get going. The messenger should be getting to Kon Malopy soon," Millites said.

"As you wish. I'll see you soon," Onaclov promised.

"And Onaclov, good luck. If these are the final days, then your winning the Ocean War may be crucial," Ram informed him.

"Wow, you're really making me feel better. No pressure," he scoffed.

"Oh, and we'd like to give you this ring, just as a token of our appreciation." Usus handed him the ring he'd been carrying ever since Ram's brother had stolen it.

"Thanks. You know, I want to look my best for battle."

They all laughed, even though they knew it could very well happen. There was a very big chance they'd never see each other again.

As they left the volcanic fortress, the crowds were as big as ever. The farmers who lived outside the volcano were this time joined by dwarves from inside. Ore was right in the middle of them, bold and heroic as he left with royalty on a deadly adventure. Many people patted him on the back, and Ore beamed each time. The crowds swarmed and laughed and cheered until the kings, Second in Command, general, dragon, and dwarf left the green valley and stepped onto the cracked, brimstone wasteland. The only one not with them was Teews. They had to leave her in the Lavalands to be escorted back to Kon Malopy.

Teews knew just like everyone else that the prophecy didn't call for her just as it didn't call for Onaclov. They had a different destiny to fulfill. For Onaclov, it was to lead an attack on the seas. For Teews, it was to help defend Kon Malopy. But for Speilton, Millites, Usus, Ram, and Ore, their destiny would be to fight the final battle between the Calorians and the Milwarians to victory or death.

Back in the volcano, the great dwarf fleet was rolled out from a dark chamber under the fortress. Their deep red, triangular sails stood tall and straight. They slid off their rollers and drifted into the water. Farmers scurried along the deck as the crew checked to make sure everything was functioning.

Food was brought on board as were cords and cords of rope, two extra sails, wood rods of all sizes, and other nautical necessities.

By the next day at midday, the ships were ready, all eight of them. One by one they took off across the calm sea. The ships met and waited about a mile from the shore. Then they sailed into the horizon.

Back at the dock, crowds were cheering. Children ran up and down the black sanded beaches, imagining the life of a sailor going out to battle on the seas. The wind was strong and blew the ships away swiftly, so that in a few minutes, they had disappeared from sight. Slowly, the crowd died out, and only a few of the children remained, digging in the black sand and leaping over waves. Not one of them would've guessed that the dwarf fleet would never touch dry land again.

Night had fallen as they finally exited the charred black Lavalands, though they continued on through the night. They needed to get closer to the desert before setting up camp. The ground in between the two territories - the Lavalands and the Desert - was covered in short, weedy grass, and tangled shrubs grew up out of it. Plateaus and rough, rocky hills rose and flowed across the landscape.

They remained quiet while hiking. In the distance was the howling of coyotes and wolves, though there were never any encounters. Ore had to walk quickly to keep up with Millites, Speilton, Usus, and Ram, but he never complained.

Finally, after a few hours of walking, they came to an area where the grass was crumpled over and dead. The shrubs were reduced to rubble. All that was left was sand.

"We make camp here," Millites declared. "At daybreak we can hike into the desert, but for now, we must rest."

The air was warm, dry and thick, but that was only to be expected near a desert. Luckily, they had come prepared. The Dwarves had supplied them with thick, heat-resistant tents, and jugs and jugs of water. They also gave them a supply of their new invention, blankets strong enough to hold water overnight to cool off the user.

After the long day of hiking, they fell asleep easily. The wind whistling off the dunes, and the howling of coyotes lulled the five to sleep.

The next day, they woke up early and started off into the desert. Light glared off the sand, as heat radiated down on them. Even though it was spring, they were hot.

Sweat dripped from their skin, as their legs strained to trudge through the sand. Ore had the hardest time. The sand reached above his knees, and he had to dig through it to move. As Speilton peered through the haze of heat, he thought he could see a vast area where there were no dunes. Sand blew toward them, then disappeared. He thought it could be the hole that the snake creature had crawled from half a year ago when he passed through. Luckily, they went nowhere near the bottomless pit in which the creature had first emerged.

The later it got, the hotter it became. They each carried a jug of water, but they were soon empty. After a few hours, the sand began to pick up and blow against their clothing. Though it wasn't bad, the sand sill whipped across their body and flew at their eyes. The travelers had to tear off the sleeves of their now gritty, dry clothing, and tied them around their mouths to keep out any sand. Though, compared to most journeys through the desert, it was fairly easy. No random sandstorms arose, and there weren't any attacks. They reached the palace by nightfall. After many stops, and multiple jugs of water, they reached the centaurs.

Speilton had never seen their palace before. Millites and Usus had only been there a few times. Out of all the regions in Milwaria - Rich Woods, Mermaid Cove, Lavalands, Jungle of Supin, Icelands, and Desert, the desert region helped the least. Each region was inhabited or mostly occupied by a different race. There were the humans, mers, dwarves, elves, giants and centaurs. Since the inhabitants of the desert, the centaurs, helped the very least, there was no need to check on them very often. Unlike the other territories who helped with a variety of tasks even simple things like gathering fruit or gemstones, the centaurs made no contributions. Milwarians had no reason to interact with them. Though, it was fine since the Centaurs enjoyed solitude.

The Centaurs tried to stay out of most affairs and kept to their own lives. In the beginning of Liolia, they weren't even considered Milwarians. They were wild tribes and began their civilizations in what is now the desert region, but at that time the area was just plains and grassy hills. After many droughts caused by the tall mountains on the peninsula of Milwaria across the ocean, the plains began to slowly dissolve into dust and sand. The centaurs tried to ride it out, but the desert just grew larger, hotter, and deadlier.

Still, they wouldn't leave. The site was a holy place since their ancestors had founded the land, and it was one of the only connections the centaurs had to them.

None of the Milwarians wanted to fight the centaurs for the land. At that point, they already had enough trouble trying to keep peace with the Calorians. They couldn't begin another war.

So they accepted the centaurs who assisted in battle, but mainly stayed to themselves. Besides, the centaurs were unlike the other races. They had different customs, and were able to function in a way that no other race could. And, they were probably the strangest of all the species with the exception of the minotaurs that lived peacefully in Milwaria. Centaurs had the torso, arms, and head of a human, but below the waist was a four-legged body of a horse.

As they neared the palace, they could see small dome-shaped huts and a flat rocky castle. They trudged onward and were soon met by centaurs, although their welcome was very different from the one in the Lavalands with no cheering and laughing. The centaurs saw them and bowed which was difficult though since they had to get down on one knee, while stretching the other one forward. Though they were mostly silent, some were overheard whispering, "My Kings."

The noise came after they walked through the vast village of dome-shaped huts. As they reached the castle, bowing centaurs formed a line on either side of the two great doors. They each held a long, twisted trumpet and faced the centaur across from them. As Speilton, Millites, Usus, Ram, and Ore stepped through the trumpets, the centaurs began to play a magnificent, proud tune as the doors were quickly opened, and the five stepped through. The door slammed behind them.

"Welcome, my Kings," a voice echoed through the area.

The room where they stood was large and very oddly shaped. Two staircases wound completely around the rectangular room, leading down into the main area. Down below, the room seemed larger and more grand, but from up high, at the top of the stairs where they stood, the room seemed flat and crowded.

The ceiling dipped down, leading to an enormous hour glass that served as the central column in the middle of the room. Sand ran off the roof and down into the top of the hour glass. On all sides of the room were doors. The palace itself was vast … but flat.

They walked down the wide stairs that wrapped completely around the room. They reached the central area and walked around the hour glass to find the King of the Centaurs. He stood since he was unable to sit in a throne and wore a turban made of gold linen. He had dark, chocolate skin and a beard so black it almost appeared blue. His horse body was grey, and in his strong arms he held a long golden staff.

As the kings came into view, he bowed in an awkward, yet magnificent way. There were two centaurs standing up one flight of stairs behind him, and they bowed, too. "For what reason do you come?" the King asked.

That's just like a centaur-orderly and straight to the point. Again, much different than when they arrived at Igniaca in the Lavalands.

"We have come due to the fore-shadowing of a prophecy," Millites began. "It indicated that we need six creatures to accompany us on a quest. One, as you can see," he gestured to Ore, "is with us right now, and four more are on their way. The other we need is a centaur," Millites said promptly.

It's best to be quick while talking to a centaur. They are easily bored and take it to be patronizing if you take too long. Annoying a centaur is not a smart move.

"You need only one centaur to accompany you?" the king asked.

"Yes."

"Hhhm... Equus!" the King called.

They heard a clatter of hooves on stone, one of the doors was flung open, and a centaur stepped out. He had bronze skin, a white, shaggy furred horse body, and a single braid of brown hair ran down his back. "Yes sir?"

"You have been chosen for a quest. You are strong, brave, and an excellent warrior. You'll do well," the King announced.

"Thank you," the centaur nodded and went to stand off to the side.

Whoa! Speilton thought, *That was too simple. That centaur, Equus, accepted the journey that easily without question. Does he understand what he's facing?*

"Um, Equus, you might want to know that at least one of us won't make it. One of us will perish on the journey according to a prophecy," Speilton confirmed.

Equus looked at Speilton with sad knowing eyes. "If that is the case, one life is a small price to give if it means saving others." These were probably the deepest, most meaningful words a centaur has ever said.

"Now that that is resolved, I have a request," the King Centaur announced.

"What is it you require?" Usus questioned.

"Generations ago, we joined Milwaria under one condition. We would supply them with warriors, if they would supply us with necessities, one of them being water, which is hard to find out here. We are in great need of water."

"Oh, if that's all, we can get you some soon," Usus agreed.

"No, we need it now. After you leave here, you'll be on your way on a quest. You'll forget about our needs, as you try desperately to survive yourself. And if you die on the quest, so does our last hope. Centaurs are dying every day. The thirst and heat drive many mad, but this is our land, the only place we've able to live."

"I'm sorry, but this is a bad time. We'll help you as soon as we can, but right now the fate of Liolia rests in our hands," Millites argued.

"So does the fate of the centaurs."

After a long pause, Ram spoke up to break the deadly silence, "We have sent many men carrying loads of water."

"We know, we found the wagon abandoned in the desert. The water has long since dried from them, and the corpses of the horses pulling the wagons is all that remain. The drivers have fled from the desert."

"I'm sorry, we didn't know," Speilton tried.

"I try to believe. We all do, but every time we ask for help, no one is willing to help. We've tried to get water ourselves, but many of our weakened men never make it back. We drink from the small bits we are able to forage."

"From now on we'll make sure that you don't go thirsty," Millites agreed.

"You better come up with a solution fast, because you're not leaving until you do," the king said.

"Why are you doing this?" Speilton asked. "We're your kings, you can't imprison us."

"I'm sorry, it must be done, for the good of my people."

"But what do you expect us to do?" Usus asked. "We can't just create water magically. None of us have that element."

"Then we'll send a messenger to get water. We've tried this many times, but without any success. You're always out fighting helpless battles, and even when the Centaurs are listened to, you only send a single wagon, and as I said, they never make it."

"Well, why can't you do it yourself? You're strong, brave. It's easier for you to get water than us." Millites argued. His patience had ended; the centaurs hardly ever did anything for them. Why does this king suddenly think he has superiority over them?

"That was the deal we created many years ago. You must live by it."

"We sent men. Many of them have reached you or at least they tried. We have focused on the war, and if we waver from destroying the Calorians, Milwaria will die."

"If you don't help, the centaurs will all die."

"Are you telling me to just stop the war so that we can get you water?"

"It's much more than that. Every single one of us will die without water. My land is dying. See that hourglass?"

They turned and faced the hourglass. "That hour glass is a funnel in the roof, the sand from the top of our palace flows down into it. In other words, it shows the time until we will once again be free, and the Centaurs will once again be a mighty civilization. But for now, the sand keeps flowing, never lessening. So we wait for the day when the sand will pass, and we can once again live in peace."

"I'm sorry, but right now, I'm too busy helping a greater cause, not just thinking about myself."

Now Millites had made the King angry. "If that's the way you are. GUARDS! Take them away until they can decide what to do."

Centaurs emerged from all around. They followed the command of their king without question. The only one who didn't move was Equus, who had a petrified, scared expression on his face.

"You can't imprison your kings. We command you!" Usus yelled at the king while drawing his sword.

"Weapons can't help you now. Tell me, after destroying us, what would you do then? There's no escape."

"This is wrong. You can't do this!" Speilton screamed.

"You no longer have domain over me. You have broken the pact created years ago, so we break our deal also. We are now our own nation and are unchanged by your commands."

They all wished that Teews was still with them. She'd be able to merely pull out her wand, use a little magic, and the king would bend to her will. But they didn't have that power, and would have to fend for themselves.

Speilton reached inside his pocket. His wand was no help. Like the king had said, there was no escape in the desert. The same was true with his sword. His shield could possibly protect him, but he didn't see any reason for the centaurs to attack. He had the Eye Stone and the other ring from the Island of the Wizard Council. The Eye

Stone might show them a way out of the prison cell where they were being taken, but after getting out, they'd be back in this same situation. The ring from the Island of the Wizard Council... Then it struck him, for the very first time. Why was the ring on an island of magic? It *must have a magical property.*

He pulled it out and began to examine it. There were three lines spaced evenly apart on different sides of the ring. One was straight and plain. Another was squiggly and curved like a river. And the last one consisted of six tiny dots that were spaced perfectly apart in a line.

But before he could examine it any further, two strong hands grabbed around his arms. "Hey, watch it!" Speilton tugged loose and stared up at the stunned Centaurs. But they quickly recovered, and their horse-ish, flat noses flared in anger. If he was going to use the ring, now would be a good time.

He slipped it on, pointed at the centaur, and... nothing. The centaurs laughed as Speilton drew back his hand to examine the ring. As Millites, Usus, Ram, Prowl and Ore were dragged away by two centaurs each (one for Ore and four for Prowl) they gave him questioned and confused looks. Prowl leapt at one of the centaurs, knocking him to the ground.

"No, Prowl, don't attack!" Speilton commanded. The blue dragon froze reluctantly and began eyeing the centaurs suspiciously.

Time was running out. He had to act fast. That's when he realized that the symbols were glowing. Speilton slipped off the ring and the light flickered off. He shoved it back on and the light reappeared.

The centaurs moved back toward him, obviously not noticing or caring about the ring. *Uh oh, maybe if I just pressed the dotted line...*

The symbol glared brightly and a beam of gold light flashed from his finger and hit the wall. The sandstone bricks disappeared completely, leaving only steam.

Millites, Usus, Ram, Ore, Equus, and all the other centaur's in the rooms leapt back in surprise. Speilton pointed at the ceiling and tried again. This time he pressed the wavy design, instead of the dotted line. A chunk of the roof dissolved into clean, pure water, and crashed down onto the head of the King Centaur.

"Uh oh," Speilton apologized. "I'm sorry, I didn't mean to do that. You see I just found it, and I didn't know how to work it-"

"Stop!" the king commanded. "Where did you get that?"

"At the Island of the Wizard Council."

"Give it to me!"

"Why would I?"

"You're under my rule. You're my prisoners. You must give that to me."

"Whoa, wait! It seems that you want something, and we want our freedom." Millites blurted.

"I don't need it," the soaked king bluffed.

Speilton dropped the ring on the floor and held his foot over it. "Then you would be fine if I just crushed it?"

"You wouldn't actually destroy it," the king sneered.

"Wouldn't? You see, we don't need it. But you do."

"You did see it turn that ceiling into water. This is what you need," Ore lured him.

But the king looked uninterested as water dripped from his beard.

"Fine, your loss," Speilton murmured drawing his sword and holding it over the ring. In a sharp movement, he plunged down, the king screamed "NO!" and Speilton made sure to strike... three inches away from the ring.

Speilton reached down, picked up the solid ring, and held it up to the king. "It looks like we've got a deal."

"Wait, but first. We need one more thing," Millites broke in. "Since we are giving you this... water-making ring, we are fulfilling the promise, the pact. Which means, you have to keep your end of the deal. To supply us with warriors."

The king scowled and turned away. In order to get water, he had to enter back into the deal.

"Uh, I believe there is a question on the table," Usus urged the king on.

"Why do you need the warriors?" the king asked.

"Only to protect Kon Malopy in the final battle," Usus said.

"Kon Malopy is your capitol, not ours. Why can't you defend it yourself?"

"We are fighting a battle elsewhere. And, if you want the ring, " Speilton held it out, "Kon Malopy *is* your capitol."

"We don't need Milwaria," the king decided.

"Then I guess you won't be needing this." Speilton said pointing right above the King and tapping the squiggly line again. The King's gold turban melted into water that soaked him once again.

It was a very risky move, but it luckily worked out.

Now Speilton knew how the ring worked. Each symbol represented a different stage of matter, solid (the straight line), liquid (the curved line), and gas (the dotted line).

Behind him the two centaurs that had been holding him rushed forward. But Speilton pointed at the ground and touched the curved line, turning the ground into a puddle. Then he pressed the straight line, and the water instantly turned to ice.

The centaurs' hooves slipped across the flat surface, and they tumbled into each other. But they soon were able to get back up.

"Stop! Okay, I agree. I get that ring, and you get our warriors," the king decided with finality.

So the troops were arranged, the ring was given to the centaurs, and the six creatures had been chosen. But the danger was just beginning.

SIEGE AT THE RUINS
~ 13 ~

Equus had been silent ever since he left the palace. He didn't seem mad or sad or scared or happy or anything at all. His face was still and expressionless. It was understandable, since he never had a say about whether he wanted to die on this journey since he'd been assigned to the mission without being asked.

At least everything was decided. The centaurs were still Milwarians, and Kon Malopy had a defending army. All they had to do was meet the other four creatures, travel across the plains, through the jungle and into the Icelands to let the army catch up, then travel across Caloria, sneak into the most heavily guarded castle in Liolia, destroy a raging fire, then prepare for a battle to decide their fate.

Pretty simple.

After leaving the desert they hiked into the Rocks of Tior, a spectacular land of gravity-defying rock structures. Like the desert, it is hot and dry, though many small shrubs dot the landscape. The earth is more stable and varied, unlike the flat expanse of nothing in the desert. In the beginning, it was considered part of the desert, as it was so close. But over the years, it was decided that it should be its own land. Though it was never appointed a King, and no race decided to live there, the area was never under any major threat of being attacked. The area could not be reached by water and was not close to Caloria in any way.

The Rocks of Tior was a land that would always stay preserved in its natural form. The forces of man would never be allowed to change it as long as the Milwarians were in charge of it. No houses or trenches or walls or barriers had ever or would ever be created. No, the Rocks of Tior was a national landmark, an area of supreme beauty.

Before the war, people would go to see the amazing formations, but now it was deserted and most likely a perfect spot for run away bandits looking for a safe haven.

The sun was rising when they first entered. There were large red rock faces that stretched up on either side of them like a large door. The pure blue sky adjacent to the flaming rocks cast light across the path. They walked along the trail, the two walls still rising and dropping around them. Finally, the walls came to an end, and they stepped onto the edge of a valley. Below them, down a steep hill was nature at its best. Deep emerald trees clustered across the red sand and arches of rock stretched across the landscape. A canyon was hidden in the center, and tall hoodoos and spires of stone etched into the sky. The two walls they'd walked through to get inside were part of a long chain of towering, red, jagged-faced mountains that circled the valley. The far end was so far away, it was nearly impossible to see. The mountains were like an amphitheater filled with people, encircling and looking down onto the stage. And the valley put on a fantastic show.

As they walked down into the valley, they passed an arch that had formed right out of the hill and trailed down thirty feet below. They hiked down farther and entered a maze of hoodoos that rose up and broke off in sections. Red light glinted off the spires causing them to appear to be glowing. They swerved and back-tracked down steep drops, and even had to climb over some of the smaller hoodoos before exiting the maze.

When they stepped out, they found themselves near the bottom of the valley. They hiked underneath an arch with two thick legs and stopped to get water in a cluster of pines that blocked out some heat. They continued on, walking for hours though each minute was thrilling. Gnarled trees grew into others as if in a four hundred year old fight. A cool breeze wafted down to them, and by midday they reached a spring where they drank. They came to the canyon shortly after and had to walk along parallel to the gorge until they reached an old rickety bridge made of worn rope and wooden boards.

"Is it safe?" Ore asked.

"Only one way to find out," Ram announced.

"Whoa! I'm not going across and risk plummeting to my death. That's a bad idea," Usus backed away.

"Okay, So there are two ways to find out," Ram agreed, "but this is what I had in mind."

Ram grabbed a large stone from the ground and tossed it onto the bridge. It shook but didn't break. "One more thing," Ram said, grabbing onto the rope attached to a tall stake next to them that kept the bridge up. He pulled down on it. But again it did not break and stood firm.

"Okay. I think it'll be good for two of us to cross at once, but only one when it comes to Equus. Prowl can just fly across."

They marched across and continued through the valley. The sun began to set, and the stone all around them changed colors from orangey-red, to deep, blood red, to mahogany, to purple. The world changed colors, until it turned black. They finally found a place to sleep out on a flat area without trees or any large rocks. Here they could light a fire without worrying about catching a tree on fire. The night was warm and a light breeze blew through the area as they lay down their gear and rolled a few logs and rocks over for the fire and for a place to sit. They dusted out a circle, ten feet wide and ringed it with rocks.

In the center they lay out small twigs, thicker branches, and then three logs. "Speilton, you may do the honors," Usus instructed.

It took Speilton a moment to notice what he meant. "You want me to start the fire? With my wand?" he asked.

"Um, yes." Usus said.

"No, thanks," Speilton said simply.

"Speilton, what's wrong?" Ram asked sitting next to him.

"You remember what happened last time I used my wand. I nearly got us all killed. Your legs are still injured, and I don't see how you'll be able to walk all the way to Skilt."

"But that was only one time. Accidents happen," Ram said.

"But they don't happen over and over again. I nearly burned down the Island of the Wizard Council, caught my bed on fire a month ago, and nearly killed Selppir last year with my anger." Speilton was close to breaking down at this point.

"Well, Selppir pretty much deserved it," Ram tried.

"I think I know what's wrong," Millites spoke up. "Let me talk to him."

He sat next to Speilton as every one else moved away to start the fire with flint and steel.

"Why was I given fire?" Speilton asked.

"That's not for me to answer."

"It makes no sense. It's as if the Wizards are mocking me. I have to control the element that destroyed my old life, my whole world."

"Or maybe they were trying to tell you something. Maybe they were trying to help you."

"Well, it hasn't worked so far."

"Speilton, when you channel fire, what memory do you use?"

Speilton stared down at his feet, "I think of my village...in flames."

"You see, that's the problem."

"What do you use then. What image creates your light?" Speilton asked hurriedly.

"Well, I think of the sun, and the moon, and the stars, all shining their light as brightly as possible. I think of darkness cowering behind me as I step forward. Light all around me."

There was silence, interrupted by Equus speaking for the first time. "You mustn't fear. You must embrace it to overcome the pain."

"What he says is true. You can't keep thinking about and dreading the past. The Calorians can use that against you. The image you use is of a raging, horrible fire that destroyed your home and that's how the fire comes out - savage, unstoppable."

"What do you suggest, then?" Speilton asked.

"When you imagine an uncontrollable fire, your wand responds. Try to imagine controlling it. Don't let the fear take over your mind. Picture yourself wielding flames. You're the master. They bend to your will," Millites instructed.

Speilton pulled out his wand and stared into the bonfire Ram had just created. A shiver went down his back as he pictured each twig of burning wood, as a hut of one of his neighbors crumbling into embers.

"No one else is going to get hurt. I'm not a wielder of fire," Speilton grumbled as he tossed the wand into the flames.

"No!" they cried as it began to smolder in the ashes. But Ore was fast and plucked the wand out of the flames.

"Are you okay? Were you burned?" Ram asked.

"Just a little. Back in the Lavalands I would have to start the fires. You get used to it." He offered the wand to Speilton who shrugged it away.

"I'll take it," Millites said, shoving it into his belt. "When you need it, just ask."

Speilton nodded his head solemnly, and stared into the flames remembering his village turning to ash before his eyes.

The next day, they continued walking through the rusted world. They walked under an arch over three hundred feet wide. They crawled to the top of a stone cliff where even more arches branched off like the limbs of a huge, orange tree. But to Speilton, it was all the same. He walked along, thinking about the curse, the flames, and how they were going to survive the next few days.

They began a steep climb out of the valley, passed between two pine covered mountains and exited the Rocks of Tior at midday. The air grew cooler the farther away they got from the valley. The hiking was easier now that they weren't tripping over sand and rocks. They passed through villages and the crowds swarmed around them, welcoming them and offering food and supplies. A few times they reached abandoned towns that had been struck by illness or viruses. They finally settled down in a village to sleep that night and began hiking again early the next morning. They walked all day and finally came to the ruins late in the afternoon. They found a river that rushed by the ruins and a tall, single tower branched off into four walls. One was facing north, another east, the third south, and then west. This tower was unlike the one they destroyed in the Rich Woods. It was once used for attack and to stop intruders that sailed down the river. But now, it was a great landmark at the site of an old battle.

They set up three tents for sleeping, and a tarp was tied up into the air to store the rest of the food, supplies, and weapons. But they kept the more important things, like the ring and the Sword of Power close-by for safety. Everything was ready before sunset, and it would be a day or so before the other four creatures would arrive. So, they had time to kill.

They played games and held competitions. First things first, since the food supplies were low, they tried to see who could catch the most fish in the river. Usus won after spearing three fish in only four minutes.

Next, they tried hatchet throwing, using a nook in a tree for the bullseye. Ore was the winner from the very beginning. He picked up the hatchet, flipped it in the air to get a good feel for it, then chucked it at the tree. It spun in the air three times before planting itself right in the bullseye.

Sword fighting was the next game. Millites took on everyone and never lost. Each time, he either disarmed his opponent, caused him to stumble, lodged the opponent's sword in a tree, or broke through the others' defenses and pinned them with his sword.

After eating all the fish, they decided to get some more food for later which lead to game four - hunting. Usus and Equus carried bows and arrows, Millites and Ram carried spears, and Ore used his hatchet. They crept through the woods for an hour. Millites threw his spear at a squirrel but missed. Ore took out a squirrel, and Prowl tore through the trees to pluck a plump hare off the ground. But Equus was the victor after shooting a wild turkey and chasing down a rabbit, though Usus was able to find some edible berries and roots.

They skinned and cooked the turkey, squirrel, and rabbit, in a fire. They packed them into a bag before hanging the meat up in a tree so that animals couldn't get to it.

All this time, Speilton sat in his tent. He ate some cooked fish, but mainly lay on his cot, thinking - thinking about what to do about the curse, how they were going to navigate through the castle, if they were going to win the final battle. But most of all, he was thinking about whether or not all of this was worth it.

Outside, the sky grew dark. The stars began to twinkle in the sky as the others talked around the campfire, discussing battle strategy.

Inside, Speilton lit a lantern, finished the remaining fish, and lay back down on his cot. His eyes drifted closed, and slowly, slowly, he fell to sleep.

When he woke up, he had no idea how long he'd slept, what time it was, or even if he'd fallen asleep. Everything was a mix of confusion and fear, as he scrambled to his knees and peered outside. Three dark shapes tore out of the sky. A trail of blackness dissolved behind them as they swarmed down upon the five sitting around the camp fire. They didn't stand a chance. There was a whinny, many grunts, a scream, a growl from Prowl, and then a streak of fire as one of the Versipellis flew through the campfire. But in only a second, everyone was unconscious, or dead - Speilton couldn't tell which - on the ground. The flaming Versipellis spun in the air, extinguishing the flames.

The three stood there, hovering in the air, staring at their handy work. Speilton could see their profiles against the light of the stars and moon. Dark pieces of linen and decaying flesh were stripped from their moldy bones as the wind blew through them. All was silent. Then, slowly, very slowly, the three simultaneously turned their heads...and looked right at Speilton.

He wanted to scream, cry, run, but all of those meant certain death. Instead he pulled the tent close and flung himself into the front wall of the tent. Sweat poured down his face as he began to hyperventilate. He closed his eyes, trying to wake up from this horrible nightmare. But just like much of his life, it wasn't a dream. *You can not run from death.* The voice of the Versipellis said, again sounding as cold and close as ever. *Eventually, it will catch up to you, and when it does…* It let that thought hang in the air.

Speilton's eyes flashed open, and he turned his head as a decaying, clawed hand slowly parted the two sheets of cloth that made the doorway. Bits of moldy linen swirled into the room, sending the smell of death up Speilton's nose. Lit by the lantern in the corner of the tent, Speilton watched as the Versipellis' head slowly peaked through the doorway. In the dim light, he saw the last bits of skin and flesh melt away into a cloud of dust, leaving only the cobwebbed bones. *There's no escape!* The Versipellis hissed, both finishing his sentence, and making a true point.

He didn't dare breathe. He wanted to close his eyes, but they remained open. His heart pounded so loudly, he was sure it could be heard outside. He looked for a weapon, though they were on the other side of the tent. There was no way he could make it.

The Versipellis' head didn't move since it didn't need to. The piercing eye slowly wound around the linen wrapped head and peered straight into Speilton.

In those eyes, he could see chaos. All the people dying, cities burning to the ground, worlds crumbling into nothing. This eye had seen it all. It had all happened at the decaying hand of this creature. And now, it was his turn to fall. The eye was ready. Ready to watch the end.

Before Speilton could even react, the bony hand reached toward his throat. He was swung into the center of the room and held a foot off the ground. Speilton gasped for air, but his wind pipe was being blocked by the icy hand. He clawed at the arm, trying to break the grip, but the Versipellis was strong, much stronger than Speilton. "*Hello Speilton,*" the creature hissed. "*It seems you have something I want.*"

Get to the point! I can't breathe. Speilton screamed in his mind, hoping that the Versipellis could somehow hear him.

"*Ferrum Potestas. I need it. And if you want your life, and their lives spared, you'll give it to me.*"

Speilton couldn't breathe. His head spun, his lungs ached, and the cold eye of the Versipellis brought back memories of his flaming village. But through all of the pain, he was able to hear the Versipellis and point in the direction of the sword. The Versipellis dissolved, dropping Speilton. Even though he he was only a foot off the ground, he fell flat on his back, his legs numb. He lay there, breathing in gulps of fresh air and rubbing his neck where the Versipellis's hand had been. It occurred to him that the Versipellis could've killed him in only seconds. It could've snapped his neck or even turned one of it's arms into a machete as it had in his dream. But it didn't. And he was still alive. Which could only mean one thing. The Versipellis didn't want to kill him. They wanted to use him to inflict a slow and horrible death to Liolia. And they were going to use Speilton to make that happen. It would all be Speilton's fault.

In other words, Liolia rested in his hands.

He looked up, to see the Versipellis lifting the rod that somehow concealed the Sword of Power.

The eye flashed back on Speilton. "*Thank you for your help. We would never have been able to do it without you.*"

And on that ominous note, the Versipellis circled the room, knocking out the rods that held up the tent and threw the lantern onto the ground.

The lantern burst open, and flames went everywhere.

"I'll see you in Skilt!" the Versipellis announced before breaking out of the tent and taking to the night sky. Outside Speilton heard a loud explosion as the other two Versipellis crashed into the tower ruins, toppling it into the river. Two ancient ruins destroyed in two weeks.

But Speilton had other problems as he became engulfed in a flaming tent.

Seagulls called as they took flight over the ships. The sea was peaceful and the sky spotless. It remained that way for three days. Turquoise blue skies with a lazy cloud drifting by every once and a while.

The weather was warm all day and continued into the night. Onaclov hardly ever went back into his quarters, instead choosing to stay out in the warm spring weather. The rest of the Dwarves checked the sails, swabbed the deck, and took lookout. There were never any problems. On the other seven boats that sailed along round them, life was just as easy - no problems.

But it would all change. On the third night, a cold blast swept through the ships. The sailors were frigid and huddled in coats and blankets. When the sun rose, there was a sheet of grey clouds that spread all the way across the sky. An icy, howling wind chilled the crew. The waves tossed, which made the work for dwarves and humans especially difficult. The flames from the torches had been extinguished, and the dwarves' beards became frosted with sea water.

The dark clouds held, not shattering into rain or dissipating. They just remained there, day and night. The stars and moon were covered by the clouds, so they were unable to establish their location for many days.

And then, after five days, the clouds burst and a storm began. Blankets of rain enveloped the ship as rain howled and lashed at the crew. The rain pounded the ship, rocking the sea vessel like a piece of driftwood. Waves two stories high crashed onto the deck. Men were swallowed up by the ocean and disappeared into the churning water. The wet boards creaked and moaned as more waves tackled the ship. Claps of thunder and lightning split the air, as more rain, and even denser, blacker clouds covered the sky. There was no difference between day and night, only the swirling dark waves that threatened to crush the boats. The men huddled below, taking turns going up onto deck to toss out water, and check to see if the ship was intact. Many men were never seen again. And in all this chaos, the seven boats were separated, each juggled away from the others on crashing waves.

Onaclov flung open the door that led out of his quarters. He peered through the haze of rain to see five brave sailors rushing around on deck, dumping water out of the boat and into the ocean. As a wave swallowed the deck, the five brave soldiers became only four.

That's when he saw it. A grey-green tentacle slithered onto the deck through the railings. It coiled around a sailors leg, and before he could even shout for help, he was pulled off the ship. It had happened so quickly, Onaclov wasn't even sure what he'd seen. But his thoughts were quickly distracted by a horrible *BOOM!!!* The railing of the ship exploded leaving steam where it had once been. *BOOM!* Another explosion left steam coiling out of a hole in the ship where the railing had once stood.

EEEER, BOOM!!! This time the sound was much closer and louder. That was because the explosion had occurred right behind him.

Onaclov spun around to find a gaping hole in the side of his room. Fragments of a shelf, the boat's wall, and many trinkets were scattered across the floor. Onaclov realized what had happened - cannons, one of the greatest inventions of the era, supposedly only used on the

Night Seemer and the Avenger, had caused the damage.

Onaclov ran to the two-foot wide hole in the wall and peered out. Rising over the crest of a wave was a ship with black sails. He saw a flash of fire, followed by another, *BOOM!!!* as a cannon ball crashed into the ship ten feet below him on the ship. Water began pouring in through the hole. Onaclov heard shouts as the crew scrambled to get away from the rushing water.

Onaclov looked back up at the ship, and glared. His ship was going down, and in this storm, there would be no way to survive.

A single green tentacle arched into the air, and wrapped itself around the middle of the Calorian ship. Even though they were over one hundred yards away, he could see Calorians frantically scrambling around deck. But it was too late. The tentacle plunged into the water, and the Calorian's ship snapped in two. Another wave rose and crashed down on the ship. Only a few pieces of driftwood were left.

More tentacles rose from the water, and turned...toward them.

Onaclov's finger twitched, though he didn't know why. All he knew was that the tentacles had found a new target. His ship was next. He flew down the slippery steps, as he held on for dear life as another wave hit, then darted down the hatch and under the deck.

It was just as wild down there. Water rushed up to his knees, and all around him people were desperately using buckets to pour out the water. But at this rate, they'd be sunk in about five minutes.

"Everyone listen!" Onaclov called, "We're under attack!"

"We've kind of noticed that," one man said. "It's the Calorians, we saw their ship."

"No, the Calorians aren't a problem any more," Onaclov started.

"Then how are we under attack?" another man called back.

"There's something else out there. It crushed the Calorian ship," Onaclov told them.

"What was it?" a sailor asked.

"All I saw was a tentacle. It was a greenish color, and-"

"Ha! A tentacle, as in a sea monster's tentacle? Please, those legends are so old," one of the sailors mocked.

If only he'd been able to see what was behind him. The man was too busy laughing, and everyone else was just too stunned to say anything. A slimy green tentacle snaked its way through the hole in the wall, though it was so massive, it broke and crushed the wood, almost doubling the hole's size.

It groped around trying to find its victim. The tentacle slithered slowly, but once it had wrapped itself around the laughing sailors leg, it pulled back sharply, like a frog's tongue catching a fly. The man's echoing scream faded away as he was dragged down to his watery grave.

The boat shuddered and tipped, throwing everyone off their feet. "It's here," one of the men screamed.

Onaclov, followed by a few other brave sailors, climbed onto the deck and peered at a most amazing sight. Something was rising out of the water. Water rushed off of it as it ascended into the sky. At first it appeared to be a mountain rising up into the air. In ten seconds it had reached two hundred and fifty yards tall.

Then, it moved and flipped back to reveal its head. The top of the 'mountain' had really been the demon's back, and now it revealed its face.

It was far from human. Water cascaded from the head, smashing onto the deck. It had two flame-red eyes with narrow slits that gleamed with chaos. Its mouth was a cave of teeth the size and shape of swords that glittered with blood. But it was the face that was the most horrifying. It was contorted and seemed to be overrun with warts.

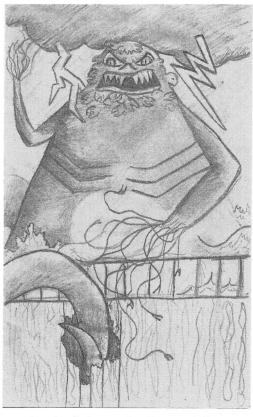

But warts don't have teeth, and they can't grow, move, and sink back into the skin in only a few seconds. The face seemed to be growing and bubbling, as if tiny faces tried to grow out of its scales, but then were forced back into the creature. The face alone was almost one hundred feet tall and wide.

Then, there was the body. It was muscular, covered in scales, and over seven hundred feet tall. The torso was long and narrow, like a mutant human-snake body. Two massive arms held in the air, and the hands, branched off into a thousand writhing serpents, each ten feet long.

The water reached his waist from where he stood, and tossing and turning under the waves were slimy green tentacles like the one that had crushed the Calorian ship.

Onaclov's finger twitched as he stared up at the beast. All around him, terror took over the men. They leapt overboard or collapsed to the ground. But one of the men remained standing, staring up at the creature next to Onaclov. "Cetus..." he muttered. It was the last thing he ever said.

Through the torrent and howling gale, the creature heard that single word. His eyes flashed onto the man, as if it had heard its name. The beast growled, and a tentacle shot out of the ocean, spraying water everywhere, and thudded onto the deck. Just as it had done under the deck, it snaked forward. The man stood there staring at the tentacle, his face, expressionless. It reached the man, and within a second, he had been yanked down into the water.

Onaclov's whole hand shook. A voice in his head whispered, *You are the master. Let go, and let your powers flow.*

Onaclov closed his eyes, and let his mind relax. His hand slowly lifted into the air. He didn't know why, but it felt natural, like that was what was supposed to happen. His hand was pointed out at the sea monster.

Onaclov opened his eyes to find a tentacle, as thick as a tree and covered in barnacles, raised high above the ship. The surviving dwarves and men tried desperately to cut it down throwing hatchets, axes, swords, spears, harpoons, and anything else they could find at it. The tentacle remained, hardly flinching, as the blade of an axe pierced it straight through.

Say the words. The voice in his head commanded. *You know the words.* Onaclov's mouth opened, and he began to scream through the pouring rain, and clashing and crashing of waves, "Stop, Cetus, Lord of the Seas, Creator of Storms, Ally of Chaos, and Slayer of Mer," the words flowed from his mouth as if someone was saying the words for him. "I have supreme power over you. You must bend to my will. And so, I command you to..."

Suddenly, the words stopped flowing. It was like a blank in the speech. It was his turn to decide the command.

"I command you to help."

Cetus shuddered. His eyes turned from red to gold. And Onaclov's voice was taken away by the storm.

The tentacle crashed down. Despite the desperate attacks by the sailors, it landed. Dwarves and men scurried for cover, but there was none out in the tempest. The tentacle wrapped around the ship, and with a tooth shattering *crack!* The ship buckled, moaned, and was crushed in half.

The tentacle disappeared between the two halves of the ship, and the ground fell out under Onaclov. Despite the commands that had magically come to him, Onaclov, the crew, and the ship plunged down under the waves in a storm at the hand of Cetus.

SCARS OF THE WAR
~ 15 ~

"Speilton!" The voice sounded distant as if shouted from miles away. "Speilton!" the voice came again.

Suddenly, Speilton woke up in a sweat. The first thing he saw peeking through a hole in the roof of his tent was blue sky, and a few cotton-ball clouds. He smiled, thinking he was back in his village, waking up for a hunt. "Speilton!" the voice was right next to him and urgent.

All hopes of being in his village shattered. He sat up but ended up flat on his back. A pain in his chest, a scratched throat, and sores ringing his neck overcame his body with pain. "Speilton?" the voice came again as Ginkerry crawled in next to him.

"What happened here?" Nicholas asked leaning down and setting his hand on Speilton's neck.

"Ow," he moaned.

"Sorry. Just taking a look. It's been cut and bruised. Your breathing is heavy from inhaling too much smoke. But I can fix you up."

Speilton could hardly talk. His throat was in horrible pain, his arms and legs were blistered and burned, and his chest burned every time he took a breath. A wisp of smoke passed his view of the blue sky and everything that had happened that night came back. How the Versipellis attacked, took the sword, and left him in a burning tent. He remembered pulling himself out of a hole, the fire searing his legs as he tried not to breathe. Then, he passed out.

Speilton turned to see the remnants of his burning tent with a trail of water rolling away from it. They must've put it out last night or whenever they arrived.

"When... did you get... here?" Speilton choked out.

"We heard the tower fall from a mile or so away," Ginkerry explained. "When we arrived, the tent was still on fire, and all of you were unconscious."

"Are they okay?" Speilton asked sitting up, then crashing down as he coughed deeply.

"Nicholas says they're okay, though none of them are yet awake."

"How long have I been out?" Speilton asked.

"Well, it's mid-afternoon. We arrived last night."

Speilton nodded his head before closing his eyes to rest.

"Speilton. What happened here?" Ginkerry asked after a minute.

He remained silent for a few seconds, trying to decide whether to tell them about the Versipellis. "We were attacked, by Daerds and...some type of evil spirits. A Calorian lit my tent I was in on fire and took the sword."

"A sword. They attacked you all for a sword?" Brute huffed as he chewed on some type of weed.

"It wasn't just any sword," Speilton said. "It was Ferrum Potestas. It can envelope the wielder in a shield of protection, causing him to become invincible. It grants the wielder the ability to summon a monster as large as the sky, and turn all it destroys either good or evil. Cigam, the wizard, gave it to us, and explained everything, but it's been stolen."

"Okay... I'm not sure why you didn't go ahead and use." Brute said.

"In order to become the master of the Sword, you must first touch the blood of a creature of flames streaked with darkness and light."

"Oh, so do you have the animal yet?" Brute asked.

"If we did, we probably would've already used it," Speilton said struggling to his feet.

Prowl woke up a few minutes later, and Equus an hour or so after. Millites and Usus woke up after the sunset later that day, then Ram shortly after. Ore slept all through the night and eventually had to be shaken awake the next day. They all wondered how they had slept so long. They had slept for nearly an entire day. Only Speilton knew the answer. They had been attacked by evil dream spirits. The Versipellis could easily have caused them to all fall into a deep sleep, thereby slowing down their journey.

The next morning when they were finally all together and awake, Speilton explained what had happened the night before. Of course, he changed the story, making sure that it had nothing to do with the Versipellis. They bought it, except Millites had to ask, "But why did they let us live? They could have killed all of us right then and there."

That was something Speilton had been wondering, too. Why was he still alive? Why were they all still alive?

Then he remembered something the Versipellis had said before leaving the tent. At first it hadn't fazed him. But now he realized what it must mean. "Well, before the Calorian left, before he lit the tent on fire, he said...'I'll see you at Skilt.'

At first everyone remained silent, then one at a time they realized that the Calorians knew they were coming. Either they had spies, they predicted, or..."

Millites drew his sword, leapt to his feet, and held the blade out at the creatures. "Who told them?"

"What?" Brute asked.

Behind him, Metus passed out from fear. "Was it him? Did he tell the Calorians?" Millites questioned stepping toward the unconscious faun.

"No, it wasn't him. Metus was with us the entire time. None of us did it," Nicholas spoke up.

"Then who? We're the only people who know of the plan besides Rilly and Cigam," Millites said.

"But they would never tell. They could sneak away easily," Ram confirmed.

"Then, they must be guessing, assuming that's our next move," Usus suggested.

"They probably don't even know about the Eye Stone. That'll be our greatest weapon," Nicholas said.

"I just hope they don't unlock the power of the sword before we can reach them," Speilton sighed.

After their discussion, Equus, Usus, Ore, and Prowl went hunting in the woods. Ram started a small fire for cooking the meat, and the others tossed nets, threw spears, and cast lines, hoping to catch a few fish. In a few hours, they had five fish, two turkeys, a rabbit, and three squirrels. They feasted on two of the fish, a loaf of bread that had been given to them back in the Lavalands, and half the turkey.

After breakfast, they filled their jugs in the river and swam across it. Prowl flew Ore over since he wasn't a strong swimmer. Then, they took off hiking over hills and into valleys. As they went, Ginkerry fell a few feet behind. Metus began muttering to himself and stood off to the side. Brute kept grumbling about wanting to finally stop walking. "There should be a few villages up ahead," Millites kept telling him, though it never helped.

Millites finally had enough of the complaints, so he brought up a new subject. "So, what do you think the creature of the sword is?"

"I've been thinking," Usus spoke up." I don't know that there is any type of creature made of fire and darkness and light."

"So, it may mean a creature that can use fire or maybe it's even flammable," Ram suggested.

"You don't think it could be...?" Nicholas stopped as they all came to the same realization.

Well, almost everyone. "Whoa! What are we talking about. What creature?" Brute asked confused.

"A Daerd," Speilton said.

"But more importantly, Worc, the King of the Daerds," Millites explained. "His wings are flammable, but it doesn't hurt him. And he's completely black, which would be the darkness."

"But your forgetting light. That's the one thing that it doesn't have. And, from what you've told me, it's supposed to have small streaks of darkness. Worc is completely black," Ore said.

"What creature has darkness, fire and light?" Ginkerry asked.

"Maybe fire, light, and darkness refer to colors, not the actual element," Equus suggested.

"Yeah! Fire could be red or orange, darkness is black, and light..." Speilton stopped.

"The opposite of black. White," Millites answered.

"What creature is orange, with stripes of black, and slightly white?" Usus asked.

Speilton and Ram's eyes met and they both came to the same realization.

"What? Do you know what it is?" Millites asked.

But before they could answer, Brute said, "Someone must really be smoking!" The satyr quickly disrupted their thoughts by his strange announcement.

But then they saw it too. A cloud of smoke coiling into the sky far ahead of them. "That can't be good," Metus whimpered.

They ran toward the smoke. A few hundred yards ahead of them was a hill. Once they reached the top, they were able to gaze down on another stretch of grassy land. A river wound through the hills, and next to the river was a village with about a hundred houses, a mill, and a tall mansion. Flames engulfed many of the homes and the mansion. The odd thing was that there was no one making an effort to extinguish it.

"Is this your idea of a resting place. If it is, I'm never going on a quest with you again," Metus argued.

"What caused this?" Nicholas asked what everyone else was thinking.

Down the river, sailing quickly away was a tall small ship loaded with furniture, mounds of food, weapons, and...Calorians.

"They've been attacked. Come on we've got to help them," Millites commanded.

"How do we know they're not already dead?" Usus asked.

"The Calorians wouldn't have killed them. They want the people to suffer."

They ran down the hill as fast as possible. They could feel the intensity of the heat as they grew closer to the flames. They could hear strangled, choked screams.

"This way!" Ram said taking off down one of the streets. Everyone followed, and they came to a house with a man lying next to it. The man almost smiled, seeing them. His face was pale, and most of his blood had escaped from a wound in his leg.

"Help..." his voice was strangled as he gave his final request. "Help them... In the mansion...trapped...he...help," the man closed his eyes and the others stood back.

"The mansion. We need to get there fast," Millites confirmed. They turned around and began running back down the road, when they saw Speilton. He hadn't entered the blaze but stood at the end of the road, his face pale and wide with fear.

It wasn't fear of the fire. It was the sight of a village, just like his on fire … just like Lorg. He was having deja vu. Speilton half expected to hear his mother or his best friend, Faveo, calling out his name. Calling for help. Calling for help that would never come. But for these people, there was little chance of survival. They may survive, but their families, their village, and their old lives wouldn't. He could only stand there, overcome with survivors -guilt, staring at the ruins.

"Come on, Speilton. We can't help them by standing here," Millites said as the nine rushed toward the mansion. Speilton followed reluctantly, but looking at every house as he thought about his village.

Millites, Usus, Ram, the six creatures, and Speilton reached the burning mansion, and here, they could hear the screams - high and pained - over the flames. Fists pounded on the door from the inside.

"I've got it!" Millites announced just as much to the people outside as the ones in the mansion.

Something triggered inside of Speilton that didn't within the others. He felt it before it happened. Something wasn't right. Fire was weakening the structure, and ... "Millites! Watch out!" Speilton screamed. Millites stopped short, as a huge piece of the wall crumbled and crashed down right in front of the two doors.

The screaming grew louder, even more horrified. Then, "Help! Somebody, Help!" rang out above the others. The thing that stunned Speilton the most was that the voice was so young. It came from a little child, whose life rested in their hands.

"What are we going to do?" Millites asked.

"We can't climb into it. The structure is coming down any second," Nicholas said.

"What about our elements?" Usus asked. "We could create something to stop the fire."

"I don't see how stone or light is going to do anything," Millites said. "But wind ..."

"No wind," Ram interjected. "It may shake the foundation, and there's a chance it'll only spread the flames further."

"Speilton," Equus said simply.

Millites nodded his head, "Speilton, you can do this."

He handed Speilton the wand, and he took it reluctantly. "Remember, you're in control, not the flames. You have to control the flames," Millites instructed.

Speilton gripped the wand's handle and pointed it into the flames. He closed his eyes and pictured raging flames. *No!* he told himself, *You're in control. You can do this! No fear.*

He imagined himself with a column of fire circling him, entering his wand, being pulled from the smokey air. The fire fought back at him, but he was too strong. It turned to smoke as it drew near him.

Speilton felt painful heat next to his right hand, but somehow, he knew it was fire, fire from the mansion being pulled into his wand. He felt confident. He was actually doing weakening and controlling the flames.

CRAAAACK! A chunk of the flaming roof toppled off the building and crashed to the ground. He lost concentration and opened his eyes which proved to be a tremendous mistake. His surroundings came back into focus as he heard the screams of the villagers and the still flaming mansion. He closed his eyes but couldn't focus. The screams still petrified him and permeated his body. And in this unfocussed moment, the flames entering his wand went out of control, spurting all around him. A strand of fire wrapped around his arm. Speilton pulled away but dropped the wand in the grass. He looked up at the mansion to see that a wave of fire had been thrown into a wall, causing flames to spray from a window. The structure groaned and cracked. There wasn't much time left. He picked up the wand, even though it was still hot and held it out to the mansion.

Speilton closed his eyes and tried to block out all noise. He couldn't fail these people. He had to stay focussed. He had to control the flames.

Speilton felt the power surge through him again, before a shrill scream echoed through his body. He dared to take a look and saw that half of the wall had given way. Just before he closed his eyes, he saw a young boy, the boy who'd screamed for help. He appeared to be about eight. The boy was so frightened and helpless, and at this second, trapped behind a wall of fire taller than him.

The site of the boy overwhelmed Speilton, as he felt the power leave his body and knew it wouldn't return. The wand dropped from his stiff, clammy hand. He fell to his knees, knowing that he couldn't save the little boy.

And at that second, there was a shattering crack as the ceiling gave way, and the entire house fell swallowing the inhabitants. To Speilton, the scream and cracking of the house was a distant echo as it imploded in a mass of flames.

He tucked his head into his knees, and wrapped his hands around his legs in a ball as he let out a sob. *It's my fault. All my fault.*

They moved out. There was nothing more they could do. The whole village was burned to the ground when they crossed the river. The last embers were slowly dying, making the site glow. They kept hiking into the night, hoping to run away from the bad memories. When they finally settled down, they were starving. The made a camp fire and warmed up the rest of the turkey and two fish. After eating they talked for the first time since the village.

"I'm so proud of all of you and your efforts to save the village. Although we were not able to rescue them, we tried our best and now need to move forward with our quest to defeat the evil that is responsible for taking those innocent lives. We must determine what creature holds the key to the Sword of Power," Millites began.

"It's mostly orange, black stripes, and a bit of white," Usus quietly replied.

"Maybe a bird, like a cardinal," Ore suggested.

"Or, it's a tiger," Speilton said simply staring into the fire, now imagining it as the mansion.

"Yeah, tiger. That works. Orange fur, black stripes, and white on the face and belly," Nicholas explained.

"But remember, it's supposed to be a fierce creature, but also very loyal. It's supposed to sacrifice itself for someone else," Millites reminded them.

Speilton and Ram held each other's gaze. "No," was all Ram could say.

"What?" Usus asked.

"The tiger… is Burn," Speilton announced.

"But Speilton, he died. He was wounded by the Calorians while trying to save you…" Ram interjected.

"Exactly. They supposedly mortally wounded him. But remember, Sinister was following us. He transformed into you, which probably meant he arrived at the camp shortly after we left.

"Sinister must've had a connection with Venefica at that point, and she would've obviously wanted him to search for the beast that would unlock the sword, then wait for the wizards to give it to us. If Sinister had known the beast was to be a tiger, then he would have been watching *our* tiger, Burn, since he played such a major role in fighting off the Calorians. And if he thought that Burn was alive at all, after the arrows... hit him, he would've tried to save him. He and Venefica would be too smart to let Burn die. I bet you anything they've been waiting for Cigam to give the sword to us. If they thought Burn was dead, they wouldn't have wanted the sword so badly," Speilton explained.

"So, Burn's alive?" Ram asked with a glimmer of hope in his voice.

"Yes, and if we don't save him, the Calorians will have Ferrum Potestas."

The next few days they struggled through the plains, a large expanse of green hills. They stretched on forever, seeming to have no end. Speilton remembered half a year ago, hiking through the plains, and how he had almost had to turn back from hunger. He probably would have, if Burn hadn't urged them on. Burn, the valiant tiger. Speilton couldn't believe he was still alive.

The food lasted a few days, but soon was gone. Not many animals lived on the plains, and most avoided it because of the lack of water. But they were able to find a stray, out of place deer, and shot, cooked, and ate it.

Water was a problem, too. Under the heat of the sun, they almost ran out of their water. After three days, a storm broke out. They ran to the base of a hill and flattened themselves to the ground. Lightning cracked and clashed around them, as the temperature dropped twenty degrees. They tried pulling blankets around them, but the icy rain soaked straight through. Setting up tents would be too risky, and the poles would be an easy target for lightning. So they lay huddled in their blankets, riding it out. And through the sound of the thunder, they could all hear Metus, playing his sweet tune. It gave them hope.

It turned out to be helpful in the end. No one was hurt, though Metus passed out from fear after ten minutes, and Brute kept screaming through the storm that his horns were wet. For someone who didn't seem to care about anything, he really was protective of his horns.

After the storm, they climbed up many muddy hills and down into slippery crevices until they came to a trench filled with cold water. They filled their jugs and drank from the water, and were even able to shoot a pronghorn that had also been drawn to the water.

They reached the Jungle of Supin late in the afternoon on the fifth day after their encounter with the flaming village. As they approached the edge of the forest, they could see that the area became wilder deeper into the jungle. With night closing in, entering the jungle would be certain death. The distant sound of hooting monkeys, and an occasional growl or howl rang out through the sound of crickets that chirped all through the night.

The next morning, they trekked straight into the vines and vegetation. Sunlight peaked through the trees, and the air became thick and humid as the sun rose higher and higher. Water dripped from the trees above them. Dirty, overflowing rivers snaked through the trees, home to dozens of crocodiles.

They walked hurriedly, hoping to reach the elves and their palace in the heart of the jungle. There they could rest and reload. But early in the morning, storm clouds rolled in and shielded the sky. Rain didn't break out, but the clouds covered the sun, and plunged them into darkness. They groped through the dark forest, stumbling over roots and rocks. Many times they fell into ditches or ran into trees. The whole time, they were wishing that the night predators that stalked the jungle at night didn't decide to come out in this darkness.

They groped along, losing their way. Soon, the small bit of heat that had been given off by the shielded sun began to vanish, showing that night was on its way. "We need to get to the palace," Usus said. "When night settles, the animals are sure to come out."

"I can't tell which direction we're heading. We're lost," Ram said.

"I can find it," Nicholas explained. "I've traveled there many times. My father used to live there."

"Good, which way is it?" Millites asked.

Nicholas pulled out a small, circular object that worked just like a compass. He looked down at it, then up to the trees, then back down again. "This way," Nicholas said, directing them to the left.

"Why did they make their castle so far away?" Brute complained.

"You'll see, if we ever reach it," Millites said.

They followed Nicholas for nearly an hour, but as the sun sank even lower, the air grew colder. Soon, the sound of jungle animals snarling and hissing closed in around them. Everyone shook in the frigid, wet air, but they trudged on.

Then, over the sounds of the jungle and the birds and the crickets was a solid thud. The trees trembled, and many of the birds and animals went silent. There was another thud, but it, too, was still far away.

Millites, Speilton, Usus, Ram, Prowl, and the six creatures began walking faster, paranoid that something was following them. But when a deep, horrible roar echoed through the trees making birds take flight, they were gone. Without planning, they took off, running as fast as possible after Nicholas who was showing the way.

Brute did find out why the palace was in the middle of the jungle. After a few minutes of running, they reached a clearing in the woods that was probably a mile wide, though it felt cramped as they came to it, since standing in the middle was a tree. This was the elves palace, a tree... that was over five hundred feet tall and had a trunk over one hundred feet thick.

They couldn't see the palace at first, but then, as they circled around the tree, they could just barely make out the shape, perched high in the trees.

But something was wrong. There was no light. The elves always had torches lit along all the branches so that people could see the edges of limbs and not fall off. Yes, the elves lived in the tree, away from the predators below. The thick branches were loaded with dome shape huts that were securely fastened to the tree. Ladders and bridges linked the branches together. And up, high in the the top of the tree was the palace, a building that stretched over many flat limbs.

But everything was silent. There was no light, no noise, nothing. "Where is everyone?" Nicholas asked as they all gazed up into the trees.

"They had to get up there somehow. Why don't we go up the same way," Ore suggested.

"Yeah, they usually have a rope ladder, but they pull that up at night."

"We don't have to climb a ladder?" Metus asked. "Good."

"I can't climb," Equus added.

"Oh, right," Ram muttered.

Don't they have a walkway? I think I walked up it once when the ladder had been blown over and stolen by... monkeys maybe?"

"Oh yeah, the rabid monkeys, um... that matter was resolved a year or so ago," Nicholas murmured. "Anyway, yes, there is a walkway that they use to lug fruit up into the palace. But they close that at night, since many jaguars and ants crawled up there to get in."

"Ants? What's the problem with ants?" Brute scoffed.

"Well, when ants are over a foot long, spit acid, and feed in groups of hundreds, they can be a problem," Usus answered.

If you ever want to know something creepy, crazy, or strange about an animal, Usus is your man.

"Why don't the ants just climb up the tree?" Ginkerry asked.

"Feel the tree," Nicholas instructed, "You see, it's slick. They coat it in flame proof oil, and sand it down every month. There are hundreds of swings and every elf in the tree helps in sanding away as far as they can reach, then coating the area in oil."

"That genius!" Usus mused.

"So, how do we get in?" Metus asked.

"There is another way, but it's no good," Nicholas stopped.

"Go on," Millites said.

"Well, it was created a long time ago," Nicholas glanced around. "It was made for anyone that was unable to make it back to the tree in time."

"That would be us," Brute muttered.

"What's the catch? Why can't we use it?" Millites asked.

"Well, for one, it's very well hidden, so that the Calorians wouldn't be able to locate it," Nicholas began.

"But you remember where it is, right?" Ram asked.

"I think I might, but that's not the problem. The real problem is that inside the passage is a maze."

"A maze? Why a maze? That's too complicated," Brute groaned.

"Well, it's partly natural. When they began digging the path, the huge roots kept blocking off the path. Cutting through the roots would've been a lot of extra work, so they left them, making the inside a maze. Many people have entered, but never made it out. Many animals have, too."

"So what's the point of it if everyone dies?" Ore asked.

"Well, all of the elves struggle to memorize it. Some of them get very creative with songs and poems. My father drew a map, and he guided me through it once."

"So, do you know the way?" Millites asked.

"Um...no."

"Great," Brute muttered.

"Well, I guess we can wait out here until... wait, did you hear that?" Nicholas paused and glanced into the jungle.

"What is it?" Metus stammered.

"Shhh!" Nicholas held his finger up to his lips.

Everyone fell silent, and they all heard the noise. Hundreds of clicking, chattering mouths and thousands of scampering feet scurried through the jungle. They hadn't noticed before, but now the noise was loud and clear and quickly getting closer.

"What should we -" Millites was cut off by Nicholas.

"Shhh, remain still and silent," he whispered.

The crawling, insect feet grew closer until they caught the gleam of the moon against their black exoskeletons. Then, a blob of acid seared through the sky, and splatted into the wall, only inches from Ginkerry's face. She squealed and jumped away, as a hole the size of an apple was burned out. But then, noticing she had broken both rules, silent and still, she clapped her hands over her mouth.

The chattering stopped, and the jungle was still. Everyone tried to hold their breath and remain completely silent. But it was too late, the ants had been alerted. And now, they wanted food.

"This way," Nicholas called, taking off to the left.

The chattering of the ants started again, this time twice as loud. Now, they had a target. Four humans, six creatures, and a dragon.

"Where are we going?" Ore called.

"Let's go up the tree," Millites said.

"Prowl can carry us," Speilton suggested as they rounded the back of the tree.

"No time for that," Ram grumbled, limping behind on his injured leg.

"Can we climb?" Speilton asked.

"Well, three of us have hooves, and the wall is slick," Brute groaned.

"The path, let's take the path! Usus suggested.

"I need time to look," Nicholas said. "I haven't been down into it in years.

"You look, we'll fight," Millites commanded.

"Okay, but be ready to run," Nicholas said.

Then, as the ants rounded the corner, he added, "Oh, and the ants are full of acid."

The elf shot an arrow into the wave of insects, and hit one in the head. Green goo spurted from the wound, just before the ant blew up completely in a ball of acid.

"Uh, oh," Millites muttered.

"Ah, they don't look so bad," Brute said, rushing forward and planting a wicked kick in an ant's face.

It crumbled backward, and Brute rushed forward smacking another up side the head with his club. He turned, and struck another ant, then another, and another.

He seemed to be doing well, when a glob of acid rushed at his face. He tried to duck, but the acid caught his horn. The tip point was burned away, though the acid didn't do much more than that. Though to Brute, it was as bad as losing the entire horn. "NO! No, this can't be happening. My, precious horn, is...is ruined!" He ran away from the ants and huddled next to the tree, stroking the remains of his horn.

"Here we go," Millites muttered, drawing a sword. It wasn't his Lighting bladed, which was far too important to risk getting covered in acid.

It was a good thing too, because the first thing he did was plunge his sword through the back of an ant. When he pulled the blade out, it had been reduced to only half its original size. The other half had burned away.

Speilton leapt on the back of Prowl, who torched many of the ants. Using his sword was useless, and he wouldn't dare use the Flame wand. He just rode it out on the back of Prowl.

Equus pulled out his arrows and sniped more than ten of the ants. His shots were direct and accurate, and he did it all without any expression.

Ore was even more amazing. He hadn't been kidding when he told them that he was strong. As they began, Ore pulled our a heavy weapon with a metal hammer on one end and a curved, axe blade on the other. The dwarf crushed two ants with a single blow of the hammer, then spun it, and sliced down another with the axe. Acid splashed against the hammer, but it didn't melt since it was a dwarven hammer with magical properties.

Metus fled to the tree as the skirmish began, but Ginkerry fought. She didn't use weapons or magic. She simply turned into a bush. But then, as the wind whistled through her branches, her roots shot out of the ground to grab hold of the ant's legs, dragging them into the earth. But the tree mode only lasted a few seconds, and she quickly had to turn back into her natural form. The power had been drained from her, leaving her weak. Before she could protect herself, the ants were upon her. Acid splattered against the tree behind her. She screamed, and tried to run, though there was no escape in sight.

As the ants approached, a shriek echoed from above, and an eagle swooped down from the sky and snatched up the closest ant. It happened so fast. Speilton, who happened to be a few yards away, wasn't sure if what he'd seen was real. But when he looked back at Ginkerry, she was smiling. The dryad closed her eyes and began humming. The song was slow and gentle, and drifted into the trees. It didn't bring back sad memories like Metus's flute song. It was hopeful and gentle, and even though the dryad was softly humming it, Speilton could hear each note.

The whole jungle heard the song and in the distance monkeys hooted. Had they been doing it before? Birds cawed and squawked in the branches, and Speilton wasn't sure, but it seemed the trees joined in.

Even the ants paused. Millites, Usus, Ram, Ore, Equus, Metus and Brute turned to watch, too. It was silent except for the gentle hum.

That's when the birds attacked.

Flocks of parrots and macaws, eagles and hummingbirds, erupted from the canopy of the jungle and swarmed down. Even Prowl was called by the mystic tune, and joined in next to the swarm of birds. Speilton pressed himself against Prowl's back as she navigated through the birds, though Speilton couldn't see what was happening.

The jungle birds formed a wall, separating the ants from them. The ants sprung at the birds but were grabbed and flown away. Some sprayed acid and caught birds flying by, but the wall was never penetrated. Ginkerry smiled at the birds, finished her song, then fell toward the ground. Metus leapt forward and caught her before she hit.

Then Nicholas announced, "I've found the path!"

They rushed down the tunnel, Ginkerry slumped over Equus's back. The birds took back into the trees at the end of the song, but the ants kept their pursuit. Though small in numbers, they would hunt to the death.

They disappeared down the tunnel, and Millites and Nicholas rolled a rock in the way of the door. Unfortunately, it wouldn't stop the ants and their acid, but it would give them time.

They took off running down the dark path. Usus lit a torch and handed it to Nicholas. Ram sat on Prowl, and Ginkerry rode away on Equus as fast as they could. Nicholas led them, picking each turn. The paths were stuffy, damp, and wreaked of dust and grime. Roots taller than Equus broke the area into paths.

The ceiling was earthen, with decaying wooden pillars holding up most of the ceiling. Many times they came to areas where the ceiling had caved in, limiting their choice of paths. They came to dead ends over and over again and had to turn around, but not reaching an end made them nervous.

They continued on, not knowing if they were heading in the right direction as the humidity and stench took a toll on them. They continued down the different paths, panting and desperately hoping to see a doorway leading out.

But the only things they found were the carcass of a jaguar and a rope someone had probably tried to use to get out. Speilton tripped on something and fell. He caught himself, but came face to face with a rotting human skull.

On the bright side, they never ran into the ants. They were as lost in the maze walking, searching, never to find an end. They stopped to rest at one point, and drank lots of water, and ate food. Anything to replenish their bodies.

But there was no rest, as they were always faced with the same challenge. They continued to stumble along the different paths. Finally, after a few hours, they came to an area where the roots had grown over twenty feet tall. Different paths were dug into the two roots that made a path on either side of them.

"That's a good sign," Millites decided.

"Yeah, taller, thicker roots, and man-made tunnels," Usus said.

"No, this isn't right." Nicholas groaned.

"What?"

"I don't remember this area," Nicholas said. "The end should have...the symbol of a tree etched into the roots, I think. But this isn't part of the *right* path."

"Great, so should we go back?" Millites asked.

"Wait," Ram interjected. "Look at these tunnels. They're freshly made and look very recent."

"A short cut?" Metus asked.

"Maybe, but there are so many paths. Which one should we take?" Speilton questioned.

"I don't...wait, do you see that?" Nicholas asked peering into a tunnel.

Millites glanced into it, too, "It's a light. Maybe fire."

"Is it just me, or is it getting closer?" Usus asked.

"That's never a good sign," Millites muttered.

They stepped back and looked into the other tunnels. "There are more," Ore mused.

Everyone peered through a passageway, and noticed at least one or two dim orbs, slowly getting closer. "What could they be?" Usus asked.

"Pixies or fairies, maybe?" Millites suggested.

"No, it must be human," Nicholas said, "Listen, I hear footsteps."

Just like the orbs, a jumble of footsteps grew closer. They weren't the scratching, rapid footsteps of the ants, but crisp, clear footsteps that could only be created by humans. But the sound that echoed to them could only be created by *hundreds* of humans.

Their thoughts were interrupted. "The dryad is gone, " Equus said with the slightest bit of shock.

"Wait, what?" Millites asked as they all turned around from their holes.

Ginkerry was no longer on Equus's back. "Where is she?" Speilton asked.

"I am not sure," he answered solemnly.

"How do you lose someone who's on your back?" Brute asked.

"In the rush, I didn't notice her ever leaving," Equus said.

"She probably fell," Usus exclaimed.

Everyone got a sick feeling in their stomachs. Ginkerry could be anywhere in the maze. She could've fallen far behind them.

But Speilton was mainly thinking about the prophecy. Only nine of them could live. Prowl was an exception on their mission. They would probably have to drop her off with the rest of the Milwarian knights once they met up later with them. Prowl wasn't supposed to reach Skilt, Speilton was sure of that. He would've noticed the giant dragon out of the nine of them. And now that he thought about it, he was pretty sure Equus or Brute weren't the ones to die either. He remembered a very tall, and very small person there, too. But he didn't recall seeing a dryad.

While he struggled to remember who he'd seen, the others discussed what must've happened. Metus had been lagging behind Equus and said that he had not seen Ginkerry fall off. That meant that she left while they were peering down into the paths.

"We know you're there," Millites called to the darkness, as they all drew their weapons.

In response, the lights froze in midair and the footsteps halted. There was silence until an arrow was launched right at Millites' sword. It caught him off guard and came so suddenly, the sword was thrown from his hand. Speilton reached for his sword, but an arrow was already on its way. It made a thin cut along his finger. It wasn't severe, but just enough for him to pull his hand away from the weapon.

They were surrounded. Arrows could come at them from any direction at any time, and the enemy had already shown that they could shoot an arrow. They could be finished at any second, and with only Equus and Nicholas's bow and arrows, and Ores' hammer, the chance of surviving the attack was small.

"Stop, hold your fire. Show yourself, cowards," Millites commanded to the darkness.

Silence again, then the first voice spoke, "Millites, is that you?" A man with a pale face and sunken eyes stepped out from the gloom.

"Arbustum?" Millites asked.

"Is it you? Have you come to save us?" the man asked.

"Us?" Usus asked, "Who are the others with you?"

An elf appeared behind the man holding a tall torch. The flame was small and round, obviously charmed with some magical property. But at the time, they didn't really care, "So that's what the orbs were." Ore said, "Torch lights."

The elf with the torch bowed on one knee, then tapped the fire against a block on the ground.

The flames spread out along a very straight path then turned sharply once reaching a certain point. Speilton backed away, thinking the passage had caught fire. But then, realized it was lighting the area, tracing the walls to reveal the rest of the room.

The different archways that they thought were each it's on path were actually columns, lining the outside of a vast room. The flames raced down the wall, spreading out so far they weren't even visible. Only then did they notice the occupants of the two vast rooms on either side of them. Hundreds and hundreds of elves of every age and size were hiking up to them.

"We've been waiting for you to come," Arbustum said.

"Release the girl," the King commanded.

Ginkerry stepped into the light, imprisoned by an elf. She rustled free and ran up next to Equus.

"I'm sorry for taking her. We heard someone coming and expected the Calorians. We didn't expect you to come this way." said Arbustum.

"Well, we had to. The ants attacked and there was no other way up."

"Oh, I understand. I am glad you made it past them. So, where is the rest of your army?"

"What do you mean?" Usus asked.

"You know, to help us fight. You got the message, didn't you?" Arbustum asked with a look of confusion.

"We never got a message. What's going on here?" Ram asked.

"If you didn't get the message, then why are you here?" Arbustum asked.

"We're on a quest," Millites said. "And we needed supplies. So we thought we would come here to refuel."

"Oh," Arbustum said solemnly.

The crowd went silent, except for a few crying babies.

"Arbustum, what are you hiding from?" Speilton asked.

Arbustum looked up, his eyes full of sorrow. "It's the Chimera."

"The what?" Brute asked.

"The Chimera," Usus began. "It's a magical beast one hundred feet tall, and three hundred feet long. It's like a huge fire breathing lion with dragon wings and horns."

"So it's from the Cave of the Magmors?" Millites asked.

"No, but good try. Most huge creatures are born from that cave. Dnuoh and Cetus both came from the Cave of the Magmors. Something about it gives power to the creatures it creates. All Liolian records show that the Chimera just appeared here one day. Nothing shows proof of it having come from the cave. All we know is that for decades it slept in a cavern beneath the Jungle of Supin. But recently, it awoke, and it has been preying on my people for a month," Arbustum said.

"So, what are we up against? A giant?" Ore asked.

"The Chimera is a huge beast. It has the body and head of a lion, and the back legs of a goat. It has the two horns of a ram, the wings of a dragon, and its tail is that of a viper," Usus explained.

"Sounds pretty tame. Anything else we might want to know?" Nicholas asked.

"Oh, and remember, it's three hundred feet long, one hundred feet tall!" Usus began.

"And it breathes fire," Arbustum finished.

"So, how do we get out of here?" Millites asked.

An elf ran out into the hallway, carrying a map in his hand. "We follow the map, my Kings," the elf said.

They began walking down the narrow tunnels, the way they'd come. In front was Arbustum, Millites, and Nicholas, who were discussing their journey and the attacks of the Chimera.

"So, when did you create that room?" Nicholas asked. "I know it wasn't there before."

"You're right, this is a new addition to the maze," Arbustum said.

"But why did you add it?" Millites asked.

"Under the tree was the safest area. The Chimera can never find us under here. After a few nights of trying to defend ourselves against it, we just retired down here. Now every night, for a few weeks, we've stayed in those two giant rooms."

"Why didn't you send messengers?" Millites asked.

"We did. Several actually. And you didn't get them?"

"Not one, unless they arrived after we left," Millites said.

"I doubt it. We've seen the Chimera rise from the jungle with its large wings. It must have been after our brave messengers."

A few minutes went by as they walked through the twisted tunnels. Finally, they came to an area where the road widened, and as they got closer, the earthen floor became stone. In the stone, the image of a tree had been etched. The path divided one last time into three paths, and they took the one on the far right. This path was well lit with lanterns on either side every five feet. They walked down the path for a minute or two, then stepped into a very large room. In the middle was a single ladder that led to a trap door.

"But Equus can't climb," Millites interjected.

"Well, it's a good thing we don't use the ladder then," Arbustum said. He walked to the far side of the room and tapped three times. Behind the wall, Millites could hear the scurrying of feet, and suddenly the door lifted up like a draw bridge. Two elves stood there, pulling on ropes that lifted the wall. Arbustum walked through the opening and up a ramp, and the rest followed.

They entered the inside of the trunk. About seventy yards wide and fifty high, the room was vast and filled with vegetation. Vines covered in flowers grew across the walls, mixing in to the brilliant paintings. They arched to the stained glass ceiling. The vines crawled around terraces that decorated the walls overlooking the place. These terraces protruded from the rooms of the most noble elves. Sometimes, a few were used for when the Kings and Queen came. But there was one thing missing - people.

As the elves entered the room, they went to work. Many headed to the far walls and climbed up winding staircases that wound up the trunk. Others walked out of two heavy bolted doorways and went to pick fruit in the jungle acting like nothing had happened, and life was normal as always. But inside, everyone knew the same thing. They were prisoners, without escape. This very instant they were being watched by an enemy that could overcome them in seconds.

They broke up into three groups. Speilton needed to think, and just wanted to relax. Millites, Usus, Nicholas, and Arbustum went up a tall spiral of stairs, walked out on a limb, then climbed a rope ladder. The ladders were simply built but were very sturdy. To keep them from swaying in the wind, two large stones dangled at the bottom, keeping it in place.

At the top of the ladder, perched on three thick branches was the castle. It wasn't very big, but it didn't have to be since the tree was big enough for all of them to live safely and comfortably.

As soon as they entered the castle Arbustum began, "You can't leave until the Chimera is dead."

"Are you forcing us to fight?" Nicholas asked.

"No, I mean that if you try to escape, the Chimera will hunt you down for certain."

"Well, we got in without any trouble from the Chimera," Millites explained.

"That's because we were a minor threat," Usus said. "We were going into the jungle. Going into a trap."

"So, we must fight it to escape?"

"To fight it would be certain death," Arbustum summed up.

"We can't die before even reaching Skilt," Usus groaned.

"And besides fate showed at least nine of us reaching the castle," Millites offered

"But this creature is powerful, and some evil spirit has been messing with it. It is no accident that the Chimera picked now to attack, when Milwaria needs you most," Arbustum explained.

"Which means that it may have the power to change the future?" Nicholas asked.

"Possibly," Ram said.

"But to reach Skilt, we must fight," Millites said.

"Then we must have a very good strategy," Arbustum decided.

Meanwhile, the other six creatures, who hadn't been to the palace, were given a tour by an elf named Sirene. She explained the architecture and showed them that each terrace led to a different guest room. Then up the stairs to the second floor, she showed them the kitchen where chefs scrambled around, preparing gourmet meals from many tropical jungle fruits. Right next door, they grouped the fruit and loaded them into bags. Since the Chimera hadn't allowed any escape for weeks, there was an overload of fruit piled there that should've been shipped to other areas across Milwaria.

Sirene continued the tour and explained that the holes in the bark allowed them to peer into the jungle. The village was amazing since it was built right on the limbs of the tree. Rails outlined the area and gave the elves some protection from falling off the cliff. The huts were dome-shaped, like the omens in the desert, so that they could allow strong winds to blow around them. A thick layer of branches and leaves that grew on the outside of the village shielded much of the wind and sunlight.

Next, they climbed up the outside of the tree, and walked up to the palace. A single dome-rose from the center, in the same shape as the huts, except twenty times larger. Two thin obelisks stood erect on either side, and behind it all was a square building covered in towers. This was the palace.

They entered into the dome, and found it to be wild with paintings. From the outside it was pretty simple with white marble, and vines scaling the dome. But inside, color was everywhere. Starting from the top, there were rows of pictures that circled the room, enough to nearly cover the entire dome.

"Each of these rows of pictures that rings the room tells a story of our history. The farther up near the top, the farther back in time the stories are, but closer to the base are the newer stories."

A man was painting a new mural while standing on a ladder. So far, all that was visible was the tree and the image of the Chimera, not yet finished. But the man was painting away, recording it in a web of stories.

"Just above the newest line, now under construction, is the battle at Kon Malopy," Sirene showed them.

"It's beautiful!" Ginkerry announced.

Metus groaned and turned away. In that battle, he had lost his family, his friends, and watched his people die. It was because of that battle that he was the way he was.

"So, moving on," Sirene announced, "in these next rooms-"

Suddenly, hooting and hollering erupted from one of the hallways. A flood of baboons and chimpanzees fled from the hallway and into the circular room, holding spears and frothing at the mouth. "I assume these are the rabid monkeys Nicholas told us about?" Brute asked.

"They aren't going to hurt us are they?" Ginkerry asked.

"No, no," Sirene explained. "We're on good terms with them now. We've just got to... give them some space."

The rabid monkeys charged through the room, howling at one another and continued out. Finally, all was quite once again, and they continued the tour.

After quickly seeing some of the public areas in the palace, they came to the most amazing place yet. A large landing led to a few flights of stairs above the palace. There was a large rope ladder, over one hundred feet tall that was planted in place by two large stones, tied together around a thick limb.

"Now, this is the tallest ladder in the entire tree. Though, don't be scared, it won't break any time soon. We used extra strong fibers, and each rung is replaced with the densest wood every other month. And the large stones at the base hold it in place. There's hardly any swaying."

"I can not climb," Equus said.

"Oh, that's right. I'm sorry, do you mind staying down here for a little while?" Sirene asked.

The centaur nodded his head.

"Yeah, uh...I'll stay down here with him," Metus whimpered, as he stepped away from the group.

"Okay, what about the rest of you?" Sirene asked.

"I'll go," Ginkerry said.

"Fine with me," Ore shrugged as Brute just muttered something under his breath.

"Great," Sirene declared, beginning the climb.

The rest followed her up the ladder, crawling higher and higher up in the air. Ginkerry tried not to look down. They were suspended over the tree, and if they fell, it was a long drop down. As promised, the ladder didn't rock and sway in the wind. It was held taut, which made it easy to climb.

Sirene reached the top and helped the others out on a branch with rails on either side. Sirene led them across the branch and onto a platform. Vines and leaves covered the outside, camouflaging the area from the ground.

They were met by a spectacular sight. The jungle was laid out all around them. They could see every tree, every bird taking flight, every wisp of a cloud. Up here the evening sun seemed huge and radiant. "This, is the tallest peak in all of Milwaria," Sirene announced to them. "However, it's not the tallest area in all Liolia. That would be Mt. Flig in Caloria"

"Wow, it's incredible," Ginkerry mused.

"Now, what's that?" Ore asked pointing down at the palace far below them.

"Uh...that's the palace, remember?" Brute answered, annoyed.

"No, not that, the metal rod coming out of the top," Ore said.

"Oh, yes. I forgot to mention that," Sirene explained. "Well, many years ago, lightning kept striking the tree. We thought it was because it was the tallest thing around. The lightning probably strikes the closest object. So we experimented some, and came up with this. The metal rod seemed to attract lightning."

A metal spire stood on the tip of the palace. It's tip stood thirty or forty feet below them, and the tip was a sharp point.

"I knew it," Ore exclaimed. "In the lava lands, we've been experimenting, too, with electrical currents. We're still not sure what it all means."

"Neither are we. All we know is that the lighting is directed to that metal rod and then, we continued the rod down, dividing it into four different rods. The four sections go out on different sections of the dome, then go down chambers in the tree trunk to the ground."

"And it works?" Ore asked.

"So far. It's a new installment, and we're not sure if it'll hold. It's only three feet wide at the base, and over fifty feet tall."

"Ingenious!" Ore exclaimed." I'd been wondering how it held against storms."

"Yeah, yeah, really great," Brute exclaimed sarcastically. "Now, can we go back down to the kitchen area?"

While the others toured the palace Speilton was led up a flight of stairs by an elf and into a thin corridor in the bark of the trunk. A little way down was a guest suite, and as soon as he entered, he crashed on the bed. Prowl laid down next to the bed, and flipped Speilton's hand onto her head with her nose.

Speilton hadn't had time last night to think, because at the time he was worrying about reaching the elves. On the Plains, he could only wonder about what he should've done differently to save those people. Maybe he should've relaxed more, felt sympathy for them. Even tried talking to them. Maybe, if he'd only held on one second longer. . .but he'd never know.

Now, he had to think about the curse. His brain told him to keep it to himself. It was too late to tell them how everything was his fault. But then again, maybe they would be supportive. Maybe they'd be forgiving and realize how hard it was to fight against a curse. He had to tell them. Yes, it would be hard, and they would be angry. But it would be worth it, knowing someone else knew what he was going through and could help him determine what to do. Right?

He fell asleep wondering about the future, wondering what his next move should be. But when he woke up, he had an answer. "I've got to tell them," he decided.

He sat up, and noticed Prowl had left his side. Speilton climbed out of bed, and walked down the empty hallway. Torches lit the wall, giving the only light, so it was impossible to know if it was day or night outside. He started into a run, hoping to find someone as he fled down the stairs and into the main chamber that led outside. There was no one there, and the doorway was closed.

Now where to go? Maybe he could go up the staircase in the center of the room. That had to lead to something. He began climbing as fast as he could. The King was soon worn out, but he had to keep going. Then suddenly, it dawned on him. The Chimera must've attacked. The others must've fought, but lost. And now, he was the last one left, forever imprisoned in this castle.

It seemed like a plausible explanation. What else could explain the lack of sound and...people.

He reached the top of the stairs, panting. But just before he climbed through the hole in the ceiling, another thought shook him. What if this was a trap like when they first entered that room. Arbustum said it would fire arrows at whoever entered. What if this would do the same thing when he entered.

Speilton strained to remember if people had entered this way before. He'd seen someone climb these stairs before. Right?

He had no choice. Slowly, he reached his hand up through the hole. He half expected an arrow to impale his palm, but nothing happened. He stuck his arm up higher, but still nothing. He was a little more hopeful, as he pulled his entire body up through the hole, and began down a hallway.

Torches lit the walls though the light was little, and it was hard to see. It was enough to prove no one was in sight. Speilton almost wished there was no light at all. That way, there could be someone hiding in the darkness.

Doorways opened up on either side of him, every few feet. They showed beds, all ready and neat but empty. That meant that it wasn't night yet if people weren't sleeping. Unless, they had all fought and lost, and were now in eternal sleep. Speilton found himself running down the hallway. He no longer wanted to look in the rooms. Each one was forbidding, and seemed to be haunted. He began panting as he ran on down the hallway. Finally, he came to where the hallway ended. But he was faced with a new challenge. He was at an intersection. Which way should he go?

Speilton walked a little down each path, but found they were all long hallways full of beds. Each way could lead to no where for all he knew.

He'd decided to go forward, when a bird suddenly flew down the hallway, going down the path to his right. That was the first living thing he'd seen since waking up. It was the first clue to where everyone might be. So he followed the bird.

Luckily, the bird seemed to want Speilton to follow it. Speilton had begun running down the hallway, and thought he'd lost the bird, when suddenly, he saw it, sitting on the ground and staring up at him. The bird took flight again, and Speilton followed.

Finally, after a few minutes, he began to climb up a flight of stairs. But before he reached the top, he came face to face with an elf. Speilton screamed and leapt backwards. The two stood there, staring at each other for a second, letting their heart rate fall back to normal. The elf spoke first, "Speilton, we have been looking for you."

"I was..." Speilton gasped for breath, "in my room. Where is everyone?"

"Right in here. They sent me to look for you."

"What's going on, why's everyone in there?"

"It's the Chimera, we're getting ready for battle."

They raced up the stairs and entered a huge room filled with elves. The area was plain and rectangular, but one wall was made entirely of glass looking out into the jungle.

Sitting amongst the elves were Millites, Usus, Ram, Nicholas, Metus, Brute, Ginkerry, Ore and Equus. The dove that he had followed was perched on Ginkerry's shoulder. "The Chimera is coming," she announced.

"How does she know?" Speilton asked the elf.

"She's been sending out those birds to report the Chimera's whereabouts."

Prowl suddenly flew down next to Speilton. "Where did you go while I was sleeping?"

"BOOOM!" the sound echoed through jungle. The elves hurried to the glass wall, and saw the mighty wings of the Chimera reach into the air out of the thick of the jungle. The wings pumped once, and the body of the Chimera was revealed. In the red light of the setting sun, the Chimera seemed covered in blood. Everyone in that room would agree, it was huge.

The elves fled from the window, and hid in the back of the room. Speilton ran up to Millites, "So, what's the plan?"

"We attack from here. Another army, led by Arbustum, attacks from the branch over there. Our target is the mouth.

"What do I do?" Speilton asked.

"You ride Prowl. Attack the Chimera but don't use fire."

"You know I won't."

"Prowl, too," Millites explained. "Fire will only make it angry.

"Got it,"

"Oh, and this has to end tonight. Some of the elves may think about fleeing to the maze. If they do, you have to get there first. Destroy the passage so that they won't have a choice but to fight. Because if they go down into the tunnel to hide, there will be no way we can fend off the Chimera."

"Agreed," Speilton said.

At that moment, there was a loud thud, and the entire tree shuddered. They were all thrown from their feet. Outside, the Chimera landed. It turned towards the tree and began searching for movement. They could see the blurred image of the huge head of the Chimera outside, looking, smelling the air, and planning their deaths.

Every elf drew his bow, ready to fire at the head. But they held fire, waiting...waiting.

The Chimera turned and faced them. The deep red eyes stared straight at them, its prey. It opened its fanged mouth and let out a roar. It was much louder than any roar they'd ever heard. Speilton clasped his hands over his ears, but the elves held steady.

The glass wall shattered, raining down the edge of the tree, and the elves let their arrows loose. They soared into the Chimera's mouth, stabbing into the tongue.

The Chimera howled and turned away, but was met by another row of arrows from Arbustum's army. Many elves leapt from branches high above, and landed on the Chimera. They held spears and drove them into the skin. Though to the Chimeras, they were merely pin pricks.

Speilton ran to Prowl, and was about to leap onto her back, when he caught sight of Metus, balled up in the corner. "Hold on," Speilton told Prowl as he walked over to the faun. "Are you okay?" Speilton asked.

Metus nodded his head. "Hey, I don't blame you for being scared. I've seen everyone I love taken away. I know what it's like." Metus slowly nodded his head. "But one thing I decided after that, was that I wouldn't back down. I wouldn't let evil win out. After they died, I vowed to stop it. And that gave me hope."

"But I'm not like you. I'm not brave."

"Yes, you are. Remember how you fought off all those Calorians last year. That bravery is still inside you. You've just got to use it."

"I can't," he mourned.

"Yes, you can. Fight for me. Fight for all those elves who are going through exactly what you are. Your fighting may save another from dying. You may be able to stop someone else from having to go through the pain you did."

Metus looked up at the chaos. The Chimera snarled and cut through a tangle of branches with his paw. Then it lowered his head and rammed a branch with his horns. He charged again, and the branch buckled. Elves scrambled off the branch as it gave way, plummeting towards the earth.

Speilton ran over to Prowl and climbed onto her back. He turned back to Metus one last time. "Be brave!" he shouted as Prowl raced into the sky.

Metus sat there, staring up at the battle. Speilton and Prowl darted through the sky, flipping and twirling away from the Chimera's huge paws. Speilton pulled out his sword and slashed the beast across the nose. It growled, but they were to quick to escape. Prowl went into a dive down the creatures back. Suddenly, the serpentine tail lashed up at them, and Prowl had to backflip to escape the poison fangs. They circled back into the sky and perched on another limb up away from the creature.

Metus continued to watch all of the brave warriors risk their lives to destroy the beast. Meanwhile he sat there, hiding.

That's when he decided, no one else was going to die. Not if he could help it. Slowly, he drew his flute from around his neck. He pressed the wooden tip against his lips, the way he always did. And slowly, he blew into the instrument.

His mind went somewhere else. He was now in the forest, his parents were calling him in for supper. The other fauns were playing in the trees, running free. He looked to them and knew that many of them would not survive. Then he looked to his parents and knew the same for them. He ran to his parents and hugged them.

Everything was normal, the way it should be. This was the memory he always held onto. That one day. But now … this last time … it ended differently. "Goodbye," he whispered.

The song ended, and he was once again sitting in front of a war. This was his life. There was no changing it, and to hold onto the past would only drive him insane. He took one last look at the flute, made by his father so long ago. It was hard to let go, but he cast the flute aside and walked toward the beast. "Be brave," Speilton's last words echoed in his head.

Metus picked up a spear, and took off towards the open wall. In one powerful leap, that could only be reached by a faun, he landed on the Chimera's snout. The creature was too distracted to notice at the time. Metus crawled up onto the monster's head, and slid down it's back.

Watching Speilton in the air gave him an idea. He held the spear out before him and pointed it at the snake tail. It hissed, as green poison dripped from it's sword-long fangs. "Brave," Metus whispered to himself as he approached the serpent. It lunged forward and struck, but Metus blocked the blow back with his shaft. The snake pulled back, then sprung again. This time, Metus swung the blade out in front, and cut a line down the snake's neck. It reared up into the air and struck down on the faun. He held up the spear in front of him, and the snake bit around it. The head thrashed, tossing Metus to the side, and snapping the spear in half. Metus lay on his back, and the blade lay under the snake. The serpent lashed out at him, but Metus ducked under the attack. He clasped the tip end of the spear in his hand, but before he could move, the head batted him away.

Venom dripped from the fangs as the Serpent lunged one last time. Metus could't move. He was certain the fangs would pierce his body. The faun closed his eyes, ready for the blow but realized he was out of the snake's range. The fangs had fallen short, and it would be the serpent's last mistake. Metus swiftly grabbed the blade and embedded it in the snake's skull.

It hissed, swung wildly, and then collapsed at the Chimera's side. "AAAARGH!" the Chimera roared in pain. It twirled around and faced Metus. The two red eyes stared down into him, and the faun felt the weight of a boulder. As he began to run, the Chimera pounced forward, shaking the ground, and knocking the faun from his feet. He lay sprawled on his back with the beast standing over him.

Then, the hollering of baboons rose, as hundreds of them dropped from the tree. They scrambled across the Chimera's face, brandishing spears and frothing. The Chimera reared up, and Metus had enough time to scramble away.

Up in the tree, Arbustum scrambled out onto one of the branches. "Drop the ladder! Drop it!" he commanded.

Two elves shoved the end over the branch. The two stones on the end of the ladder caused it to plummet to the earth, and land only a few feet away from Metus.

"Climb!" Arbustum screamed down.

Metus grabbed hold and began climbing. His hooves slipped on the rungs of the ladder, but he soon reached the top. A few elves helped pull him up onto the branch. "I've got a plan," he declared.

"Then let's go," Arbustum said.

"No, just me. I don't want to be responsible for all of your deaths if something goes wrong."

And with that, he took off up the stairs.

The monkeys soon had to fall back. The archers were slowly losing more and more arrows. Soon they would be out, and so far all they had done was destroy the tail. Speilton and Prowl took to the sky once again, but the Chimera was now more angered, ready to fight, ready to destroy them. The arrows were now just getting stuck in its mane, and many branches had been broken off by its giant paws and horns. Things weren't looking good, and time was running out.

Metus reached the landing. Above him was the tall rope ladder that led to the top. He quickly untied the rope ladder's stones from the limb, so that they now dangled high over the ground, hundreds of feet below. He leapt for the ladder and grabbed hold. Slowly, he pulled himself to the top, though it was harder than when the ladder was firmly planted by the stones. It rocked and swayed, leaving him suspended high up in the air. And it didn't help that his hooves kept sliding off the rails.

He reached the top, though he couldn't head to the main platform yet. He had to move the ladder out farther from the platform below. He scooted the ladder over ridges in the bark, until it was far enough away from the platform. Slowly, the limb began to bend. As he got out farther, he had to balance. To slip, meant to fall from the highest area in Milwaria. Finally, the rope ladder was hanging on the very edge, threatening to drop.

Now he crawled back over to the top platform. "HEY!" he screamed at the top of his lungs. "I'M UP HERE YOU BIG BEAST! REMEMBER ME? THE ONE WHO DESTROYED YOUR TAIL!"

The Chimera opened up its huge wings, larger than the sails of the Night Seemer. In one puff, the Chimera took flight. Below, the elves cheered. They thought it was retreating, going back into the jungle. But they were so wrong. The Chimera flapped its wings again, and glided across the top of the tree.

This was it - the final moment. Metus walked out onto the branch. In a thundering crash, the Chimera landed on the platform far below. It raised it's head upwards and roared as loudly as possible. Metus clasped his hand over his ears and nearly tumbled over the edge. But luckily, he regained his balance and was able to crawl over to the end of the branch. And at that second, the Chimera unfurled its wings, took one mighty flap and struck at Metus. The faun lunged for the rope ladder, and pushed the last ropes off the branch. It snapped in half, as the rope ladder and end of the branch plunged into the Chimera's throat.

It gagged and twisted. Its back and goat legs kicked the air in anger, as it swung its head around violently. It tried a strangled roar, though nothing would get the wood and rope from its throat. Metus noticed the flames spurting from the deepest part of its throat. It was trying to burn the wood out.

This wasn't good. It could catch the entire jungle on fire. Then, Metus would've failed.

Flames streaked from the demons throat exploding into the sky. The Chimera pumped its wings a few more times, until it was high up in the night sky. It thrashed once, twice...

...then was suddenly hit by a flood of arrows.

That's all it took for the monster to relent. The wings stopped pumping, and the body thrashed as it fell.

Something caught its fall. The lightning rod impaled the Chimera straight through. It growled, and kicked furiously, one more time before going still.

But the kick was just enough to snap the branch where Metus was perched. The faun fell. Suddenly, the roles had switched. Now Metus was the one falling to his doom by the Chimera's hand (or hoof). And as Metus fell, something caught his fall, too. But it wasn't nearly as painful as a fifty foot tall spire.

It was an eagle, a huge, grey, Harpy Eagle, that soared under the faun and landed him gracefully in front of the palace. He slumped off the back of the bird. Ginkerry approached the Harpy Eagle and patted him on the head, then went forward and hugged the faun. "That was amazing!" she declared.

Arbustum laughed and patted Metus on the back. "Now, that's a plan!" the king announced.

Speilton flew over next to the faun and said, "You were so brave."

"Thank you," was all Metus could say, before he was swept away by a mob of cheering elves.

THE FROZEN TUNDRA
~ 18 ~

The next day, the elves began repairing the tree. Fallen branches were chopped up to use for rebuilding. Many more wagons were constructed to take out the overload of fresh fruit to other places in Milwaria. The broken ladders were repaired, and the Chimera'a bloody carcass was removed and dragged deep into the woods on hundreds of rolling tables.

Slowly, the Jungle of Supin began coming back to life. Elves were once again happy, and all around, people were building, repairing, and helping one another. New houses were built for those who had lost theirs during the battle with the Chimera.

Speilton, Millites, Usus, Ram, Prowl, and the six creatures stayed for two more days. During these days, they rested, filled up their supplies, and supervised the rebuilding of the jungle. They ate some of the most exotic and juicy fruits that the jungle had to offer. In all, it was very relaxing, though they couldn't go more that a few minutes without being reminded of their journey.

Late on the second day, they began packing for the rest of their journey. They were supposed to meet the rest of the army in the Icelands in only a few days and needed to hurry.

Since they were going into the Icelands, they needed to dress for the frosty terrain. The elves wove thick jackets with hoods and pants and supplied them with many dry pieces of wood tucked into water-proof bags. Thick tents made of animal skins were made along with many new blades and arrows.

Then early on the third day, they packed hunks of rich meat, dozens of loaves of bread, and bags full of dried exotic fruit. After everything was packed and ready for the last leg of the trip through Milwaria, they left hoping to escape the jungle before the sun set.

Though they didn't make it out as early as they hoped, they still were close. Only an hour after twilight, they arrived at an area where the trees parted, revealing a large meadow. It was there that they spent their first night since their arrival at the tree.

The next day, they walked endlessly through the meadows, though the grass here was much more fertile and brightly colored than it was on the dry Plains. They walked on into the night, finally reaching the edge of the Icelands.

The temperature had dropped fifty degrees since they had left that morning. But now, as they made camp at the edge of the icy, glacial Icelands, the temperature was at its all time low. The air was frigid as they began to build a campfire. Ginkerry pulled on her jacket and huddled next to the glowing embers. Prowl shook and began to turn pale, and eventually had to lie down directly by the fire to keep warm.

They all knew that the blue dragon wouldn't be able to stay with them for much longer. If she went into the Icelands with them, she would surely freeze to death. They decided to let her stay until the army came. Every few hours she flew high up into the air to check to see if the army was anywhere near. Once they came, she and Hunger would be able to fly around the Icelands, together, therefore decreasing their changes being attacked. They could fight better together than alone.

The eleven awoke the next day, and after saying goodbye to Prowl, they began across the frozen tundra. Each wore a thick jacket, hood, and scarf. Equus also had blankets wrapped around his horse body. The ice cracked and slid out from under their feet as they became buried up to their shins in the deep snow. The frigid wind blew across their faces, and soon they had to pull their scarves over their noses to protect their skin.

All around them, the world was pale. The sky was a dark grey, not allowing any rays of sunshine through, and the white ice continued on forever and with the constant flow of wind, it was impossible to tell the difference between earth and sky. They had seen no sign of the Milwarian army.

Unlike before, they never came to any towns or villages. Everyone knew to stay out of the Icelands. People only entered it if they were completely desperate or seeking assistance from the giants, the creatures that ruled this area.

They would spend the next two days trekking to the Castle of the Giants where they would meet up with the rest of the army before entering Caloria. They all knew that the challenges they would face there would be much worse than anything they had been through so far.

The ice came up to Brute's thighs, and Ginkerry's joints were stiff and rigid. This harsh weather was difficult for dryads, in both tree and human form.

Equus was soon forced to carry Ginkerry, and after much complaining from the satyr, Equus agreed to carry Brute, too. The journey was cold and miserable as their faces were stung from the ice shards that whipped through the air.

Both nights, they were only able to create a weak fire as they huddled up with their backs, which worked as a shield against the wind. They tried to heat the meat quickly before the flames were extinguished but had to eat just the bread and dried fruits.

Late on the third day, they could make out the castle in the distance. From where they stood, it appeared to be a long slab of grey stone. As they hiked into the night, the whole structure began to take shape.

The castle was probably the largest building any of them had ever seen. It was all one level with the exception of turrets that rose up on each of the four corners. The structure was probably a mile wide and was constructed entirely of grey stone blocks giving the appearance of a prison. Each wall was nearly twenty feet high. In front of the castle was an overhang that was supported by a row of columns.

"This is the castle," Millites announced.

"So, how do we get in?" Ore asked.

"Each side has a revolving door in order to control the amount of cold air allowed inside," Ram explained.

The ten passed through two of the columns underneath the overhang. It was definitely warmer here, away from all of the ice. The ground was made of cobblestone, and although it was slippery, it was much easier to walk over than the ice.

In no time, they had reached the large door that led into the castle which stood nearly twenty feet tall and turned turned on a center axle connected to the ground. Millites grabbed the large iron piece and banged against the door. There was no reply for a few seconds, then suddenly the doors began to move, spinning lowly in a circle. Suddenly, a giant stepped out from behind one of the doors and bowed down to their level as he saw his guests.

"My Kings, do you wish to enter?"

"Yes, please," Millites responded. "And there will be more men coming soon."

"Come with me," he said, as the ten of them stepped into the doorway with the giant. The ten-foot-tall man pushed against the doors, causing it to spin.

The main chamber was vast. Doors fifteen feet tall covered the walls and led out to a separate part of the castle. Each door was marked with a sign. Signs included "battle preparation", "village," since everyone lived inside the castle rather than in the cold, "market", "schools", "excavation sight", and hundreds more.

It was mostly silent since it was nearly midnight. The only giants stirring around at these hours were the guards who led the questers to their rooms.

They slept late the next morning in the comfort of the warm castle heated by hundreds of fireplaces. There was one in nearly every room.

After explaining the mission to the King Giant, they spent the next two days exploring the castle, visiting friends in the village area, and trying some of the giants' customs. It was a welcomed break from their adventure and challenging events.

Late in the afternoon an army suddenly appeared on the horizon which the giants soon realized was the Milwarians. Nearly five hundred men inched along, their sloppy, torn jackets frozen stiff. Many rode on whimpering horses carrying thick bags.

In the center of the army was a huge machine that rolled on eight wheels and was drug through the thick tundra by a dozen horse.

Millites, Speilton, Ram, and Usus rushed outside through the revolving doors toward the army. Rorret leapt forward and tackled Millites. As the King began to pull him to his feet the lion began to lick his face. Millites laughed. Andereer ran up to them as Millites wiped away the slobber.

"My King! I'm so glad you're alive!" the Battle Strategy Chief exclaimed

"Thanks, and I presume that you didn't run into any trouble on your journey here?" inquired Millites.

"No, except for the Avenger. It is so heavy that it cracked through the ice many times," Andereer explained.

"So how does it work?" Speilton asked as he walked up behind them.

"The design itself is pretty simple," Andereer said. "The Avenger is an incredibly powerful catapult. Men push the wheels in a circle, pulling the rope attached to the catapult which brings the basket down. Then, a rock rolls in and as the level is pulled down, it fires. I can show you if you'd like."

"Sure!" Speilton agreed.

"Wait. We first have to get all the warriors inside to defrost. Then we can begin to discuss the remainder of the journey," Ram said

The men filed in to the separate door cells and were guided inside to let the warm castle melt off the snow and ice. Giants walked into the room, carrying large platters of bread and soup which were distributed among the men.

For the rest of the day, most of the warriors laid around rubbing warmth back into their stiff legs and arms after they had gulped their soup and gorged their bread. As the sun began to set, the warriors were fed large mugs full of warm milk with bread and cheese. The men ate all the food ravenously, before slowly drifting off to bed, one by one.

The warmth of the castle and food slowly restored and refreshed them. With their bellies now full of good food that wasn't covered in ice, the men had peaceful dreams. And they were well deserved because what they were going to encounter next, would completely erase all of those happy memories.

While the men sleep, I'll give you a little more back ground on the Avenger. In the front of the machine is a tall metal wall. Small gaps in the shield wall allow cannons to be fired out at the other army. The sides of the machine are covered in slits for crossbows to fire out of, so that the enemy could not climb up without being impaled by a wave of arrows. Still, the most important mechanism of the Avenger is it's high tech catapult. Since it needs to have an extremely tall pole to be able to hurl a rock at a far distance, the catapult has a joint about halfway up the pole. The top part of the pole can unhinge, and move backwards.

In the far back of the Avenger is a steep slope that holds the chunks of rock that the catapult can throw. They are kept down under the slope, and are lifted up to the top of the slope by a pulley. The men can pull down on the rope, lifting the rocks into the air, and empty them up on top.

The moment the basket touches the slope, a rock rolls down into the basket.

Once everything is ready and the Avenger is positioned towards it's target, all they have to do is pull down on a lever, and the catapult would return back to it's straight pole form, and snap forward, tossing the rock forward.

As the catapult moves forward, it tugs on many ropes. Many of these ropes are attached down under the main deck and are tied around the triggers of the crossbows. As the Catapult snaps forward, the trigers are pulled, and the arrows are fired out.

The catapult's launch signals the men to fire the cannons. Like that, dozens of hard stones hurtle out into the army.

And then, the whole thing is repeated again. The men spin the two wheels, pulling in the rope and lowering the catapult. Other men jump up and down on other areas, pumping air down into the machine. In only a few minutes, the Avenger is ready to fire again.

The men awoke the next morning, feeling rested and relaxed. They were served loads of chicken, sausage, baked pastries and warm drinks. The men gulped down every last bite. That day many walked around the castle, exploring it for the first time. As they all worked on taking their minds off the future. They tried to stay focused, not allowing fear to overtake them and like the day before, the men slept peacefully.

Early in the morning, Millites, Speilton, Usus, and Ram packed up and dressed in their thick snow clothes. The other six creatures were ready, too, covered from head to toe or hoof in the animal skins.

The Milwarians cheered as they left, and the giants wished them a safe journey. They wouldn't be leaving with them. Cigam had told the army to linger behind so that if the army was spotted, the other ten could continue on in secret. Speilton, Millites, Usus, Ram, Nicholas, Metus, Ginkerry, Brutus, Ore, and Equus gathered their courage and prepared for the harsh weather ahead. Then, very reluctantly, they set out into the snow. Prowl stayed behind.

Immediately, a storm began to pick up. The wind was stronger than before, blowing them sideways onto the ground. They had to huddle closely together to preserve body heat and keep each other from falling over. Not only had the wind gained strength and grown much colder, but it was now snowing so hard that they could not tell which way they were going. They could only inch forward, up to their knees in ice, hoping that they were heading south.

After awhile the storm died slightly and the snowfall wasn't as thick. Yet the wind still whipped around in strong waves as they reached the river, the river that divided Milwaria from Caloria.

Speilton and Ram had crossed it once before nearly half a year ago when the river's ice cracked. And that's how it remained today.

With the strong wind, the waves were wild and choppy. They clashed together, spraying water into the air. The waves splashed up onto the ice, instantly freezing into a slippery sheet. "Now, how do we get across?" Usus asked.

"Didn't the giants build a bridge across recently?" Millites wondered.

"Yes, I think I remember that, too," Ram agreed.

"But where is it?" Brute groaned.

"I say we split up. Half of us go left, the other half goes right. Once someone finds it, they send up a flare of their element," Speilton suggested.

"But if the snow begins to fall again, we won't be able to see the flares," Ore said.

"Then let's spread out," Metus suggested. "Each of us could be within eyesight of each other, but try to move out as far as possible."

"Good idea. I guess that'll work," Speilton agreed.

"But after five minutes, or if the storm begins to pick up again, we should all come back," Usus said.

The ten spread out walking a short distance away from each other. Everyone could just barely see the others in the snow. After a few minutes passed, down on the far end Nicholas announced, "I think I see it!" The others rushed down to him, and after walking a few feet further, they could all make it out, too.

The bridge was made of the same dark grey stone as the castle. Steps led above the icy water. There were hand rails on either side, though they only gave minor security. The walkway across was frosted over, and every once and a while, a large wave would crash against the side, spraying water up, which froze on the bridge.

"Do you think it's safe to cross?" Metus asked.

"Probably not, but we have to go over it one way or another," Speilton sighed.

"No," Ram said, "It's too risky with the high wind. We should wait for it to die down."

"But we can't wait," Usus said. "The rest of the army is coming soon. If we wait, they will catch up, which means our plan will be ruined."

Before leaving the castle, they decided that the ten would leave first and the army would follow about an hour later. The army could follow them closely, so that they would reach Skilt around the same time if the everything worked out as planned. But if they stayed here, the army would eventually reach them, therefore ruining their strategy.

In the end, they decided to cross the bridge before any other storms could come. Ginkerry rode on Equus's back, and although Brute slipped off once, there were no other incidents. The wind *did* blow them into the rails a few times, but it could've been much worse.

Finally, they reached the other side, and even though it was a pleasure to have gotten off the bridge, they were now faced with a strange feeling.

It was a feeling that caused their spines to tingle. It was a feeling of loneliness, and dread, and fear. It was a feeling that meant they could no longer rely on the Milwarians to help because here and now, they were in Caloria. The tables were completely turned.

After two days of hiking, the Milwarian army finally escaped the frozen death trap of the Icelands. But now, they were faced with an even greater challenge. They were in Caloria, the wasteland of death and hopelessness. The next two days, the warriors spent hiking through woods. Here the trees were darker, not nearly as bright and colorful as the Milwarian trees or those in the Rich Woods. They were still surviving, which wasn't very common in Caloria. Most of the trees closer to the castle had been cut down. These woods were closer to Milwaria and had been spared by the Calorians for now.

On the fifth day, they reached the end of the trees. The landscape changed very suddenly and drastically. The ground was wet and sludgy in this area of the forest where the trees disappeared all together. Before them was a flat landscape of knee deep mud, green pools of moldy water, and a few dead, decaying trees. Termites had eaten away whatever bark and vegetation those few trees had, leaving them naked and decaying.

The wind whistled across the bog like an imprisoned soul, forever chained to this dead land. Thick fogs of odiferous steam hung in the air like a shadow of despair.

As the warriors began to hike across the silent landscape, the devastation took ahold of them, too. They could feel the despair of all the Calorians that had died out here, lugging back entire trees to their castle. They could feel the hopelessness the treeps and dryads felt as their trees were cut down, ending their lives so that the Calorians could build a fortress. Many lives had ended during that time. There had been a battle out here, a battle that no one would ever know about. Though neither side *wanted* to fight. So after all the deaths that came of that battle those many, many years before, there were no winners.

The warriors hiked up to their knees in mud and molding ponds. Countless snakes and leeches writhed through the mud popping up every once in awhile for blood. Vultures flew overhead waiting for one of them to fall.

The Avenger was slowly pulled through as its wheels sank in the mud, and the horses strained to pull through. Many of the warriors tried to push from behind without success.

They finished the day finding a long slab of rock that rested at the top of a hill where the mud had been washed away. There they ate their first meal since breakfast and set up tents to sleep, though even their dreams were full of despair and hopelessness. Their minds had been affected by the landscape, and in their dreams, they faced horrors that only a nightmare could bring.

The next morning they awoke to the worst horror of all. Reality.

Five days through the bog they had traveled. The ten of them had been affected by the despair, just like the warriors. For once, Brute remained silent, as though the imprisoned souls had stolen his voice. Ginkerry was close to tears while looking out upon a land once overgrown with dryads and treeps and nymphs. To the other nine, it was a place of dread, but to the small dryad, it was a graveyard that stretched on for miles and miles.

It was still early on the sixth day when the thick mud began to lessen. There were more trees, though all of them had been stripped of their bark and leaves and left to die.

Soon, they came across a hill, with a grove of black leafed trees standing a little way up. They had knotted roots, thin, broken limbs, and large, grotesque tumors lumped up at their bases. The bark that clutched the tree was old and frail, and much of it had fallen away. Though depressing, they were a good sign. They meant that they were almost out of the bog. Very soon they'd reach the Evly Forest.

As they walked to the top of the hill, they saw the gorge below them, a deep crack in the earth nearly twenty feet across.

"Now this, could be a problem," Usus announced.

"Look, there's a bridge!" Ginkerry announced pointing a distance away.

"I don't know. It doesn't look very sturdy."

"We should at least check it out," Millites said.

They walked down the other side of the hill and along the gorge before coming to the bridge. It hung there, two stakes holding it up from either side. Decaying wooden planks lay on top of the two bottom ropes, while two more ropes made handrails higher above.

"Do you think we should try?" Metus asked.

Ram looked at it carefully. Then, he dug out a rock the size of his hand from the ground. "Let's find out."

The general tossed the rock out onto the bridge. The moment it landed on the bridge, the wooden plank cracked in half and tumbled down into the green river below.

"Maybe it was just a faulty board," Ore suggested.

Ram grabbed another and tossed it on the bridge. This time, instead of the plank collapsing, one of the ropes snapped. The bridge tipped sideways, letting the rock tumble off the side. But now, the other ropes were having to carry extra weight, so in no time another had popped.

The bridge dangled sideways, and after a few seconds, the third rope burst. The bridge tumbled out of the sky, only connected by one rope. But as it fell the last one broke, and like that the bridge was gone.

"Well, does anyone have any other ideas?" Speilton asked.

"What about your wands? Could you create a bridge with those?" Nicholas asked.

"My light is to weak to walk across, and Speilton's fire would only burn us to a crisp," Millites said.

"I could create a bridge with my wand," Usus announced, "but I'm not sure how long it'll last."

"We can't take any chances," Equus said solemnly.

"But what about Ram's wind. Can you blow us over?" Nicholas asked.

Ram shook his head, "Wind is hard to channel and control. I could blow you over, but I can't necessarily promise you a *soft* landing."

"How else can we get over?" Brute asked.

"Just think," Millites commanded.

There was silence for a minute as they all pondered over what to do.

"I know!" Ginkerry announced, taking off back up the hill.

"What's she doing?" Millites asked, though no one had an answer.

The rest of them followed her, and once they reached the top they saw her standing next to the five gnarled trees. "What are you - " Brute was cut off.

"Ssshhh!" Ginkerry put her finger to her lip before approaching the trees.

"Um, hello."

There was no response.

"My friends and I need help getting across that gorge. Will you help us?"

Again, there was silence.

"Please, sirs, I know you've had a difficult life, but may you please do this one favor for us?"

Silence.

"Ginkerry, I don't think anything is going to happen," Speilton said.

Suddenly, one of the trees began to move. Two pieces of bark slid back like a eyelids, revealing the white underside. Two of the tree's branches suddenly dropped to its side. The roots began shift and turn in the ground, ripping up through the muddy surface. The lower portion of the trunk separated itself in two.

The treep raised its twig hands up into the air in a yawn as four others began to awaken. The the tallest treep who was first to rise approached the dryad. "What is it you want?" he asked with a snarl.

The treep was nearly twenty feet tall and slowly took a step toward Ginkerry. Millites rushed between them pointing his sword directly at the treep.

"Now, now," the treep countered with his voice as dry and crackled as the bark that fell from his body. "Put away that weapon. We don't mean to threaten you."

The other four had finally awakened and were peering around at the other eight adventurers.

"Please, sir," Ginkerry stepped back in front of Millites. "We need to pass over the bridge. Would you help us?"

"And why should we help you?" the treep asked leaning forward over Ginkerry.

"It will help Milwaria win the war!" Ginkerry announced.

The treeps eyes narrowed and his eyebrows furrowed. "Milwaria? We are Calorians!" he growled. The other four marched up behind him, holding long, fallen tree limbs in their hands like swords.

"I'm sorry," Millites apologized. "She didn't mean to say that."

He turned to Ginkerry and whispered, "Let's keep going. They can't help us."

"No," she said as she pulled away. "You don't understand, do you? If Milwaria wins the war, that means that we would control Caloria, right?"

Millites nodded his head.

"And you, the great kings of Milwaria, will order this area to be cleaned and protected. If Milwaria wins, everyone in Caloria, besides the Wodahs, will be positively affected."

"Is this true?" the treep stared at the dryad.

"Of course," she promised.

"And this journey, is it truly to win the war?"

"Yes," Millites stepped in.

"Then we will help."

The treeps moved toward the the edge of the gorge. Their eyes closed like massive shutters and their roots dug down into the earth. Nothing happened for a few moments as the five treeps stood there.

"Are you sure this is going to work?" Brute asked.

"Positive, now just watch," Ginkerry whispered.

There was silence for a few more seconds. Then, suddenly, the edge of the gorge exploded as lashing roots broke out of he ground and darted toward the other side. Once reaching the other wall of the pit, they dug into the soil, reaching deep under the ground.

All five trees entangled their roots together creating a lumpy but sturdy bridge across. The trees opened their eyes to examine their work.

"There," the largest treep declared, "you may cross."

Millites, Speilton, Ram and Usus crossed first, followed by Equus, Nicholas, Ore and Brute. The roots did not dip or slide as they walked across, but instead held strong and straight like stone. The path was wide, nearly five feet, but they still felt dizzy as they peered down at the river that rushed hundreds of feet below.

Ginkerry was the last to cross. Once every one was on the other side, Ginkerry started across. "Thank you for helping us. I promise, not a single treep or dryad will die by the hand of the Calorians ever again." She raised her hand and waved goodbye, but as she did they all stared with fear and amazement at the dryad's hand.

Ginkerry's hand was slowly turning black. it started as a small black dot on her hand, but then grew and grew until every part of it was a dark blackish grey. The dryad gasped in shock as she looked at her hand. Her face became white, pure white, not just pale, and suddenly she collapsed to the ground crying in pain.

Speilton, Millites, and Usus rushed across the path to her, but suddenly the root bridge shook, as the trees pulled back their roots. They tossed the three leaders of Milwaria back to the other side of the gorge as they brought Ginkerry into their clutch.

"What have you done to her?" Usus shouted.

"*We* have done nothing."

"Then why is she dying?" Metus commanded.

"This dryad is beyond your saving. Her human body is melting away."

219

"But why is it dying and how?" Speilton asked.

For the first time, the other trees spoke. "Her soul tree, has died," they all said in unison.

They were all silent. "So, that means-" Millites began.

"Her soul has been released from her body. Now she may rest."

Ginkerry was laid onto the ground before the five treeps. Her entire arm was black and seemed to be melting away. Her skin was tight, and as white as a dove. Ginkerry's eyes stared, open, but her pupils vanished. She was seeing her tree crumbling apart. She was watching the end, her end.

Metus turned away, tears filling his eyes, and pressed his face against Speilton's chest. It was too painful for him to watch. He couldn't stand to watch the light leave her eyes.

Silently, the others watched as she melted away. Her pink hair and white skin, her burned arm and torn dress, all slowly melted away in a shower of petals that drifted up into the air. The petals swirled once, before disappearing into the sunset. And as if on cue, the light from the falling sun hit the clouds, turning the sky a brilliant rose shade.

The treeps solemnly moved away without a single word. The others stood and watched as the pink sky grew darker and darker, fading into the night. Tears were shed for the beautiful dryad who had inspired them, and given them hope in the icy cold and thick jungles. Because of Ginkerry, they could go on from this place, able to save the rest of Milwaria. Now, she could be with the hundreds of trees chopped down to build a ruthless empire in Caloria.

They hiked for only an hour that night, just far enough away from the gorge. They made a campfire and set up the tents. No one spoke for a while as they cooked some of the meat and ate the bread and dried fruits. Their supplies had dropped rapidly, and they were now left with only a few more servings.

After eating, they began to talk again knowing that they couldn't become too overwhelmed with grief of Ginkerry's death that they forgot the purpose of their mission.

Speilton shattered the melancholy silence, "She was the one to die," Speilton moaned, "Ever since she disappeared in the maze, I knew it was her. The image in the prophecy never showed her reaching Skilt. And I knew it," Speilton paused, staring into the dying fire with dread. "I could've stopped it. I could've done something."

"Speilton," Ram stopped him, "what is done is done. There is nothing you could've done to help her. If destiny showed her dying, then that is the way it was meant to be."

Speilton stared into the fire, his eyes blurred with tears. He felt such sorrow and guilt for her loss that he was relieved to finally know who would not continue with them on the journey.

"I know this is very difficult," Nicholas said, "but we have to move on. We can't let this affect us or our chances of victory will be depleted." The other eight agreed.

"When Ginkerry died, her arm became black," Millites said.

"What about it?" Brute asked.

"Her arm turning black probably symbolized something. Something that was happening to the tree. If a dryad's soul is connected to it's tree, then the mortal body must die the same way."

"So, however she appeared to be dying in her human form, was probably the same way she was dying in tree form," Ram clarified

"It looked like her arm was being burned black," Metus suggested.

"That's what I thought too," Usus agreed.

"So what if her tree was burned? What does that mean?" Ore asked.

"We must take into account that Ginkerry's soul tree lives in the Rich Woods. And, if one tree was burned..." Millites let the thought linger in the air.

Speilton, Usus, Ram, Ore, and Nicholas gasped.

"Wait, what?" Brute asked staring around at them.

"Who else would have cut through the forest, burning down trees than the Calorians," Millites announced.

"Then, that means that Kon Malopy must be under attack," Ore said.

Speilton bit his lip. "Let's just hope that the centaurs can hold them off," he said.

Equus began to squirm. His hoof scraped at the ground and for the first time they all noticed that his face showed apprehension.

"They are going to fight the Calorians, aren't they?" Usus asked nervously.

Equus remained quiet, but eventually he cracked. "There are matters that even our King can't control. When he told you that the centaurs would separate themselves from Milwaria, it was not an empty gesture. Everyday, the centaurs have wished to be free, not having to fight the hopeless battles of the Milwarians. The Centaur King has tried to hold the army together, but they have been deviously plotting against you, my Kings."

"So they're going to abandon the Milwarians in their darkest hours?" Ram asked with anger boiling up in his voice.

"Most of them will leave and join Caloria," Equus answered solemnly.

"But what about you?" Speilton asked. "Where do you stand?"

Equus didn't respond right away, "Once, I stood with the other centaurs. After awhile, we forced the King to change his opinion on this matter by threatening to overthrow him. Then, he assigned me to fight only for Milwaria, if the time ever came."

"But why? Why did he want you to go with us?" Millites questioned.

"He commanded me...the others commanded me...to declare ourselves Calorians by destroying the Milwarian Kings."

THE EYE STONE
~ 20 ~

Millites, Speilton, Usus and Ram leapt to their feet and unsheathed their swords. "So, this whole time, you were plotting our downfall," Millites questioned, furiously.

"I *was* planning to turn on you, but now I realize how much this journey means to you and the Milwarians," Equus said.

"We can't know for sure," Usus muttered. "This could all be a trick. While we're sleeping he could come and slit our throats."

"I could, " Equus said, "but I won't. I have finally realized that many people will be affected if this journey is disrupted, and it seems it would happen for the worse."

"Promise. You must promise to be and stay loyal to Milwaria, unless all you have is empty words," Speilton announced.

"I promise that I am and forever will be loyal to Milwaria, and follow every command."

"Then, drop your sword and quiver and bow. And that's an order," Millites commanded.

Equus dropped the weapons onto the ground.

"And," Ram added, "you must give your word to never harm a Milwarian or turn your back on one in need."

"Yes sir."

Speilton spoke up, "Since you're a Milwarian, once we… get back - "

"If we ever get back," Millites muttered.

"You have to persuade the other centaurs to join us. You are the only one they will listen to."

"I'm not certain they will listen," Equus said doubtfully.

"If you are truly going to join the Milwarians, then you will do as we say," Usus said

There was silence, when Speilton suddenly realized, "It doesn't even matter if we win this battle at Skilt. Even if we destroy the Calorians at Skilt, they will have still beaten us at Kon Malopy. Our two countries' capitols would have been destroyed."

"I guess we can only hope that our men can stand strong and defend Kon Malopy," Usus said solemnly.

"But what men? All of the warriors are following us. We were relying on the centaurs to help us," Millites said.

"Not all of them will turn. Many are still loyal to Milwaria and will still stay and fight, even if it means death," Equus explained.

"Teews!" Millites suddenly realized. "We sent her back to Kon Malopy! She's having to fight the Calorians alone!"

"Wouldn't they hide her? Maybe she's been taken deep into the castle near the prison," Ram suggested hopefully.

"No, that would be too risky," Usus explained. "If the Calorians win, they will probably destroy the castle, and if Sky Tower crumbled the levels below would trap Teews."

"And besides, she would never just wait in hiding while a battle is raging," Speilton said.

"So, she's fighting, alone," Equus muttered. "I am sorry for what my centaurs have done, and I promise, if we live, I will bring them back to our side."

They continued their hike the next day. The sludgy mud had begun to lessen, and there were more and more trees. Though they were all sickly and black with over sized lumps and knots growing in their trunks. The tree's leaves were either black or grey, as if each leaf had been singed.

In the distance they could see shapes like steep brown hills which were known as the Mounds of Waste. Many years before, Skilt had become overrun with waste and trash from the gluttony and carelessness of the Calorians. Disease was spreading like wildfire, and the Calorian race was dying. The king commanded many men to carry the refuse out of the Evly forest into the wood of black pines that surrounded Skilt. Over the years, the landfills piled up into huge mounds of horrible, smelly waste that decayed and contaminated the surrounding areas.

Luckily, the Milwarian travelers weren't close enough because the smell was said to be almost unmanageable to endure. It was late in the afternoon when they reached the Evly Forest. Tall black pines loomed before them. "The Evly Forest is our last stop before reaching Skilt," Millites announced.

They entered the dark forest. Nearly all light was blocked by the thick trees that stood next to the other. Unlike most healthy forests, the trees were pressed so closely together that they had to walk around clusters.

SInce there was very little light showing through they lit torches to guide their way. They stopped to rest that night after cooking dinner. When they woke, they had no idea if it was even morning, since they couldn't see any light, and there were no birds chirping. The Evly Forest was abandoned, and they were possibly the only living beings there at the time.

The next day they stopped and took a break about mid afternoon. Speilton burrowed through the supplies. "We only have probably two meals left," Speilton told them, "and we have three torches."

He handed one to Millites, and the other to Nicholas. "I'll keep the other," Speilton told them, shoving it into his pocket.

"What about the Eye Stone? Do you think we're close enough?" Usus asked.

"I guess it's worth a shot," Speilton said.

The king reached down into the bag of supplies and pulled out the ring. He held it up to his eye and looked through.

"Do you see anything?" Usus asked.

"No," Speilton said, spinning in a circle.

He moved it away from his eye and slipped it around his finger. "I'll just hold onto it and check every once and a while," Speilton suggested.

After everyone was given a slice of bread to supply them a little strength, they began again. They hiked for a few hours, dodging the close trees. They hadn't seen any wildlife since they had entered, unless you count treeps, though none of them had moved which was probably for the best.

They finally reached the other side as the sun had just set and the sky was darkening. Before them lay a vast open area of dusty, flat earth. And far in the center, nearly half a mile away, stood Skilt, the stone castle. The Evly forest wrapped around this entire area in an oval.

"Okay, we must've passed the cave," Nicholas decided.

"I've been looking through it every few minutes, but nothing seems to indicate a path. Everything seems normal," Speilton explained.

He slipped the ring off his finger and held it up over his eye. And then he saw it. Across the flat expanse of dusty ground, on the other side of the forest he saw a red, shimmering light in the shape of a half circle.

Speilton removed the ring, and the light was gone. But when he replaced it, the light was there as if it had never left. "Here, on the other side of this area. I see the cave," Speilton announced.

Millites took the ring and looked for himself. "Speilton is right. I see it, too."

"So, should we try running across?" Ore wondered.

"No. The Calorians will see us," Ram said.

"Then we must walk around," Metus agreed.

They began the trek around the dusty area, staying just in the cover of the trees since they couldn't risk being seen. The night came fast, and soon they had to fumble in the dark to light one of the last two torches. Speilton kept his as a last resort.

"So, what do we do when we reach the portal?" Metus asked.

"Cigam said that only four can enter." Ram recalled.

"That means Millites, Speilton, Ram, and Usus, right?" Ore wondered.

"Yes," Millites said, "It's probably safest if we are the ones to go inside."

"So what do we while the four of you are inside Skilt?" Brute asked.

"Stay hidden. The army should be by soon, and try to meet up with them. Whatever you do, don't let the Calorians know you're here. And if we don't come back out, don't go inside." Speilton instructed.

"Fine," Metus said.

"But are you sure you won't need our assistance?" Nicholas asked.

"There is no way you *can* help us," Millites said. "There are only four vials of Aqua, and the four of us are the carriers. If you follow us, you will only be caught."

"Speaking of the vials, do you still have them secured?" Metus asked.

"Good idea. Everyone, check to see that your vials are still secured," Millites requested.

Millites, Speilton, Usus and Ram all pulled out their Vials of Aqua that hung on chains around each of their necks underneath their clothes. "Good, they all survived," Speilton said.

Suddenly, an arrow whizzed out of the sky. They all heard it coming. Luckily, it didn't hit anyone, but the arrow still hit its mark. The tip of the arrow shattered Ram's vial as he held it out to inspect the contents, and the liquid splashed to the ground.

"We're being followed!" Equus announced. "Run!"

A dozen Calorians rushed out of the woods around them. The nine questers took one glance and took off. Trampling over fallen branches and roots, the eight ran on. Brute fell behind, and Equus had to run back and lift him onto his back.

As they ran, arrows flew around them with many planting into the mess of trees which added to the confusion. The nine were quickly separated while diving away from arrows and swerving past trees. Finally, Speilton and Millites met.

"Speilton, look through the ring!" Millites told him, panting.

"Millites, they...they know about the Vials!" Speilton told him while huffing and puffing, "We have to... destroy them or Sinister will know."

Millites realized that even if they escaped, Sinister would be alerted, and the entire Calorian army would know they were there.

Millites suddenly stopped. "Everyone, stop running. Stand your ground and fight," Millites commanded.

The others froze. "Is he insane?" Usus muttered.

"It makes you wonder," Nicholas agreed.

The Inferno of Erif

Millites, Speilton, Ram and Metus drew their swords. Usus drew his khopesh. Ore held up his hammer. Equus and Nicholas drew back their arrows, and Brute, well, he hid behind a tree. The Calorians approached with a storm of arrows. Millites led them forward and quickly knocked down a Calorian with his Minotaur faced shield. Nicholas tossed his torch onto the ground, sending up a wall of fire. Unlike the soft wooded trees on the mountains in Milwaria, these trees wouldn't go up in flames.

Nicholas and Equus both took down a Calorian with a single shot. Ore smashed one into a tree with his hammer. Metus leapt up into a tree then pounced down onto a Calorian, sword first.

Speilton backed away from the fight, and held the Eye Stone up to his eye. There he saw it, only fifty yards ahead.

"Everyone, come on, I found the cave!"

The other eight turned and began to run, but Millites was stopped. An arrow flew down from the trees and caught his sword, knocking the lightning-bladed weapon to the ground. The king turned to see his attacker drop out of a tree. Millites was knocked to the ground as the Calorian planted his knees on Millites' chest. The Calorian's eyes darted to something laying on the ground next to him, as Millites looked to see the Vial of Aqua. But before he could stop the Calorian, it had shattered the vial with an arrow.

Millites quickly grabbed his sword and knocked the warrior off him before running after the others. In just a matter of minutes, two of the four vials were destroyed.

As they ran, the surviving six Calorians pursued. These had been more cautious or better skilled than the others. They soon began to catch up with Millites who was the farthest behind, but the king narrowly dove through a grove of trees and disappeared from their sight.

Usus, however, was not so fortunate. After a while of dodging around trees, he didn't know which way he should be going or where the others were. That's when three arrows struck the trees around him. Usus dropped to the side as another flew by him. He began to run, but tripped over a large root.

Then two Calorians stepped into sight. One carried a sword, the other, an axe. Usus stood and blocked the blow of the axe, before disarming the man with the sword.

As the warrior with the axe attacked, the other ran behind Usus. The Second-in-Command swung his sword at the armed Calorian, when suddenly, he was choked from behind. The Calorian grasped the chain that contained the vial. Before Usus could defend himself, the Calorian crushed the vial in his hand.

Gasping for breath, Usus prepared himself as the other Calorian approached. He swung the axe, but Speilton quickly kicked him in the chest. Millites suddenly appeared from behind a cluster of trees and swiped down the other Calorian. Usus began rubbing his throat and taking deep breaths.

"They destroyed the vial. That is what they were after the whole time."

"I know," Millites said. "They destroyed mine, too."

"But that means..." Usus began.

"Speilton has the last Vial of Aqua," Millites confirmed.

The two ran out of the trees toward Speilton. When they reached Speilton and the others, they knew that the young king had found the cave. Except, it wasn't a cave.

The entrance was a very old black tree. It was nearly eight feet wide, and probably the most knotted and gnarled tree they had encountered yet. Arrows flew down at them from somewhere in the foliage. Equus and Nicholas stood next to it, firing arrows up into the tree. Metus fought a Calorian down below on the ground, but there was still no sign of the Ore, Ram and Brute.

"Should we go back and look for the others?" Usus asked.

Suddenly, the roots at the base of the old tree began to shift and turn. A dark pit was revealed. "Yes, I found it. I found the entrance!!" Speilton announced.

Ram showed up only a second later. "Come on, now! I can't hold it open much longer!" Speilton called.

"What about the others?" Millites asked.

"We'll be fine, just go!" Nicholas commanded as he shot one of the Calorians out of the tree.

Millites, Usus and Ram began running to the portal.

Suddenly, Speilton looked up to see a Calorian coming at him. His sword was drawn, ready to swing. Speilton shuffled for his sword, but the Calorian was faster. He swung the blade, and...

CRACK!

Brute charged forward between the two, thrashing his head upwards, impaling the Calorian and his metal armor. The two stumbled to the ground, and Brute's right horn snapped clean off.

The moment the satyr hit the ground, his hands went up to check his horns. When his hands reached the small stub, he cried, "NO! My horn. Speilton, YOU OWE ME! Now go before you get killed!"

Brute shoved Speilton backwards into the portal, and he disappeared inside. The other three were there a second later, and they all dove into the portal.

There was a flash, and then a cry of pain from above. Then they were gone.

Immediately, the four felt weightless. None of them were sure if they were falling, or rising, or flying, or just floating. Their bodies felt light and loose, as if they had somehow dissolved into liquid or even vapor. All around them were different colors, both light and dark. They swirled and changed as they swam through the air.

They had just begun getting accustomed to the feeling, when ground suddenly appeared beneath their feet. They fell to the ground, and the lights vanished in a bright flash, leaving them alone in the darkness lying flat on their backs. They stood up, brushing dust off their clothes.

"That was...bizarre," Usus said.

"So, I guess this is inside the cave?" Ram wondered.

They looked around, and slowly their eyes adjusted. They were inside a dark tunnel, carved out of craggy stone. Light spilled from cracks in the rock, throwing blue light into the area giving it an under water feeling.

"So, where do we go now?" Speilton asked peering down the tunnel.

Suddenly, a voice erupted through the air. It creeped from cracks and seeped from the stone. The voice was sly and old, very old.

"Four brave souls. Four different tests. One soul for each. If one soul fails, the other three will be deposited outside the cave. But the failed soul...dies," the voice was thin and cut across the air.

"We die?" Speilton asked as fear slowly began to seep into his body. All four of their hearts sank, and their stomachs churned. It was a feeling they had many times before giving a speech in front of a large crowd. Except this time it was fear from something much worse than embarrassing themselves. It was fear of life or death. If they failed in here, it didn't only end their life, but end their chances of destroying the Inferno and the Calorians.

"Don't worry," Ram told them, trying to urge the bravery back into them. "We will all survive. We've been lucky this far, and I'm sure our luck will not decay when we need it the most."

Despite Ram's words, they still felt dizzy with fear and responsibility. But the General was right. They couldn't stop now.

"So, what happens when we all pass?" Millites called to the disembodied voice that had spoken to them before.

"You gain access to the great Castle of Skilt."

"Fine, then. How do we start?" Ram asked.

A light poured from an archway that suddenly opened at the end of the path. Blue light, like that spilling from the cracks, poured from the doorway and a ghostly fog slowly rolled from the mouth. Above the archway was a blue circle with an eye in the center.

"What's this?" Usus asked.

"The first challenge, agility," the voice said.

"Agility?" Millites echoed.

"I'll go," Usus said.

"But Usus, are you certain you are prepared? We don't know what to expect. Are you sure you want to go first?" Ram asked.

"I have to," Usus answered casually. "We know the other challenges. Battle skill," he gestured to Millites, "Strength," he gestured to Ram, "and Decision," as he pointed to Speilton.

"Are you sure?" Millites asked.

"No, but I have to do it, don't I?" Usus shrugged as he marched up to the doorway.

"Now, what do I do?" Usus called.

"Enter," the voice seethed.

Usus took a step closer and reached out his hand. The blue curtain of light fell around it, and slowly spread up his arm. Behind him, the fog began to swirl up around his body. Speilton, Ram, and Millites saw the blue light encase his arms and torso. The funnel of smoke threw Usus through the archway, as they heard the Second in Command scream. Then, he was gone, and the blue archway collapsed.

Once again, they were left in the darkness.

Usus felt the ground leave his feet, and he tumbled through a sky of blue. The next thing he knew he landed on his back, staring up into oblivion. Slowly, he lifted himself to his feet and glanced around.

To his left was a sheer cliff so deep that it seemed to drop off to an endless pit. Over to his right was a thick, stone bridge that led to the only source of light. Two torches with blue flames stood on either side of an archway, just like the one he had just traveled through.

"Wow, is it really that easy?" Usus asked the air, half expecting the strange voice to hear him. It seemed too simple. He stood on the flat top of a circular rock pillar. A wooden bridge connected him with the portal to get out. *I don't see how this is agility?* Usus thought, "Oh, maybe I have to do backflips or something across it," he wondered sarcastically. He walked forward and was about to step onto the bridge, when he remembered how Ram taught him to be certain that the bridge was secure.

Usus walked over and kicked a chunk of rock off the pillar. He tossed it across the bridge, and the second it touched the stone, cracks quickly appeared. Piece by piece separated from the rest of the bridge. But the chunks of the bridge didn't fall. They hovered in midair, suspended over a deep void.

"Oh, so that's where the agility part comes in," Usus said. "Yeah, I'm not doing backflips on that."

Hundreds of rocks were scattered between him and the portal. Some were tiny, the size of pebbles. Others, about a foot wide. A few were over three feet across which, of course, Usus decided would be the best to use.

Slowly, he rested his foot on the stone hovering closest to him, which was a rock about two feet in diameter. He put a little weight on it, and it still stood strong. He shifted over his other foot, and reached his arms out for balance. The rock didn't tumble from the sky, but instead, it slowly moved away from the rock pillar. Usus squatted so he could balance better. Beneath his shaky feet, the rock floated and moved by the sudden weight Usus applied.

The moving of the rocks was both a good thing and a bad thing. Yes, he was getting closer to the other side, but when he bashed into other rocks, they were knocked away and floated farther out over the void. And, every time he hit a rock, his stone was forced backwards, farther away from the other side.

At one point, he found himself gliding far away from the other rocks, alone in the darkness. As he floated away, another rock suddenly appeared out of the gloom. This one was long, but only half the size of the one he was on now. It was his only chance. If he stayed on this rock, chances were he'd end up sailing on to eternity.

So he lunged forward and grabbed hold of the rock with his hands. It tipped and turned, but he held on, just long enough for it to take him back into the main cluster of stones. As soon as he could, Usus grabbed hold of a different rock. This one was much larger. Usus pulled himself up onto his feet. He knew better than to try to ride one rock to the other side. He needed to go from rock to rock. Usus jumped for another stone and landed on his knees. It was difficult business, leaping over a pit that dropped to oblivion, trying to land without tipping over the edge. Usus made it though from rock to rock. It almost seemed too easy. There had to be a catch.

Usus only had one rock left before he reached the other side, and things were looking pretty good until the rock before him fell out of the sky. Usus could hardly believe it. After making his way through the flying rocks, it was stunning to see a rock fall.

Usus cautiously turned around to see other rocks were falling too. One moment they were there, then they shook violently and dropped. Now was the time to freak out. Would his rock drop? No, no of course not. It wouldn't.

But then, if his didn't drop, all the others would, leaving him on the only one left suspended over death. He had to jump off quickly. The problem was, there weren't any large rocks between him and the other side. Usus could only wait for one to come close.

So he sat there, waiting, waiting, for a rock that would never come. Suddenly, his rock began to rumble beneath his feet. Usus remembered the other rocks had done this, the second before they...

Without hesitation, the Second in Command scrambled to his feet and leapt for the other side. Halfway across, his foot kicked off another rock, the size of a coin, and landed on the other side. For a few minutes all he could do was lay there, panting, and trying to regain his breath. Finally, he pulled himself to his feet and looked back over the void.

Not a single stone was left. Every single chunk of the bridge had fallen down into the abyss. But Usus was safe.

The Second in Command turned away from the cliff and walked up to the mouth of the archway. This time, he let the light swarm around him and shove him into the portal.

"Miss me?" he asked stepping out of the doorway and into the tunnel.

Ram, Millites, and Speilton's eyes were wide with fear as they shrank back away from him. "You... you did it?" Millites questioned.

"Yes. Why are you so surprised?"

"You've only been gone for about ten seconds," Ram responded.

"Ten seconds? It was more like an hour," Usus argued.

"Really?" Speilton asked. "Because we just saw you leave, when suddenly you appeared again."

"Well, maybe time is different in the two worlds," Ram suggested. "To Usus, it could've been an hour, but to us it only was a few seconds."

"Well, at least we don't have to wait very long to find out if we survived," Millites offered.

Suddenly, the light in the mouth of the tunnel changed colors. Gold light spilled from the portal, and the eye changed colors along with it. "Battle skill," the voice announced.

They turned to face the opening. "I guess that's me," Millites muttered.

"Are you ready?" Ram asked.

"Yes," Millites said. "Usus, do you have any suggestions?"

Usus thought for a second, "Head for the portal. And, when you think you've completed the task, and it seems too easy, then it's not yet over."

"Oh, and don't die," Speilton added.

"Thanks, that's really helpful," Millites said sarcastically walking toward the portal.

But he didn't wait for the portal to take him away. Instead, he leapt into the golden light and was whisked away.

The tunnel collapsed, and Millites began the challenge as he found himself on a field of burned grass. He sat up, and quickly noticed the portal sitting on the top of a hill less than a hundred yards away. The golden light spilled down the hill.

The next thing he saw were two turrets sitting a few feet farther down the hill on opposite sides of the portal. They were two stories high, constructed of limestone. They were empty with no one patrolling the edges. In short, Millites knew something was wrong.

Slowly, he approached the towers. But everything remained still and quiet until he touched the side of the turret. *Thunk!* Something struck the ground only feet from him. *Thunk! Thunk!* Two more landed around him.

Millites stepped back and pulled his shield off his back. "Who's there?" Millites called.

In response, dozens of projectiles began falling around him. Just in time, he lifted his shield above his head for protection as three of the objects splattered against it. As they slid off the shield, Millites caught a quick glance at the objects.

"Teeth?" he whispered.

Inch long razor blade teeth fell from the sky and tore into the burned soil. Like tiny arrows, they pelted the ground, tearing up the ground and reflecting off the tower and Millites' shield. Finally, the teeth ceased to fall, leaving the area quiet. Millites let the shield drop to his side and peered out across the field. He looked for the teeth in the soil, but none of them could be found. It was as if they had buried themselves deep in the earth. *Well, that was easy,* he thought.

But as he began walking up the hill to the portal, he remembered Usus's last words. 'When you think you've completed the task and it seems too easy, then it's not yet over.'

At that precise moment, the earth began to rumble. It wasn't a horrible shake that threw him from his feet, but a deep vibration. Millites turned around to see deep gorges forming in the soil. Cracks split through the dirt, and grass and other dead plants toppled into it. The king should've run, but he stayed to watch what was happening.

The gorges grew wider, as more cracks appeared. Dirt erupted into the air, like poisonous gas bubbling out of a swamp. Craters formed, and the place completely tore itself apart.

Then, just as fast as it had started, the shaking stopped, the cracks stopped spreading, and there were no more explosions.

Millites turned to leap in the portal, but found a very unpleasant sight. It was gone.

The king turned, and far away saw the portal. The golden light was hard to see, but he could still make out the distinct shape. It was far down the hill, nearly five hundred feet away, located in between two large gorges.

"Really, a decoy portal?" Millites grumbled.

He began walking back down the hill, when he thought, '*So, what's the catch. This is supposed to be battle skills, and watching ground explode doesn't fit under that category.*'

Millites soon understood the challenge. A sudden explosive noise broke out over the ruined wasteland. It was the roar of a thousand men, screaming a horrible battle cry. The sound was so loud and seemed so close, but Millites couldn't see an army anywhere. The noise abruptly stopped but was replaced by the sound of hundreds of scampering feet. He thought about running to the portal as fast as possible, but wondered if the men could be coming out of there.

That's when the first skeleton appeared. The bony fingers reached out of a gorge and pulled the rest of the body up. Dust and the remains of cloth stretched across the bones like skin. The stretched material layer was so thin, a slowly beating heart could be seen through the chest.

The skeleton wore a metal helmet and held a rusty axe in one hand. Slowly, the demon limped forward, as more of the skeletons appeared. Each one appeared the same: unhinged jaw, deep, eyeless sockets, cracked bones, and the internal organs all intact inside their chests. Each wore armor or held a weapon of some sort.

Millites had no time to think before the skeletons were on him. The first to attack was the skeleton with the axe as it screamed a raspy, ancient voice and held his axe up over his head. Millites met the blow with his sword, then kicked it in the chest. As the skeleton stumbled backwards, his thin cloth layer ripped, and half of the ribs cracked.

A skeleton with a spear leapt forward and stabbed at Millites. The king side-stepped, spun, and caught the demon in the side with his sword.

Another skeleton, wearing a metal eye patch and wielding a bola (a weapon with a spiked ball hanging on the end of a chain) rushed toward him. Millites didn't stay to fight. Instead, he fled to the turret.

Behind him he could hear the skeletons rushing towards him, their bones clattering and cracking. Luckily, the undead weren't very fast, and Millites made it to the top before them. Many more were crawling out of the ground all around him. As the king finally reached the turret he tried to open the door.

"It's locked!" he grumbled kicking at the door furiously. He turned around since he had no other choice, and came face to face with the bola skeleton. Millites rolled to the side as the spiked ball crushed the ground where he'd been only seconds before. Millites struck the skeleton in the arm as the bone splintered and cracked off.

But the demon was quick to react. With his other hand he swung the bola, and Millites only had a second to drop to his knees to survive getting hit. And as the spiked ball soared just over his head, it crashed into the door, shattering the wood to thousands of pieces. Millites struck the skeleton through the chest as it fell back landing sprawled on it's back.

Millites rushed through the broken doorway and raced up the stairs. Behind him, skeletons followed, climbing the stairs to the top. As soon as the king came to the open at the top, he slammed the trapdoor closed and locked it. It didn't take long for the skeletons to reach the door and begin banging away at it. At the center of the turret stood a single pillar about a foot wide, piled with rocks. Millites thought about using the rocks on the pedestal to pelt them as he crossed over the edge of the turret as he peered down at them.

"Oh, no," he whispered with his eyes wide with fear. His stomach plunged even lower than when he first entered the cave. From up here, Millites could see most of the army, but since the portal was the only source of light, many more demons could be hanging in the darkness.

For the time, he was safe from the skeletons. He had time to think about escape.

He recalled that on the Island of the Wizard Council, Cigam told him to remember the old stories of heroes. Was that a clue, or was he just telling him to continue studying or something? But when Millites thought about it, he realized that Cigam was trying to help him prepare for this moment.

Millites thought about all the famous stories he heard as a child from his caretakers and advisors that had raised him. He remembered a story about a witch that could turn people to stone with one glance. There was another about a giant red snake that battled a falcon-headed god through the night. But Millites didn't see how those would help.

Maybe there's a story about a hero that fought skeleton warriors. Then I could destroy these the same way that hero destroyed the warriors. That may be what Cigam had wanted me to do.

There was a story about Heracles, Hourus, Athena, a man named Arthur and a half human creature called Anubis, but nothing had to do exactly with skeletons. But Millites was still sure that at least one story had zombie warriors.

And then, it hit him. Jason, the leader of the Argonauts, had to fight an army of undead warriors to get the golden fleece. The skeletons were created by … dragon teeth. That's what had fallen from the sky! And the teeth created the skeletons.

This was good. Everything was making sense. Now, for the last piece. How did Jason destroy them?

All he could remember was that it was some object, charmed by a witch that helped Jason. But what was the object?

Millites didn't have enough time to figure that out, because at that moment an axe shattered the trap door. The skeletons climbed out and rushed forward. Millites kicked one to the side, chopped one in half, then batted the other over the edge. Three more climbed up onto the top and rushed at Millites. Two of them leaped for his arms and wrapped themselves around them. The other leapt at his chest, knocking the king on his back. His sword skidded away from him, and the three warriors towered over him.

"Goodbye," one of the warriors said holding a weapon to him.

Millites landed a kick right in the skeleton's chest and it tumbled backwards, knocking over the pedestal of rocks. The king jumped to his feet and grabbed a stone from the ground. He tossed it into the skeleton's eye socket, and then reached for another. But it turned out, one was all he needed. As soon as the stone hit the skeleton, the other's attacked him. The three fought viciously for a few seconds, until there was only one left. That skeleton held the stone like it was the most valuable thing in the world.

Even though the sudden fight was strange, Millites quickly recovered and shoved the skeleton over the edge. The warrior fell with the stone still clutched tightly in his hand. As he hit the ground, the rest of the warriors rushed his broken body, destroying whomever was in their way to get the stone.

And that was when the story came back to Millites. He remembered how it ended. The witch gave Jason a stone that had been charmed. When he tossed the stone to the skeletons, the magic caused them to desire it, causing the warriors to attack each other for it. They all fought until no one stood.

Somehow, someway, the challenge was a replica of Jason's fight with the skeletons. Everything in the challenge was set up for the participant to use. He just had to know what to do. And now, Millites understood.

Quickly, he shoved as many rocks as he could inside his pockets. Holding his sword in one hand and a stone in the other, he raced down the stairs. Outside the door was chaotic, but Millites ran out ready for the battle. As soon as he stepped out of the turret, he tossed a rock. Every skeleton in a twenty yard radius took off toward it fighting off any who tried to stop him.

And that's how it went for many minutes. Every few yards or every time Millites came to a large cluster of warriors, the king would throw the rocks, and the once allied skeletons would turn on each other.

Even though he was cautious not to use the rocks unless it was imperative, he found himself fifty feet away from the portal with only one stone left. Millites took off running past warriors taking out as many as possible without slowing down the least bit.

'*Too easy,*' he thought only feet from the portal. And of course, that's when things got harder.

The ground began to shake again. Cracks formed only inches from the mouth of the archway, and one more warrior formed. This one was huge. It was ten feet tall, coated in armor, and holding two bolas, each two times larger than the one wielded by the other warrior.

"This is the final test," the giant skeleton seethed in a voice that was all too familiar. It was the same voice that had directed them inside the cave.

"So this is what you look like, "Millites taunted. "I never expected you to be so... old."

"Feel my wrath," the voice said as it began to spin the spiked balls.

Millites saw the attack coming and was able to dive out of the way as the foot wide bola crushed the ground. Millites jumped backwards as the second ball landed at his feet.

At this point, a small group of skeletons formed to watch the final test. But besides these, there were hardly any more warriors alive. The only survivors were the ones with the stones, or those that had not been involved.

Millites sprang for an attack, but the chain of the bola caught his sword, tossing it from his hands. The king backed away as the giant began spinning the bola again, like an enormous set of deadly nun chucks.

In a flash, he brought one down, inches away from Millites. The next one soared right over his head, and while Millites ducked he pulled out the last of the stones from his pocket. Millites sprang to his feet. The giant skeleton realized what had happened only seconds before the stone landed in his mouth and rolled down his throat.

The rest of the battle was fought by the surviving skeletons, all attacking the giant for the stone. Millites ran for his sword before entering the portal. As the golden light swirled around him and picked him off his feet, the last thing he saw was a skeleton warrior holding up the stone with triumph, before being attacked from behind.

Then, there was a flash of gold light, and he was back in the cave.

ALONE IN THE DARK
~ 22 ~

It was Speilton's turn. The cave mouth turned red and the eye along with it.

"The third challenge is Determination," the voice announced.

"Thanks for trying to kill me!" Millites called back.

Speilton crept closer to the red light that resembled roaring flames. "What should I expect in this challenge?" Speilton asked, facing the portal.

"We don't know," Ram said, walking up behind him. "You'll just have to be brave and strong."

"And determined, apparently," Usus announced, trying to lighten Speilton's spirits.

Just a few days ago, Speilton told Metus to be brave. Now, it was his turn to face his fears and banish the horror from his mind.

"Here, just in case I don't make it through, I want you to have this," Speilton handed Millites the flame wand and the Eye Stone which he had been clutching in his pocket.

"No, Speilton! The wand is yours. You have to keep it," Millites argued.

"But if I don't make it, then my wand will no longer have an owner. I don't want Sinister to be able to get it."

"Speilton, I know you will succeed. I have faith in you. I'll hold onto the Eye Stone but you keep the wand. There's nothing to worry about. You'll see. You'll be back. And who knows, you may need the wand in there."

"Doubt it," Speilton muttered under his breath.

"Good luck," Ram said as he hugged Speilton's shoulders.

"And remember, this is a test of determination. They'll push you to the limit, but don't give in," Usus added.

"Thanks," Speilton said, reaching into the red light.

It wrapped around his body like dozens of snakes. Snakes coated in flames. He was floating, floating, then...the first thing he noticed once touching ground was that all of his weapons were gone. *Good,* he thought, *at least I won't be fighting.*

When he tried to move forward, he noticed his legs felt heavy, and it took extreme effort to move them. It was as if someone had replaced the bottom of his boot with lead.

Moving is out of question, he thought.

But then a shiver went up his back. If he couldn't move or fight, then what was the challenge? Torture? *Oh no.* Speilton was starting to panic. What was going to happen to him?

Then, he looked more closely at where he was standing. And in that second, he knew it was going to be much worse than torture. He'd been here, in a dream, a dream that still haunted him to this day.

The long hallway was dark and cold. There were windows along the side, but no light came through. At the end of the hallway was a door about twenty yards away. An eerie, blue light was the only thing that lit the way, but the source of it was unknown. Speilton took a step forward, and everything shook as if it would collapse. Then it stopped. He took another step forward and again everything shook. In the distance he could hear a tapping noise coming from … everywhere. It grew louder and louder until Speilton noticed that it wasn't a tap, but a laugh - a horrible laugh coming from all around him, filling his mind. It wasn't just one laugh, but thousands, all high pitched and cold! Then, they all stopped.

The Inferno of Erif

A cold breeze crept through the hallway and extinguished the light. In the pitch blackness, small red eyes loomed from the windows. He heard footsteps walking down the hallway and wanted to run, but he couldn't. He seemed to be running in the air. Then, as though it had never stopped, the laughing came back. The light appeared again, and he noticed he was even farther down the hall than before, and now about forty yards away from the door. On the other side of the hallway he saw a boy. He suddenly noticed that the boy had the same eyes, the same hair and nose, the same mouth, the same…everything that he had. He was looking at himself or a reflection or a twin of himself.

The other boy silently strolled up the hallway with his face growing darker and darker the closer he got to Speilton. A splash of black, as dark as the bottom of an endless pit, began to coil onto his face, turning the face into a Calorian. In a few seconds the figure was inches away from Speilton's face.

Speilton wanted to run far away, but couldn't move as the laughing stopped and a cruel voice echoed from everywhere.

"Join me, and I will spare you and your friends. Join the Calorians, and you won't die. We'll protect you and your friends. You could be a hero."

Speilton clenched his fists and looked the Calorian in the eyes, "No. I will never join you!" he said with as much bravery as he could muster.

The Calorian smiled, and at this point the dream changed. A cloud of smoke suddenly erupted around the Calorian's face. As it slowly drifted away, the Calorian's face tuned into Sinister. The man grew taller, more muscular. "Are you sure about that Speilton?" Sinister asked. "I thought you were wise. I thought you knew the difference between bravery and foolishness."

"What do you mean?" Speilton asked.

"Fighting for the Milwarians is not brave. You're a fool to fight for a dying cause. In the end do you want to be remembered as the boy who died for Milwaria or the boy who *lived* for Caloria?"

"I'm a Milwarian. And I'll always be a Milwarian," Speilton announced. Suddenly, the three Versipellis appeared behind Sinister. The Dark King smiled as he saw Speilton's face in shock.

"The Versipellis are on our side, Speilton," Sinister said. "And if you joined us, they could end your curse."

Speilton's throat went dry. "You could end the curse?"

"Of course!" the Versipellis growled.

"And you wouldn't hurt my family or my friends."

"They will remain unharmed."

"And the Sword of Power. Will you give it back to the Milwarians?" Speilton pleaded.

Sinister's smile suddenly dropped, and his eyes became dark and fierce. "That is not part of the offer. I am now the owner of the Sword, and its allegiance has change. Even if I gave it to the Milwarians, it wouldn't work."

"You've already unlocked it?" Speilton asked with his heart racing.

"Not yet. All I need is the blood of the beast. Then, I will be the master."

"No, don't harm Burn! " Speilton suddenly gasped, realizing what he'd just said.

"Burn? So that's the beast that will unlock Ferrum Potestas?" Sinister's grin returned, more devious and deadly than ever.

"You must promise not to harm him," Speilton commanded.

"Do not worry, King Speilton. Once you have joined us, you will be glad that I have the

Sword. You will be happy that your...leader, has possession of the most powerful weapon."

There was silence as Speilton thought it all over. Everything that the Versipellis were suggesting crossed through his mind, *'Milwaria is dying,' he recalled the* Versipellis say. '*In two years, it'll be nothing more than a barren wasteland. Believe us.'*

Speilton looked at the four rulers of darkness as Sinister reached out his hand. "Do you wish to die?" Sinister asked, "Or do you wish to live...forever?"

Speilton looked at Sinister's hand. The whole scene had become so real. Speilton no longer remembered where he was or how he got there. Yet he didn't even wonder about it. All he knew was that here he was, faced with an opportunity that may never come to him again.

His mind was so focused on the future that he hardly had anytime to think about the present. And right now, the future was a choice of either living or dying.

"No one else will die?" Speilton asked.

"No one else will die," Sinister responded, sticking his hand out further.

Slowly, cautiously, Speilton reached out his hand, too.

Suddenly a flash of golden light appeared to whisk by, just outside one of the windows. Speilton was suddenly reminded of his mission and what would happen if he made this decision.

But this time, the light was too late. Sinister's hand wrapped around his. Speilton had already committed to the Calorians. All of the lights turned off. As the ground dropped away underneath him, there was a scream. Speilton wasn't sure if it was his or someone else's. Then there was laughing, a deep, horrific laughing that echoed through his body.

And in that instant, Speilton had failed his task. Immediately, the other three were deposited outside the cave.

Four brave souls. Four different tests. One soul for each. If one soul fails, the other three are deposited outside the cave. But the failed soul...dies.

"I'm dead! Oh, I'm dead," Speilton muttered.

Darkness surrounded him. There was no light. Not a single noise or a single peek of light. Just darkness. Darkness enveloped him as the only thing around him besides the hard stone floor.

"No, you're not dead...yet," a voice said.

The voice was young, and fresh, but horribly scratched. It came so abruptly from the silence, Speilton jumped. He reached for his sword, his shield, something to protect him, but they were all gone. "Weapons can't help you here. Trust me, I've tried."

Speilton stopped fidgeting and remained silent. "How did you-"

"Know you were reaching for your weapons that you do *not* have?" the voice responded. "I can see you."

"Prove it," Speilton called to the darkness.

"Really, you want me to prove that I can see you. Fine, you have dark brown hair, not very long. Your eyes are...wait, I can't see them. Oh, green. You're wearing a simple brown shirt, and forest green pants. Both of which are torn in many places."

"Okay, so you can see me," Speilton agreed. "Now, where am I, and who are you?"

"As for where you are, right now, you're sitting in a prison cell, deep down under Skilt."

"I'm in a cell? No, no, I'm supposed to be dead. I failed the challenge. I should be dead."

"No, unfortunately you're just trapped here," the voice stopped. "Regarding your second question, who am I? I am the person-who's-been-sitting-down-in-this-prison-for-over-half-a-year! No, that's not really my name. That, I'm not going to tell you. First, you have to tell me who you are."

"Me?"

"Well, you are the only other person here. Besides me, and long deceased Dane over there."

"   "I'm… King Lux. "

"Seriously? Aren't you a little young to be a King?" the man stopped to chuckle.

"I am a King. You have to trust me."

"Well, you can't be a king since I've never heard of you," the voice said stubbornly. "If you're a king, how did you end up down here in this vault?"

"I don't know really. I was supposed to - "

"Be dead. Yes, you told me," said the voice.

Now, Speilton was starting to get annoyed. "So, if you know so much, tell me what you saw. If I don't know how I came here, then how did you see me appear?"

"I didn't. I was asleep when there was a loud crash. The next thing I knew, you were lying there unconscious."

Speilton thought for a second, devising a plan. "Fine. I'll tell you my story, or at least what I know. Then you tell me how you got here, and help me escape."

"Go ahead, but just so you know, there is no escape from here."

Speilton excused those last words, not letting the creeping feeling of confinement overrun him.

Speilton began his tale, "Half a year ago, I lived in a village called Lorg on the island of Kal."

"Kal?" the man whispered under his breath.

"Yes," Speilton continued. "One day, I went out . . . to shoot a deer for my people, but when I returned, Lorg was on fire. Everything, was falling apart. My own house was caved in, my mother was missing, and my best friend's house was destroyed, too. Everything I had ever known was smoldering under the flames."

Suddenly, the voice drew in a sharp breath. "What?" Speilton asked, hoping that the man wasn't only faking his affection.

"Wait a second," the voice whispered with excitement and fear. "Is ... is your name Speilton?"

"How did you know that?" Speilton wondered.

"Speilton, it's me, Faveo."

Speilton couldn't say a thing. For a second, he thought that the man was only trying to annoy him, but when he thought about it, it seemed very unlikely. "Faveo? Is that...really you?"

"Speilton, it is you!" the man who claimed to be Faveo announced, "I can't believe you survived. When I heard you had gone out into the woods, I was sure you would never come back."

"I can't believe *you're* alive!" Speilton announced, "I finally shot a deer and as I was going back to Lorg, I saw the flames. I ran through the village but everything had crumbled to the ground. I didn't see any living thing, except for Saul, the old man that lived close to my house. You won't believe this, but he was a wizard."

"A wizard? That's a new development," Faveo said, considering the possibility.

"So you're saying that you believe me? You trust me even after all this time?"

"Speilton, I have seen things and experienced horrors that I could only have gone through in a nightmare. These...creatures came and attacked Lorg. Our men were all slaughtered, and those of us who had survived were enslaved. The creatures threw us in here."

"There are more of you?" Speilton began, optimistically.

"There were, but now I'm the last one. Well, except for you. Anyway, my point is that I've been through ... so much. Right now, anything I hear, no matter how crazy it sounds, I am forced to believe it.

Just one day I hope all the pieces will fit together."

"Well, keep believing everything you hear, because I know the complete story. I know everything that has happened."

Speilton told about his journey, meeting Ram, fighting Sinister on the boat, saving Kon Malopy, and discovering that he was a king.

"My real name is Visvires Lux, though please, I like Speilton better."

"Is it true?" Faveo asked, "Are you really, truly a king?"

"I know, it sounds unbelievable, but it's true."

"Then I guess, I must believe you," Faveo said. "How did you end up here?"

Speilton began the rest of his story. He told Faveo how he slowly became accustomed to becoming a King, how they went to Rilly's hut and got their mission, their battle at the Island of the Wizard Council, and then Millites' kidnapping.

"So all of this is true? You've fought battles and slain beasts all this time, while I've only been sitting down here?"

"Ever since the attack, you've been down here?" Speilton asked.

"Yes. There were four others from the village that kept me company. There was the old baker, and Dane, who lived next door to me, one of the builders, and a hunter who I'd only seen a few times. They had all been wounded in battle and did not survive down here for long. So how'd you end up here?"

Speilton was about to begin again, when he remembered something. The Vial of Aqua. The other three had been destroyed, but not his. He reached for the necklace, and there it was, still there.

At least it hadn't been taken. It wasn't a weapon, so didn't pose a threat. Speilton excitedly explained to

Faveo, "This is the Vial of Aqua that I told you about. With this vial I can destroy the Inferno of Erif and end the war."

"Speilton, no offense, but I really don't care about the war. It has only destroyed Kal and gotten me stuck in prison. And, by what you've told me, it doesn't seem like it will end in Milwaria's favor. To be honest, I don't really care who wins, because in the end, I'll still be stuck down here."

"Well, Faveo, I care, and so do thousands of Milwarians and every person risking his life to fight."

"Speilton, but why should I help Milwaria? I was born and raised in Caloria. I've never even seen Milwaria. Why should I help them when they haven't done anything to help me?" Faveo questioned.

Speilton was taken back by Faveo's words. This cell and all the pain he had suffered had changed him, turned him against everyone. All he wanted was to live. "Well, Faveo, haven't you ever thought about a world ruled by darkness and evil? Don't you care about other people in the generations to come?"

"I did care, once," he paused, as he was reminded of a horrible thought. "You may not have seen the villagers after the battle, but I encountered them, firsthand. I saw them injured, and saw the flames tear up into the sky. I saw my parents, your mother, and friends and neighbors, slaughtered at the hands of the Calorians. Now, I can't really feel sympathy for anyone but me."

"Faveo, I know that must have been very hard for you to go through."

"Oh, I'm sure. But you could never know what it was like down here in prison. I had to watch, yet again as my only friends died away. Dane was the last to die, and since then I have been alone.

Luckily, that's when a new Calorian began feeding me. This Calorian wasn't nearly as savage as the one before. The second Calorian guard felt sorry for me and told me his story. He told me how the Calorians are mistreated. They're abused by their own kind. It's horrible. The Calorians aren't even allowed names. The Calorian disagreed with Sinister. He told me the horrible things Sinister had done, the unfairness of the corrupt government ruled by this dictator, and how one day, he sought to over throw it.

I told him my story, too, and in return, he gave me additional food. Every day, he risked his life hoping to keep me alive.

And then one day, I heard someone coming. But once this Calorian came into view, I saw it wasn't him.

The Calorian held a knife with smoke coiling from the blade. I shrank to the far side of my cell as the creature's eyes stared into mine.

'Too bad, what happened to your friend,' he sneered. 'He was overheard speaking against the king.'

"After that day no one has come down here. They excused me as dead, and I was soon forced to drink the water that leaks from the ceiling. I eat, well, you don't really want to know." Faveo concluded.

"I'm sorry about what you had to go through, but..." Speilton didn't know what to say. Faveo had been imprisoned by an enemy he had never even known he had. Speilton understood his hopelessness.

So how could he encourage this boy, this boy who had once been his best and only friend, this boy who was struggling to stay alive.

Speilton knew that if *he* was to stay alive - if Milwaria was to stay alive - he would need Faveo. The prisoner knew the way out, if there was one and could see in the darkness.

"Faveo, if you help me escape, if you help me rejoin the army alive, I promise you I will make sure you are once again granted a life and family. You could live at Kon Malopy with me. I would do anything in my power to make sure that you could live with out fear."

"So you really are a king, aye? Well then, tell me how a King ended up in a jail like this."

Speilton finished the story, all the way to when he grabbed Sinister's hand, and subsequently fell into this cell.

"And that's all I know. Technically, I should be dead after failing."

"But you're not dead, which means some force is working against it. Either you have been given a second chance, leading you to victory, or Sinister has tampered with it and is trying to direct you to him."

"Let's just hope it's the former," Speilton said, and for the first time in years, Faveo laughed. It was weak and hoarse, like the clanging of rusty chains, but the feeling was still the same for Speilton's old friend.

They remained silent for a few moments, pulling their minds back on track. "So, you know this place better than anyone. Is there any way to escape?"

"Well, there are doors that lead out. The main one is over there to your left, but our jail bars are too thick to allow us to get there."

"Is there any other door out."

"There is another, used many years ago. In the beginning, the Calorians set up a network of paths that crossed over all the cells. These paths are ten feet above us and used to be monitored. They put up the wooden bridge, to allow the guards to watch everything in the cells. They could also throw down food from there. It actually wasn't that bad of an idea, until the prison itself began falling apart. Then, prisoners began throwing stones that had fallen from the walls up at the guards. After that, the bridges were retired, and the guards just came into the room."

"That seems too easy of a way to escape."

"You're right. There is a catch. Underneath the wooden planks are spikes so that if someone tried to climb out, they'd run straight into blades."

"Couldn't you lift someone up onto the wooden areas?"

"Oh, it was possible, but we never got the chance. By the time the wooden planks were retired, there were only three of us left. One of my jail mates tried climbing it, but was caught and terminated. After that, it was just me and Dane. Our cells were separated, and helping each other was impossible. But our cells are next to each other."

"So do you think you can push me up onto the ledge?"

"Only if you come back for me."

"It's a deal," Speilton agreed, hopeful for the first time since entering this prison.

"Oh, wait, what about the spikes? How are we supposed to get through those?"

"I've got that covered. For a while, I've been carving a tool out of a piece of the rock wall. I think its finally perfect."

"Okay," Speilton went over the plan. "So you raise me up, and I remove the spikes with your stone tool. Then I pull my self up onto the bridge ... and then what?"

"Well, the guards used a door just past the bridge to store their weapons, and, if we're lucky, extra keys."

Speilton agreed to try the escape.

"So, are you ready?" Faveo asked.

"Definitely ready to get out of here, but I just wish it were easier to see."

Speilton had become accustomed to the darkness. He could barely see in it at all, but he'd come to expect it. "Do you have any source of light?" Faveo asked.

"No, but my shield would've really come in use if it hadn't been taken. All I have left is... oh, wait, I do have a torch, the last one," Speilton pulled out his pack and reached deep inside. There it was, the last torch along with his flint and steel. "You may want to look away," Speilton said lighting the flame.

"Where can I put the torch?" he asked Faveo.

"Here, just give it to me," he said, taking the torch in one hand while shielding his eyes with the other. Faveo tucked it into a gap in the metal bars where the light could easily spread across the room.

Speilton could now see the man. He had long black hair, a pale, white face, sunken cheeks, and wild eyes. It was his friend.

"Let's go," Faveo said, shoving his arms through the metal bars and into Speilton's cell. Faveo positioned his hands into a table for Speilton to stand on. The king propped one leg on the arm, then pushed off the ground, grabbing hold of the bars. "Ready," Speilton announced.

Faveo slowly raised his arms, lifting Speilton higher into the air. When he got high enough, Speilton began chipping away at the deadly spikes. One by one, they fell to the ground.

It was unsettling to balance while knocking away the enormous blades. But finally, Speilton had chipped away enough for him to pass. "Okay, I'm ready. Now give me a boost." Speilton was thrown a foot higher into the air which was all he needed. He gripped the edge of the wood board, and pulled himself up onto the bridge. "Thanks, I'm up,"

"Good, so now go left down that board then take a right."

Speilton crawled across the board lessening his risk of falling unless the bridge broke. But nothing bad happened. Speilton reached the door with Faveo's instructions in only a few minutes. He stepped into the dark room, and once again fell into darkness. The torch's light couldn't reach him here.

Speilton scaled the room, using his hands to guide him. The room was cluttered with swords and shields and bows and arrows, all strewn across the floor. Cobwebs filled almost every square inch of the room that wasn't already occupied by dust and mites. Speilton raced his hands across the walls searching and finally touched a round ring covered in keys.

"I've got it!" Speilton called, "I found the keys!"

"Yes! I can't believe it! We did it!" Speilton rushed out of the room and slowly climbed down the metal bars onto the main hallway. From here, all of the doors could be unlocked, and that's precisely what he did. Faveo flew from the prison, overjoyed to be a free man.

Though, they were far from being free. Ahead of them were more troubles to come. Their lives would be at risk every second in the world above. Because, even though they'd escaped the prison, they were still in Skilt.

They fled through the doorway and up the stairs. The paths were dark and silent since they'd left the torch because it would've drawn too much attention.

They came to a large room with doorways covering the walls. Between each door was a staircase leading down. Speilton had no doubt that each of the rooms were filled with prison cells. "Wait, Faveo, should we stop and let out the other prisoners?"

"SHHH!" Faveo put his finger to his lips. "Just because my prison was no longer watched doesn't mean all the others aren't."

They crossed through the room and went up another staircase. Up and up the stairs they traveled the many levels of the jail. Finally, the stairs ended, and they were at an intersection of wide hallways.

Every wall was made of black stone, covered in cobwebs and cracks. Burned draperies and banners hung next to intricate torches along the wall. "So, where exactly are we going?" Speilton asked.

"I don't know," Faveo answered.

"I say we continue this direction for now. We'll at least know which way we came," Speilton suggested.

"Good enough."

They walked along the deserted hallway that seemed endless as they walked. Paintings of ruthless Calorian kings and bloody battles covered the walls. As they continued they heard a distant noise. As it got closer, they realized it was hundreds of feet dragging across the floor, and the clanging of chains.

"That can't be good," Speilton said.

"It may be going away from us. We don't need to jump to conclusions so fast."

But as they continued walking, the noises got louder and louder. Along with the noises from before was a horrible groaning, the crack of a whip, and a few people screaming orders.

"What's happening?"

Faveo turned even paler than before. "Prisoners. The Calorians are bringing in prisoners."

Speilton was silent as he let the thought sink in. "Then that's why no Calorians are out here. They're all herding the prisoners to the dungeons."

"Which means they're coming this way!" Faveo realized.

Up ahead, a shadow began to creep into view. The Calorians and the prisoners were entering, and would be on them in only a few seconds. "Over there," Faveo pointed, "There's a door!"

They rushed to the narrow hallway as the Calorians were growing closer by the second. Speilton could only hope that the prisoners didn't round the corner before they were safely inside.

Faveo yanked open the door, and they scurried inside. Speilton gently closed the door and they both threw themselves against the wall, not even daring to breathe.

Outside, the Calorians passed, screaming at the prisoners as their chains rattled and the whip snapped.

Finally, as the sound died away, they exhaled. "That was close!" Speilton announced, but then saw Faveo's face.

He was staring, open mouthed, straight ahead. Speilton followed his gaze, and soon saw it, too.

They were in a small room that seemed to be used for storage. Wood planks, cinder blocks, old furniture, used torches, cobwebs, and a Calorian were in the room. He had been asleep, but after Speilton's outburst, he was wide awake.

The Calorian held a long, curve-bladed scimitar. "You aren't supposed to be in here," the Calorian grumbled.

Faveo suddenly dropped to his knees. "What are you doing? You have to help me," Speilton pleaded.

The next second was a blur. Faveo leapt back to his feet, a rock clutched in his hand. Then, the prisoner pulled back his arm and hurled the stone at the Calorian's head. The warrior collapsed to the ground, either unconscious or dead. Speilton couldn't tell.

The next second was even more strange. Faveo scrambled across the room and grabbed the scimitar. Then he turned and held the blade out at Speilton. "This is where I leave."

"Are you crazy? I saved your life, now you're going to destroy me?"

"I'm not going to hurt you, Speilton. *I* just want to live and going on this suicide mission won't help my chances."

"Faveo, don't be a coward! How can you think about yourself now?"

"You know, maybe that's because I'm alone in this world. You are a Milwarian and you have a family. You have an entire country at your disposal. Me? I have nothing but the clothes I wear. This is your war, Speilton, not mine. I can not help you."

"But Faveo, you could come back with me! You could have a new life."

"Yeah, but what if we don't make it out. What if we die. Speilton, you have a family, and friends, who will all mourn over you. But I'll have no one, no one that cares or even knows who I am. I will have been forgotten forever, while you will forever be remembered. I can't die that way." Faveo said.

"Well, I care. I care about you as my friend. And I also care about everyone in Milwaria. That's why I have to do this."

"Then you're going to have to do it with out me."

Faveo turned away and scoured the Calorian's body for anything useful. He found a map, a ring of keys, and took the warrior's helmet.

"Wait, Faveo, if you're going to go, at least give me the map."

"Yeah, and risk getting lost myself? No thank you."

"Can I at least look at it?"

"Fine. I'm not unreasonable, but expect this to be the last favor you ever get. I've got to get out of here quickly."

Faveo handed him the map. Speilton unrolled it and began to study.

Skilt had four outer walls, and just like Kon Malopy there were four towers connecting them. A draw bridge was the only way out, since a moat of molten lava circled the castle. There was a central tower, not as tall as Sky Tower, but it had a thick base and a thin tower on top.

Located close to where he stood was the Treasury Room. Chances were, he'd find weapons there.

Finally, he found the Inferno of Erif on the map. It was located two stories up and a fair distance away. Oddly, there was something surrounding it that was only labeled with a symbol. Whatever it was, Speilton knew he'd have to go through it.

"Okay, okay, that's enough time," Faveo pulled the map away and shoved it in his pocket.

"One last thing before I leave. I don't mean to abandon you, but you must understand that I have to start a new life. I'm sorry, but this is what *I* must do."

Then he left, running down the hallway.

Speilton sat down on a broken, moldy bench, stunned. Now he was alone, in the most dangerous area in all of Liolia. Before, he'd been glad that at least there was someone else there with him. But now, he felt open, vulnerable, and mostly lost.

His hands began to get cold and clammy, and even though it was cold inside the castle, sweat began to drip from his scalp. Tears began to form in his eyes as he felt incredible disappointment in the one true friend he thought he had. Was there anyone he could truly trust?

The weight of the mission pressed on him. He was going to die, no doubt, or get thrown into a prison for the rest of his life. And then, he realized what would happen to so many others if he did not survive. If he failed, there would be no way to stop the Calorians. Milwaria would be unable to continue the war.

The fate of the world weighed down on his shoulders. It was a feeling that he couldn't explain. Worse than pain, more terrifying than the worst nightmare. And, it was a burden he couldn't share with anyone else. No, he had to do it alone. There was no other way.

Slowly, he rose to his feet, trying to keep himself from falling apart. Clenching his fists, he opened the door and stepped out into the hallway. Speilton began running down the hallway, passing the corridor the prisoners had passed. He continued down the hallway listening carefully for any activity.

Speilton took a right down a smaller hallway, then a left at an intersection. And there it was, a tall wooden doorway covered in gold leaf. Speilton approached it and put his ear to the door. On the other side he could hear stomping. *Maybe they're guards.* Speilton thought.

But there were too many feet. There had to be twenty, at least. "Men! Bank right." The footsteps shifted pace, and began growing louder.

They're coming this way! Speilton realized.

Slowly, he peeked through the crack in the doorway and saw a squad of Calorians marching toward him. Speilton threw himself against the wall. He was sure one of the warriors had seen him since, for a split second, they had held eye contact. Now, Speilton could only wait for the Calorians to rush him before he could even retrieve his weapons. "Men!" Speilton waited to hear the word, *charge!* "Men, halt!"

What? Speilton exhaled as the stomping ceased. *Maybe the Calorian hadn't seen me.*

"Sir, I saw a human over there!" one Calorian shouted out.

Speilton went numb. He *had* been seen. Suddenly, there was the crack of a whip, followed by a yelp. "You may not speak unless given permission. Understand?" the commander screamed.

"Yes, sir," the Calorian moaned.

The commander walked around the squad, and pointed a finger at one of them. "You, go check outside."

Speilton heard a warrior run forward, and swiftly ducked behind the door as it opened. The Calorian glanced around, then walked back inside. "There's nothing outside, sir" the Calorian announced.

"Of course," the commander drooled. "Men, attention. Forward march!"

The Calorian squad marched forward and exited through the doorway. Speilton pressed his back against the open door as the men passed. If one turned around, they just might see him standing there.

But as the group marched away, Speilton was feeling optimistic. Until...

"You there," the commander pointed at a warrior. "Close the door. And you over there, make certain that it is bolted."

Speilton's heart leapt up into his throat. The two turned around and began walking towards the doors and towards him. They didn't seem to notice him, but once the doors were closed, he was sure to be caught.

Speilton had to think quickly. There were a few stones on the ground at his feet. He reached down and picked one up as the two Calorians reached the open doors. The first went around to the left door and began pushing it closed. Then, the other came to his door.

The Calorian didn't have a second to be surprised, before Speilton smashed the stone into the side of the warriors head. As the Calorian slumped to the ground, unconscious, Speilton caught him to avoid any loud clatter and gently laid him on the ground.

He picked up the wounded warrior's staff, then with all of his courage came from behind the right side door. Just as the other Calorian closed the left door, Speilton struck him in the chest, and he collapsed to the ground.

This time Speilton didn't try to catch the Calorian, but instead ran through the doors into the Treasury. He looked back only for a second to see the rest of the Calorian squad marching away, unaware of what had happened.

Inside the doors was a large room with exits on both the left and right of Speilton that were bolted shut. Directly in front of him was a tall archway with ancient letters etched across the ridge. Through the archway Speilton saw a vast room with mounds of sparkling, glittering jewels and gold.

Speilton could not believe the piles of stolen treasure the Calorians had amassed as he stepped into the Treasury.

Speilton half expected a guard to rush out and attack him, but since the castle was already protected so well it wasn't necessary for the room to be constantly guarded. The thick bolted doors would keep out any unwanted guests, but even still, Speilton had foiled the rooms protection.

The Treasury was a large room stuffed with mounds and mounds of gold, jewels and valuables. A single flaming chandelier hung from above, lighting the entire area. The sparkle from the flames caught the gold and jewels, throwing light across the room.

As Speilton entered, he knew that finding his shield, sword, and wand in here would be nearly impossible. He approached the gold and reached his hand into a pile of coins. He brought up his hand, watching the coins slip through his fingers. *All of this could be yours...* the voice of the Versipellis whispered inside his brain.

Speilton shuttered in fear as he glanced around. He wasn't sure, but he thought he saw the tip end of a black cloak disappearing over the edge of a mound of gold.

He cast away the last coin and continued into the room. *If you joined us, it could be yours.*

"No!" Speilton whispered. "I'll never join you."

That's not what you said in the tunnel. You gave up in there when you reached out your hand to us.

"That wasn't me. That isn't what I wanted." Speilton was growing weak as he collapsed to his knees. Speilton shut his eyes closed and clenched his fist. *You could be great. You could be King here. Worshipped and feared by a nation. A nation that won't fall. Ever.*

An image appeared before him like the eye of the Versipellis floating in a ball of flames. Fire raced across the pupil, searing the eye. Somehow it seemed to be feeding the eye, causing it to grow stronger.

'*Join us…. Join us… Join us…*' the voice repeated over and over again.

"No, no, never!" Speilton muttered.

He stumbled to the ground landing flat on a disk as bright as the sun. Speilton broke away from the Versipellis' grip, and opened his eyes only to be blinded by the radiance of his shield.

His shield! Speilton opened his eyes again and saw it was true. He had fallen onto his shield, and only a few inches away was his rusty sword. Speilton picked up the shield and strapped it to his arm as he reached for his sword with the other hand. As Speilton turned to the door, he saw his wand.

Millites should've kept it. Why had he trusted Speilton enough to give him the wand in the cave? Now Millites probably regretted it.

Then, he realized that the others must think he's dead since he didn't return from his challenge. The others must have been deposited outside of the cave, left to wonder what had become of Speilton. Hopefully, the Milwarian army had reached the clearing in the forest by now, and they could join them. News of his 'death' would cause chaos. They were all probably mourning him this second. If only they knew.

Speilton knew he couldn't trust the wand, but he also knew he couldn't leave it. He reached down, picked it up, and shoved it deep into his pocket.

That's when the next round of Calorians showed up. "What happened here?" he heard the commander ask after they entered one of the side doors. The mass of Calorians marched over to the open doorway littered with the bodies of the Calorians.

Speilton concealed himself behind a mound, then slowly peered around to observe that the squad found the unconscious bodies of the guards in the open doorway.

"We've been breached!" the commander announced. "Men, go check the Treasury. You two, stay back and don't allow anyone to escape."

The Calorians rushed into the room and broke up into many groups. Speilton slid down the hill of gold. He needed to escape, but the only open exit was guarded. If he stayed here much longer he was sure to get caught.

I have no choice but to fight them all! Speilton decided, then realized that if he attacked them, an alarm was sure to go off and then every Calorian would be after him. He had to sneak out, quickly.

"Hey, up here! " a Calorian called from just a few feet away. Speilton quickly buried his legs in the treasure and held the shield over his head.

Speilton heard the Calorian approach. "I think he's right down here." Speilton clenched his teeth and hoped the Calorian wouldn't see him.

Suddenly, the warrior tumbled down the hill, rolling down to the bottom. Speilton dared to take a glance and saw the Calorian rubbing furiously at his eyes.

Of course! The shield burned the Calorian's eyes. That would be his opportunity to escape.

Speilton pulled himself out of the pile and slid down to the base. Then, he held the shield on his right side to blind and protect himself from any

Calorian as he quietly crept by the wall sneaking by easily.

Finally, the wall turned and Speilton followed it a short distance before reaching the archway where he stopped. His plan was far from easy or even possible, but Speilton had no other choice. He would flash the shield in the Calorian guard's eyes, and while they were distracted, Speilton would slip by through the open door. It all depended on the Calorians seeing the shield, and light catching the shield at the right time.

If not timed perfectly, there was a huge chance he'd be seen and the warriors would recognize him. Speilton was cautious, hoping the Calorians would see the shield. Speilton held the round disk of light out in the doorway, waiting for the warriors to see it. But the longer he waited, the less likely it seemed. As Speilton waited he began to hyperventilate. At any second, a Calorian could walk up.

"Ah, there's nothing here." Speilton heard a Calorian announce from deep inside the Treasury.

Speilton thought that he would certainly be caught in only a matter of seconds.

But then, "Argh," one of the guards stumbled to the ground.

"What's wrong?" the other asked, rushing to the fallen Calorian's side.

That's when Speilton lunged forward and ran past the two warriors and through the doors. He quickly rounded a corner outside, and darted away from the Treasury. Speilton continued running, not daring to stop to breathe. He turned random corners, hoping to get as far away from the Calorians as possible.

Finally, he stopped to rest inside another storage room. Thankfully, this one didn't have a sleeping Calorian. Speilton sat down on a stack of wooden planks, and inhaled sharply to catch his breath.

The worst still lay ahead, and he knew it. Now he had weapons and ways to defend himself, though he still felt just as vulnerable. He had a mission and couldn't back down now - not after all that had been sacrificed and all the lives that had been lost for this moment.

Speilton clutched the vial of Aqua that hung around his neck. It was their last hope. Though it was such a small object, it could be the difference in life or death for so many.

He breathed in deeply, then carefully peered out of the room. After a short glance around, he began running down the hallway. Speilton concentrated on what he could recall from the map. While escaping from the Treasury, he'd taken many random paths. Now, he wasn't sure which way he should go to the Inferno. All he could remember was that he had to go up two floors. A good place to start would be finding some stairs.

After winding through several narrow passageways and into a larger corridor, Speilton finally found a staircase and darted up two levels. At the top, he didn't have to wonder which way to go. The path led directly ahead with no other options. There were no doorways littering the walls. The entire area was an endless hallway that turned and wove through the castle. Speilton ran on his tiptoes down the path, listening carefully for any sounds of oncoming Calorians. If anyone appeared, there would be nowhere for him to hide.

But when Speilton rounded the next corner, everything changed. There was no longer silence or emptiness. The air was stiff and hot, and reeked of smoke. Shouting and screams rang through the air, and the path was no longer endless. There was a dead end with smaller paths on every side of him leading to dozens of rooms. And from the doorway on his left, came an orange-red light that could only be cast from a fire. But this fire was too large and full to be a torch. It could only be … the Inferno of Erif.

Speilton slowly moved toward the path when the horrible pained shouting began again. A group of Calorians suddenly bustled through one of the doors. A tall, muscular Calorian stood behind them, cracking a whip at their backs. "Keep moving!"

Speilton whipped around the turn in the hallway and flattened himself against the wall. Had he been seen? Surely one of the dozens of Calorians saw him?

Speilton held his breath waiting for the Calorians to com after him, but the leader proceeded to herd them into the room on the opposite side of the hallway.

"Now we'll determine whether you're warrior material," the leader announced. "Defend yourselves if you want to live."

They all disappeared into the room. Speilton cautiously rounded the corner and continued down the hallway entering the room that the Calorians had just exited. He knew that at least one of the guards from this room was gone. There was no one there, but he found a desk in the center littered with pages of paper. Speilton glanced at one page in particular. It was a map but not of the castle.

Speilton continued looking around the room and realized that he was in a registration area where the Calorians were documented and sorted. The pages on the desk seemed to classify the most likely and least likely warrior categories.

Across the hallway in the training room, the Calorians first had to prove themselves worthy to be warriors. And next to that, somewhere out of view was...

Speilton gulped as he read the words. A scream echoed from somewhere to his right. "The Execution Room," Speilton whispered, "where those who fail the test finally rest," Speilton read.

For a second, Speilton imagined himself living the life of a Calorian where the first few minutes of life may be your last. You're born without a name, without an identity and are dead to the world. And then, even if you survive the first trial you are still destined to die for the cause of another. Tossed into war like a dull arrow, you must do whatever necessary to survive.

Speilton shook the thought away and looked back at the map. There it was, the Inferno of Erif, just a few steps away.

Speilton closed his eyes and wrapped his hand around the vial, the last hope. This was it - the final moment. Speilton crossed the room and opened the door.

The heat of the Inferno overwhelmed him, but Speilton had to continue. Forcing each step, Speilton moved in where flames took up almost every inch of the room. They danced across the walls and spurted from the ground. All around the room were more doors that most likely led to more rooms like the one he'd just left.

But at the time, Speilton was entranced by the fire in the very center. Ram once told him, very long ago, that the Calorian flames look like any other except, if you looked closely, you could barely see the face of the Calorian.

But this was much different. The inferno of Erif wasn't a small bonfire. It was a chain of massive fires, each five times larger than his old hut in Kal. Each one licked the top of the three-story-tall room with its flames. All around the room were more flames. They spread across the ground and up the walls, covering every square inch.

Speilton moved forward into the room. Magically, the flames that spread across the ground slipped back away from Speilton's feet like the water in Mermaid Cove.

Except, something was different with this *fire.* It seemed afraid as if were aware that something was about to happen. It sensed an enemy.

The flames danced up into the air around Speilton, warding him off. They hissed and seethed like dozens of fiery snakes.

Speilton tried to ignore them although he was surrounded by his worst fear. The flames seared his legs and hair and eyebrows. His skin burned.

Speilton continued to move closer as the smaller flames around him died down. They now seemed to know that there was no way to stop him.

Looking into the tall flames, he saw something moving inside. The shadow writhed and tossed and turned inside. Speilton knew something else was wrong. Something that seemed so obvious, but yet, he couldn't put his finger on it.

The smoke! Speilton realized, *There's no smoke.* All of the smoke created by the fire simply didn't trail off into the sky, but instead coiled back into the flames, feeding and creating the growing Calorians inside.

Speilton knew he had to end it right then and there. He pulled the vial from around his neck, and held it in one hand.

"This reign of terror ends now!" Speilton pulled back his hand to throw, but something stopped him. A pain as sharp and devastating as the stab of a sword ran through his body. It ran through his chest, as if the flesh and skin were being ripped from his bones. Speilton collapsed to his knees, shaking uncontrollably as the pain died down.

Speilton was panting as sweat dripped from his face. His body burned from the heat of the flames around him. For a second, the pain was gone and everything returned to normal. Speilton had experienced enough of this castle and flames threatening his destruction. Speilton tried to leap to his feet, but he couldn't move. His hands and legs stayed firmly planted on the ground.

It was the strangest feeling, being unable to control his body. *What's going on?* Speilton wondered, applying all his effort to move his hand.

"You are mine. We are one. There is no escaping it," the Versipellis's voice cried through his head.

"No," Speilton muttered. "This can't be happening.

"But it is. I now have possession over your body. We are now one.

Speilton felt another sharp pain, though it didn't course through his body like the first one. Instead, it ran through his brain, numbing his senses, stealing every good memory.

Speilton's strength gave out, and he collapsed to the ground. "This must be done," the Versipellis seethed.

Suddenly he felt a surge of strength. He was powerful...extraordinarily strong. And with this power, he could be invincible. Speilton suddenly realized. *Why should I fight for the Milwarians? With this power, I could become great, the leader of the Calorians. I could be on the winning side. I wouldn't die.*

"No," Speilton found himself saying. "Don't give in. Those thoughts aren't yours. They're the Versipellis'.

Why shouldn't I listen to them? Speilton thought, *They could give me power. More power than anyone before.*

"You must help the Milwarians. They're counting on you. Just throw the vial!"

Why should I help Milwaria? What have they done to help me. My own parents cast me away when I was too young to defend myself.

"That's not true. They loved you. They were trying to protect you!"

What? Suddenly, the Versipellis's grip on Speilton's mind began to shatter, and a single memory seeped back in.

Speilton saw the image so clearly. He was being cradled in his mothers's arms. Her tears dripped down onto his forehead. His father's face appeared above him. "Goodbye, my precious son. I promise, we will see you again."

His mother held back her tears for only a second to kiss him on the cheek, and say, "Speilton, be brave. And know, we will always love you."

The memory began to dissolve, as a scream broke out. Speilton's body jerked violently and suddenly, the screaming stopped. Sweat poured down his face as he moved his hand to wipe it from his eyes. *I can move!* Speilton realized jumping to his feet.

But his heart suddenly dropped as he saw the Versipellis floating only feet away. "This isn't over." It muttered, "It will never be over, until the end of Liolia."

And with that, it vanished.

Speilton sighed with relief. It was over. He had won. Clutching the vial in his hand he pulled back, once again ready to throw.

This time it left his hand sailing through the air, but it would never again touch ground. A hand snatched it as a Calorian stepped out from behind the Inferno. When Speilton saw the arm and long, curved horns, he knew that it was all over.

Sinister stepped out into the light, the vial in his hand.

"You should've known Speilton, that if the Versipellis didn't destroy you, I would,"

"How did you know I was here?" Speilton asked.

"Two Calorians reported seeing a round disk of light. Two ended up unconscious. I knew you were here."

"So now what? You found me."

Sinister smiled. Then, he blew a silver whistle. From every doorway a Calorian rushed out.

"Now Speilton, dId you really think that you were going to succeed?"

The Calorians laughed, and Speilton's stomach churned.

"I'm surprised at you *Sinister*. You have me alone against you and hundreds of your minions. That's pretty pathetic even for you."

"But it's also a victory for me and that's all that really matters, now isn't it, boy?"

The Calorians cheered. Speilton clenched his fists. "What did you do to the portal? It should've killed me."

"Ah, so that *is* how you got here. Well, there are some benefits of having a Sorceress on your side. Venefica charmed it so that if a person failed in the cave, they would be deposited here in my dungeon."

"Why? Why bother bringing me here? Wouldn't it just have been easier to let me die there?

"Yes, but once a person dies in there, every part of them stays."

"What do you mean?"

"You naive boy, you were never actually in a cave. Well, at least, not an actual, physical cave anyway."

Sinister must have seen the udder confusion on Speilton's face because he smiled even more deviously than before. "While you were hovering in the air, intertwined by light, the cave tapped into the deepest areas of your brain. Your worst fears, your greatest desires, even your destiny. All of it, the cave knew. And once you entered your challenge, the cave created an area that could test your mind. Therefore, if Millites were stabbed in his test, he wouldn't have actually been killed by the blow. His human body would be unharmed. But instead the cave would've destroyed him, deep in his mind."

"So why did Venefica charm the portals?"

"If you had actually died in the portal, all of your weapons, and everything else would be lost forever in there. But once you survived, we knew you would come here, and bring us this." Sinister waved the Vial of Aqua in the air. "And I'd have the pleasure of destroying you myself."

Sinister drew his sword and went at Speilton, who blocked back the blow quickly then ducked to the side. Sinister spun and his sword smacked against Speilton's. Speilton stumbled backwards, his sword skidding away.

"What do you suppose your brother thinks of you now? What do you think your parents think of you?"

"My parents are dead!"

Sinister smiled, a smile as knowing and horrifying as the fire that swirled around them.

Suddenly, a figure appeared between Sinister and Speilton. The second Speilton saw the pure black, long hair, he knew who it was. "Faveo?"

Faveo lunged at Sinister and cut him across the cheek. Steam rushed over the king's face.

"Such a brave warrior. Too bad you'll have to die, too," Sinister sneered. Faveo struck again, but this blow was blocked easily by Sinister.

"You're too weak," the king said.

"Maybe, but I know my place. I know my destiny." He stared Sinister in the eyes, "And it's here, between you and Speilton."

"Then you will meet your doom."

In a single blow, Sinister disarmed Faveo and in the next blow he cut the man across the chest.

Faveo collapsed to the ground. He groaned as his hands pressed over the wound.

"Now it's just you and me, Speilton." Sinister grinned.

Suddenly, Faveo grabbed his scimitar from the ground, sprang forward, and sliced at Sinister's legs. The King collapsed to the ground, smoke coiling around him as the rest of the Calorians rushed to his side.

Speilton ran to the wounded Faveo. "What made you come back?" Speilton asked.

"You were right. I realized that even if I lived, I would return to a new world that was in peril. What's life without family or friends or a future? You are my only family, and you needed me, even if it meant that I didn't survive. At least my life was given for a greater good. And that's when I understood my future. All of the time I spent in the Calorian prison was for this moment. My destiny, the meaning of my life, was to save yours. And therefore, I could be saving hundreds of others. It's just like you said."

"NO, you don't have to die. You could come with me."

"I'm sorry kid, but I have no fight left in me. I'm so proud of you, Speilton."

Speilton saw it, too. His shirt was now soaked red with blood. His lips were tuning blue, and his dark eyes were now as deep and lifeless as a black hole.

"It's okay. Go, get out of here. Milwaria needs you."

"I won't leave you here."

"You have to. Now go. You're no good to Milwaria dead."

Speilton reluctantly stood up and ran off. He only looked back once to see the person-who-had-been-waiting-in-jail, close his eyes.

Now, Speilton truly was, the Last of Kal.

THERE'S NO ESCAPE
~ 24 ~

Speilton fled from the Inferno of Erif hoping he'd never return. Behind him there was a scream, but he didn't know whose. Speilton took off down the hallway that seemed to never end. He came to a squad of Calorians with their backs to him. Not even then did he stop. Instead, he shoved by them and ran past, leaving them stunned.

Speilton's body ached and his lungs begged for air. But he never stopped. They all knew he was there, and at any second now the entire army of Calorians could be on him.

Speilton tried to shake that feeling away. It would only distract him and cause him to fail.

But what is there to lose? The Inferno of Erif was still burning strong. Speilton had already failed. Faveo had died for nothing. Every Milwarian who had died fighting for justice, had also died in vain.

"No! There is still one more way. I can destroy Sinister. I will end this once and for all." Speilton promised not only himself, but also Faveo and every other Milwarian.

Speilton reached the end of the hallway and ran up the stairs. If he went down, there was a chance he'd run into the Calorians from the Treasury.

Speilton climbed two levels, not even considering where he was going. *Why didn't I take the map from Faveo?* Speilton regretted.

He climbed another level, when suddenly, the staircase changed. It slowly wound around in a large circle. Speilton climbed higher and higher, wondering where he was going. Rooms broke off to his right, though they were all empty except for old furniture. Speilton continued climbing, his legs begging his brain to stop with every step.

Then he came to a landing much larger than the others. Through the archway, all Speilton could see was a small chamber covered with doors on each wall. But to his left, there was a window.. Speilton glanced out and saw a heart-wrenching sight.

As he looked through it, he saw the black trees of the forest and the wasteland surrounding the castle. He was high in the only place elevated in Skilt. Speilton was climbing Skilt's center tower with no way down.

Speilton thought about surrender, but something kept him going. Whether it was adrenaline, or just to prove to Sinister that he was willing to fight no matter the cost, Speilton continued.

Speilton nearly gave out a dozen times, but finally the stairs ended. As he walked out into daylight, clouds shielded most of the sun's radiance, but the feeling of its heat baring down on him was nourishing and consoling. He was glad to have its presence during his last few seconds.

Speilton ran out across the roof area of the tower, which was much wider than Kon Malopy's but not nearly as steep. There was a walkway that circled the point, unlike Sky Tower.

But Speilton had no time for comparing. Quickly, he scrambled up the side of the roof. Chunks of rock and panels broke off and fell beneath his feet, yet it was easier than he expected.

He was halfway up when the doorway exploded with Calorians. They rushed out, swords and bows in hand. Those with swords began rushing up the side after him. The rest threw spears or shot arrows. All around him, Speilton heard arrows ricochet off the rocks. His shield was slung over his back and gave him some protection as the swarm of arrows splattered around him.

Speilton looked to the top of the tower to see his target. There was a hole where the very tip of the tower should be. The hole was about three feet in diameter and black smoke coiled from the opening.

There Speilton would end his life before anyone else could. It must end this way, but first he had something to say. He reached the top, took off his shield and held it out in front of him. Then, he faced the Calorians.

"Stop!" he commanded.

Many of the archers stopped, just to hear the King's final request. Others continued shooting, but none were in range. Speilton continued, "I've seen how you've been treated. Your life is dictated by a ruthless king. And I...feel sorry for you. My people do not want war. They mean you no harm. You have nothing to gain by destroying Milwaria. *Retsinis* will continue to torture and mistreat you long after he has won. Please, I beg of you to stop this savagery against my people. We understand that you have been brutalized by a dictator, but this can end now! You just have to believe in a greater world."

"Don't listen to him!" One Calorian shouted. "He's the enemy!"

"No, I'm not your enemy," Speilton argued. "I know that the way you've been treated is wrong. It's unfair that you must go through such horrendous trials the second you enter this world. But I want to tell you, it doesn't have to be that way. You should have control over your lives and your decisions - not Retsinis, not anyone else. This isn't the life you would have chosen for yourselves. And, if you change your ways and join me, you may be granted a new life, with the Milwarians." This was Speilton's last hope. If he could convince the Calorians to help him, he may be able to escape. If his plan failed…

"You speak bravely," a Calorian growled, "though what you are asking is treason. What happens if in the end, the Calorians do win? We'd have a chance to live *a* life in Caloria if we survive the war. But if we join the Milwarians and your Nation of Light falls, we will be terminated with your people. I'll take my chances with Caloria since we have you overpowered and outnumbered!"

"Yeah!" the other Calorians cheered in raising their weapons and beginning the chase again.

Speilton's heart dropped. His last idea had shattered like a sheet of glass .

Speilton knew that if he was going down he wouldn't let a simple Calorian arrow or the blade of a sword be the one thing that ended his life. If he was leaving this world, he wanted to make sure that his last seconds would leave one last impression on the Calorians.

"Just remember," Speilton told them, "You're not fighting alone. Be brave and stay true to what's right and just. Things will change. Your pain doesn't have to lead to the suffering of others."

"How are you so sure," a Calorian muttered.

"Just wait. You'll see," Speilton finished, now satisfied. He looked up to the sun, then closed his eyes.

This is it. Speilton reached his arms out on either side of him, and fell backwards, down through the hole. His stomach flipped, and he felt weightless, as he fell, down, down down...

Retsinis won't be the ruler of my life. Speilton thought to himself. *Neither will the Versipellis. I am the master of my destiny for the good of Milwaria.*

"Squawk!"

Speilton heard them before he saw them. A bustle of feathers and the snapping of fanged beaks.

He'd been wondering where the Daerds were. They always appeared at a moment's notice. And yet, he hadn't seen a single one until now. It seemed that every Daerd was cooped up inside this area like it was a giant bird cage.

They swarmed and dove through the room that was almost three times taller than the vine-covered room at the base of the tree in the Jungle of Supin

Speilton suddenly landed on the back of a flying Daerd and was flown a few feet before slipping off. He fell a few feet before smashing into another one. Speilton tossed and turned through the sky, batted back and forth by the swarm of Daerds.

As he fell, he noticed that despite the crushing blows of the giant birds, there may be hope. Speilton wasn't sure how long he had been falling, when suddenly he was dangling from the legs of a Daerd only a few feet from the ground. He was alive and unhurt.

But he had fallen right into their trap. A dozen archers stood ready on the ground. All he remembered was a stinging sensation. It was almost as bad as when the Versipellis first entered his body back in the Inferno. He looked down to see an arrow planted deep in his leg with blood oozing out around it.

Speilton groaned before nearly fainting from the pain. His leg throbbed, and his whole body began to shake. His mind became dizzy and unaware. Slowly, he began losing focus of where he was and who he was, just as he saw Sinister's evil face peering down at him.

"I respect your ... near escape. But you've forgotten. This is Skilt, my realm."

Speilton could hardly move. His eyes teared up and desperate groans escaped his mouth. Speilton noticed the metallic taste of blood filling in his mouth.

"Ah, so sad. Speilton Lux, the all powerful King," Sinister growled with mock affection. "Bring him to his feet. Speilton, I want to show you something before you're executed."

Two arms grasped him by the shoulders, lifting him to his feet. The moment his foot touched the ground a nauseous, poisonous pain shot up his leg and ran through his body. Speilton collapsed, as the Calorians all began to laugh.

"Such a pity," Sinister smiled. "Fine, I guess you'll just have to walk him."

The two Calorians grabbed him again and threw his arms around their shoulders. They dragged him along behind Sinister, carrying him like a wet sack. Speilton couldn't help but wish that he had died falling down the tower.

Speilton was dragged down countless hallways, up and down many flights of stairs. Slowly, the pain eased ever so slightly. Speilton was able to think more clearly.

The black-tipped arrowhead had completely sunk into his leg. Around the wound, the skin was bright red and twice it's normal size.

Now that the pain had lifted somewhat, Speilton made a point of remembering which way they were going just in case he was able to make an escape.

But as they rounded a corner, it seemed that it wasn't necessary. Before them was the exit, a large drawbridge that was the only passage over the lava moat outside.

"Why are you showing me this?" Speilton asked, trying to stay strong.

"Look at the edge of the forest," Sinister commanded.

Speilton looked to see the outline of an army, standing just outside of the shadow of the woods. Above the tree canopy was the top of the Avenger. The blue Prowl and the Red Hunger dove through the sky, spitting flames up into the air. Below, Speilton saw the golden manes of Rorret and Flamane and the distant image of Millites and Usus riding the two animals.

What's going on? Speilton wondered.

"They're preparing for war. Hoping to 'Avenge,'" Sinister smirked, "your death."

"Why did you show me this?" Speilton asked trying to untangle Sinister's twisted mind.

"This is the last time you'll ever see your brother and friends. They await the same fate as you. Death."

Speilton glanced back out at them. If only they knew. He was alive, and so was the Inferno of Erif. Tears welled up in Speilton's eyes, both from the pain in his leg and the sudden realization that his brother wasn't going to make it. If any one deserved to live, it was Millites and definitely not Sinister.

The Lord of Darkness saw the longing on Speilton's face. "Raise the draw bridge. Young Speilton here has to meet his doom."

A Calorian rushed to the side of the drawbridge and began cranking up the chains. The door rose in the air, being pulled upwards by a long link of chains feeding into the contraption.

Speilton held his breath, watching his last chance of survival disappear. Soon, the door had covered up his view of the woods and the dragons, leaving only the grey sky.

The dark clouds were suddenly illuminated by a flash of golden light. In only a second it was gone, but in that second Speilton was given an idea. If he failed, there would be certain death. He had nothing to lose.

Speilton screamed as he wrapped his hand around the arrow still protruding from his leg and pulled it out. A surge of pain coursed through his body as he plunged the weapon into one of the Calorians next to him, then shoved the other aside. Speilton wobbled around, and before the warriors could rush to kill him, he threw the arrow at the Calorian working the draw bridge. The Calorian dodged as the arrow lodged in the hollow of a chain. The Calorian began cranking the machine furiously attempting to raise the bridge, but it was useless. The arrow was pulled down into the machine and splintered. The arrow caused the machine to become clogged, stopping the warrior from continuing any further.

Speilton climbed the drawbridge door quickly, using his one good leg. Once he reached the top, he turned around and caught a glimpse of the Calorians before leaping out over the lava on his uninjured leg.

Speilton felt a surge of heat and was certain that he'd hit the lava, when he landed on hard ground. Speilton breathed deeply, amazed that he had made it this far, then carefully lifted himself to his feet and began limping as fast as he could away from the castle.

Speilton's entire body throbbed. Every time his leg brushed the ground, it exploded with pain. His arm was now aching from his rough landing off the bridge and his head throbbed. Ahead, the edge of the forest was about two hundred yards away. Speilton turned around to see how close the Calorians were in pursuit of him, only to find that there weren't any. It seemed too simple. Why were they letting him go? Were they trying to repair the drawbridge, or were they letting the Milwarians see their King once more before they hunted him down? The last choice seemed more likely.

Or maybe, Speilton thought, *They'll just let me go. Maybe they'll just prepare themselves for the battle and plan to crush me then.*

Then the ground shifted. It was a sudden jerk as though the ground had jumped a foot. Speilton stumbled as did the others in both armies. Whatever had caused the movement was massive and close.

Speilton had just picked himself up when the ground shook again. This time it was a deep rumble that thrashed the ground for many seconds. As Speilton fell to the ground, he saw an eruption from the ground only feet in front of the molten moat.

Fierce red eyes shadowed by a round wolfish face erupted from the ground followed by a massive body. The creature shoved it's way up through the rocks and stone, as chunks of dirt stuck in it's thick black mane of hair.

The creature put it's front paws on the hard bare ground, and pulled the rest of it's body out of the ditch. Then, the monster shook furiously like a wet dog, throwing dirt and rocks as large as cannonballs into the air.

It was Dnuoh, the flame spitting, massive dog born from the Cave of the Magmors. This was the Calorians wild card. A beast so powerful, not even an entire army could take it down. And here it was, up against a wounded, weaponless thirteen-year-old boy.

Speilton started running, even though it was hopeless. Every ounce of adrenaline had been used back in Skilt. Now, he was defenseless as Dnuoh took two steps forward and stood looming over him. Speilton looked up at the ugly face. It was like a hound's, except with a flat snout and eyes close to the nostrils. Smoke hissed from its mouth, drifting up into the air.

And then, Speilton saw a sight that no man had seen and lived to tell about it. It started as a distant light deep in the beast's throat. Then it grew brighter, and larger, until the flames flooded from the hound's mouth.

Speilton saw purple, red and orange swirl around him, just before the heat reached him.

Millites saw it from a distance. Speilton, flat on his back, staring up into the mouth of Dnuoh, then a flash of fire. Speilton put his hands up over his face for protection, but Millites knew, Speilton knew, every Milwarian warrior knew, and Sinister knew, it would be of no use.

ONLY EIGHT SHALL LIVE
~ 25 ~

The flames began to lift off the ground. There was the slightest gap between the purple fire pouring from Dnuoh's mouth and the bare ground. "What's going on?" the warriors began asking, as the flames moved up even higher into the air.

It was as if once reaching that certain point, the flames vanished. No one knew what to make of it. Not even Dnuoh was sure. But Millites could only smile. He understood. Speilton was finally in control.

Speilton stood under the torrent of flames, though none of them had touched him. They fell in a dome around him. The heat burned his hair and eyebrows, but none of the fire touched his skin. Not even the smoke touched him.

The reason why? His wand.

Speilton had pulled it out the second before the flames left Dnuoh's mouth. He'd imagined himself guiding the flames and causing them to move at his will.

And they obeyed. His wand wasn't creating any flames, but instead, moving them ... making them turn against their creator, Dnuoh. Little by little, the flames began to lift from the ground and shift directions, flying against their master. *No, Speilton realized, Dnuoh is not their master. I am.*

The flames slithered up at Dnuoh, wrapping around the demon's face like a blanket. It traveled back up the creature's throat. Even the smoke lashed out, forming a cloud around the giant hound's head.

After only a few seconds, the flames died away. The attack had been enough to subdue the animal for a while, as it collapsed backwards down its cave. A puff of dirt and smoke rose from the cave like a mushroom cloud, and it all went back to normal.

A cheer erupted from the Milwarians as a group of five men galloped toward Speilton. In only a minute, Speilton was at the base, surrounded by all those that he loved.

It seemed like only a second ago, that he was alone in a prison cell, running through the castle lost, hiding from Calorians, facing Sinister, and ready to take his own life.

And now, it was all worth it. He was safe again, and alive.

Speilton was quickly carried away to the infirmary. The best doctor checked his leg. After washing it out with water and a certain medicine, he applied ointment, stitched it back up, and wrapped it in a gauze. Then, he was given some food and water for the first time in forever, and fell asleep.

He woke and fell back asleep countless times. Every time he rolled onto his wounded leg, pain surged through his body. But the soft, cool bed felt good, and he continued sleeping for many hours.

Finally, Speilton climbed out of bed and limped out of his tent. Everywhere, men were training. Warriors practiced sword fighting with wooden dummies. Others threw hot arrows at targets. Some threw knifes or axes at trees. Many others fought each other, showing off their skills. But the war hadn't started … yet. Speilton walked through the trees and warriors, before he was grabbed from behind. It was Millites.

"I can't believe you're alive. When you entered the portal, we waited and waited and waited, but you never came out. And then, we were suddenly transported outside of the cave. We thought you failed," Millites exclaimed.

"Technically, I did." Speilton began to tell what had happened, leaving out the parts that included the Versipellis.

To tell Millites now would completely undermine his amazing escape, and everyone was so happy right now. Besides, with the threat of war hanging around them, knowing about the Versipellis would surely cause them to freak.

Speilton had just gotten to the part about Dnuoh standing over him when Millites said, "And you did it. You used the wand and took control,"

"Yeah, it was a good thing you forced me to keep the wand."

They walked through the groups of training warriors, many of which bowed as the Kings passed by. "So, where are we going?" Speilton asked.

"Headquarters. We're working on battle strategy there."

"What's the plan?" Speilton asked.

"Well, we don't exactly have one yet."

"Do you have any ideas?"

"Andereer is thinking about a formation-less attack. Everyone rushes out of the woods suddenly, catching them off guard."

"What's the problem with that?" Speilton asked.

"There's about five hundred feet between us and the castle. Once we leave the shield of the trees, we'll be easily taken by arrows," Millites explained, "In a sudden, random attack, it would be hard to protect the army."

They walked a few more steps and came to a very large tent nearly the size of Rilly's hut. "Here we are," Millites announced as they walked into the tent.

Speilton had just set foot inside when Usus leapt forward and hugged him. Speilton stumbled backwards from the sudden force, but Ram was quickly there to stop him from falling.

"So, how did you survive?" Usus asked stepping back.

Speilton began again, telling everyone in the tent. Andereer, Nicholas, Equus, Ore and Metus sat around a table in the center of the room. A sketch of the area had been laid on the table, and many different colored rocks scattered the page.

It was difficult for Speilton to explain how he lost the vial. If only he'd thrown it a moment sooner. The battle would've been over, and the Calorians finished.

But he hadn't and now, he couldn't dwell on the past. They had different matters to deal with.

Speilton finished the story and everyone tried to act happy. Though inside, they all knew that they were fighting a hopeless battle. Sinister was waiting to destroy them. And they had to be ready... or die.

They discussed strategies. A triangular formation wouldn't work while rushing out of the forest. The warriors would have to dodge trees and break out of their ranks. They could form lines of men and have them march out, though that would take too long, giving the Calorians more time to shoot them out.

In the end, they decided to get creative. The groups would divide up, each attacking at separate times to throw the Calorians off. They would also surround the Calorians to add to the confusion. The plan seemed good enough, but the question still stood. 'Would it be enough to destroy the Calorians?'

But all of them knew, even the knights knew, that in the end it wouldn't be the strategy that would help them to succeed, but the men and their courage. And that meant that every one of them had to be ready. The battle wasn't going to be easy.

The next day at sunrise, the men were told the plan. Warriors congregated into their groups with the feel of battle in the air. Soon after, the Calorians began coming out of their castle. They filed in before the walls and molten lava. But as the day wore on, the Calorians kept coming, filling the area around the castle.

The Milwarian knights stood frozen watching the Calorians. They found their friends and shook hands, hoping it wouldn't be the last goodbye. As they passed each other, they could only wonder if they'd see their face again.

At noon they were called in before the large tent. A platform had been assembled, and Millites stood atop the structure.

The crowd of warriors were silent and ready to listen to more inspirational words. Words of comfort and bravery. But as Speilton stared down at them, he couldn't think of anything to say. What could he say? This was the final chapter. They either won here or died trying ... every single one of them.

"This is it," Millites managed. "The final battle. This is where we take our final stand. Now, all that matters is that we try our hardest, and show Sinister that he cannot overcome us. Fight your hardest to destroy the Calorians. Give them the pain they have given us. Today the roles will change. The Calorians - the predators - shall become the prey. Today we must stop them, we must destroy every single one of them."

The Milwarians cheered. But Speilton interrupted as he leapt up on to the stage and shouted, "NO!" The stunned crowd grew silent.

"No, we're not going to needlessly inflict pain on them. Then, we'd be no different than they are."

"What?" Millites looked confused.

"I've been in that castle," Speilton announced. "I've seen the way they've been treated. As they're born, they're forced to fight each other. Many die in the first few seconds, and if they fail or refuse to fight, they're terminated. If they survive, they're thrown into battle to kill before being killed. They're given no life, no name, no future. Many can't even talk. All they know is to follow Ret - I mean Sinister's command. And while living their horrible, miserable lives, they take their frustrations out on others. That's why they're so ruthless. It because they have been oppressed and mistreated. They have never been given the opportunity to care for anyone or anything.

And if we go into battle and cause needless pain and suffering, what is that proving? Our problem is not with the Calorians. They are merely pawns." Speilton paused and stared into the crowd.

"There's only one way to end this, and it's not by destroying the Calorians. We have to destroy Sini... Retsinis!"

The crowd gasped, "You dare speak his name?"

"Retsinis is his name, and we better begin using it. Calling him *Sinister* only empowers him and shows him we're afraid. We have to destroy Retsinis, and after he's out of the way the Calorians will no longer have a commander."

"But then what? After Retsinis's gone, then what do we do?" Ram asked.

"We forgive them. We accept them back into Milwaria and give them an opportunity of a new life."

The forest was dead silent as the warriors pondered Speilton's words. They all realized they couldn't fight the battle in the same manner as before. But then, how were they going to win?

"Speilton, but how are we going to destroy Retsinis? In the first place, we can't even penetrate his armor. Secondly, if we go after him, every Calorian in that army will attack us. If we can't take the Calorians out, then they'll take over," Millites said.

"But we can still defeat them without destroying them." Speilton turned to the warriors and said, "Disarm them, wound them enough to take them out of the battle. Do whatever you can to disable them, but try not to inflict any deadly blows upon them. I know that we can't save them all, and there will still be casualties on both sides, but if we at least try to save them, we can show that we aren't as ruthless and demonic as Retsinis. That's not the way it should be. That's not the way any creature should have to live."

The warriors began talking amongst themselves. Speilton could hear many of them whispering about how impossible the fight was, how hard it was going to be to only wound, and how many of them wanted to escape. "It's impossible!" Many men shouted out of the crowd, "It's practically suicide!"

But Speilton wouldn't back down from what he knew was right, "Many of you may think this is impossible. Who knows? Maybe it seems impossible, but by the end of the night I promise you, one way or another, you will have seen the impossible. Because tonight, we take back Milwaria and end Retsinis' wrath. By the end of tonight, all of you will be in a better world. And how do I know? I know because we're fighting for the right side. We're fighting to restore the light and bring back justice. Tonight, we make it all happen.

Tonight, we take back not only Milwaria but Caloria, too."

"But to do that, we need you, all of you. To do that, we must be brave, and loyal, and true."

The Milwarians were silent. They looked upon this boy, only thirteen years old, and saw more hope than any of them could ever manage. If this young boy was brave enough to venture through the belly of the beast, and had the wits to come out alive, they could surely fight this battle... and win.

Millites stepped onto the platform and raised his sword. "For Milwaria!" he announced.

Usus, Ram, Andereer, Equus, Nicholas, Metus, and Ore stepped up onto the platform too, and raised their bows, clubs, and swords into the air, "For Milwaria!" they shouted.

One by one, the Milwarians raised their swords and spears and arrows and bolas and axes. And all at once, they shouted, "For Milwaria."

And it was so loud, brave, and triumphant, a shiver went down the Calorians' back as the cheer echoed all the way to them.

The Milwarians walked out through the forest, taking their positions. Their stomachs were tight and tense like they were before every battle. Though they tried not to show it, they were all horribly frightened. Not only were they worried about survival, but they were also scared that they would fail. What if they couldn't do it. What if they did not make it, leaving the Calorians free to destroy the rest of the Milwarians?

The sun was setting when the battle began. The Calorians who had appeared human most of the day in the sunlight stood still, motionless. As the sun slipped behind the cover of the trees, casting a shadow over the two armies, the

Calorian's faces shimmered, then became black voids with two eyes of red.

The Milwarian Leaders knew that it would be crucial to fight during the night. They knew that the Calorians were better off fighting in the dark. But with the Daerds, they would be in the darkness no matter what time of day it was. This way, the Milwarians weren't allowing the Calorians the satisfaction of turning night to day, and controlling the outcome of the battle. This way, the Daerds would have no effect.

Everything was ready to begin. The warriors looked at one another, hoping it wouldn't be the last time. Now they could only wait for the signal.

Millites appeared at the edge of the woods. He held his wand in one hand, his sword in the other. Millites rode on the golden lion Rorret, who had assisted him in many battles against the Calorians.

The king shot a spark of golden light up into the air, and the first warriors showed themselves. They walked in straight lines, led by Millites. They walked straight forward, facing the drawbridge leading to the castle. To the Calorians it all seemed too easy. A volley of arrows were fired at Retsinis' command. They arced into the sky and began showering down on the men. But the Milwarians showed no fear. As the arrows closed in fast, not a single one lifted a shield. It seemed strange, and the Calorians soon found out why.

As the arrows reached a sudden point, ten deflected on some invisible force. As they snapped and broke in the air, cracks began forming over the Milwarians, as if hovering in the sky. It was a light shield, cast by Millites. The broken arrows slid down the sides of the transparent dome. Millites summoned the shield back into his wand. Then Rorret rose up on his hind legs, roared, and leapt forward. The first line of warriors followed quickly behind on horse back. The rest of the men walked forward slowly, and then, once reaching a certain point rushed forward, row by row.

The warriors roared as they rushed out into battle, but suddenly, their cry was matched with another.

Many of the Calorians turned around to see more Milwarian warriors rushing from the trees behind them. They had no lines. No formation, but were merely rushing forward.

And for the first time for many of them, they felt outnumbered and surrounded. And in that moment of shock, the Milwarians met the Calorian army.

Millites reached the Calorians first. Rorret, clad in silver and emerald armor, didn't leap onto the first Calorians but instead plowed over them warriors, knocking them to the ground. Millites disarmed Calorians on all sides.

Behind the Calorians, the other Milwarians began their attack. Many let arrows fly in the air, but before they could reach the warriors, they were pulled into a thick vortex that Ram had created. The twister of air also crawled through the Calorian army, blowing Calorians to the ground. The second army of Milwarians attacking from behind, were shielded by a wall of flames that crept ahead of them as they ran. As soon as the two armies met, the flames vanished.

And the final battle between the Milwarians and the Calorians began. There was no turning back.

Speilton took to the sky, flying over the Milwarian army, the Calorians, and over the walls of Skilt. Prowl spit a ball of flames, setting the Calorian archers into a frenzy. Prowl and Speilton continued into the air, dodging between towers. They drifted and soared over the black rooftops. Calorians shot out of windows, trying to strike Speilton and Prowl out of the sky. Though none came close to the blue dragon.

Prowl shot up, up, up into the air, nearly climbing the steep center tower. They continued up over the half way balcony and drifted to the top point. There, Daerds had begun to spill out like black smoke from a volcano. They chattered and squawked as they took to the air, covering the darkening sky in a black blanket. Prowl glided onto the roof, and Speilton leapt off. He disarmed the first Calorian that came to stop him, then spun and knocked the other in the shin. Though he was injured, it wasn't anything that couldn't be fixed. Prowl growled and hissed at the Calorians, warding them off. The Calorians retreated down the stairs, hoping to find reinforcements.

After all of them had left, Prowl blew the small structure that encased the stairs into a fiery blue blaze. "There. We got them out of the way. Now we have to get by them!" Speilton muttered as he and Prowl stared up at Daerds.

Speilton climbed on Prowl's back, and she leapt into the air. The moment they approached the cloud of black feathers and teeth, the Daerds swarmed them. Prowl hissed flames at the surrounding birds, while Speilton chopped them down. He held his wand in one hand, summoning flames. It was all going as planned, until a wounded Daerd tumbled out of the sky and bashed against Speilton's chest. The King was thrown off Prowl's back and momentarily felt himself falling. Then his back banged against stone, and he slid down the edge of the roof of the tallest tower of Skilt. His wand and sword left his hand as he tumbled to the floor. As soon as he reached the bottom, he dizzily pulled himself to his feet. The first thing he noticed as the world stopped spinning was a large Daerd swooping down for him.

It was only feet away when a blast of gold light entangled its wings. The flightless bird tumbled over the edge and fell down the side of the castle. Hunger landed before him, flame red, and Millites jumped off his back. "Are you okay?" Millites asked.

"Yeah, great," Speilton wobbled over to Millites.

Prowl suddenly rushed out of the swarm of Daerds. She landed next to Speilton, who cautiously climbed on her back.

Speilton looked up at Millites to find him staring at him.

"What?" Speilton asked.

"You're going back into the castle," Millites noticed.

"No, I'm not," Speilton tried.

"Speilton, I can tell that you're scared. You're planning to go back in there."

Speilton sighed, "I have to do it. Burn is in there. He saved my life, and I have to repay him."

"Then that means that Retsinis has already used his blood. He has unleashed the Sword of Power?" Millites asked.

"No, not yet. Retsinis said something about experimenting. He's unsure of which tiger it is. But I know. I'm sure it's Burn.'

"Then let's go."

"No," Speilton said, "I have to go alone." Speilton decided.

Suddenly, the smoldering ruins of the stairs exploded as a group of Calorians archers rushed out. Millites quickly blinded them with flashes of light, and Hunger rushed forward, growling. The king knocked the bows from the Calorian's hands and cut many down in the knees.

For the time being they were incapable of fighting, though soon reinforcements would be on the way. "See," Millites said, "You need me in there."

He turned around to see Speilton staring, entranced on something in the battle below. "What?" Millites walked to Speilton's side.

"Nicholas," Speilton whispered.

Down below, Nicholas rode on the back of a Daerd. A length of rope was tied around the bird's neck like a harness. The elf dove to the left and right flying closer and closer to Worc.

The giant bird hovered over the battle field, the Lord of Darkness standing triumphantly on his back. Worc cast a horrible shadow on the battle below, as Retsinis began creating hounds of darkness from his wand. The dark dogs leapt down onto the warriors below, biting and clawing through their armor.

Nicholas dove in, momentarily letting go of the reins to shoot one of his fine tipped arrows at Retsinis. The arrow missed his ear by an inch, but it was close enough to draw the King Calorian's attention.

Retsinis turned to face the elf and blasted a stream of darkness his way. Nicholas dove under the churning wave. The Daerd began to pull and thrash away, but Nicholas held on tightly. Nicholas darted back up into the air, grabbed his bow, and leapt off the Daerd. Midair, he launched an arrow at the King. Retsinis merely blocked the attack away with a wave of his wand, though the attack had been enough to land Nicholas safely on Worc's back.

The elf stood and launched three arrows at the king. Retsinis blocked them with his shield of darkness.

Now it was Retsinis' turn. He pulled out his sword and rushed forward. Nicholas drew a dagger and barely blocked the blow. The elf swerved and ducked and dodged and kicked, but in the end.,Retsinis disarmed the poor elf by cutting him across the arm.

Nicholas launched a few arrows, though without success. He was tired and injured. Retsinis made his move. The King Calorian sent darkness swarming and billowing out over Worc's back like a thunder cloud. The darkness bit and wrapped around the elf, pulling the arrows from his quiver. In the darkness, Nicholas fell, unable to see anything. Then two red eyes appeared, and a horrible pain cut across his chest.

Nicholas could feel the sticky, hot blood rush from his wound as the darkness melted away. Retsinis stood over him, a bloody sword in his hand. "You're a fool elf. Just like your parents."

Nicholas clutched his bleeding chest. "Don't say a word about my parents."

Retsinis smiled, glad to have been able to make the elf mad. "I destroyed them you know. And now you will meet their same fate."

"You will die, someday. And it will be because of my arrows. Someday you will be brought to justice. I will avenge my parents."

Retsinis smiled, "Ha! You fool! I will never go away. No one will ever destroy me. Great power like mine is invincible and will never die."

Nicholas stared up into those horrible red eyes, the bronze horns, and the one human arm. Now it was his turn to smile. "But evil does!"

The roles switched as it usually does before every death. The smile dropped from Retsinis' face. The elf closed his eyes, and the King struck.

This time there was no last minute miracle. There was no sudden wind of luck. The sword entered the elf's body, and his story ended.

"NO!" Speilton screamed rushing to Prowl. He'd already leapt on the blue dragon's back and gotten ready to leave when Millites stopped him. "Speilton, don't go. There's nothing you can do. Nicholas … he's dead."

Speilton felt tears welling up in his eyes, though he wouldn't let them fall. "I'm going to get him. I'm going to destroy Retsinis before he harms anyone else." Speilton promised.

"Not yet," Millites commanded. "If you go now, he's sure to be waiting for you."

"We can't just sit here. People are dying. We are outnumbered three to one. We have to end this!"

"We will. I promise. But right now, we have to save Burn. If Retsinis' gets his blood first, we're all doomed."

"Then let's go."

The two flew up, back into the torrent of Daerds and dove down into the castle.

Retsinis stood atop Worc, staring down into Nicholas's blank eyes. A smile spread across his black lips. "Such a pity." he mumbled.

He drew his wand and thought about devastation. People dying, screaming, crying at his hand. He brought them their worst fears, their deepest longings, then took them away. He took away their life, their freedom, their compassion.

Darkness shot from his wand, entangling the boy in a web of fear, then pulled him over the edge.

Nicholas tumbled to the ground, his body becoming lost in the battle.

"Let us go back," Retsinis muttered. "The sword is waiting for its master."

The Daerds rained down on the army as the Calorians unleashed the trolls. Scaly, hairy creatures around fifteen feet tall with thick over sized fore heads, long, clawed forearms that brushed the ground, and piercings and tattoos covering their grey bodies. They brandished clubs and axes, and wore thick, round helmets, and some had body armor.

In all with the Calorians, the Daerds, and a few trolls, it was too much for the Milwarians. The Milwarians could only disarm or slightly injure the Calorians, but when it came to the others, they were allowed to destroy the beasts of darkness and evil that would never be thankful or be redeemed. Besides, it would be pretty hard to disarm or slightly hurt a troll.

It was the trolls that presented the biggest problems. It took at least ten knights to take one down. The thick scales and skin made normal sword blows useless. The back of their skulls were their weak spots, but it was very difficult for the Milwarians to reach. The trolls could easily crush a man with a single blow of his axe or club. And even without weapons, trolls had huge, gorilla-like arms that could swat men or even feed them to their nasty, yellow, fanged mouths.

But then, out came the game changer - the Milwarian's last hope - its purpose was to avenge. The Avenger was pulled out by a dozen sturdy horses. Ram was seated inside the main controls of the machine, next to the mechanic and Ore. The enclosed area was filled with many levers that when turned, triggered different artillery weapons.

Atop the machine, men worked to turn large wheels to pull the ropes. Others jumped up and down on planks of wood that pumped air into the machine. The moving air helped many of the artillery weapons function.

The machine's front shield protected it from many Calorians and arrows. The horses pulling the Avenger were clad in amor, and warriors stood around them, fighting off Calorians.

In only three minutes, the Avenger was ready for battle. All of the cannons had been loaded ahead of time. The main huge catapult was pulled back and loaded, and the crossbows that dotted the metal sides were ready. They waited for the right moment.

"Okay, everything is ready for battle," the mechanic said.

"Ram, do you want to fire the main catapult?" Ore asked.

"Sure, it would be my pleasure," Ram said.

"Good, we'll tell you when to fire. After you shoot, everyone else will follow."

Ram raced onto the top of the Avenger. The men were ready at the cannons. He grasped the main lever, which when pulled would unleash the giant catapult. There he waited for the signal.

In the area underneath him, Ore and the mechanic waited while losing patience by the second. They peered out at the battle. Three trolls were slowly getting closer. Two held axes, while one held a sharp pitch fork. In the distance, he saw many archers lined up, shooting at each other. On the other side of the battle, warriors clashed together in a frenzy, attacking people from all edges.

"NOW, FIRE!!!" Ram immediately pulled down on the lever. The ropes went slack, and the huge catapult thrust forward. A stone the size of the top floor of Sky Tower hurtled through the air. As it completed its arc through the sky, the crossbows fired, taking out the Calorians surrounding the Avenger. Then, in a deafening series of booms, the cannons fired into the Calorian army.

Large chunks of rock crashed to the ground. As they rolled, the troll with the pitch fork and nearly fifty Calorians were taken down. Dirt and stone went everywhere as the cannons crushed into the ground, knocking many creatures onto their backs.

Ram's stomach churned, and he momentarily lost his ability to speak. Ore ran up from behind yelling something, though it was lost in the chaos. Ram had just killed nearly fifty Calorians with a single pull of a lever. It was the very thing that Speilton had commanded them not to do. He could never erase the chaos he had just caused.

The rocks fired from the cannons thudded into the ground, forming deep craters and blowing Calorians to smithereens.

"Ram!" Ore cried, "I'm so sorry. It was my fault. I was the one who told you to fire."

"No, I was the one who pulled the lever. I could have waited. My hatred and anger toward them blinded me." Ram had never admitted this before. It was true though. Ram had never seen himself as an ally to the Calorians, the ones that took his brother away and killed him. The creatures that caused his parents' deaths. He could never trust them again and never intended to.

"I know you didn't mean to pull the lever Ram. I know you were only following orders, and so you aren't to blame for their deaths. I am," Ore said, trying to comfort Ram.

Though, it only made Ram unsure. Did he really mean to kill that many Calorians? Was that what he wished to do? No, no surely he hadn't been able to tell where the rock would hit. He was probably only listening to orders. Though, if Ram *had* gotten the chance to destroy those Calorians, would he have fired?

Ram wasn't sure, he could never be sure. Though he did know that if the Calorians had been given that chance to end the lives of fifty Milwarians in only a second, they would certainly fire.

"Don't worry. I promise that it won't happen again, Ore." Ram said as the dwarf nodded solemnly and left.

All around them, Calorians rushed away from the Avenger to regroup and ready themselves for the next round. Amazingly, the Avenger was ready to launch again in a matter of minutes. The catapult crushed two more trolls, the cannons tore through a flock of harpies that had erupted from the Dark woods to fight, and the crossbows cleared out the Calorians that had charged toward the Avenger.

Four more times, the Milwarians launched their unstoppable attacks, and four more times they struck fear into their enemies.

Hunger and Prowl wove through the long, empty hallways of the castle. With the Calorians outside fighting, to Speilton the place was like a cemetery - a cemetery where he had many supernatural experiences. A nightmare to relive.

Millites saw it more as a maze. He had no idea what to expect and what lay behind every turn.

But as they traveled, the only life they saw were bats and spiders and rats. Many of the torches had been extinguished, so Millites created a ball of light that traveled a few feet in front of them as they flew on.

"Speilton, do you know where we are going?" Millites asked.

"To be honest, I have no idea," Speilton said. "We need to find Retsinis."

"So, what exactly are we trying to stop him from doing?" Millites asked.

"Retsinis has Ferrum Potestas. And by now, with the final battle on him, I have no doubt that he will try everything he can to unlock the sword right now."

"So, you think he's got Burn?"

"I know he's got Burn," Speilton corrected.

"But Speilton, what if Burn was killed? What if the one creature that was able to unlock the sword is already dead?"

"If Burn was dead, Retsinis wouldn't have seen any reason to have the sword. Yet he sent out the Ver-, I mean those spirits to take the Sword of Power from us at the old fort. If Burn is alive the Calorians must have possession over him."

"So, Sinister -" Millites began.

"It's Retsinis, Millites." Speilton corrected.

"Sorry. So *Retsinis* only has to touch Burn's blood, and he can use the sword?"

"Yes. I'm almost sure that's what Cigam said."

"Did Retsinis give you any indication where he was keeping Burn?" Millites asked.

"Why would he? If he did tell me anything or give me any signs, they would most likely lead to a trap."

"Your right," Millites mumbled. "Well, let's think like Retsinis. Where would he most likely be if he didn't want anyone to find him?"

"Well, he has to be inside the castle," Speilton began. "And he most likely has guards."

"Guards? But all the warriors are outside."

"I know. But when you really think about it, Retsinis is a coward. He always has protection and others to fight for him so that he can escape, if necessary. You remember a few weeks ago, when we were fighting in the forest where Toroe perished. When we fought Retsinis, he had all of the Calorians swarm around and watch. Then, when Hunger and Prowl came, he was able to escape while the Calorians ran around in a frenzy," Speilton recalled.

"That also happened when we fought on Sky Tower. He had the Daerds there to protect him. That way, if he had to escape, he only needed to jump onto one of the giant crows."

"So, if all the Calorians are outside fighting, his protection is the Calorians who aren't fighting, or even been born yet," Speilton decided.

"The Inferno of Fire? Do you really think he's there?" Millites asked.

"Let's go find out."

Deep in the Cave of the Magmors, a creature was stirring. It had been at rest for centuries, and now for the first time in centuries, the creature moved.

It was not awake but would soon be. Its master was calling. As the beast took in a deep breath, its chest pressed against the hard stone floor. Slowly, its heart began to beat. Faster and faster. It was awakening. Soon it would be ready. Once again it would vanquish its master's enemies. But for now it rested.

Its master was calling.

Speilton and Millites headed for the Inferno of Erif and as they reached the area, light spilled through the dozens of doorways. Prowl and Hunger followed closely behind.

"Should we turn back?" Millites asked as they heard voices arguing.

"No. If Retsinis is anywhere, he's down this way."

"Fine, but can you just not use ... Sinister's name ... his real name? It's chilling to hear you speak his name when we're so close."

"Call him what you want. But if you're not willing to call him by his name, his real name, he knows that you're afraid. You are empowering him," Speilton said.

Millites peered through a crack in a thick wooden door that created a peephole. "Uh, oh," Millites muttered. "Speilton, you might want to see this."

Speilton saw dozens of Calorians crammed in the room. They must've been very recently born, because many were still half smoke, dissolving below the legs like a genie. A single Calorian dressed in battle armor stood above them on a pedestal, screaming and lashing his whip at them.

"What should we do?" Millites asked as Speilton backed away.

"We must go in, of course. Retsinis must think he can cowardly guard himself behind a room of Calorians and that will be enough to make us turn back," Speilton answered.

"Well, it is enough to make me turn around. The moment we step in there, every Calorian will come at us."

"No, they won't. Remember what I told you. Don't you remember what Faveo said? The Calorians are not evil. Sin ... I mean Retsinis, is the evil one. They are not born with hatred for Milwaria - they have learned it from him. They cause harm to us because that is the only way for the Wodahs to survive the wrath of Retsinis. These Wodahs haven't been faulted with evil yet, only their leader has."

And with that. Speilton flung open the door entering into the crowd of Calorians.

Millites followed reluctantly. But the dragons were spotted by the lead Calorian right away. "What is this? Who's here?"

Millites raised his wand, and before the commanding Calorian could react, there was a flash of golden light. The lead Calorian flew backwards, thudded to the ground amongst the Calorians, and lay unconscious.

The herd of Calorians began to shuffle away from Speilton, Millites, Prowl and Hunger, as they walked through the crowd. It was strange, walking amongst their enemies. Though, just as Speilton had predicted, they didn't attack. They just stood and stared, like a group of innocent children. In a way, they were.

The two Kings and the two dragons reached the other side of the room and opened the door entered the door. Millites locked the door behind them after they were all safely on the other side.

Once again, they found themselves in a long hallway. Speilton walked ahead, "I told you it would work," he laughed.

The rest followed. This hallway was just like the other. It was about the same size in length, covered in gory pictures, and had strange objects dangling from the ceiling.

They reached the end of the hallway and knew Retsinis was inside. They could hear his horrible voice. "Do it now, before they find out!"

There was the hissing and growl of a large jungle cat. "Burn!" Speilton whispered to Millites.

Speilton went for the door, but Millites held him back.

"Wait...listen" he whispered.

A Calorian with his voice full of panic said "My King, my axe still needs sharpening. I will begin in a few moments, with your permission."

There was a loud smack, as Retsinis struck his weapon against the wall in anger. "You will obey this second."

"Yes, my lord. Of course. But -"

Retsinis cut him off. "Destroy him immediately. I need his blood."

At this Speilton flung open the door in a flash. Burn lay chained to the ground, growling and hissing at the Calorian holding a large axe over his head. But before the Calorian could bring the blade down on the tiger, he was knocked to the ground by a golden flash of light that Millites had created.

Speilton released a ball of flames from his wand, but Retsinis quickly blocked it back with darkness. Speilton tried again and again, but Retsinis merely swatted it away like a pesky fly. Then the Dark King attacked, creating a tall black cobra to keep them busy. "You really do amaze me, Speilton," Retsinis mused as the snake struck. "But this time you fail."

The King Calorian pulled out a knife and quickly cut Burn's forearm. The tiger hissed and growled as the King stepped away, Burn's blood dripping off the blade. "The beast is waiting." Retsinis said, holding his wand up above his head.

Darkness coiled around his body, and the King disappeared.

The serpent remained, though without the aid of its master the two dragons quickly did it in. All that was left was scattered dust and smoke.

Millites ran to Burn. He summoned a strong blast of light that broke away Burn's chains. He wrapped his hands around the tiger's wound to stop the flow of blood.

"Speilton, get me something to wrap around the wound," Millites commanded.

Speilton pulled out a knife and quickly cut the rugged end of his shirt off in a thin strip.

Millites wrapped the cloth around the tiger, and pressed tightly.

"Now we have to get out of here," Millites said.

Speilton pointed his wand at the ceiling and blasted a hole in it with his fire. He helped Burn onto Prowl's back.

Hunger and Millites took off through the opening, and Prowl lifted the bleeding Burn up into the air flying away from the Inferno. Unfortunately, they were still in Skilt.

The Avenger was doing its job. Six trolls had been destroyed and hundreds of craters still showed. Only four Calorians had been mortally wounded by the Avenger after cannon blasts had fractured the ground around them. The Avenger was a horrible machine. It was deadly, though it was their only hope to intimidate their soldiers.

Ram had been guiding the stones toward the trolls only and used them to form a barrier between the Milwarians and the Calorians. The booming cannons shattered the ground, scaring away many Calorians. Dirt was flung into the air creating obstacles for the Calorian army.

The Inferno of Erif

In a matter of minutes, the Calorians were retreating into the castle. Although it was a good sign, they would be able to get many reinforcements. Hundreds of Calorian warriors could be ready to fight. They couldn't let that happen since they were so close to victory.

The Avenger was pulled straight through the Calorian army by the horses. It was a risky move, though it had to be done. Out here in the open, they were more susceptible to the Calorians.

In a matter of seconds, that's exactly what happened. A troll broke through their defenses. He was taller that the others, somewhere between twenty and twenty five feet tall. He had a flat nose, one eye, one ear, and wielded a forked club the size of a tree.

The troll picked up a boulder the size of a horse and hurled it at the Avenger. The stone crushed two canons and damaged another. The wall of the Avenger was now cracked and the wood was falling apart.

That's when the troll attacked. With the forked club, he took out three men in one swing, tossing them into the air like dolls. Then he went for the horses. They neighed and kicked, but in the end the troll ate one and cripple many others.

Warriors came from all around to take down the troll but only one would succeed. Arrows and spears planted themselves in his thick skin, but none of it seemed to make a difference. The troll grabbed and ate many knights.

Then Ore stepped onto the top of the Avenger and waited for the right moment. When it came, he was ready.

The troll lifted his hands in the air in triumph. At that second, Ore threw his axe, and the blade hit the creature right in the back of the skull. The troll stumbled, injured beyond repair, then collapsed to the ground. The twenty-five foot tall beast was taken down by a man less than a fifth his size. The men swarmed Ore, shaking his hand and patting him on the back.

The Avenger continued as planned creeping closer and closer to the castle. They watched the Calorians continued to retreat.

They were ready to launch as the mechanic screamed, "FIRE!!!" Ram pulled down the lever, the main catapult snapped forward, and the rock launched into the air. The surviving catapults fired and a wave of hurtling rock and stone flew towards the castle.

Inside the castle, Millites, Speilton, Prowl, Hunger, and Burn felt the structure shake and the impact from the attack. As they flew into the base of the central tower, they saw the destruction. "What could have caused that?" Millites asked.

Prowl began whimpering and Burn hissed like a scared street cat. "We need to hurry out of here," Speilton said.

They began flying to the empty area of the tower while they heard bangs and explosions outside. Suddenly, a dozen cannonballs blasted through the tower above them. The two dragons froze, not willing to go any farther. "It must be our army attacking the castle with the Avenger!" Millites exclaimed.

"But what about the dragons?" Speilton asked, "Why won't they fly?" Only a second later, bricks began to fall where the cannonballs had torn through and the structure grew weaker.

"Come on, Prowl! We've got to go, now!" Speilton commanded as Prowl shot up into the air.

Eeeerk! a chunk of the wall fell, bending and cracking the metal bars that lay inside the castle. There was another loud bang followed by four cannonballs that were wrapped in cloth and lit on fire which tore through the stone.

Now, everything began crumbling and breaking apart. Prowl and Hunger flew right into the thick of it. They tossed and turned through the sky, dodging flaming stones and a downpour of rocks. Prowl flapped hard, giving herself enough momentum, then folded up her wings to slip by large rocks. Hunger clung to the edge of the walls to let falling debris pass.

Just then the roof of the tower began to drop in nearly one entire piece, crushing everything it touched as it dropped. Speilton pulled out his wand, clasped onto Prowl's horns in the other hand, then screamed, "Fire!"

Speilton's orange flames, Prowl's blue flames, Hunger's red flames, and Millites' golden light collided against the round roof, shattering it and turning the falling remains to dust. The ash and pebble sized remains fell around them, as they flew up into the night sky. It had grown dark since they first entered. Below them, the battle still raged.

As they glided through the cold air, they looked down into the battle there were trolls holding lit torches that gave light to much of the battle. Calorians with torches were in the battle without any other weapon.

It was peaceful up there, but the moment ended as they dove down towards the Avenger.

Greeted by a swarm of men asking questions, Millites and Speilton shoved through to find Ram.

"We found him, Ram. We have Burn!" Speilton said.

Ram turned pale with a mixture of confusion and joy as he glanced over the two king's shoulders. It was Burn. Ram ran to the tiger and wrapped his arms around Burn's neck. "I just knew you were alive," Ram exclaimed.

The tiger purred slightly and leaned into the man. Ram's eyes rested on the wound. "What happened to his leg?" Ram asked.

"Retsinis," Millites paused. "He injured him to take his blood."

Ram's jaw dropped, "And...he has the Sword, too?" he asked.

"Yes," Speilton muttered.

There was silence even from the warriors who noticed the tension in the air.

Millites looked around at the battlefield. "I'm sorry that we were not here to offer more assistance against the trolls and the Calorians. How are we doing? Did the Avenger do its job?"

Ram turned back, a weak smile on his face. "It did more than its job. They tried to retreat to Skilt, but we were able to advance and destroy the bridge and the center tower."

"So where did all the other Calorians go?" Speilton wondered.

"Well," Ram said, "since they couldn't retreat to the castle, they retreated to the ocean. My Kings, we believe they're planning to sail away."

It was a race. The Calorians ran for their last opportunity to escape with the Milwarians following closely behind hoping to stop them. The Calorians that fell behind, stayed behind. Any alliances the Calorians had formed between themselves were broken, as they ran every man for himself.

Since the trolls were not the smartest creatures, they didn't know that the boats were not large enough to carry them anyway. The hard headed, pierced giants stood their ground, and fought to the end. The Warriors quickly overwhelmed them, though their attacks did delay the Milwarians.

The Lorkin Ocean was about two miles away. Many Calorians had to run the entire distance clad in armor while others rode on horses or Hakesorsees. The two armies reached the water where the battle began anew while the Calorians waited to board their ships.

Men splashed through the green water, their boots filling with grey sand. With the endless Ocean as their backdrop, the two armies met once more. The Calorians who were waiting had to fend off the Milwarians before they were able to board.

The Avenger was dragged into the battle, but it never fired a single catapult. They had to follow Speilton's command. At this point, there were no trolls to shoot, only Calorians.

Half of the Calorian army was imprisoned inside the castle, so their numbers were few. But they still had one last chance - Duonh, the Hound of Flames.

Deep underground dwelling in an open area to the side of the battle, the ground shook and cracked, knocking warriors to the ground as the black dog crawled up out of the ground and stalked towards the Milwarians. His hind-legs were planted firmly on the fallen Calorians, as if the dog was unaware that he was trampling his own side. The dog stared straight at Speilton, who had lived through his flaming breath before the battle began. Then, Dnuoh exhaled a ball of flames that engulfed nearly twenty men in the Milwarian army. The purple flames danced across the dusty ground before disappearing.

"We've got to take him down," Speilton said.

"How do you suggest we do that?" Millites asked.

"I guess we're about to find out," Speilton said, as Prowl leapt into the air.

Hunger was close behind, and Flamane and Usus caught up after only a few seconds. They flew three across through the Daerd filled sky.

"Millites, create strands of light and wrap them around Dnuoh's legs," Speilton began. "Usus, you can cover the light with stone to make sure it's durable. Then, we get him to follow us to the edge of the ocean. As he falls, we all attack with everything we've got."

"What will you do, Speilton?" Usus asked.

"I'll distract Dnuoh. And, if he even thinks about torching the army again, I can stop his fire from reaching our warriors."

"Are you strong enough after all you have been through?" Millites asked. "Do you think you can use that much power?"

"I guess I don't really have a choice since no one else can control the fire."

"Be brave, "Usus said. "You can do this. We're all depending on you. Now, let's end this war!"

The Inferno of Erif

The three split up as they approached the Hound of Flames. Dnuoh glanced around at them, trying to figure out what they were doing. Millites dove toward the creature's legs as the hound glared down at him. Speilton surprised him as he flew in from the side, throwing a ball of flames against Dnuoh's head.

Dnouh's black fur burned to ash as it looked for Speilton, but he and Prowl had already flown away. Before the hound could react, another ball of flames exploded against the back of his head. Dnuoh thrashed around to see the blue dragon and opened his mouth wide to exhale a stream of purple fire.

Prowl flew at top speed, as the flames hissed closely behind them.

At first, Speilton wondered why Dnuoh didn't scorch them since he had them in his view, and then he understood. The hound was waiting for them to tire. With Prowl flapping frantically and the heat of the flames baring down on them, that wouldn't take long.

They flew in circles, trying to distract Dnuoh from attacking Millites while he and Usus finished tangling the hound's legs. Three legs had been wrapped and covered in stone. Speilton only wished they could go faster.

The heat from the flames burned his back as they intensified. Prowl began to slow down, her wings growing tired from the battle, and finally she gave out.

Dnuoh was weak. His flames that had scorched the sky turned against him and crawled across his face.

Prowl tumbled out of the sky, and Dnuoh howled in pain as most of the hair on his face burned off, leaving his snout a mess of scarred tissue and burned, blistery skin.

The dragon opened her wings as they fell which provided them a soft landing. Speilton pulled himself to his feet and was once again confronted by the challenge.

The hound's four legs had been wrapped completely, and now they had to lure Dnuoh towards the water. Millites and Hunger dodged the balls of fire as flames exploded against the ground around them. Hunger leapt up high into the air, flipped upside down, then swerved straight for Dnuoh's thick head. Millites shot a blast of light at the hound, though Dnuoh hardly seemed fazed. But as they passed, the beast was able to grab Hunger by the wing. It shook it's head back and forth before tossing the king and the dragon to the ground.

Then it turned to Usus, the last one standing just out of the reach of his fire. Dnuoh stepped towards Usus and Flamane and as he did the light and stone that held the legs together shattered. Dnuoh quickly pulled himself to his feet and stalked toward Usus.

From the Avenger, Ram saw smoke coil from the hound's mouth. He saw the red glow in Dnuoh's eyes and knew that as soon as the flames spurted from his mouth, Usus would be killed.

Ram pulled down on the lever, and even though the Avenger wasn't facing exactly towards Dnuoh that wouldn't be a problem if he timed it just right.

All around him he could hear the warriors gasping and groaning. *Did he really just waste that shot? Did he really just miss now, at the most important moment?*

Ram pulled out his wand, pointed it at the stone as it floated high through the sky, and channeled a wind so powerful that the men fighting on the ground were blown over.

Through the sky the rock blew like a feather, but this feather packed a serious punch.

The flames streamed out of Dnuoh's gaping mouth as the rock hit, crashing against the back of Dnuoh's skull. The moment the flames made contact with the frigid Ocean water, a cloud of smoke shot up into the air. Dnuoh fell face first into the water, the smoke filling his throat and lungs. When he tried to gulp in fresh air, all he got was salty water.

And like that, the great Hound of Flames had met his match.

A cheer erupted from the Milwarians. Warriors swarmed Millites and Hunger, while others ran to Speilton, Ram, and Usus as they cheered and laughed, but all too soon the fun would end.

The eyes of the Beast of the Sword flashed open sensing that his master had touched the blood of the tiger. Now, he held the sword that summoned him.

For many centuries, he had rested without worry. But now, he was refreshed and ready to destroy anyone who stood in his way.

His back arched, shoving against the thick rock ceiling. Chunks of stone and dust fell from the roof. He had grown since he had fallen asleep.

He lashed upwards with his tail covered in hundreds of sharp spikes that helped break away the stone. The roof weakened, and the monster thrust his body against the stone. Cracks appeared, cutting deep into the rock. But the rock stayed firm.

He tried again, and chunks of stone fell, but it wasn't enough.

The third time he tried, the rock exploded from the cave, showering all around the mountain side. For the first time in thousands of years, light shown into the cave. The demon turned his white face towards the light and hissed at the sun. He stretched his long wings up into the open hole above him and shook out the dust, stone, and vegetation that had grown over it.

The beast wrapped his talons around the side of the hole and pulled himself up as his chest and stomach broke away the thick dirt and rock. Roots and bark had even grown on him, but they broke away as he stuck his long neck up. His jaws stretched wide open as he spit a ball of green acid into the air.

As he stared out across the swampy wasteland with his black, sunken eyes, he took flight with only two pumps of its sail-sized wings. He flew away from the Cave of the Magmors to seek his master.

The cheering stopped slowly as darkness seeped onto the army like smoke. It came from somewhere in the sky as the strands wove and coiled around the men. The Milwarians stood completely quiet as it slithered through the air. It was strange, as if evil souls were wandering amongst them.

Then, suddenly, a voice issued a horrifying whisper. "You have not won," the voice seethed. "I am the master of the sword. I have touched the blood, and now the beast comes. Give up now or every one of you will meet your doom.

The warriors began muttering amongst themselves trying to convince each other that they had come too far to be afraid. Still, others thought they had done enough. The Calorians were crumbling, and the Milwarians were not in a position to fight another beast.

Speilton screamed out above all the others. "We will never retreat. We took out your trolls and you saw us take down Dnuoh. We are not afraid of you and your evil creatures."

Retsinis laughed. "I admire your bravery, King Speilton. But those are just words. Do you know what you're really up against?"

The knights fell silent. Speilton was frustrated and at a loss for words. Millites spoke instead, "We will bring the fight to you, and we will never retreat," he announced.

"Fine!" Retsinis said, his voice full of joy. "Then while you're waiting, I'll let the Daerds keep you occupied."

The warriors had completely forgotten about the Daerds that had been stalking them in the black night sky waiting to make a move.

It was as if the whole sky dropped down. A black mass of feathers and fangs bore down on the men, grabbing them and carrying them into the air. It was a frenzy. Archers were scared to fire their arrows for fear of hitting their own men in the dark.

Many Milwarians fell in that once instance with the Daerds carrying the men into the darkness. During the mayhem, three Calorian ships left the dock full of men. There was no way to stop the ships.

In a matter of minutes, the beast could be there to destroy them, and Retsinis would win. But for now, it looked as if the Daerds might end them first. And half of the Calorians had escaped already.

There seemed to be no hope. The war would end right here, and they wouldn't be on the winning side.

And that's when a miracle happened.

The water began to churn. Waves crashed against the beach, rocking the docked ships.

Bubbles floated up to the surface from deep below the sea. Warriors entranced by the waves, waited to see what was happening.

The waves slowly grew more vicious and large, pounding the shore and giving the appearance that there was a storm moving inland.

But it couldn't be. Everything began shifting about one hundred feet from the beach. Bubbles rose twenty feet from the end of the dock and many large waves lashed up against the ship.

Soon, there were waves nearly twelve feet high crashing against the beach. The boats rocked and banged against the docks while those on the beach rushed for higher land.

One boat pulled out of the dock and began sailing away as it rose up and over the waves carrying a group of fleeing Calorians. The ship had begun to disappear into the night sky, when something changed that for good.

A green tentacle rose up out of the water, shot across the ship, and broke it in half. The remains of the ship were pulled down under, leaving only bubbles.

No one was sure what they had just seen. Had they all imagined it? What had pulled the boat under?

The answer came very quickly. A huge shape rose from the Lorkin Ocean. Covered in coral, barnacles, and green scales, it rose. Tentacles snaked their way through the green water. Then, the creature opened it's yellow, gleaming eyes, raised both of its muscular arms, and roared, showing off its rows of shark-like teeth.

To their amazement, arrows began flying out of its open mouth, taking out hundreds of Daerds. Its tentacles wrapped around the dock and splintered it into thousands of pieces before destroying the ships one by one.

Speilton, Millites, Ram, and Usus stared at it in awe. Then, Speilton finally announced, "They're people!"

"What?" uses asked."

"Inside the creature's mouth, shooting the arrows. Those are people."

The rest of them saw it, too. Torches lit the creature's mouth like a cave revealing small people inside shooting arrows at the Daerds.

Suddenly, the monster moved its arms into the flock of Daerds. Each of his fingers had tiny serpents that branched off into thousands of tiny snakes. As the fanged heads attacked the Daerds, the birds scattered into the sky. The Daerds retreated and flew out across the Lorkin Ocean.

The Milwarians walked away, leaving what was left of the Calorians alone. The Milwarians had to prepare since the battle wasn't over. It would never be over unless they destroyed Retsinis.

The Milwarians returned to the battlefield to care for their wounded. A medical tent was set up, and the horribly injured were treated inside. The others wrapped cloth around their wounds to stop the flow of blood.

While the monster waded in the water, the Milwarians tried not to look or think about the dark shadow in the ocean. They were not sure if the monster was an ally. Wood and smoke drifted from the remains of the dock. The monster's eyes were trained blankly into the black forest.

Finally, the creature raised a tentacle his mouth as his opened his jaws. By the dim firelight, they saw men jumping from the slimy tongue, landing on the scaly arm, and being lowered into the ocean. Only a few feet from shore, the water was up to their chest which allowed the men to reach land quickly.

Milwarian warriors walked out to meet the men, holding swords and spears for protection.

But it turned out they didn't need weapons because leading the men out of the ocean was Onaclov.

THE DRAKON OF THE SWORD
~ 28 ~

Millites quickly pulled Onaclov into the royal tent as Speilton, Ram, and Usus gathered around asking questions.

"What was that creature?" Millites asked.

"Oh, that's Cetus," Onaclov responded quickly.

"Cetus?" Speilton thought. "Didn't Neptune say Cetus was the enemy of the mers?"

"Yes, I think so," Onaclov said.

"Then how do you have possession and command of him?" Usus asked.

"It has something to do with this," Onaclov said as he held up the ring.

"A ring? How does that help you?" Ram asked.

"I'm still not completely sure, but when I saw the monster, Cetus, from the boat, my hand began to twitch. It was the ring, urging me to talk. Then suddenly, these words just came into my head, and somehow, I knew I was supposed to say them. It was strange, like in a dream when you talk, though it isn't really you choosing the words to say. All I know is that I was commanding the monster. His eyes turned from red to yellow, and suddenly, the boat collapsed.

"I thought we were all going to die. We fell into the water and began to sink. But suddenly the monster lifted us up on a tentacle. I knew that he was listening to me, so I commanded him to take us to the other men. We found the other warriors and rescued them from their sinking ships."

"But how were you able to control Cetus?" Millites asked.

Onaclov shrugged.

"I think I know," Speilton answered. "When I was at the Mermaid Cove, I went to the top of the castle."

"You saw Cetus?" Ram asked.

"No, but remember that large disk that projects the images onto the water? Well, I was looking at the pictures and saw one with that creature, Cetus."

"What else did it show?" Usus asked.

Speilton thought back to that moment. "There was a man on a small boat, and he was pointing at the monster. Cetus wasn't fighting, but stood still, watching him."

"What do you think it means?" Millites asked.

"Could it have been a prediction of the future?" Usus asked.

"No," Speilton said. "Neptune said that Cetus had been defeated in the past. But he was awakened, and all the mers were scared."

"But what does that have to do with the ring?" Onaclov asked.

"The man on the boat," Speilton explained, "He pointed at Cetus, and something was glowing on his finger."

"Was it the ring?" Millites asked.

"Possibly," Speilton said.

"So," Onaclov wondered, "Where did you get this ring."

"Speilton grabbed it on the Island of the Wizard Council," Ram said.

"Exactly," Speilton began. "On the Island, there were many magical artifacts. Speilton probably grabbed the ring that controlled Cetus."

"That makes sense," Onaclov agreed.

"So what happened next," Millites asked. "You commanded Cetus to take you to the other ships, then what?"

"Oh, right," Onaclov continued, "So, we found our other ships, and I commanded Cetus to bring them aboard."

"Aboard what?" Usus asked.

"Well, I figured the only place where we could breathe for the time being would be in his mouth. Trust me, it wreaked in there. Like dead fish and mold. But we had to do it to survive."

"Amazing," Usus mused.

Millites continued, "How did you know we were here and needed help?"

"I didn't know for certain that you were in trouble, but with Cetus at my command I knew we would have a great advantage. We've been waiting off the coast for a few days for the battle to come to the shore."

"How did you know we were here?" Millites asked.

"When we heard the crash of Dnuoh falling into the water."

"Well, it was good that you came when you did. The Daerds were about to destroy us for good."

Onaclov smiled. "So, what's happening here. What are we waiting for?"

The tension in the air grew stronger. "Remember the Sword of Power we showed you in the Lavalands?" Millites asked.

"Of course."

"Well, Retsinis took it!" Millites exclaimed.

Onaclov gasped.

"I know, pretty frightening, isn't it?" Usus agreed.

"Well, yeah, but you just said...Sinister"s real name."

"That law has been repealed. Use it as often as you want." Speilton told him.

"Oh...," Onaclov looked around at the others trying to see if that was some kind of joke. Then he said, "So, back to the sword."

"Retsinis has it." Ram said, "And we figured out that the creature whose blood is needed to create the sword, is Burn." Ram said.

"Really? I though he was dead."

"So did we at first," Speilton said.

"Then, where is Burn?" Onaclov asked.

"Speilton and Millites rescued him. We're keeping Burn away from the others."

"Does Retsinis know?" Onaclov asked.

"Yes, and he's already taken his blood," Speilton sighed.

"So..."

"Retsinis is now the Master of the Sword, and he's summoned the terrible beast that is charged with guarding it," Millites explained.

"And that's why we're waiting?" Onaclov guessed. "We're just going to wait here for the monster?"

They walked out of the tent and into the night. Torches cast light across the area and the twelve tents were arranged in a U shape. To one side, most were filled with injured men. Across from them the tents stabled horses, Prowl, Hunger, Burn and Flamane. Two tents in the center were for strategy and to accommodate the highly ranked officials.

In the center of the tents was an arsenal of weapons, most from the fallen Milwarians and Calorians.

The warriors were instructed to choose their weapons according to their positions. The knights needed swords or knives, archers needed new bows or more arrows, the infantry needed axes and spears, and they all needed chest plates, helmets, chainmail, and shields. The Milwarians and the warriors that had accompanied Onaclov walked along the piles of weapons, picking out the best ones for fighting the beast.

Since the only way to win would be to destroy Retsinis. But first, they'd have to find the Dark King.

Suddenly, they saw blood red eyes glistened in the darkness beyond like two rubies hanging in the field of blackness only twenty feet from their campsite. The warriors noticed and couldn't believe what they saw. Through the darkness they could make out his body and curved horns as Retsinis stood in the darkness of the night staring at them.

A warrior ran to Millites and Speilton. "My Kings, Retsinis has been spotted."

"Where is he?" Millites asked at they began following the warrior.

"He's standing in the shadows, staring at us."

Millites and Speilton ran to the group of warriors, shoving their way to the front to position themselves between the warriors and Retsinis. They looked into the darkness and saw the red eyes. "Show yourselves!" Millites commanded.

Retsinis merely smiled, and began walking toward them.

"Back down or we'll attack," Speilton announced.

The Dark King laughed, "Your pathetic weapons won't help you win this battle. The Drakon would never fall prey to such weakness."

"Men, prepare for battle," Millites commanded.

As the men unsheathed their swords and drew back their arrows, Retsinis continued walking toward them into the light. "You will not survive this. There is no other destiny for you," Retsinis announced. "Are you prepared for that fate?"

The Inferno of Erif

"Fire!" Millites commanded as arrows took to the sky towards Retsinis. Men rushed at him holding spears and swords.

But Retsinis remained calm. With a wave of his wand, strands of darkness emerged around him quickly reaching into the air, snatching the arrows from the sky. Other strands of darkness grabbed the sword-drawn warriors and tossed the arrows back into the army of warriors. The men were lifted up and thrown around as they screamed in fear.

"Drop my men!" Speilton shouted.

The Dark King continued as if he hadn't heard a single word. Speilton and Millites drew their wands and summoned flames and light at Retsinis.

The King Calorian dropped the Milwarian warriors to the ground, and created a shield of darkness before him. The two spells shattered against the wall.

"Take your precious knights. But I warn you, none of you will survive," Retsinis seethed.

The Milwarian warriors scrambled to their feet and ran back into the crowd as they were led to the infirmary to regroup.

Far in the distance, there was a roar very different from any other. It was like the whisper of a snake, mixed with the roar of a lion. It was shrill and unnerving, deep and ferocious. The roar echoed to them from far away, though by the sound of it, the creature was getting close.

"And here comes the Drakon now," Retsinis announced proudly, before vanishing in a swirl of darkness.

Onaclov, Ram and Usus ran up behind the Kings. "Were you harmed?" Ram asked.

"We're fine, but a few knights were injured," Speilton informed them

"Their injuries were not too serious and are being cared for now," Usus said.

"The Beast of the Sword is coming, and Retsinis has gone to it," Millites said.

Onaclov's ring began to twitch on his hand, and his eyes suddenly became yellow as they stared into Cetus's eyes. He whispered, "Cetus, prepare to fight."

The creature suddenly rose out of the water as his tentacles began to toss and turn in the ocean, turning the water to froth. His distorted face began to shift and change as he opened his shark-like mouth wide to roar a battle cry.

"That's pretty impressive," Millites confirmed.

"So, are we ready for war?" Onaclov asked.

Ram, Onaclov, and Millites rushed into the crowd of soldiers and began shouting orders. "Load your bows and prepare the Avenger for attack!"

Warriors grabbed every last weapon they could find. Speilton rushed into the bustle trying to reach Prowl in the stables but felt someone grab his shoulder. It was Usus. "Speilton, did Retsinis give any clue about the creature he had summoned?"

"Why do you want to know?" Speilton asked.

"Well, if we know more about this beast, maybe we would have a better chance to destroy it."

Speilton thought for a second, "He called it Drakon, I think."

"A Drakon?" Usus asked.

"Yes, I think that's right. Do you have any idea what a Drakon is?" Speilton asked.

"I think so," Usus announced. "I believe it's a dragon, without legs. It has the body of a snake and the wings of a bat."

"Well, a legless dragon doesn't seem so threatening."

"It is. Drakons are huge creatures. They can fly at super speeds and breathe acid."

"You mean it spits balls of burning liquid?" Speilton asked, frightened.

"Yes, it can breathe that, but it can also create clouds of green gas."

"Is it poisonous?"

"No, but instead it brings people's worst fears upon them. The green gas taps into their minds, and brings out their worst fears."

"So we are not only fighting a monster, we have to overcome our worst fears, too."

"It would seem so," Usus sighed.

Speilton rushed into the stable tent where Prowl was being kept. The moment he flung back the door, the horses began to neigh knowing that something was about to happen.

Speilton grabbed a hunk of meat from a bucket on the far side of the tent and opened Prowl's door. "Here, girl," Speilton said, tossing the meat to the dragon. "You'll need all the strength you can get."

The blue dragon gobbled it up in only two bites. Licking her lips, Prowl looked up at Speilton with a look of confusion on her face. "What's wrong girl?" Speilton asked.

Suddenly, his mind began to melt. He felt his body go weak as the world became hazy. He fell backwards, and his banged against something hard. Then his body was whisked away from the tent.

Like a shadow of death, and an image of evil, the Drakon descended. His eyes were like two black holes, dark and sunken into the face. There was a long snout that curved up into two horns with spikes protruding from his chin and forehead. Two thick ridges swelled up behind its jaw, as a long neck connected the ugly head to an extended, snake-like body.

Roots, soil, and chunks of rock hung from the underside of the Drakon. A line of spiky ridges went down its flat back, leading to a tail coated in thorny spikes. His back was a pale, grey color, and the belly was a dark black. The only other color on him was the red blood stain that coated its jaw. And then there were the two large wings, each the size of a huge sail from an enormous ship.

The men scattered as the Drakon touched down. He hissed, breathing out a cloud of the foul smelling gas. The green substance ran across the ground, entangling the army in their own nightmares. The men fell to the ground, their worst dreams and fears driving them insane.

A distance away from the Drakon, the Avenger was being prepared. The cannons were ready, and the catapult was loaded as they positioned the machine to fire. While the men worked to arrange the machine, their eyes were glued on the monster. In a single breath the monster spit a ball of acid that burned down an entire stable tent.

Retsinis summoned a hurricane of darkness above the monster that pulled in every arrow the Milwarians shot at the Drakon. Hardly any of the warriors were fighting, since most had been consumed by the gas.

The Avenger had been aligned and loaded, but just before they were ready to launch, the Drakon spotted them. "Fire!" the mechanic ordered. Ram pulled down on the lever and the catapult snapped forward. But midway up, the catapult's long metal pole that held up the stone was hit by a glob of green acid. It only took a second for the substance to melt the metal and cause the beam to fall, broken to the ground. The stone fell short crashing only a few feet in front of the beast.

The men fled from the Avenger for fear that the Drakon would attack again. The injured men and the medical supplies were carried out of the tents and into the forest since it wasn't safe in the tents with an acid spitting Drakon outside. The knights who hadn't been entangled in the cloud of gas rushed to the stables to free the animals.

In the frantic mix of the nightmare gas and horses, Ram found Onaclov. "Have you seen Speilton or Millites?" Onaclov asked.

"No," Ram said. "Are they missing?"

"Well, no one has seen them since before the Drakon arrived."

"Maybe they're devising a plan," Ram offered. "Right now we really need to focus on destroying this beast."

Onaclov's hand twitched, and his blue eyes became a bright yellow as he stared at Cetus and whispered, "Cetus, attack."

The sea monster rose from the water as his tentacles thrashed biting at the Drakon's scales. The Drakon roared and bit at the tentacles before slithering into the air. Cetus lunged out of the water just high enough to grab hold of the Drakon's wing.

The Beast of the Sword writhed in the air like an angry cobra, hissing and biting. Cetus wrapped his tentacles around the Drakon, causing the creature to fall into the water.

A cheer erupted from the Milwarians, but they predicted victory too soon. The Drakon tossed around in Cetus' clutch but was able to breathe a ball of acid hitting the at the sea creature's arm.

Cetus roared as his scales burned off, and the acid seared into his flesh. His grip loosened and the Drakon slithered away. As Cetus regained his strength, the Drakon lashed out at the sea monster with it's spiked tail. The long, thin tail wrapped around Cetus's other arm, pulling it up into the air.

Cetus moaned as the thorny spikes tore through the scales and barnacles, cutting across the skin.

Then the Drakon inhaled, and spit another glob of acid that burned a hole in Cetus' chest. Cetus roared and pulled his arm away from the Drakon's tail as he sank down under the water, hoping to extinguish the burning acid.

A roar echoed from the Drakon as he spit a cloud of gas over the area where Cetus had sunk. The Milwarian knights fell silent as the Drakon glided over. They saw Retsinis drop strands of darkness into the army, and after a few seconds a voice erupted. Though the exact words were indistinct, they obviously understood the meaning as the rest of the Calorians charged with swords drawn.

"Ram, what are we going to do?' Onaclov asked, "Most of our men are still stuck in the gas."

"Where's Millites?" Ram asked. "We need him."

Usus walked up behind them. "I think I found him!" he said, pointing up into the sky.

Millites was high in the air on the back of Hunger going straight for the Drakon.

"What is he doing? Has he lost his mind?" Onaclov wondered.

"Millites will do anything to protect Milwaria and end this war," Ram sighed.

Speilton found himself standing in the center of the empty battlefield. In the distance he could see the smudgy outline of the crumbled Skilt. Speilton walked away from the castle through the fog, stepping carefully over swords and arrows and the remnants of war. The dense fog made it difficult to see where he was going.

"Hello?" he called as he heard something shuffling around nearby. Speilton drew his sword but found nothing as he moved toward it.

"Show yourself!" Speilton called.

A dark shadow crossed behind him, but when he turned, it had vanished into the fog. "What do you want?" Speilton asked.

Then, a voice echoed in his head. It was a voice that was cold and evil. "We are giving you one last chance. Join us now, or we'll never leave. Never..."

Speilton stumbled to his knees and pressed his hands against his ears to muffle the voice. "You will lose everything that matters to you. Your family, your friends, your country. We won't stop until they are all gone."

Speilton ran away, hoping to escape the Versipellis' grasp.

"You cannot run from us. We're always watching you, always."

Speilton tripped over a sword and stumbled to the hard, dusty ground. The voice vanished in his head, and Speilton slowly began to regain focus. He looked around to find that the smeared image of the castle was gone, and there were no signs of life.

When he turned around he found his friend Nicholas who lay before him. Speilton crawled to his knees and sat beside the fallen elf as he tried very hard to contain the tears that begged to fall. But he couldn't cry. For nicholas' sake, he couldn't cry.

The elf strived to end evil down to his very last second. He had been an inventor, a dreamer, and someone who worked hard to help others. As he stared into the elf's young face, he recalled Ram finding his dear friend, the last King of the Icelands, mortally wounded in a battle with the Calorians. As Ram left him, he had taken the man's sword so that he could remember him always.

Speilton felt compelled to do the same. He couldn't allow Nicholas to be forgotten after he had risked so much for Milwaria.

Speilton softly picked up Nicholas' quiver of arrows that lay beside him. He slung it over his back, as he reached for the elf's bow that lay on the ground. Then, he touched Nicholas' head lightly, before turning and walking away.

There was a weak light ahead of him, and Speilton quickly knew that they were torches.

Holding his sword out firmly before him, Speilton approached the light. The torches slowly came into view, though he couldn't make out the entire structure until he was right under the rocks. Two tall walls of stone stood before him. The torches were attached inside the two walls showing him a path.

Speilton knew that there was some force causing this. With the dusty, strong wind, and no one around, the torches shouldn't have been burning strong. He was sure that the two stone walls hadn't been there before.

Even though the path seemed dark and forbidding, Speilton knew that if he wanted to escape this place, he had to enter and face whatever challenges ahead. He held his sword up high, listened carefully, then entered the path. There was only silence as he continued down the path with no end.

"Versipellis?" Speilton called, "Come out of the shadows. I know you're devising this!" There was no reply as Speilton realized he had entered a crater, with very steep, craggy rock sides. The top was open, and he could see the foggy, night sky overhead.

The bottom of the crater was made up of jagged rocks that lay on top of the other like choppy waves. Speilton continued with his sword drawn. The area was empty. Or at least, that's what he thought. Speilton smelled the decaying flesh before he heard or saw it.

"Take in the view now," the Versipellis said from behind him, "for it will be your last."

Millites darted through the air on the red dragon's back as Hunger blasted the Drakon with flames. The serpentine monster snarled, spitting out a ball of acid that Hunger was able to dodge the acid that soared into the Lorkin Ocean.

Hunger turned sharply to the left to avoid the massive spiked tail as Millites fired a blast of light at the King Calorian. Retsinis, now standing high up on the Drakon's back, quickly blocked the attack and fired his own spell of darkness at the King. Hunger darted ahead as it exploded behind them. Another was fired, this one closer but still too far behind.

Retsinis continued to throw every bit of darkness he could conjure at the dragon and the King but each time he missed. The Drakon was too busy blasting clouds of green gas and burning down tents to fight against the king. Below them, the battle continued. Equus ran back and forth through the cloud of gas, pulling men to safety. Usus and Ram led the men into the battle while Onaclov roused the dwarves. The Milwarian army was still weak and many were were still under the affect of the nightmare gas.

Suddenly, a Calorian fired a chain-net which Millites saw only two seconds before it hit. He had just enough time to steer Hunger away, but it was too late. Millites slipped off the dragon's back as the chain entangled Hunger's wings. He saw the frightened look in the dragons bright eyes, before he disappeared into the darkness. Millites fell too, but his last second effort put him over the

Drakon. He fell fifteen feet before hitting against the Drakon's hard scales.

The fall knocked the wind out of Millites, but after a few seconds he began to pick himself up. Suddenly, a biting, scratching substance wrapped around his body as he struggled with deep cuts that darkness gorged into his skin. Millites lay flat on his back, peering up into Retsinis' eyes as he reached up his hand to wipe the blood from his face.

"I propose a duel," Retsinis began. "The winner gets … to live."

Retsinis pointed his wand at Millites, and before Millites could prepare himself, darkness enveloped his body and sliced into his skin.

"Sounds fair enough," Millites said wincing in pain.

Retsinis smiled pointing his wand, "Good. It begins now!"

The darkness shot out, but this time Millites was ready with a beam of light created from his wand. Darkness and light connected, spraying up into the air. Millites was stronger, and the light pressed hard against the darkness. Retsinis was knocked backwards, as the light extinguished the darkness and wrapped around the evil king's body. Retsinis stumbled backwards.

Millites drew his sword. "No, Retsinis," Millites decided, "the challenge starts now."

Speilton's sword collided with the Versipellis' machete tipped arms. "You can not win this fight, Speilton, you know that there is no way for you to survive," the Versipellis snarled.

Speilton tried not to listen to the creature as he deflected another blow. The Versipellis pounced at him knocking the King in the chest. As Speilton fell backward, he pulled his invisible shield from his back out in front of him as he watched the Versipellis bring its two bladed arms down.

Speilton leapt to his feet, and with his shield in front of him he ran toward the demon to land another blow. The Versipellis fell backward, off a tall rock spire. Before it hit the spikey rock, it evaporated into a trail of smoke. Speilton cut through it with his sword, but it merely kept swirling around and around through the air.

"Come back here and fight me, you coward!" Speilton ordered the smoke.

"If you insist!" the voice echoed in his head.

The smoke dove down out of the sky and wrapped around Speilton like a tornado. As it tossed and threw him around, the smoke began to condense into the decaying, smelly form of the Versipellis clutching his throat. Speilton was lifted off his feet, dangling by the demon's cold hand. "You must've known, Speilton Lux, that if you did not join us, you would give us no choice but to destroy you."

Speilton wrapped his arms around the Versipellis' stone-cold fingers, hoping to loosen the grip. But the Versipellis would not give in.

The gruesome, bloodshot eye turned in its socket and stared straight into Speilton's. The King was suddenly overcome with dread - the dread of all of those who had died by the power this eye represented.

With one hand, he clutched the Versipellis's bony hand, but with the other, he reached for his sword and raised it to stab into the eye. But the Versipellis as too quick. He tossed Speilton out of his grasp.

As he fell, Speilton bashed his head against a rock and rolled off the edge of another. He lay moaning in a cavity in the rock, as he reached for his sword that was only feet away. His fingers tightened around the sword handle. He looked back up into the night sky to see that the Versipellis diving down at him. Speilton raised his sword and swung with all his might as the Versipellis came closer, and the two blades collided in a deafening clang. Speilton's had struck harder. The Versipellis' blade shattered at the base as tiny shards flew everywhere, and the blade clattered to the ground.

The Versipellis screamed with pain. Speilton pulled himself to his feet, his body still shaking from his narrow escape. He swung his sword again at the demon, as it cut straight through the Versipellis like butter. The demon hardly seemed fazed by the attack.

"Ha!" the Versipellis sneered. "You missed your chance, boy. You can't harm me without destroying my eye. Better luck next time, but there won't be a next time."

The Versipellis caught Speilton by surprise and knocked the sword out of his hand. Speilton was now unarmed.

Millites lunged toward the Dark King while still on the Drakon's back. Retsinis raised his sword, colliding with Millites' blade.

"You know, Millites, all it will take is one cut, one tiny moment of my blade piercing your skin, and you will become an indestructible leader of darkness. You could live forever, conquering all lands," Retsinis said as if it was an amazing offer.

"Why do you want me to become the all powerful king? Did you ever think of using it on yourself?" Millites asked.

"It delights me to know that you think I'm that foolish. Of course, I thought about it, but then, I realized that I am already all powerful. I am already the ruler of an army. So instead, I decided to use it on you. The famous King of Milwaria, now you will be the Prince of Darkness, and my ally. With you, Venefica, and the Versipellis, I could be the leader of an army that could conquer the galaxy."

"Wait, you've seen the Versipellis?" Millites asked as the color drained from his face.

"Oh, you didn't know that they have been here?" Retsinis asked with mock concern before nearly cutting off Millites hand.

Millites rolled out of the way as Retsinis' sword shattered one of the Drakon's scales. The King leapt to his feet blocking back Retsinis' attack.

The Dark King spun and struck, as Millites held up his sword. The two swords held, one pushing against the other. Retsinis suddenly reached for his wand and channeled a snake of darkness to wrap around Millites' waist. The King fell over, as the snake hissed and bared its fangs in Millites' face. It struck, but the good king held up his sword just in time for the snake to thrash and dissolve into the blade. The serpent still had enough strength to toss the weapon out of Millites' hand. The sword skidded across the Drakon's leathery white scales.

The king scrambled to his feet, but before he could reach the sword, Retsinis stepped before him. Millites tried to see if there was anyway around, but there was no escape from Retsinis's blade.

"Come here, and face your destiny," Retsinis cooed.

Instead, Millites ran in the opposite direction. Spreading his hands over his head, Millites leapt off the Drakon.

For a second he plunged down the side of the Drakon, then his fingers grasped around the tangled mess of roots and stones still on the creature.

His feet dangled high above the ground, and he knew if his hand slipped on a root just once, he would hurtle to the ground. Millites had to climb across the Drakon's filthy stomach quickly, so that he could reach the other side before his arms began to grew weak.

Many times he slipped and grabbed the end of a long vine. He had to pull himself back up into the thick of the roots. The places where the roots were bundled together were stronger and thicker, making the chances of them breaking off much less likely. Finally, as his arms began to go numb from exertion, he reached the other side of the creature's stomach.

He reached up the side, grabbing onto a ridge of spiked scales. As he pulled himself up on to the Drakon's back, he noticed his sword only a few feet away. He dove for it, and as he rose to his feet the Lord of Darkness suddenly appeared out of the night sky flashing Ferrum Potestas. The good king raised his blade, deflecting the blow with a loud *clang*. Then, he swung at Retsinis' hand, throwing the Sword onto the Drakon's back. Retsinis stood weaponless.

Then, he slowly backed up. Millites let his sword drop to his side, ready to run if Retsinis tried to escape. But instead, the King of Darkness charged. He lowered his head like a charging bull.

Millites was so surprised, he hardly had any time to defend himself.

Retsinis' ridged helmet cracked against his chest as Millites was thrown backwards. Before he hit the ground, Retsinis threw up his head letting his sharp horns stab into Millites.

The horn ripped a hole in his leather armor and shattered his chainmail. Millites felt a horrible pain as he collapsed. His body shook as blood spilled out of his wound. Millites was coated in sweat, blood, dust, and ash, and his body ached horribly. His arms were numb, his chest screamed with pain, and his mind begged to fall asleep.

But he had to fight. He had to keep going. All of Milwaria depended on him this moment. It had to end here.

Millites pulled himself to his feet. One hand clutched his wound, hoping to slow the flow of the hot, sticky blood. The other clutched his sword, his last chance at survival.

Retsinis was also ready with the Sword of Power back in his possession. The two stared at each other, slowly walking around in a circle. "We're going to end this, right here," Millites said, trying to conceal sharp cries of pain.

"I agree. Only one shall walk away," Retsinis announced.

The two then ran at each other, and their swords clashed, signaling the beginning of the end of the war.

The Versipellis turned to smoke and swirled through the air. Every once and a while it would materialize next to Speilton, hoping to catch him off his guard. But Speilton was always ready, reflecting every move. Speilton climbed to the top of a tall rock, so that he was able to watch the Versipellis more easily.

Speilton focused on the Versipellis' eye, but it twitched around the face. Each time he took a swing, his sword drifted through the demon as if it were smoke.

The battle continued with Speilton unable to breach the eye, and the Versipellis drifting around him as smoke. Finally, the Versipellis traveled high up into the air as a trail of darkness before morphing into the black wolf that Speilton had first encountered in the Rich Woods. The howling canine leapt out of the air as Speilton moved to the edge of the rock just as the wolf crashed to the ground. He raised his head and stared at Speilton with one eye that was the horrific, bloodshot eye of the Versipellis. The other was a torn, scarred, milky-white eye.

Froth dripped from his blood stained fangs, and his wet nostrils flared with anger. The wolf pounced, as Speilton swung his sword through the wolf without harming the beast a bit. But as the wolf fell, his claw caught Speilton's arm ripping a gash in his skin.

The good king pulled back, clutching the gash in one hand. Speilton knew that there was no use in fighting. Instead he lifted his shield, let the wolf bang against it, then he ran. Speilton jumped up and over rocks, running for his life. He could hear the canine behind him. Quickly, he hid under a rock where he was concealed.

Speilton heard the wolf on the rock above as he sniffed the night air. "Aaaawoooooooh!" he howled to the sky before dropping his nose to the ground to smell for his scent.

Speilton suddenly had a rush of adrenaline knowing that if he stayed much longer, the dog would soon pick up his scent. He silently climbed from beneath the rock and out of the ditch as he caught a glimpse of the beast facing the other direction. His foot shuffled, knocking a rock over the edge, and as it pattered to the ground the wolf turned. Speilton's heart leapt into his throat as the beast knocked him away with one paw. Speilton was thrown backwards but was able to escape.

Speilton soon met the wall at the edge of the battleground and ran along it, hoping it would lead him out. But the Versipellis wolf pierced Speilton's shoulder, throwing him against the rock wall.

The king collapsed as blood rushed from his shoulder. Speilton opened his eyes for a moment to see that the wolf had transformed back into the Versipellis and was standing high over him. The King scrambled for his sword, using whatever strength he had left, but the Versipellis disarmed him, tossing the blade away.

"You should've joined us while you could. Now, you will always be the king who died mysteriously. The weak one." The Versipellis lifted its machete arm, as the red eye moved and turned to stared at Speilton.

In that second, Speilton finally understood that the Versipellis needed its eye to see Speilton. While fighting, Speilton had always been standing in front of it. The Versipellis had been able to shield its eye and use it only when needed. So to destroy the Versipellis, he had to surprise it. *But how?*

Just as the Versipellis struck, Speilton tumbled under it. Nicholas' arrows began to spill out of the quiver strapped to Speilton's back. The king grabbed one as he landed on his feet like a cat.

The eye had moved with him and was now staring straight at Speilton. And the king who had *survived* the Versipellis' attack, was the last thing the Versipellis saw as Speilton drove the arrow straight into the beast's black pupil.

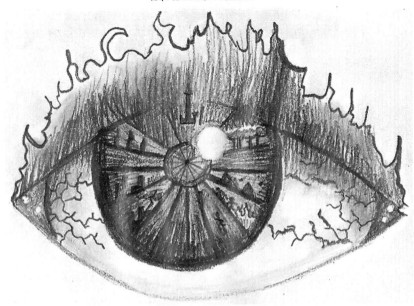

The Versipellis screamed, a roar so loud that the earth began to shake. The walls began to crack as thousand pound chunks of stone dropped out of the sky. The ground cracked into thousands of pieces around them, like a delicate webwork.

But the most horrible sight of all for Speilton was the Versipellis. It tossed and turned in the air, and the decaying linen that wrapped around his body began to melt off. The eye was burning with fire, then dripped with water, then shone bright as a star, as it continued going through each of the twelve elements. It finally became a crippled, dead, black color, and detonated. A whirlwind swarmed around the Versipellis, breaking each of its bones to dust before seeping into the cracks in the ground like dirty rain water. Then, the cracks resealed and the shaking stopped. Everything was quiet. It was over.

Speilton awoke on the dark, burned grass. The back of his head hurt and his left arm and shoulder were bleeding. He opened his eyes, and the first thing he saw was Prowl staring down at him with concern. He reached up his hand and lay it on her scaly snout.

"That's a brave dragon you've got there." Speilton heard Usus' voice say.

Speilton sat up to see the Second in command standing above him. "What happened?" Speilton asked peering at his wounds.

"We're not really certain," Usus answered. "The Drakon attacked and began burning down tents."

"The Drakon has already attacked?" Speilton wondered.

"Yes, nearly two hours ago."

"So, how did I get out here?" Speilton asked.

"Well, you must've passed out in the tent or something, because Prowl had to drag you out. The tent was covered in the the Drakon's green acid, and it had begun to collapse. Prowl raced in there and when you came out, you were unconscious. You were holding these," Usus held up the bow, the quiver full of arrows, and the Versipellis' machete arm, the one that Speilton had broken off. "How did they..." Speilton whispered under his breath.

"Speilton, aren't these Nicholas' arrows?" Usus asked." How did you get them?"

"I..." Speilton thought for a second, "Prowl and I flew over to the castle to find Nicholas's body. I didn't want his weapons to be forgotten forever. So I took them back with me."

Prowl looked over at Speilton with one eyebrow raised. She was obviously confused. But Speilton quickly began to pet her head to keep her quiet for the time being.

"But where did you find the sword?" Usus asked holding up the Versipellis' machete-blade.

"It was...lying next to him, and it looked interesting," Speilton explained.

"So how did you become unconscious?" Usus wondered.

"When I came to get Prowl some food before the war, I heard a roar that surprised me. I tripped and hit my head. That's all I remember."

Of course none of this was true, but Speilton couldn't explain all of it to him right now. That would take at least an hour. And besides, he'd destroyed the Versipellis, right?

"So where are the others?" Speilton asked.

"Everyone that is left is still fighting. Many of our warriors were engulfed in the green cloud. With the Drakon gone, the poisonous smoke is slowly dissolving away and more warriors are recovering," Usus explained.

"Wait, the Drakon has left?" Speilton asked.

"Yes, but it isn't gone from the battle. Last time we saw it, Millites was fighting Retsinis on the back of the beast," Usus said.

"Why is no one helping Millites?"

"We were, but the Calorians attacked us. Once we regained our position, the Drakon was gone. All we know is that it went out over the Lorkin Ocean."

"Thank you, I'll go look for him." Speilton ran to Prowl and climbed onto her back.

"Wait, Speilton," Usus ran up to them. "Be ready and aware. Retsinis has the Sword, and if he has already defeated Millites...your brother will no longer be on our side."

"Trust me. Millites would never let that happen."

"Just...don't get cut by the sword," Usus told him.

"Of course," Speilton promised as Prowl darted up into the air.

Millites knew that he had to find an opening in Retsinis' armor in order to destroy him and end the war forever. He knew that he wasn't just fighting Retsinis, he was plotting the end of the Lord of Darkness and the Calorian domination. Millites made sure that every swing of his sword was intentional. Every time he swung, he was testing the Dark King's defenses. Which side he covered more, which side of the armor was weaker, and so on.

After dueling for a while, Millites was able to cut a long gash in Retsinis's leg. The dark King fell, clutching the smoking wound and the good King was able to get a glimpse of the back of Retsinis' armor. Four strands of leather attached in the middle by a small ring held his armor to his chest. Millites thought about trying to stab through the ring but knew his sword blade was too wide to fit.

Retsinis suddenly whipped around, knocking straight into Millites. The Dark King rose to his feet and pointed his sword into the air. *CRACK!* a bolt of lightning shot down out of the sky only a few feet between the two.

Millites ears rang after the sound of the clap of thunder, and the Drakon growled as the bolt bounced off his scales. *CRACK!* another bolt flashed down only feet in front of Millites. The heat of the lightning singed his hair and eyebrows.

As Millites stumbled, Retsinis spoke. "The power of the Sword goes far beyond summoning creatures and turning warriors against their own men. No, with this sword I can do anything...be anything."

"Why are you doing this? Why do you take pleasure in others pain?" Millites asked.

CRACK! another bolt cackled down and Millites had to dive out of the way.

"I was born not by the fire like every other Calorian. I'm a mutant, the offspring of two species that should have never been brought together. And because of that, I was forever taunted and unaccepted by neither Wodahs nor humans. But after today, there will be only me and those who have chosen to follow in my path."

Bolts of lightning showered down around Millites as the sky roared with thunder. He raised his sword and rushed at Retsinis, hoping to reach him before...

CRACK! Millites noticed what was happening just in time. He held his minotaur-faced shield in front of his face and chest, and let go of his sword. The lightning bolt hit his lightning shaped sword in midair. They held for a second, lingering in the sky as Retsinis cried a cackling laugh. Then, the sword shattered and burst into tiny particles and flaming shards blasted into the air.

Millites heard the metal shatter against his shield and felt the eruption of flames that thrust him backwards. Pieces of burning metal struck at his legs, the only areas not covered by the shield.

But Retsinis felt the full explosion of the sword. The pieces tore straight through his monticore armor as it was engulfed in flames. Every part of his vulnerable skin was pelted with the shower of fragments from the sword. Ferrum Potestas was knocked to the ground a few feet away from Retsinis.

Millites fell back clutching his bleeding legs. They caused nearly as much pain as his chest. He didn't even have the stomach to check his wounds.

Retsinis was still recovering too. Half of his face was still smoking. His powerful armor was almost completely burned off, and only a few clumps still remained. But it wasn't long until he was back on his feet. Instead of rushing straight to his Sword, he picked up a shard of Millites' sword off the ground.

"What are you going to do now?" The Dark King asked. "Without your weapons, you are nothing." Millites scrambled backwards as he approached. "Are you prepared to die? Are you prepared to be the end of an entire nation?"

Millites knew what he had to do. Retsinis charged at him with the dagger-shard in hand.

Millites rolled to the side, avoiding the blade, then made it to his feet though his legs screamed with pain. Retsinis swung the blade wildly trying to scare the King, but Millites thrust his shield at Retsinis, bashing the Minotaur horns into him.

The two struggled against each other and without even realizing, they had approached the edge of the Drakon's side. Retsinis charged into Millites and his shard-blade ricocheted off the shield and dropped down into the waves far below. The Dark King instead grabbed onto the shield and jerked it to the side, bending Millites' arm backwards. They both heard the crack, and knew it was broken.

Millites fell to the ground, his arm swelling up in pain. As Retsinis reached for the Sword of Power, Millites knew that he could not defend himself with a broken arm and no weapon other than his shield.

Unable to run, Millites knew what he must do. Slowly, he crawled to the edge of the Drakon and peered into the water far below. Before rolling over the edge, he wondered if it would hurt to die.

He never hit the water. Black strands of darkness wrapped around his arms and attached him to the Drakon's side. The strands of darkness were the only thing keeping him from crashing against the waves below.

Retsinis appeared above him. "Did you really think it was that easy? Though you are brave, Millites Lux. Courage will be a positive trait when you're my ally."

Millites struggled against the darkness, though it was nearly impossible since his left arm was numb with pain. "Relax, Millites or my hand may just slip."

Retsinis pretended to drop the Sword on Millites head. As he Millites reeled back, the Lord of Darkness laughed at him.

"You will pay for all of the horrible things you have done," Millites promised. "One day all of the words of hatred and innocent lives you have destroyed will come back to haunt you. You won't ever get away with this. One day...one day...you're going to be the one begging for mercy."

Retsinis smiled as he leaned over the Drakon. "And just when will that be?" he asked with mock affection.

Millites didn't say anything. He merely closed his eyes and prepared for whatever destiny awaited him. "Millites Lux!" Retsinis announced, "Prepare to meet the beginning of a new age!"

As he approached the Drakon, Speilton heard these last words. Following the bolts of lightning, he and Prowl had been able to locate the Retsinis, but it seemed he was too late.

Speilton knew the fate that awaited his brother, but he was still too far away. Prowl was nearly thirty feet above the Drakon but still not close enough. Speilton could only watch as Retsinis raised his sword above Millites head.

Then, his fingers wrapped around the bow that had been hand-crafted by Nicholas and

Speilton had one last idea. "Dive!" Speilton commanded Prowl.

The blue dragon darted for the Drakon. Speilton grasped an arrow and pulled back on the string. He closed one eye, aimed, and found his target.

The Sword came down. Millites closed his eyes and readied himself for the impact. But the only thing that came was a weak, surprised groan from Retsinis. Millites opened his eyes to see that the Dark King had fallen to his knees with a fine tipped arrow protruding from his chest. The King's face was blank and smoke coiled from his wound. But this time the wound didn't reseal. For the first time, something more than smoke came out. Blood rolled down into the remains of the monticore armor.

Speilton had pierced the heart, the source of Retsinis' power. Without his heart, he was just as vulnerable as anyone else.

The Sword of Power rolled from Retsinis' hand and clattered onto the back of the Drakon. Then, silently the King of Darkness, the Lord of Death, Retsinis, tumbled off the Drakon and plummeted into the water below.

Millites glanced over the edge to see the red tail of the arrow planted in the center of the ring that held the four straps of Retsinis' armor. Then, there was a splash, as the water turned red and the sky filled with smoke.

As Retsinis disappeared in the Lorkin Ocean, so did the strands of darkness that held Millites. Millites, the Wielder of Light, slipped off the edge and fell into the green waters below.

Far away, deep in the heart of Skilt, the Inferno of Erif began to shake. There had always been two ways to destroy the Inferno - by pouring the vial of

Aqua into it or by destroying the Dark King since he was the protector of the eternal fires.

The fire thrashed and snapped. The souls of the Calorians waiting for birth thrashed as they tried to escape, but it was too late. The Fire was dying, and so were the ones it created. For over one hundred years it had grown and thrived, but now it had met its end.

Suddenly the flames imploded, leaving only an ash covered room. The souls of those who had never been given the chance to live, charged at the walls causing the entire room to implode. With the castle already crippled from the battle, walls throughout began to crumble and the stones from the remaining towers shattered through the roofs. Skilt crumbled. It's endless maze of hallways became rubble, and years and years of work were destroyed in a matter of seconds.

Millites dropped out of the sky. He tossed and turned in midair, his broken arm throbbing so badly it brought tears to his eyes.

Above, Speilton and Prowl took off from the back of the Drakon after Millites. Prowl caught him just as Millites' hand skimmed the top of the water, spraying salt water up at Speilton.

As they flew to safety, they couldn't stop thinking about what had happened. Retsinis was dead. The battle against the Calorians was over. It seemed like a dream. And to think that Retsinis was taken by an arrow shot by possibly the worst archer of all - Speilton Lux.

Prowl finally reached the beach to find the Calorians had been surrounded. The Milwarians stood with their swords pointed at them. The gas cloud from the Drakon was completely gone, along with the creature itself, who had disappeared over the Lorkin Ocean. Prowl drifted over the army, and

Speilton cried to them, "Retsinis is gone! The war is over! Retsinis is gone forever!"

The Milwarian warriors cheered, throwing their helmets up in the air. Everyone screamed as they rushed to find their friends. The cook pulled out wagon loads of bread and steaks were passed out to everyone. The kings shared their finest things with the warriors.

The war was over. The darkness was gone. As Speilton, Prowl, and Millites touched down, Ram, Usus, and the others rushed to embrace them. Even Brute was smiling. "You did it?" Usus asked.

"It's over, my friend!" Speilton announced, and all the warriors around them cheered. And at that precise moment, the first rays of the sun shone down on them. Dozens of golden lights flashed across the sky like a shower of shooting stars. They started at the sun, and flashed over the sky in golden streams.

Speilton, like many others had seen those flashes before. They had always come in his darkest hours, bringing hope and joy. He had never really wondered too much about what they were or why they were there. It just felt...right.

It had always given Speilton a sense of assurance and reminded him that there was something bigger, something more powerful than him out there. They were a sign that there was someone always watching him, always there to help. As he and the others watched the golden flashes of light cross the sky, they all knew that wherever they went or whatever they did, they could always find hope if they looked to the light.

THE RETURN TO KON MALOPY
~ 30 ~

The Calorian's numbers were low. The survivors had clustered together and waited for the Milwarians to attack and slay them all. They believed that just because their king was gone, the war was not over.

But the Milwarians didn't attack. Instead, they surrounded the Calorians, who appeared human in the sunlight, and brought them food. The Calorian warriors stared cautiously at the food, suspecting poison. But soon their hunger overwhelmed them, and they began to eat. They'd had no food in days, and for most this was their only meal that wasn't overrun with mold and disease.

One by one they began to eat, feasting on the soft, warm bread, and paper thin slices of rich cheese. After they had all eaten, Speilton left the crowd of Milwarians and approached the Calorians. "Drop your weapons. We mean no harm."

Many dropped their weapons reluctantly, but a few held on with indignation.

"How can we trust you?" a Calorian asked.

"We just fed you when you all were starving. We have kept you and your wounded alive," Millites responded.

"If you want to help us, then why did you destroy nearly all of us?" another asked.

"We never intended to cause you harm. Since the beginning of this battle, our only target was Retsinis. But to do that, we had to keep all of you occupied," Speilton explained.

"Then where are our wounded?" the Calorian who had spoken first asked.

"We have sent our men to collect all of the fallen warriors, both Milwarian and Calorian," Ram told them.

"But why?" one of the Calorians asked. "Why are you helping us?"

"Because, we know how you have been treated," Speilton announced. "We know that Retsinis, your king, treated you very poorly."

"So now what?" A Calorian asked. "Are you going to place us all in your prisons for the rest of our lives?"

The Calorians began to talk over each other plotting to rebel against the Milwarians. "They are going to terminate us all now."

"They've been waiting for this moment!"

"No, their going to enslave us and torture us!"

"No!" Speilton cried over them. "We are not here to hurt you in any way. We only wish to accept you and allow you back into Milwaria. If you agree to be peaceful, we will help you establish a future for yourselves," he told them.

The Calorians were stunned. Many suspected a trick, though most were just stunned.

"There is one condition!" Millites said. "You must promise from today on to join Milwaria as an ally. We shall put an end to the war."

"No longer will you have to risk your life for your king. From today on, you will be able to live your own lives. You can own your own houses and land. You can use your abilities to do great things. You no longer have to only serve as warriors," Ram promised.

"And the centuries of feuding between our two countries will finally come to an end," Millites announced.

"If you promise to abandon the ways of the Calorians, we will forgive you. And you may live peacefully and whole in this place."

Nearly every Calorian dropped his weapon and began to approach the army. The Milwarians retrieved the weapons and carried them back to the camp. The Kings led the Calorians to a row of tents for them to rest.

For the Milwarians, it was a peculiar sight. The ruthless enemy that had struck fear into their hearts since birth now looked frail and helpless. The enemy only minutes before was now their ally.

But for the Calorians, it was just short of a dream. For all of their lives, however short they may have been, the Calorians had wished and hoped for this moment. A time where they could be free and live without fear. And to think, it came in the least likely of times. Their numbers were low and everyone was slowly growing weak. Their king had been slain and left them to die. That one shining moment came like the golden flash. It was a promise to them and to the world that hope, forgiveness and the light in the world would always win in the end.

Messengers were sent out on horseback to spread the news throughout Milwaria. "The war is over, Retsinis is dead, and the wodahs are now our allies."

The horsemen broke off one by one, each going a separate way. One went to the Jungle of Supin, another to the Icelands, others to Mermaid Cove, another to Lake Rou, one to the Lavalands, and the rest went to either Kon Malopy or small villages that lay nestled in the plains.

The word spread like wildfire, and families traveled across Milwaria to visit their families. It was an amazing time. The war that had raged for centuries was over.

Millites, Speilton, Usus, Ram, the four creatures, the two dragons, Burn, Rorret, and Flamane all stayed in Caloria for several more weeks. The

Calorians that had been trapped inside Skilt when it caved in were evacuated from the rubble. The survivors were accepted into Milwaria just like the others.

Houses and other structures were constructed for the Wodahs, and each was given a proper name. They swarmed into lines, anticipating the moment when they would have a name, something that made them different from the hundreds of other wodahs. Many of them suggested names for themselves that they had heard.

And like that, the Wodahs had their own nation. They were now treated as human beings. Without the tyrannic rule of Retsinis, they had nothing to fear and no reason to want revenge.

The Inferno of Erif was gone, and with it the Wodahs' chance for future generations. It was for the best. Without a high demand for warriors, they had no need for the Inferno. Instead, small fires were created and charmed so that they could produce more Wodahs. Only one Calorian every week or so would come from the small flames. That's all they needed.

Once the rebuilding was well underway, the Milwarian rulers and the others began their return to Kon Malopy. When they reached the thick mud of the wasteland, they came across people for the first time. Wodahs had carried out wagons full of seeds and seedlings for planting. Once the wagons were emptied, they would cut and load slabs of mud into the wagons and return to Skilt. Rather than use the trees from the sparse forests to build the houses, they would use the mud to create stone houses.

The kings took a different route to return home and had to travel farther north to avoid the bridge over the gorge that had been destroyed.

They soon reached the woods and entered Milwaria bypassing the Icelands this time. After crossing the plains, they headed straight into the Rich Woods. Though it took nearly 10 days, they finally reached Kon Malopy.

They weren't sure what they would find when they arrived since there had been no communication from Kon Malopy for weeks. Had they been able to hold off the attack from the Calorians? Their hearts nearly beat out of their chests as they drew their swords and prepared for the worst.

They stepped out of the trees and onto the beach that lay between the woods and the lake. At first, they couldn't see much since there was a cloud of smoke lingering in the air like a fog, covering their view of the castle. The only part they could see was the top of Sky Tower. Half of the roof had been burned and there was a gaping hole in the side of the wall below.

"This doesn't look promising," Millites muttered as he climbed on Hunger's back.

Speilton boarded Prowl, Ram leapt on Burn, Usus took flight on Flamane, Brute and Ore grabbed onto Equus' back and Metus leapt on Rorret.

"Stay close behind me," Millites instructed.

Hunger flew into the sky and flew a few yards off of the ground, blowing away the smoke with his powerful wings. Speilton and Usus followed Millites in the sky, helping to clear the way. The others followed on the ground running behind the kings.

As they came to the end of the path, they stepped out of the smoke into the village, busy with life. The villagers carried long planks of wood and hammered roofs back together. The ground was singed, and there were a few houses that had been completely destroyed. But the village seemed to be coming back together. Everyone helped each other with repairs, and even the young kids brought tools and supplies to the older workers.

As the eight adventurers and their leaders appeared, the villagers gathered to celebrate. Everyone cheered and clapped, offering their finest things to them. Their gifts were refused by the kings, knowing that it would be a selfish act of power. They did accept the gratitude and well-wishes the villagers offered.

As they began up the hill to Kon Malopy, Teews rushed out. She had a cut on her lip and a gash just over her left eye, though she was alive and healthy.

They hugged her, as Teews kissed them all on the cheeks before asking, "Is it really over? Did you finally destroy Retsinis?"

"Yes," Speilton announced. "The war is over. The Wodahs are now our allies."

"What? They've joined our side?" Teews asked.

"It was Speilton's plan," Millites said before explaining what had happened. He told her that Speilton entered the castle and saw how horribly the Calorians were treated.

"So you forgave them? And now, without Retsinis they're loyal to us?"

"You won't believe how desperate they were to be able to live and begin their own lives," Usus said.

"What happened here. Equus told us that the centaurs were going to turn against you. We expected to find Kon Malopy in shambles," Speilton said.

"You're right. We were tricked by the centaurs. As soon as they saw the Calorians only a handful stood with us. The Calorians and the centaurs started to attack us with arrows. Our men had no way to protect us so the even the women and children of the village grabbed weapons and prepared to fight. And yes, even *I* fought. I did pretty well too, thank you."

"So what happened?" Millites asked.

"Here, follow me. I'll show you," Teews said as they continued up the slope. When they reached the top, they were greeted by the guards who opened the door and welcomed them into the courtyard. Stones from the towers and walls lay crumbled in the center of the grassy, open area. The damage was in no way as extensive as the previous battle.

They walked across the courtyard, down a hallway, and eventually emerged in the Banquet Hall. Trays of food had been set up along the cross shaped table. Breads and fruits and cheeses and steaks covered the table. Occupying the chairs in the hall were none other than the Isoalates. Many Tawii warriors sat at the table, decorated in red and yellow war paint. Stone spears and knives lay at their feet as they dug into the food.

"There are many more Isoalates, though most are still recovering in the hospital."

"How did they know you needed their help?" Ram wondered.

"They told me that they were following an ancient prophecy. They were responding to a call," Teews explained.

"A call from whom?" Millites asked.

"They said that it was a king who requested their assistance."

"A king? I didn't ask any of them to help us," Millites said.

Speilton also responded, "Neither did..." Suddenly Speilton remembered that the Isoalates had taken care of him. "Wait, now that I think about it, back in the Lavalands I told the Tawii man that we were looking for warriors. Then he said...something about a call and said he wouldn't fail me."

"Do you remember what he looked like?" Teews asked.

"I think so. But I don't seem to see him here in this room," Speilton said.

"Then let's check in the infirmary," Millites suggested.

They crossed the room and entered a door on the left. "While you look for the Isoalate, we'll check on the villagers," Usus said as he and Ram walked back out of the castle.

Speilton, Millites and Teews continued to find row after row of beds occupied by the wounded. Village women rushed around tending to the warrior's wounds.

"Do you see him?" Teews asked.

Speilton drifted down the aisles, looking at the men with bandaged arms ands legs. Others were drinking medicine or just trying to rest.

Speilton finally found the Tawii he was seeking as he was slowly sipping a cup of green medicine and gagging. It was heart-wrenching to see that his right hand was only a stub. Even with a bandage wrapped completely around his wrist, the handless arm was still gruesome.

"That's him," Speilton told them gesturing to the man.

"Ask him," Teews said.

"Ask him what?" Speilton asked.

"Ask him how they knew to come here to protect Kon Malopy," Teews suggested.

"Is this really necessary?" Speilton asked.

To be honest, Speilton was nervous. He was nervous at the thought of facing this man who had come to help him, but in the end, had lost his hand.

But the look in his sister's eyes told him that she wasn't going to leave unless she got some answers.

Speilton approached the bedside of the man and sat down. "Hello," he said.

The Tawii man sat down his cup on the table beside him.

"I'm sorry to disturb you," Speilton said apologetically.

"Oh, it is fine. If it means I am able to put down that drink, then I am happy," the Tawii said.

Speilton smiled. "I don't know if you remember, but you were the one that took care of me in the Lavalands."

"How could I forget meeting the king? You gave us the call," the Tawii announced.

"Well, that's why I came. We aren't exactly sure what you mean by 'the call'." Speilton said.

"Of course, you do not," the Tawii said simply. "Many years ago one of our people saw great troubles ahead. Very soon after, many of the tribes began to flee. The man who had predicted this change told us that the only way for us to survive would be to answer the call to battle from the King. And then you arrived and said you needed men to help you fight."

"And that was the call?" Speilton asked.

"Precisely."

"So, how did you convince all of your men to fight?"

"Why, King Speilton, our people had been waiting for years for the day when the Kings would come. The man who told us the prophecy knew only that you would need our assistance on the mountains on the night of April twenty-third. Each year, on that precise day, we sent men to search the mountains. Then finally, we found you. When I told the others about the call, they believed me, and we prepared for battle," the Tawii explained.

"Thank, you," Teews said. "Without you, we wouldn't have been able to hold off the Calorians."

"You are welcome, kind lady. Now, I have to finish my medicine."

The Tawii lifted the cup with his one hand and drank from it as Speilton, Teews, and Millites left the room.

"The Centaurs and Calorians had surrounded us," Teews explained to the two kings. "A few of the village men, women, and older children were willing to fight. Counting a handful of warriors, it was still ten too one," Teews explained. "Since we couldn't fight with that few, everyone came inside. We bolted the doors and loaded catapults, but the Calorians kept getting in, flying on the backs of the Daerds. Others shot flaming arrows at the castle and tossed catapults.

"And then the Tawii attacked them from behind. While they were all distracted, we fired the catapults and crushed many of the Calorians. Though the Tawii fought the most, and soon, the Calorians had been defeated."

"What happened to the centaurs?" Millites asked.

"We're not sure. We think they may have gone back to get the other centaurs, because recently, none of them have been seen. They've left for good, hopefully."

"Looks like Equus is going to have some trouble persuading them to come back and join us as allies," Speilton said with a slight grin.

"Now tell me what happened after I left the quest? How did the final battle with the Calorians end?" Teews asked.

Speilton and Millites looked at each other deciding who would go first. Speilton began the story. Millites told about the Chimera until the death of Ginkerry. Speilton explained about his adventures in Skilt and meeting Faveo once again. And Millites told the end, until the second they arrived at the castle.

"What about Ferrum Potestas?" Teews asked. "What ever happened to it?" she asked.

"I saw it fall," Speilton said. "Retsinis tumbled into the Lorkin Ocean and the Sword dropped with him."

"And what about the Drakon?" Teews asked.

"It's gone, hopefully forever, too," Millites said.

"Without a master, it was no longer able to serve a purpose," Speilton told them.

"I wonder what would've happened if we had the sword. Wouldn't it be great?" Teews said as she imagined herself as the master of such a powerful beast.

"Not really," Speilton disagreed. "I wouldn't want to have something that powerful. There would be far too much responsibility to have that much power. I think the power itself would drive me insane."

The others laughed. It felt good to laugh. Now they really could laugh without having to hide the sorrow that ached inside of them because they were now free. Free of the worry of destruction and chaos. The war was over and now they could sleep peacefully at night.

Or so Speilton thought.

That night, as he lay down in bed with Prowl curled up beside him, Speilton was happy and peaceful. Finally, for the first time in seven months, he could lie in bed with worrying about what awaited him tomorrow. His soft, silky bed-covers and cushioned mattress had become almost a reward to him. Up until now, if he were able to lie down that meant he had survived one more day.

But that night, the sheets felt like the greatest prize of all as Retsinis and the Versipellis were gone … forever.

Speilton drifted to sleep very content, though he wouldn't feel that way for long.

He stood at the end of a long hallway. It wasn't like the hallway in the cave or Skilt or Kon Malopy or any where for that matter.

The walls were smooth and grey and continued on far, far, far into the distance. The room was lit from what seemed to be natural light, but when he looked up, all he could see was a dark void.

"Hello?" Speilton cried to the hallway.

There was no response. Speilton moved ahead as each of his steps landed a crisp, clear tap that echoed down the hallway. Speilton continued walking down the bright, grey hallway. The place looked safe enough and clean, though something about it caused a shiver to run down Speilton's back. "Hello?" Speilton asked the hallway again.

No response. Speilton continued on, picking up his pace. He had a feeling that he was being watched, followed, but when he turned around, all he saw was the endless hallway.

Speilton walked faster and faster, hoping to escape whomever was behind him until he was running. Speilton whipped around quickly, and there he saw it. The two Versipellis stood, one next to the other.

Suddenly, the lights flickered, then went off off, leaving him alone in the darkness. Speilton heard a scurrying of feet somewhere in the void.

"You are ignorant, Speilton Lux," the voice of the Versipellis snarled in his head.

Then as if it were an echo, the other Versipellis said, *"You are ignorant, Speilton Lux."*

"There were three of us."
"There were three of us."
"Now, we will not rest until you..."
"Now we will not rest until you..."
"And all of your allies, are dead."
"And all of your allies are dead."
"Our job is not yet finished."
"Our job is not yet finished."
"Neither are your troubles."
"Neither are your troubles."
"This will never, never be over."
"This will never, never be over."
"Never ... Never!"
"Never ... Never!"

Two fiery red eyes appeared before Speilton. They carried the devastation and hatred of the Versipellis, but they were not the eyes of two separate creatures. These were the eyes of one beast, one wielder of death. Speilton couldn't tell who or what it was, but it was obvious that its evil and horror was matched only by the Versipellis.

The eyes stared into Speilton, and even though he shut eyes the image of the dark slits, masked by a red as deep as blood still stared into him. *"This will never be over."* The creature snarled in a voice that was all too familiar. *"We have only just begun."*

The Inferno of Erif

ABOUT THE AUTHOR

Will Mathison is a 6th grader who loves to share his stories and draw. In 2nd grade, he drew a map of a fantasy world and a story soon evolved. In the 4th grade Will was motivated to begin developing the story of <u>The Last of Kal</u>. Earlier this year, he published his first book to benefit Relay for Life and his friend's little brother in his battle against Leukemia. Will has just completed the second book in the <u>The Battles of Liolia</u> series, <u>The Inferno of Erif</u>, with the proceeds again benefiting Relay for Life.

Wonderful teachers have encouraged his ability and his love for writing, as well as his little brothers, Charlie and Jack, and their dog, Lolly, who have offered inspiration for several of the characters. Will is a Boy Scout and loves playing sports. He especially loves watching the Georgia Bulldogs. Always ready for an adventure, Will draws inspiration from his experiences on family road-trips across the USA. Will plans to continue to share the adventure in the five part series of books, <u>The Battles of Liolia</u>.

To learn more about the characters, please visit <u>www.battlesofliolia.blogspot.com</u>.

Made in the USA
Charleston, SC
10 December 2011